P9-CCU-662

NANCY RICHARDSON FISCHER

WHEN ELEPHANTS FLY

ISBN-13: 978-1-335-01236-4

When Elephants Fly

Recycling programs for this product may not exist in your area.

This edition published by arrangement with Harlequin Books S.A.

For questions and comments about the quality of this book, please contact us at CustomerService@Harlequin.com.

Printed in U.S.A.

This book is dedicated to Henry.
There are more stars to wish upon
More dreams envisioned and fulfilled
More adventures near and far
Since you took my hand.
I love you beyond infinity times eleven.

This novel is a work of fiction.
Mental health challenges manifest in myriad ways.
Every individual has a different journey.
The commonality is the courage it takes to survive and thrive.

Heal my splits
Make me whole
Wrap me in blue-velvet folds
—SWIFT JONES, *RAZOR*

Letting go can set you free
Drowning might just let you breathe
Surviving means so many things
Live Leap Love Sanctify
Never ever say goodbye
—SWIFT JONES, *ELBOWS & KNEES*

Turn your back to change the view
Keeping eyes closed nothing's new
Spread your arms to let her fly
What doesn't break solidifies
—SWIFT JONES, *THE STUDIO SESSIONS*

The Pennington Times

SEPTEMBER 1

BY T. LILLIAN DECKER, INTERN

New Arrival at Pennington Zoo

The Pennington Zoo is expecting! Thirteen-year-old Asian elephant Raki's due date is October 5. Her twenty-two-month-long pregnancy was the result of a live breeding with Lorenzo, an elephant on loan from Wild Walker's Circus in Haven, Florida.

Dr. Addie Tinibu, director of the zoo, began its elephant breeding program. "Asian Elephants are on the endangered species list," Tinibu said. "The addition of Raki's calf is not only good for the zoo's herd, but for the protection and continuation of the species."

Visitors of the Pennington Zoo can expect to view the calf by Christmas. For more information visit: penningtonzoo.org/elephants.

The Pennington Times

SEPTEMBER 15

BY T. LILLIAN DECKER, INTERN

Contest: Name Raki's Calf!

Have you ever wanted to name an elephant calf? Now you can! Raki, one of the Pennington Zoo's Asian elephants, will give birth to her first calf in early October. The *Pennington Times* is holding a contest to pick that newborn's name.

Zoo officials don't know the sex of the calf. But if you'd like a chance to name him or her, go to www.penningtontimes.com/namingcontest to make a $5.00 donation to the zoo and enter your name of choice for Raki's calf. You can enter as many times as you'd like. The most popular name will be the winner.

"All proceeds from the contest will go toward creating an even better home for our growing Asian elephant herd," said the zoo's director, Dr. Addie Tinibu.

*Contest ends September 28. The winning name will be announced October 5.

1

Crazy is genetic. It's the house I was born inside. There are no windows, just two locked doors. One door leads to *Normal*, the other to *Insanity*. At some point, I will inherit a key, but I don't get to pick which door it unlocks. Even if I did, there's no guarantee I'd understand the choice, or realize where I was when I got there.

The minute hand on the Paddington Bear clock my mother, Violet, gave me when I turned five clicks to 12:01 a.m. I hold my breath, wait. The loft I share with my dad in downtown Pennington is silent. I'm not sure what I expected. A roar in my ears like waves punishing rocks; the whisper I'd never heard before, curling like smoke through my brain; a steady stream of nonsense dripping from my lips?

I'm one minute into my eighteenth birthday, twelve more years to go before I'm relatively safe. A text pings my phone.

SAWYER: You good?

ME: Still me

SAWYER: Want to talk?

ME: No

I roll onto my back, stare at the ceiling. It's white now. Years ago, the month before she tried to kill me, Violet covered every inch of my room, including the ceiling, with posters of Escher drawings. Violet was going to be an architecture major before my dad got her pregnant during her freshman year of college. Escher was her favorite artist. His work explored infinity, and the print Violet taped over my seven-year-old self's bed was called *Relativity*. It showed a room with seven stairways, and people going up or down depending on their own gravity source so everyone traveled a different path. That's probably what it was like in Violet's head.

My finger traces the scar above my right eyebrow. A well-meaning doctor said he could make it smaller, possibly invisible. My dad was all for it. But it's a gift, a reminder stitched into my pale white skin that if I don't remain vigilant, keep my head down, avoid all triggers, stick to my Twelve-Year Plan, I could turn into Violet.

Carefully, I withdraw a yellowed newspaper article from beneath my mattress. Once a year, always on my birthday, I read it to remind myself of the stakes.

The Pennington Times

Oregon Mother Guilty of Attempted Aggravated Murder

Friday a Pennington County jury found Violet Hanover Decker, twenty-six, guilty of attempted aggravated murder of her seven-year-old daughter,

T. Lillian Decker. She faces up to fifteen years in prison. Sentencing will take place next month.

On September 17, Decker attempted to push her daughter off the eleven-story rooftop of their Pearl District apartment building, according to police and a crowd of eyewitnesses.

Decker's husband, Calvin Christopher Decker, age twenty-eight, and Mike Gomez, a lieutenant in the Pennington Police Department, gained access to the rooftop moments before the incident unfolded.

"I didn't know if we were dealing with a mother who was a meth addict or someone who'd just snapped," Gomez said. "All I knew was that I had to get to that little girl before her mom killed her."

As previously reported, Gomez grabbed the child's ankles as she fell. Decker caught his wife. The child was treated at Emmanuel Hospital for a concussion and a deep laceration to her forehead that required twenty-nine stitches. Violet Decker was taken to the Samaritan Institution for assessment. She was later diagnosed as having paranoid schizophrenia.

Pennington district attorney, Alfred Bench, charged Violet Decker with attempted murder despite that diagnosis. "Decker was first diagnosed as having schizophrenia at age twenty-three. She knew she was mentally ill and stopped taking her medication," Bench said. "She understood there

> might be terrible consequences. But she did it anyway. That makes her culpable."
>
> "I really feel for the little girl," Lieutenant Gomez said after the guilty verdict was read. "Crazy is genetic."
>
> At the time of this article Calvin Decker could not be reached for comment.

After folding the article, I replace it beneath my mattress and hope that when I read it next year, I'm still me. My heartbeat is a pointed finger jabbing at the truth. Today, on my eighteenth birthday, I've officially entered the danger zone, ages eighteen to thirty, when females with my genetic history are most likely to manifest symptoms of schizophrenia. Violet's condition began in her teens with hearing voices, but the illness can also start with bizarre behaviors, a lack of emotion or disconnected speech.

When Violet went off her meds, she quickly unraveled. She answered questions I didn't ask and read J. M. Barrie's *Peter Pan* over and over again, because she said there were messages in the text written expressly for her. In addition to my bedroom, she wallpapered every inch of our loft with Escher posters and scribbled quotes from Barrie's book on our walls. Her temper was short, her memory shorter. If she hit me, five minutes later she'd wonder about a red mark or bruise, then kiss it to make it better.

But it wasn't always bad. On the drugs, Violet never smiled. She paced nonstop, had brutal muscle spasms in her back that made her cry and had facial tics that scared me. Off the meds, she giggled a lot; made elaborate desserts, including a very detailed pirate ship cake; wove flowers through my hair and sang songs in Italian. At least I think it was Italian.

Grabbing my phone, I send another text.

ME: I wish

SAWYER: If wishes and buts were candy and nuts we'd all have a Merry Christmas

It's a quote from my school counselor, Ms. Frey, from when she was just starting her career and fell back on tired clichés. I laugh aloud. Big mistake. My dad knocks on my door like he's been lurking in the hall. When I don't respond, he peeks his head in.

"Hey, Lily. You're still awake?"

I look up from my phone. "Just doing some research for a reporter at the *Pennington Times*."

The lines around his faded blue eyes deepen. "Awfully late. You sure that internship isn't too much on top of schoolwork?"

This is the game he plays, never saying what he really means. If he did, he'd tell me that my internship is a threat.

"I'm sure," I say.

This is the game I play, pretending not to notice the way he watches me, waiting for crazy to smash into our lives again.

My dad glances at his watch. "Wow. Hey. Happy birthday."

I smile. "Thanks."

"I know you don't want a party, but how about I pick up a carrot cake from Peyrie Bakery for dessert?"

I haven't liked carrot cake for years and steer clear of refined sugars. "Sure. That'd be great."

The door closes with a soft click. It's now 12:09. I go over the core tenets of my Twelve-Year Plan: No drugs, alcohol, boyfriends or stress until I'm thirty years old. Closing my eyes, I attempt to grind my subconscious's voice beneath an imaginary heel. It's asking what could possibly go wrong. We both know the answer.

Everything.

2

"I'm not talking to you." I slam my locker shut and give the combination a rough spin.

Sawyer grins. "Happy eighteenth and you just did." He leans in. "Come on. It's pretty much the best birthday present ever, and it'll make you look good at the *P-Times*."

"I don't celebrate birthdays." I try to glower at him, but it's impossible to stay mad at Sawyer for more than three seconds because Sawyer isn't just my best friend, he's my only friend, and he pretty much has the greatest smile in the universe. Plus, what Sawyer did will indeed make me look *really* good.

"How many times do I have to say it? All I have to do to get into community college is keep breathing." We're seniors, and college applications are due this month. Most of the kids in our grade are hoping to leave Oregon, or at least our city. I'm staying put. But I'm good with it. Sawyer, on the other hand, is applying early admission to Stanford. He'll get in because he has a 4.5 GPA, is captain of the lacrosse team and his grandfather's money built one of the libraries. I don't blame him for wanting to get away. But if Sawyer were a body part, he'd be my toes or thumbs or the smartest part of my brain. Without him I'm going to be off balance, uncoordinated, challenged. Basically, I'll live but it'll suck.

Yesterday is history, tomorrow a mystery and today is a gift. That's why we call it the present. That's another pearl of wisdom from the early iteration of Ms. Frey that still pops up. She also used to say things like *Worrying is wishing for something bad to happen.* Forcefully, I squelch her voice.

Sawyer tugs me down the hall. The kids rushing to class part in a way they never do when I'm walking alone. People wave to him. They slap his hand or grab his shoulder like he's the touchstone of cool and it might rub off. If there were a picture of a high school guy in Wikipedia under the entry for *cool* it'd be Sawyer with jeans hanging off his hips, broad shoulders beneath an old flannel shirt, killer smile and Converse sneaks.

"Hey, Sawyer," Carla Bonani calls out.

Carla, the editor of our yearbook, is traveling in her usual pack, Dawn, Claire and Bethany at her heels. The entire crew is what the guys at our school call librarian hot—lip gloss and mascara only. Artfully unbuttoned tops hint at cleavage and their skin tones, ranging from pale white to deep brown, are blemish-free. The orange blossom perfume they all wear wafts over me. It would smell good on one person, but as a collective, it's overwhelming.

"Lily, we've been looking for you," Bethany says, her long-lashed eyes scanning me.

"We heard you have an internship at the *P-Times*," Claire

explains. "We really need someone to write human interest stories for the yearbook."

"If you're game," Dawn explains, "we'll give you writing credits."

"How about it, Lily?" Carla asks.

I shake my head. "Sorry. I've got too much going on."

Carla gives her friends a look. "Told you." She turns to Sawyer. "Secret?" She puts a hand on his arm. "You were voted most likely to break a girl's heart."

Carla has been crushing on Sawyer since forever. She has great taste. But he's dating a model named Wyn who he met in Europe.

Sawyer runs fingers through light brown hair, gray eyes in a lightly tanned face momentarily downcast. "Thanks?"

Carla turns, a little smile on her lips. "By the way, Lily, you were voted most fun to give a makeover."

Sawyer puts his arm around my waist and propels me away. "And I need a makeover, why?" I ask over my shoulder. I will pay for my snarkiness later.

"You *could* wear some of your own clothes," Sawyer says, glancing at the oversize Stanford sweatshirt I swiped from his bedroom. He pulls the hood over my head.

"Careful! You'll ruin my hair." We both crack up. I've worn my hair in a knot since I was eight. Otherwise the curls sprouting like twisted macaroni from my scalp would make it impossible to see. A freshman running by squashes my little toe. "Ow!"

"The danger of wearing flip-flops out of season," Sawyer notes, giving the kid a light shove.

I watch the guy ricochet off a locker. "We're a long way

from Gary Haycox." Gary was back in second grade. I was taller than Sawyer and popular because I kicked ass at dodgeball. The fact that I used the bigger kids as shields eluded the brainiacs in my class. Sawyer wasn't coordinated yet, probably because his feet were almost as long as he was tall. He was picked last for every gym team unless I was captain. We weren't friends yet, but I had a thing for underdogs.

Sawyer had another strike against him. Back then he liked to wear superhero costumes to school for no reason. One day he came as Wonder Woman. He liked the golden lasso and bracelets. Gary tripped him during recess, then tried a move he'd seen on WWE wrestling. He straddled Sawyer's back, attempting to twist my friend's leg around his own neck. It looked impressive but überpainful, so I punched Gary in the nose. It broke.

My dad upped my therapy with Ms. Frey to twice a week. Sawyer and I became best friends. We stayed that way even after he became insanely coordinated and effortlessly popular.

"It's a good day to have a good day," Sawyer says.

I snort again. We wouldn't have Freyisms to share if I hadn't broken Gary's nose. I nudge Sawyer's shoulder. "Seriously, why'd you do it?" Sawyer turns to wave at Jonah, a pencil-thin freshman with ginger-colored hair. Jonah wears a JV Track T-shirt, even though he's been kicked off the team by his own teammates. "How long before he gives up and puts on a different shirt?" I ask.

"He just wants to fit in."

"That ship has sailed." Jonah told his dad that there was a keg at a preseason track party. His dad called the principal. Jonah is now a pariah.

"Hey, Jonah," Sawyer calls.

The kid's super fair cheeks turn bright red. Sawyer is probably the only person talking to him in the whole school even though they have the least in common. I nod at Jonah. Sawyer's position in high school is a lock. I have to keep my head down.

"Lily, I'm just trying to give you possibilities," Sawyer says. "If your internship goes great, you'll have more options for college."

"I'm not going to apply to USC." The University of Southern California Annenberg School for Communication and Journalism is one of the best in the country. It's a five-hour drive from Stanford, or a short flight, which I can't afford but Sawyer Cushing Thompson, heir to countless pulp and paper mills responsible for decimating Oregon and Washington state forests, can.

"We could hang out on the weekends," Sawyer says. He whispers in my ear, "'When no one knows you, you can be anyone, anyone, freedom from everyone, everyone.'"

Sawyer is quoting a Swift Jones song. I am not a fan of pop star SJ, because I don't relate to her particular brand of teenage angst. But she's Sawyer's favorite singer. When I hang at his house, which I do a ton to avoid feeling like I'm an amoeba under my dad's microscope, Sawyer picks the tunes. Those tunes revolve around Swift Jones.

"You do realize that I hold your popularity in the palm of my hand. If anyone else heard you quoting SJ, you'd be screwed. Guys do not quote SJ without serious hazing." Sawyer scrunches his forehead. He sucks at feigning worry. I stamp my foot. "You have to pick a different name."

"It's my money. I adhered to the elephant-naming contest rules: five dollars per entry. Shall I do the math?" He pretends to count on his fingers. "Five dollars times twenty thousand entries, each with the same name, equals $100,000. I win."

It's unreal that Sawyer has access to that amount of money. But he does. It's a drop in his oversize bucket. "What if the baby elephant is a boy?"

"The name Swift Jones is unisex. Another reason SJ is perfect."

I'm not going to win this fight. "I'm sure Dr. Tinibu will be thrilled. And if blowing a hundred grand doesn't make your father talk to you, nothing will."

The bell rings. Sawyer walks into the doorway of his AP physics class. My class is across the hall: math for dumbasses.

"After school?" Sawyer asks. "Betty is making apple tarts."

Betty is his family's cook. My mouth waters. "Can't," I say. "Internship."

"Still going okay?"

"Yeah. They hardly know I'm there."

And that's how I need to keep it.

3

"The boss wants to see you," Shannon says when I arrive at the *Pennington Times* after school.

"Um. Why?"

She looks at me over the top of her bifocals. "He buzzed for you. That's all I know."

Shannon McDaniels is a thirty-eight-year veteran news reporter at the *Pennington Times.* She sits five feet to my right behind one of the desks that form rows of five in the open space that is the *Pennington Times* newsroom. The minute I walked into this place, I was drawn to the sense of order. The linoleum floors are a no-nonsense gray, and there's perfect symmetry in the metal desks, halogen lamps and matching laptops. I'm an intern working three afternoons a week, starting last month. Except for a few tiny stories, I've mostly made phone calls for reporters to double-check facts and quotes. There's no wiggle room in reporting. Everything must be truthful, verifiable. I like that, too.

Right now there's a deep crease between Shannon's eyebrows. She wasn't happy to be saddled with an intern, even though she's the one who interviewed and hired me. Her beat is politics and big legal cases. Shannon turns back to her screen. Its glow illuminates a constellation of freckles and washes out her pasty skin. Without looking at me, she pulls the pencil stuck in her strawberry blond braid free and throws it like a dart. It whizzes by my right ear.

"Don't keep the King waiting. Rumor has it he has hemorrhoids. Scoot."

With each step toward the editor in chief's office my skin tightens. I wish I'd worn something other than Sawyer's lacrosse T-shirt and worn Levi's. The newsroom is a pretty informal place, but I've never met the big boss, who from a distance looks like a football linebacker, except he's bald. Maybe he asked for Lucy in Accounting, not Lily.

"Kid, grab me a coffee?" Bart Jacobs calls. He's on Sports. I think he used to be a pro athlete. But maybe that's just because he chews tobacco then spits it into a Diet Coke can.

"Sure. Americano. But I need to see Mr. Matthews first."

"Oooh," Bart says. He tosses a Nerf football at my head. I duck. "Your eye-hand coordination sucks."

The editor in chief of the *Pennington Times* is the only person at the newspaper who has an office. Right now it smells like take-out Vietnamese from Silk, the restaurant one block away. On his desk is what looks like a #7, crispy duck rolls. I knock on the glass of his open door.

Mr. Matthews is focused on the oversize foam box containing his lunch. He stabs a duck roll with the end of one chopstick and drops it into his mouth. "Come in," he says between chews. "Those articles..."

"Um..."

"The zoo ones."

That's my internship news beat—really, really small local happenings. I've covered a few restaurant openings, a visiting children's book author (who answered all my questions in rhyme) and the impending birth of Raki's calf, which, stunner, a few people actually seem to care about. Mr. Matthews looks up. Deep-set, hazel eyes set in a light brown face squint at me like I'm next on the menu.

"Have a seat."

I sink onto the wooden chair across from his battered desk and remind myself that I don't really need this internship. I'm attending Oregon Muni College next year. It's small, state run, a bus ride from our loft, and everyone who applies gets in.

Mr. Matthews holds up an issue of the *P-Times* folded open to the elephant-naming contest. "Whose idea was this?"

"Mine," I admit, wincing a little.

"It was a great idea."

The bunched muscles in my back release. I'm a skydiver who just realized she has a parachute. "Cool."

"What made you think of it?"

"The Pennington Zoo has one of the largest elephant habitats in the country. But Dr. Tinibu, the zoo's director, said that their exhibit still needs work. Her short-term goal is to create new features in the elephants' habitat so they don't get bored. Eventually she wants to build a sanctuary separate from the zoo where elephants can be rotated out of the exhibit to a nature preserve where they'll roam almost free." I suck in a lungful of air because I forgot to breathe.

Mr. Matthews toys with a duck roll. "Back to my question."

"Sorry. I thought a contest might hook the public into caring about elephants, help raise some money for their exhibit."

"How'd you know anyone would pay to name an elephant?"

"People like to name things—boats, buildings, even their cars. I know a guy who named his pinkie toes."

"Why?"

"So they'd feel as important as his other toes." That was my father, when he still had a sense of humor.

"What names have been popular?"

"Daisy if it's a girl. Duke for a boy with Buddy a close second."

Mr. Matthews almost smiles. "How much has the contest raised?"

"Until yesterday? Eight thousand, three hundred and twenty-five dollars."

"And a few hundred more today?"

"Um. One hundred thousand more."

Mr. Matthews shakes his head like he heard wrong. "What?"

"Someone sent in an anonymous check for $100,000 this morning."

"Must be a hoax."

"It's real."

Mr. Matthews whistles. "I'll be damned. Me? I hate everything about zoos," he says, fiddling with his brass nameplate. "Remind me of prisons for animals. What'd you think of the current elephant exhibit?"

"I didn't see it. Dr. Tinibu and I talked over the phone."

Mr. Matthews leans forward. "Why?"

"I don't, um, drive?"

"Ever heard of a bus?"

I sit up straight, because he sounds annoyed. "Um. It's quicker to get the information by phone?"

Matthews tosses the empty foam container into a can beside his desk. "Easier, you mean. That's the problem with your writing."

He's actually read my writing enough to know there's a problem with it? My face gets warm. "It's not that it's easier," I try to explain. "It's…more unbiased."

"It's a local-happenings beat. People want to get jazzed about a new restaurant or their favorite author, even if she's annoying as hell and speaks in rhymes. They want to be excited about the birth of a baby elephant after a two-year wait for the little bugger."

I've stretched the tiny hole in Sawyer's shirt to the size of three fingers. I should just nod, agree, thank Mr. Matthews and then scram. But he's messing with the Society of Professional Journalists' Code. The Code is something I researched after Career Day my freshman year pointed me toward journalism. It's a large part of my Twelve-Year Plan.

Silently I tick off the four major tenets because it's the life preserver I cling to whenever waters get turbulent.

1. **Seek Truth and Report It.**
2. **Minimize Harm.**
3. **Act Independently.**
4. **Be Accountable and Transparent.**

Nowhere in the Code does it say I have to make people excited or that it's important they care. What it does say is to be logical, emotionless, responsible and balanced. If anyone asked me what superpowers I'd want, it'd be those four traits.

"But if I go to the zoo, I won't be able to write an objective article."

Mr. Matthews frowns. "Why's that?"

My palms are instantly damp. Violet used to take me to the Pennington Zoo. She was fascinated with the tigers. She'd make me stand in front of their exhibit for hours to hear them roar, and then we'd practice our own throaty growls. Violet also loved the bats, and we'd stay even longer to watch them fly. She said it was research. "I hate everything about zoos, too."

Mr. Matthews narrows his eyes like he's trying to see me better. "Kid, you don't have to love every aspect of a story. But when it's a human-interest piece, you do have to figure out a way to infuse life into it while still reporting the facts. You want to be a great reporter?"

I took this internship because Ms. Frey harangued me into it. All I want is to learn the basics about being a reporter so I can work for a small-town paper with a beat that covers parking tickets, jazz bands, maybe G-rated movies where an animal doesn't die. It's the perfect job for me, at least for the next twelve years. "Maybe," I say.

"Then figure out a way to connect with a story no matter what it's about. Despite your flat prose, you've already hooked readers with that elephant contest. Do a follow-up."

"About the elephant?"

"No, about the Pope's visit to the US." Mr. Matthews turns to his computer screen. "What are you waiting for?" he asks. "Get the hell out of my office. It's late, but call the zoo lady and try to get that interview today."

4

Dr. Addie Tinibu sits at a desk piled high with files and folders. "Budget cuts," she says with a wave of her long fingers. "I'm now the director of the Pennington Zoo *and* head paperwork pusher."

Dr. Tinibu's voice lilts like a song. She's very pretty with high cheekbones, dark brown skin and a smile that takes up half her face. "Thanks so much for letting me interview you on such short notice," I say. My plan is to ask a few quick questions, give her the check, then head home to write my article. "So. Dr. Tinibu, where did you grow up?"

"Call me Addie. Please."

"Okay. Everyone calls me Lily."

"Lily, I'm from a very small village in northern Kenya." She walks over to a faded map on her wall and points. "It's near the Nairobi National Park."

"How'd you end up in Oregon?"

"It's a long story."

All I need is one good quote about elephants. I take a step closer. "I'd really like to hear it."

Addie unzips her red fleece vest. "I had seven brothers and sisters. We were the kind of poor that I can still feel in my belly. My father supported us by poaching elephants."

My breath sticks and I look up from my notes. "Killing them?"

"Yes. Then selling their tusks on the black market. An elephant's two full tusks can be worth as much as $10,000 if a poacher is willing to kill the animal illegally and hack its face off to remove the ivory. The rest of the animal is left to rot."

A chill creeps down my spine. "That's horrible." Crap. I've just insulted Addie's father.

She sits down, gesturing for me to take the chair across from her, then rests her elbows on the cluttered desk. "Yes, it is pretty horrible. Poachers illegally slaughter up to thirty-six thousand African elephants annually."

"Are there enough elephants for them to survive?"

Addie twists the gold ring on her thumb. "Birth rates can't keep up with the rate that they're being slain. Up to a hundred are killed each day."

"How many are left?"

"Approximately four hundred thousand, which means that wild elephants in Africa may become extinct as early as ten years from now."

My shoulders sag. "That's a depressing thought."

Addie nods. "The situation is even worse for Asian elephants, like the ones we have at our zoo."

"Poaching?"

"Yes, but also Asia is the world's most densely populated

continent. Every day elephants lose more of their natural habitat. As a result, they've destroyed property and had deadly interactions with people. So they're killed with guns or poison. They're also captured for illegal wildlife trade."

"How many Asian elephants are left?" I ask.

"Only about forty thousand in the wild."

I stare at my notes, not sure where to go from here. "So your father?"

Addie runs a hand over her cropped hair. "It's the only life he knew. But when I was nine, I got a job cleaning pots in the kitchen of the Henry Shaw Wildlife Trust. The people I met there, and the animals I watched them rescue, changed my life. I earned a scholarship to an all-girls' high school, then to a college in America. Grants allowed me to get my PhD in zoology."

"You dedicated your life to protecting animals, but do you ever feel bad that they're in cages?"

Addie sighs. "It's not perfect. We do the best we can with the money we have to give each animal the highest quality of life possible."

Silence stretches between us. I wait for her to say more. She doesn't, so I dig into my backpack. I had a whole speech ready for presenting the contest check, but instead I just give it to her.

Addie looks from the check to me. "Is this a joke?"

My face heats up. She thought it'd be more. "Sorry. That's it."

"Sorry?" She grins. "I was expecting a few hundred dollars! This means the community really cares. It means we can raise even more money and create the type of sanctuary our elephants deserve."

Addie bounds around her desk. At first I think she's going to hug me but instead she puts her hands on my shoulders. Our eyes meet. Hers are shining.

"Lily, this is so great! Thank you!"

I try to stay professional but can't help grinning. "You're welcome." I don't tell her that the Pennington community only cared about $9,000 worth of the total. It's breaking the Code, but I don't want to ruin her moment.

"What is our calf's name?" Addie asks.

I wince. "Swift Jones."

"Like the pop star?"

"She sings country music, too," I say. *Pathetic.* "If you don't mind, I kinda need to quote your reaction?"

"'I love my pickup truck more than you,'" Addie sings.

It's a Swift Jones song. Addie has a good voice made prettier by her accent. Sawyer is going to eat this up with a spoon. "You like Swift Jones?"

"Very much. She sings from her heart."

"So you're good with the name?"

Addie holds up the check. "I'd have been okay with Daisy or, God help me, Buddy for this much money."

"So. Um. Good luck with the baby elephant."

A handheld radio on Addie's desk crackles to life. "Addie? It's time."

"On my way, Steve." Addie strides toward the door then stops, looking back at me. "Come on. You've earned it."

I don't know what she's talking about, but I follow her toward the stairs. My pulse quickens as we leap down the steps two at a time. Outside, Addie breaks into a jog, weaving around the zoo-goers. I jog every day, but her legs are twice as long as mine so I have to really run to keep up. We pass the bat exhibit followed by the tiger habitat. My stomach swirls. Addie veers along a train track that circles the entire zoo. I've ridden the train at least one hundred times. Violet loved it, even though the seats were so small that her knees were up at her ears. One day, toward the end, she came to my school, pulled me out of class and brought me to the zoo. Violet's hair was in pigtails like mine. We rode the train, in the dead of winter, for three straight hours. Somehow my dad figured out where we were. He showed up with my winter coat, but by then I had the beginning of frostbite on my toes.

When we reach the concrete-and-steel entrance to the elephant exhibit, employees in blue Pennington Zoo staff shirts are ushering people out of the building. Addie and I slip inside. A gray-haired staffer locks the door behind us. The smell of straw with a musky undertone rolls over me. I'm standing in the center of a massive elephant footprint that has been pressed into the concrete floor. More footprints lead down a wide hallway. The concrete wall to the right has children's drawings of elephants in brightly colored frames. There are large glass panels on the left wall that provide windows into different enclosures; some lead outside, where I can see a grassy area, a pond, some thatched sun shades and big logs chained to the ground. In the distance three elephants with dented foreheads, two bumps forming the top of their heads, stand belly-deep in the pond. One sucks up water with his trunk and sprays the other two like they're little kids at a water park.

A guy in worn jeans and a blue plaid shirt pokes his head out of a doorway set into a barred wall. He looks at me.

"Who's the kid?"

"Lily, this is one of our veterinarians, Steve Cohen. I think you spoke on the phone?"

"Hey, Lily," Steve says.

I wave. Dr. Cohen sounded older on the phone. He can't be more than thirty-five. His auburn hair is brush cut, white scalp shining through a bare patch, and his lopsided ears stick out like teacup handles.

"She raised more than a hundred thousand dollars with her elephant-naming contest. I thought she deserved to be here," Addie says.

Steve whistles. "Wow. Now we can afford to start construction on the deep pool our herd needs. Thanks, Lily. Seriously. Thank you. Okay, sure, you can watch from the corner but be really quiet and stay out of Raki's line of sight."

Steve closes the door. We watch through the bars as he walks into a room about the size of a four-car garage. There are vertical bars on all sides that remind me of the old Western jails I've seen in movies. But these bars are white and twice as thick. Steve slowly walks to a metal cage on the far right of the enclosure. He steps into it but leaves the sliding door open. Opposite him, in the left corner of the room, is an elephant. Goose bumps break out on my arms. This close, the animal is stunning and so big she doesn't seem real. "That's Raki?"

"Yes," Addie replies. "Normally, having one of our veterinarians stand so close would stress an elephant in labor. But for the past few years, since we planned to breed Raki, Steve has worked as one of her keepers instead of as her veterinarian, so that she doesn't associate him with anything unpleasant like shots or foot care."

"So why is Steve in that cage?"

"He wants to be close in case Raki or her calf needs him, but he has to stay safe."

"Would Raki hurt him?"

"They have a great relationship, but Raki is a mother in labor. Pain can make anyone unpredictable."

My eyes travel over Raki's bulk. She has gray skin covered in wrinkles that make her look like she's clothed in the worn leather of a really old book. Her tail swishes over a cream-colored sac glistening between her legs. Dribs of seashell-pink fluid drip onto the sawdust. Ears the shape of giant plates wave like fans. She sways, shuffling immense feet. Beneath steel-gray skin I can see her belly rippling as the baby shifts.

I don't know how much time passes, but together we watch as the sac grows so big it dangles halfway to the ground. Raki's tail swats faster. She hunches her back. The membrane stretches until the calf's drum-shaped feet and rounded backside are visible… In a single breath the sac expands then Raki's calf drops to the ground. There's a gush of fluid followed by a stream of bright red blood that paints the insides of Raki's legs crimson. Quickly, she lifts one back leg so that she doesn't trample her baby. The calf lies motionless half covered by its embryonic sac.

"Is the baby okay?" I whisper. My mouth is so dry I can't swallow.

Addie holds up her index finger. We wait for the calf to do something—open its eyes, move or cry. But it's inert. Raki kicks the newborn with her back leg—hard enough to move it several feet. The calf doesn't react. Raki kicks it again. I grip the steel bars so tight that my hands throb. The mother elephant uses her trunk to roughly tear away the rest of the sac. She clears the membrane from her calf's face, but it's still lifeless.

"She's dead?"

"Shhh," Addie says.

Raki kicks her newborn a third time. It rolls to face us. The calf's trunk flops onto the sawdust. Raki's ears flap against her head in loud thwacks. Her feet stomp. She raises her trunk, trumpeting so loudly that my ears buzz. Steve picks up what looks like a gun with a green dart on the end. I shiver. It must be some kind of tranquilizer gun. "Why doesn't he use it?" I whisper. Raki's eyes roll around in their sockets, electric, furious, too bright. She grabs the newborn's trunk with her own, tugs hard. I press my forehead hard against the bars. Violet's voice whispers and I'm back on that rooftop...

"Why are you crying?" Mommy asks.

My tummy flutters in a bad way. "I'm scared."

"You wouldn't be if you used your real name."

"Can we go home now?"

"No. But we can fly."

She smiles at me. Her eyes are fireworks, so bright I squint.

"Come on," Addie murmurs. "You can do it."

Raki's hold slips. The embryonic fluid on the baby makes her fuzz-covered skin too slick to grasp. The mother elephant tries again, until she's able to lift her calf's head off the ground. I don't understand why neither Addie nor Steve is stepping in to save the calf. The baby's eyes open for a second then slide shut. Instead of flinging her baby against the wall, Raki lifts its head repeatedly. Finally, its dark eyes blink then remain open. The newborn's rose-colored mouth makes gasping sounds.

I take pronounced breaths like I do at a physical when the doctor listens to my heart to make sure it's still beating.

"It's a girl," Steve calls.

Using her front leg and trunk, Raki helps her newborn stand. The calf is all wobble. The first attempt rolls her sideways. The second leaves her in a Buddha-like slump, head folded on her belly. Raki pushes her calf toward the metal barrier where Steve stands. She wedges the baby against the bars then uses her front leg under its belly to lift it. Raki steps back. The calf sways like the ground is unstable then takes her first step, pushing out her foot like a little kid learning to walk in boots for the first time, shaky but making progress, her mother hovering over her.

"Welcome to the world, Swift Jones," Addie says. She looks at me. "Holy shit! You're white as a ghost. Are you going to faint?"

All the blood has rushed out of my head. My vision narrows. My lips are numb. Knees turn to liquid. Addie grips my waist and pushes my head between my thighs. She roughly kneads the muscles of my neck. "I thought—"

"It's going to be okay," Addie says. "Raki did what was necessary to help her calf breathe. It's every mother's instinct."

Clearly Addie never knew anyone like Violet. I gulp a few more breaths then stand up straight. Swift Jones is halfway under her mother's massive belly. She's about three feet tall. Her skin is a shade lighter than Raki's, and there are tiny gray hairs sprouting along her back. Raki runs her trunk over the newborn like she's checking to make sure her baby has all her fingers and toes. Swift Jones grins.

"It looks like they're smiling."

"They are," Addie says. "Elephants have humanlike emotions. They smile. They cry. They even mourn their dead."

I think she's anthropomorphizing, like everyone does with animals, but it's not my business. "Would Steve have stepped in if Raki couldn't help her calf?"

"Yes," Addie says. "He would've sedated her, but interfering can cause a mother to reject her baby. We want to avoid that at all costs."

We walk into the late afternoon chill. There are dark gray thunderclouds in the distance. My muscles quiver like they do after a hard run. "Thanks," I say. Addie tips her head sideways like she's still making sure I'm not going to pass out. "I'm fine."

"Thank you for the donation. We will use it wisely."

My father is waiting in the zoo parking lot. I told him I'd jog home since I haven't gotten my run in today, or wait for Sawyer to get out of lacrosse practice, but he insisted. He's been hanging out for over two hours.

"Sorry," I say, as I climb into our worn Subaru. "I had no idea it'd take so long."

"No worries. I finished all of my grading." He starts the car. "Long interview?"

"Not really," I say. "It was interrupted by Raki having her calf." I try to fight my smile but it tugs relentlessly upward.

"I got to watch. Just me, Addie—that's Dr. Tinibu—and Steve, the vet."

"That's incredible," my dad says. "Seriously, Lily. A once-in-a-lifetime experience. What a birthday present, right?"

I wedge trembling fingers between my thighs. "Yeah."

"Boy or girl?"

"Girl."

My dad puts on his blinker, turns right out of the parking lot. "How'd Dr. Tinibu like the name?"

"She quoted a Swift Jones song," I say, laughing. My dad laughs, too. "They're going to use the money to make the elephants a really big pool."

"Sawyer will be happy to know that he's responsible for making that happen."

"I went by the tigers. We used to practice growling like them." My comment is a knee-jerk reaction for him giving me zero credit. I want to hurt him back. Invoking Violet in any way is something I rarely do, because my dad has worked so hard to erase her. I get it. But I wish I could tell him that she's always there anyway, at least for me. It's like my dad's act of erasing her made her seep beneath the surface, into my bones.

"Lily?"

"Yes."

"Are you okay?"

There are a million ways to answer that but I give my father what he wants. "I'm fine."

The Pennington Times

OCTOBER 1

BY T. LILLIAN DECKER, INTERN

The Pennington Zoo's Raki Gives Birth

The Pennington Zoo's Asian elephant Raki gave birth to a healthy calf at 5:32 p.m. on September 30, following a twenty-two-month pregnancy.

The calf, enclosed in its embryonic sac, was not initially breathing. Raki struggled to clear her baby's airway by grasping the calf's trunk. After several failed attempts, the calf's eyes finally opened and she gasped for air.

"It's a girl!" veterinarian Steve Cohen announced as the wobbly newborn took her first step with the help of her mother.

The calf's birth is the result of a breeding program instituted by the zoo's director, Dr. Addie Tinibu. Tinibu hails from a small village in northern Kenya. As a young girl working for a conservation group in the Nairobi National Park, she came to love endangered elephants and decided to spend her life finding ways to protect them.

"Poachers illegally slaughter up to thirty-six thousand African elephants annually. They may become extinct as early as ten years from now," Dr. Tinibu said. "The situation is even worse for Asian elephants, like the ones we have at our zoo. There are only about forty thousand Asian elephants left in the wild."

The *Pennington Times* elephant-naming contest generated thousands of potential names and raised $109,350 to aid in the creation of a better elephant exhibit and ultimately a sanctuary.

"I'm stunned and grateful," Tinibu said.

Drumroll, please. The winning name for Raki's female calf is Swift Jones. Zoo-goers can see Swift Jones as early as Christmas. For additional information visit: penningtonzoo.org/elephants.

5

"Did Dr. Tinibu really sing a Swift Jones song?" Sawyer asks as we rush to our respective classes.

"Do we have to relive the moment again?" Sawyer nods even though I've repeated the story at least twenty times in the last twenty-four hours. "Fine. Yes. The one about a pickup truck."

Sawyer beams. "Swift Jones would be so proud."

"Later." I duck into my math class, slide into a seat and pull out a math book. Dawn turns to face me.

"Did you at least think about it?" Dawn asks. "We're really in a bind."

"No."

"The crack Carla made about a makeover was totally made-up," Dawn confides. "But you could look way prettier. Everyone needs a little help." She leans in. "I took Accutane," she whispers. "Now I'm dating Travis."

The last thing I want is a boyfriend. But I can tell Dawn's

sparkly pink heart is in the right place, so I throw her a bone. "What would you do?"

Dawn reaches up, pulls one of my dark curls free. It spirals down to my shoulder. "I'd kill for that kind of natural curl," she says. "It'd look epic with highlights."

Said by the girl with perfect, long, straight, blond hair. She pulls off my round glasses, studies my wan face with its dusting of freckles like it's an unfinished painting. Thankfully she doesn't look through the lenses, because they're fakes. I've worn glasses since the trial. My dad's recollection is that I stole a pair from the grocery store after the first day in court. I don't remember that. I just remember the feeling of wearing them as Violet's jury stared at me with horror and pity. Those round circles of glass created a protective layer between us. Sawyer is the only one, other than my dad, who knows my vision is twenty-twenty.

"If you ladies are done chatting..." Mr. Boce intones.

Dawn hands back my glasses. "Your eyes are a really cool green," she whispers before turning around.

I put my glasses back on, pretend to focus on the equation Mr. Boce is writing on the chalkboard. I didn't do my homework so I have no idea what he's talking about, but I manage to make it through an entire hour of math class without getting picked on or learning anything. The bell rings and there's Sawyer, waiting outside the classroom door because he knows I'm a flight risk.

"I was thinking about skipping it."

"If you do, your dad will know."

He's right. My father teaches at Grable. As if on cue, I see him at the end of the hallway—red flannel shirt, tan cords, leather Crocs. He doesn't look up from his iPad, but I'm sure he has registered I'm heading toward Ms. Frey's office.

Sawyer grabs my backpack and hoists it over one shoulder. "At least your dad doesn't make you wear one of those ankle bracelets the police use to monitor criminals on probation."

"Just like you to find the silver lining."

We pass the student lounge. There's a sheet of paper taped to the glass door with rainbow letters stating: LGBTQIA Meeting—EVERYONE welcome!!! Two kids sit at a table for twenty. They look…lonely. "Maybe they should bring cookies," I say.

Sawyer slows. "Do you think—"

Doug Stackler pounds a fist on the lounge's door as he walks by. One of his football player buddies snickers.

Sawyer hesitates. There's a battle going on inside him. He wants to stand up for those kids but fear stops him. I get it. I didn't have any choice when I was thrown into the spotlight. Once your biggest secrets become public, there's no return. I touch Sawyer's arm. "Either way, I have your back." He looks down at the floor, his cheeks ruddy, then widens the distance between the football players and us. I pull folded pages from my backpack to distract my best friend. "I printed out the test."

Sawyer chuckles. "Of course you did."

Two years ago I found a mental screening test on psychcentral.com and instituted a once-a-month testing policy so we could form a baseline for sanity before I turned eighteen. Sawyer grades it. I can be sure about the results because I made him swear to uphold the Journalist Code of Ethics, even though he has no interest in being a reporter, which he could be because he's smart, articulate and has a face made for world news.

"You'll pass," Sawyer says, bumping my shoulder.

"I know," I say. But I don't know, because schizophrenia is a mental illness that makes it hard to tell the difference between what's real and what's imagined. People with schizophrenia might believe they're being persecuted or followed, that there are people living in their head or that the TV is sending them messages. It should be super easy to tell the difference between what's real and what's not, right? Wrong. Neuroscientists have scanned the brains of some individuals that have schizophrenia. The areas that have activity when a subject with schizophrenia is listening to a *real* person talk also respond when they're having an auditory hallucination. That's why the hallucinations seem so real. On top of that, the brain of a person with schizophrenia can fail to activate the part responsible for monitoring inner speech. So that inner voice can get attributed to an outside person, making it even more difficult for someone with schizophrenia to figure out what's real.

"Remember Confessions of a Teen Schizo?" I ask.

"Hannah. Why?"

When I was fourteen, I went through a stage where I scoured YouTube for videos made by anyone who had schizophrenia. Hannah, this girl with enormous brown eyes, her hair in pigtails like she was seven, not seventeen, posted every week. She was super unlucky because she began having hallucinations when she was only twelve. In her videos, she'd describe the worst ones. They included seeing the lower part of her face in bloody tatters each time she caught her reflection in a window or mirror. Hannah made YouTube videos from her bedroom, a rainbow poster promising a pot of gold taped to the wall behind her.

"Hey, Lily?"

"Yeah?"

"Worrying is wishing for something bad to happen."

I smile at the Freyism. "Remember that kid? The one who always wore a Dodgers cap sideways?"

"Sammy."

He was twenty-two, living in an institution. Sammy believed he was going to be murdered on his twenty-third birthday. The voices in his head told him every single day to kill himself before someone else did it for him. His birthday was March 17 and he didn't post that day, or ever again.

"He found the right meds," Sawyer says.

"Duh," I say, bumping my friend's hip with my own.

"Don't forget the good ones," Sawyer says.

He's right. There are wins in the world of schizophrenia. There was a lecture by a woman with schizophrenia who'd gone down the rabbit hole and fought her way out. Barb, or Belinda, I can't remember which, still saw a bearded man with no legs and arms sitting beside her every time she got in her car, but she'd made peace with him and didn't mind that sometimes he'd sing opera.

"I liked the girl who got the dog," I say.

"It worked," Sawyer points out. "Katherine, right?"

"Kate, I think." Kate's schizophrenia made her so depressed that she didn't want to get out of bed. So she got a dog that slept beside her. Rex. He had his own pillow. If she didn't get up in the morning Rex would pee on her sheets. "Kate tried to drill a hole in her head so the voices would leak out."

"Lily—"

"If I need a dog, get me a huge one."

"Why?"

"The bigger the consequences, the more motivating." Sawyer actually laughs—a real one that cracks me up, too.

So far I don't have schizophrenia, but my case doesn't follow Dr. Phil's oft-repeated line, "Past behavior is a good indicator of future behavior." Au contraire, Doc. Mental illness can creep up and wallop me over the head at any time.

"Ten percent," Sawyer reminds me.

That's what he thinks my chances are for contracting the illness. He's partially correct. If a close family member has schizophrenia, there's approximately a 10 percent genetic chance their descendant might have it, too. That number seems small to Sawyer because he believes I have a 90 percent chance of being healthy. I agree that those are phenomenal odds if someone is betting on a horse, a hand of poker or a basketball game. But not when you think about having your life taken away before it has barely begun.

"Lily?"

I refrain from telling my best friend about the letter I found last week. Sawyer would still be my best friend, but nobody should have to be that great. "Ten percent. That's right," I say. "I'll take that bet."

Sawyer wraps his arm around my waist and gives me a squeeze. "Twelve-Year Plan."

"Yup." My Twelve-Year Plan is a combination of the Journalist's Code, which necessitates navigating by logic not emotion, and clean living because schizophrenia isn't just hereditary. There are hosts of contributing factors. Stress, a lack of sleep, changing hormones, childhood physical, emotional or sexual abuse, alcohol and drugs can all be triggers for schizophrenia. I run three miles most days, try to meditate, don't drink caffeine or alcohol, and have never even smoked a cigarette, let alone pot.

I can't do anything about the physical and emotional abuse.

"There's a party at Ben's house this weekend. His parents are out of town," Sawyer says. "Be my wing gal?"

"You don't need a wing gal. Everyone wants to talk to you." Sawyer's smile slips. I'm a pitiful friend, but parties without parental supervision are definitely not part of the plan. "Why are you friends with me again?" But I know why we're best friends. Neither of us matches on the inside. Sawyer is every girl's dream but he's attracted to guys. I'm so bland that no one can imagine the time bomb ticking inside my head.

We reach Ms. Frey's office. There's a poster on the door that reads Do You.

"Carla keeps bugging me about Wyn," Sawyer says. "She wants her email address so she can ask her about a runway model named Kendall. Apparently Carla is a *huge* fan."

"Then it's time to break up with model Wyn."

Sawyer sighs. "But she's so hot."

"If Carla gets too nosy, she might actually figure out that the photo hanging in your locker is a Slovenian actress named Lena."

"Who am I dating next?"

"Um."

"What?"

"Are you sure you want a new girlfriend?"

Sawyer nods.

I nibble my lower lip, thinking. "The daughter of a Saudi prince who you met over summer break while cruising the Greek Isles with your parents."

"Did I cheat on Wyn?"

"No," I say, because Sawyer would never cheat, even on a make-believe girlfriend. "But you kept in touch."

"You sure? A princess?"

"Yup." Sawyer dating a princess is entirely possible. The only lie other than the obvious is that Sawyer's parents were on the yacht with him. They were supposed to be, but Sawyer's mom had a face-lift that needed revision and his dad got off the boat at some port only a few days into the cruise and never got back on. It took Sawyer days to realize his father was gone. Turns out Cushing found some guy-on-guy magazines in Sawyer's stateroom. They haven't talked since.

"So what's my princess's name?"

"Not Swift Jones."

One side of Sawyer's mouth crooks into a half smile. "Deal. If you promise to lay off the worrying?"

For a second I reconsider telling him about the letter. "Deal."

6

"Hey, Lily. Have a seat," Ms. Frey says.

She has a round table for a desk with four red plastic chairs. The walls of the small office are covered with movie posters from *Pulp Fiction* to *28 Days Later* and *Straight Outta Compton* to the latest superhero and thriller releases. Its Ms. F.'s way of showing kids she's cool. I guess she kind of is—early thirties, dead ringer for Katie Holmes, and she talks to students without sounding like she's standing by a chalkboard. I take some credit for that, because I was her first case when she arrived at Grable. She was just out of school with a master's degree in counseling, and in over her head, unsure how to deal with a kid whose mom tried to kill her. To her credit, Ms. Frey has evolved, listening more and rarely talking in clichés.

At this point, we've known each other for ten years. Ms. Frey understands that I'm a lazy student. Smart enough to get decent grades, but it's hard to care that much given my uncertain future. She gets that I skip art class because I'm uncomfortable doing anything Violet loved. My mom painted in acrylics, usually creating jagged, fractured faces on empty wine bottles. They were as vibrant and jarring as her personality. My dad shattered every bottle after the trial ended.

Ms. F. and I both share a love of documentaries. My favorite is *The Lion's Mouth Opens*, about a young actress and filmmaker confronting her fear of developing Huntington's disease. Ms. F. prefers lighter films. Her recent pick is *Twinsters*, about two twins finding each other after being adopted in different countries. She's all about happy endings. I try not to burst her bubble.

On the more serious side, Ms. Frey knows that my dad and I have a *careful* relationship, that I still have nightmares, my aversion to birthdays in general, my own obviously being the worst. But the evolved Ms. F. and I have an understanding. She makes suggestions only if I ask for them. And I usually don't, because my Twelve-Year Plan is pretty straightforward.

Lately, though, Ms. F.'s been pushing me a little bit. She's the one who talked me into applying for the *Pennington Times* internship. There were over a hundred applicants from high schools around Pennington. We were both pretty shocked when the newspaper picked me. I almost said no, but after years of listening to my drivel, Ms. F. deserved a win. Also, I could tell that my dad was a little bit pissed that she'd suggested the internship. He prefers me in direct line of sight.

Ms. Frey tears a bag of salt and vinegar potato chips open, our favorite, and offers them to me. "How're the college apps going?"

"One and done," I say between crunches.

She hands me the top sheet of the pile of papers in front of her. It's a list of colleges that have great journalism programs.

There's USC, of course, but also Boston University, Washington and Lee, Northwestern, NYU, Lehigh, Pepperdine, UC Irvine. "I'm going to Muni," I say, sliding the paper back.

"Lily, unless you totally mess up, you're going to graduate with a 3.4 average. Math isn't your strong suit, but English, French and history have saved your butt. Why not apply to a few more schools? Just to see?"

"Are you saying that I'm too good for Muni?" I ask.

Ms. F. cracks a smile. "I'm saying that maybe it's time to push a little bit outside your comfort zone. Challenge yourself."

I cross my arms. "I'm good."

"I want to share something with you." Ms. F. takes another sheet out of the folder. "Did you know that one in five people who are diagnosed with schizophrenia get better within five years?"

I don't point out that the word *better* is a relative term. Instead, I wonder what it would be like to be the person without a sledgehammer hanging over her head. "Remind me why we're talking about this?"

"Because I only have eight months left with you." Ms. F. reads the next line. "Three in five will get better—"

"But still have some symptoms," I finish, because I have the stats memorized. "And they will have times when their symptoms get worse. Symptoms can include feeling like your head is going to blow apart, seeing people morph into insects or wild animals, hearing voices telling you to kill your baby sister or your mom or a cat because if you don't something horrible will happen to you… But I digress. One in five will continue to have troublesome symptoms. All will need to find the right medication to manage their condition. Shall I go on?"

Ms. Frey leans back in her chair. "Sure."

"There are two types of drugs commonly used for treatment. *Typical* and *atypical.* Typical drugs have neurological side effects like tremors, painful muscle stiffness, temporary paralysis, muscle spasms and extremely slow movements. They can also result in tardive dyskinesia. That means facial tics, or spasms of the tongue or mouth."

"I just want to get across the point that you've spent your life worrying about something that's treatable—"

"Would you like to hear the side effects for atypical meds?" I ask, tapping into my imaginary superpowers: Logical. Emotionless. Responsible. Balanced.

Ms. Frey holds up her hands. "Go ahead."

"Weight gain, loss of motivation, sexual dysfunction." I crumple the piece of paper with all its helpful statistics and toss it at the trash can. It goes in. "Two points."

"So the plan is to make all the easy choices? Float through life?"

"I've told you." I tug an escaped strand of my hair hard enough to hurt. "The plan is to get through the next twelve years doing everything I can to avoid boarding a train to Crazy-town."

"You do realize that it's not politically correct to call someone with mental health issues crazy?"

"It's my brain," I say. "My choice. Just like floating through life."

Ms. Frey leans in. "I'm not suggesting you develop a heroin addiction or join Tinder. A date would be good, though."

Yeah, a date would be great. I'd like to at least be kissed

by someone other than John Jensen in the tunnel of love. We were ten and I let him cop a feel of my nonexistent boobs.

"Lily, I'd just like to see you take a small step toward whatever future you envision."

"Does my dad know you're on a one-woman campaign to push me out of the nest?"

"I'm not your father's counselor. I'm yours." She slides the list of colleges back to me. "Pick one other school on the list. Apply to it."

"Why?"

"Because you can."

"What are you, the Make-A-Wish Foundation?" It's a joke, but my voice comes out too sharp. I push my chair back, start to pace around the small room. "I'm not some kid with cancer that needs to live my dream before I croak. I'm not dying. I just might not have a future as…as me."

"But right now you do. As you."

I slump onto a chair.

"One more thing."

"Do your demands ever cease?"

Ms. F. licks her lips. It's her *tell.* She's nervous. Making jokes is my tell. Sawyer's is ticking his tongue against the roof of his mouth. My father's is clearing his throat. Violet's right eyebrow twitched, but not all the time, which made her more dangerous.

"Okay… Let me say that I feel like this is a huge breach of your privacy. But I also think I have to share it with you."

Ms. Frey pulls a photocopy out and I see the first lines:

Dear Calvin,

You claim that you love our daughter…

I don't need to read the rest. It's the letter I found last week but already know by heart. Now I understand why Ms. F. felt the need to dig into the drug options and possible positive outcomes of a schizophrenia diagnosis. She knows that I know I'm screwed. "Where'd you get it?"

"Your father realized it was missing. He found it under your mattress."

"So he came to you. Not me." I hate the hurt in my voice. "Why did he show you the letter?"

"To remind me of the stakes." Ms. F. reaches for my hand but stops an inch shy.

I hold my breath, frozen like a soldier who has stepped on a land mine. But no matter what I do, eventually it's going to blow me up.

"Lily, I think it's time for you to live a bit more. That way, if the worst happens—"

I exhale. "At least I'll have the memories?"

"No. You'll have something you love to fight for."

"I needed a T-shirt to go running. All mine were in the laundry. The letter was taped to the inside top of his dresser drawer. Half the tape had lost its stick so my fingers caught on the part of the envelope that was hanging down." I look at Ms. Frey. "Why do you think he bothered to keep it? I mean, if he wasn't going to share it with me?"

Ms. F.'s lips are pressed into a tight white line. I can't help it. I read the letter again.

Dear Calvin,

You claim that you love our daughter, Violet. But you

are rushing into an impossible future and your actions will end in catastrophe.

Sarah and I would love to see our daughter become a wife and mother. But some things are not meant to be.

Violet's great-grandmother (Sarah's grandmother) Mary Catherine had hebephrenic schizophrenia. She was committed to an insane asylum at age twenty-seven. She hanged herself six months later.

Mary Catherine's twin sister, Elizabeth, had schizophrenia, too. From letters, we know that at nineteen she began to hear voices telling her to commit acts of violence. She died of sepsis from a ruptured appendix before the illness fully manifested.

Sarah's mother, Carolyn, had paranoid schizophrenia Her illness was controlled by medication that left her lethargic and confused. Carolyn's drug overdose was ruled accidental.

Sarah has a diagnosis of bipolar and schizoid personality disorder. By the time we found out that she was pregnant with Violet, it was too late to abort or we would have done so. There have been periods in our life, when Sarah's mental illness took over, that were a living hell for Violet and me.

At age fifteen, Violet experienced auditory hallucinations. The voices disappeared a few months later but they can be a precursor of what's to come. Given our family history, even with extreme vigilance, Violet's chance of escaping schizophrenia is small.

Now Violet is pregnant. We are furious and heartbroken. Motherhood is an exhausting, stressful proposal for any woman. We feel certain the schizophrenia we've managed to hold at bay will manifest should Violet have this child.

Violet is accountable, but you, Calvin, will be to blame for what happens next. End your relationship. Convince our daughter to get an abortion. We will attempt to pick up the pieces.

Should the two of you decide to have this child, we will discontinue all contact. We simply cannot watch our daughter's imminent destruction.

Sincerely,

William Hanover

"She told me that no one wanted us," I say.

"Who?" Ms. Frey asks.

"Violet. When we were on the roof." This is new territory. I've never discussed that day with anyone but the judge who required my testimony. My vision blurs…

Violet and I stand on the edge of our apartment building's roof. My bare feet are really cold. A breeze rustles the edge of my nightgown, the cotton one with tiny strawberries on it. My knees shake. Police cars are parked eleven stories below.

"Don't be fooled, little bird. Nobody really wants us," Mommy says.

I shake my head. "Daddy wants me."

"Do you know where my mommy and daddy are?"

"No."

"Exactly."

"I never understood until I read the letter. Violet's parents kept their word."

"You never call her Mom."

I shrug. "It helps create distance."

Ms. F. slips into the chair beside me. "Can I give you a hug?"

"Only if it will change my life." I wipe my wet eyes and runny nose with the sleeve of Sawyer's sweatshirt. Nadine, his housekeeper, will get the snot out. "What would you do?" I ask.

"I can't possibly answer that without living in your shoes."

"Try."

"Part of me would do exactly what you're doing with your Twelve-Year Plan," Ms. Frey says, twisting the rows of silver beads she wears around her wrist. "Part of me would say screw it and live the life I want, within reason, because the future is uncertain and because, like I said, if there's nothing in your life you love, you won't fight to have it back."

Ms. F. hands me a tissue. It smells like lavender. I'm not really crying, but I blot my face to make her feel useful.

"Have you talked to your dad about any of this?"

"We have a deal. He pretends he's not watching for telltale signs that I'm sliding toward bonkers. I pretend I don't know that he's waiting for what he believes is inevitable."

"A family history, even as bad as yours, doesn't mean it's inevitable. Does anyone on your father's side—"

"Have schizophrenia? Not that I know of. But the odds are definitely not in my favor."

"Do you want me to talk to your father?"

I meet her gaze. "If you do, I'll never talk to you again."

Ms. F. helps me rip the Xeroxed letter into tiny pieces. "I'll apply to one other school," I say, because this isn't a run-of-the-mill counselor problem. There's no reason for Ms. F. to feel like a total failure.

Ms. F. sniffs. "Which one?"

"USC." I give her hand a pat. "The best is yet to come."

"Did I really say that?"

"Who else?"

7

"How was your day?" my dad asks the second I walk through the door of our loft. He's grading history papers at the dining room table, his blond hair loose, half hiding the deep lines etched into his forehead. The smell of broiled chicken fills the air.

"Same but different." I toss my backpack on the table, then pull out a French assignment. I'm supposed to learn the vocabulary in a new chapter of *The Little Prince* by Antoine de Saint-Exupéry for tomorrow's quiz. I sit down at the far end of the table and start reading, looking up words when I don't know them.

"Did you see Ms. Frey today?"

You know I did. "It was on the calendar." My father writes a *C* in red pen on the top of a student's homework assignment. Is his job as boring as it seems? I could ask him, but I don't. We are two people living under one roof, but we've become strangers. Silence is the invisible third person in our family, always standing between us.

I set the table. We both resume working while we eat. The only sound is the clink of our forks, the rustle of turning pages, the occasional throwaway comment. "Thanks for dinner," I say ten minutes later, clearing the dishes.

"Did you like it?"

What can I say about broiled chicken, brown rice and a green salad? That we eat it at least three times a week? "Yeah. New recipe?"

"I added cumin."

"Nice." I grab my backpack, heading down the hall to my room. When I shut the door it's like I can breathe again. My twin-size bed with its white duvet is on a modern black platform in the corner. Other than the limited edition Paddington Bear alarm clock, my room is undecorated. The only real artwork is in the far back corner of my walk-in closet, below rows of hanging sweatshirts, jeans and a few dresses still bearing tags that Sawyer insisted I buy. Behind a suitcase I've never used is a miniature version of Escher's *Reptiles* that Violet drew on the wall with a green felt-tip marker. I remember bits of what she said to me the day we huddled together in my closet...

"Always be waiting for me."
"Are you leaving, Mommy?"
"Never say goodbye...it means forgetting."

I click on the closet light, sit cross-legged beside the sketch and lightly trace the patterns with my index finger. As lizards climb off a sheet of paper they turn into three-dimensional reptiles then climb onto different objects until they return to the page as one-dimensional drawings.

After the trial was over, my father didn't just tear down the Escher posters from our loft's walls. He shredded them. I watched, hidden beneath the overstuffed couch that was replaced with a leather sofa a few weeks later. It was the first and last time I saw him cry. When he was done with the posters, he attacked the sentences Violet had scrawled in red Sharpie over doorways, around every window frame. He covered every word with two coats of white paint. I've never told my father about the one remaining Escher that Violet drew in the back of my closet. I don't want any part of her, but erasing every last trace that she existed won't change anything.

My phone rings to the tune of *The Exorcist*'s bells. "Hi."

"Thought you were coming over," Sawyer says.

"Sorry. Ms. Frey needed to talk. Plus, how will I fit into my homecoming dress if I keep eating Betty's desserts?" Sawyer doesn't laugh. It's a sore subject. He wants me to go to the dance with him. I've said no a hundred times.

"Lily, come on," Sawyer says.

"Sorry. I'd do just about anything for you, but I will not be your pity date."

"You know that's not true."

"Yeah, good luck convincing the rest of our class. Plus, Carla might dump a bucket of blood over my head."

"We do not live in a Stephen King horror flick," Sawyer points out.

"Speak for yourself." I lie down on the closet's hard floor. "Next subject, please."

"Cushing spoke to me."

"What?" I sit straight up. "Tell."

"He actually did notice the $100,000 transfer out of my trust fund."

"Duh."

"There's nothing he can do about it." Sawyer clears his throat. "He said that I disgust him."

I want to drive over to Cushing Stafford Thompson's mansion and light it on fire with him inside. "You are the best person I know."

"I'm the only person you *really* know."

I think Sawyer is crying, which makes my chest feel like it's six sizes too small. I do the only thing I know will make him stop. I start to sing. "'Your life is made of tight jeans, sweet smiles, easy denials… Your style is all fast cars, open bars, rubbing up to shallow stars… You think I buy magazines to see your face, curves and lace, but I'm into novels not comic books—'" Sawyer hoots. In that moment I actually appreciate Swift Jones. "More? Because I'll do it," I threaten.

"You do realize you're tone-deaf?"

"What? I can't hear you," I shout into the phone. My dad knocks on my door. "I'm fine," I call. "Just talking to Sawyer."

"Don't go to bed too late."

"Okay." I wait until I hear his footsteps fade. "Can Cushing cut you off?"

"Maybe. But most of my trust fund is from my mom's side."

"Would she care?"

Sawyer is quiet for a moment. "The good news is that my parents don't talk. Ever. They just pass in hallways wide enough that they can pretend they didn't see each other."

Sawyer's not kidding about the mansion he calls home. It's fifteen thousand square feet of exotic woods, marble, soapstone and crystal chandeliers with outdoor fountains, tennis courts and a swimming pool, all set in the tony suburb of Dunnhop. He's also not kidding about Cushing and Mirabela's relationship. I've actually never seen them in the same room at the same time.

"Where are you right now?" Sawyer asks.

"My closet."

"Reptiles?"

"Uh-huh." I trace a green lizard. "You know what Escher said about his drawings?"

"Tell me."

I read the Escher quote taped beside Violet's sketch. "'I try in my prints to testify that we live in a beautiful and orderly world, not in a chaos without norms, even though that is how it sometimes appears.'"

Sawyer clears his throat. "Ready?"

My skin prickles. "Go already. And skip to the ones that matter most."

"Bossy."

"Guilty."

"Number two. 'I hear or see things that others do not hear or see. A, Not at all. B, Just a little. C, Somewhat. D, Moderately. E, Quite a lot. F, All the time.'"

"B," I answer.

"Number one. 'I believe that others control what I think and feel. A, Not at all. B, Just a little. C, Somewhat. D, Moderately. E, Quite a lot. F, All the time.'"

My dad definitely tries and sometimes succeeds. "B."

"Number three. 'I feel it is very difficult for me to express myself in words that others can understand. A, Not at all. B, Just a little. C, Somewhat. D, Moderately. E, Quite a lot. F, All the time.'"

Doesn't everyone sometimes feel like that? "B."

"Number five. 'I believe in more than one thing about reality and the world around me that nobody else seems to believe in. A, Not at all. B, Just a little. C, Somewhat. D, Moderately. E, Quite a lot. F, All the time.'"

"A."

"Number seven. 'I can't trust what I'm thinking because I don't know if it's real or not. A, Not at all. B, Just a little. C, Somewhat. D, Moderately. E, Quite a lot. F, All the time.'"

This one is tricky. "A."

"Number twelve. 'I talk to another person or other people inside my head that nobody else can hear. A, Not at all. B, Just a little. C, Somewhat. D, Moderately. E, Quite a lot. F, All the time.'"

"Does Ms. Frey count?" I ask.

"Lily," Sawyer says. "You ask me that every time. And I tell you that when you start to have *new* people, *new* voices and *new* conversations, songs or quotes, not just Freyisms or lines from Swift Jones or *Peter Pan* popping up in your brain—which, by the way, I have, too, the latter thanks to you—those will count. Accept it. You just have a kick-ass imagination."

"A," I say.

We go through all the questions, including the ones that ask if people are plotting against me or if I have magical powers.

"You've scored a big, fat zero," Sawyer says. "Way to go, champ."

It's just an online test, but I feel relieved. "Thanks. Do you want me to tell Dr. Tinibu where most of the money came from?"

"No. I prefer for my charitable donation to remain anonymous," Sawyer says in a great imitation of Cushing's snooty voice. "Unless Swift Jones reads your article and wants to give me front row tickets to a show."

"I'm pretty sure she won't be reading my article."

"Lil," Sawyer says quietly, "how can I love SJ so much but not love her enough?"

I think about sharing a Freyism, but a cliché doesn't feel right. "I love you, Wonder Woman."

We stay on the phone for a while not talking. I can hear SJ in the background. I'll memorize a few more songs so that I can pull out different lines if Sawyer needs them. I grab a pillow from my bed and curl up on the floor of my closet. When I wake in the middle of the night, there's a blanket over me.

8

"What's this?"

My father holds up a large manila envelope that contains my application to USC. I spoon Cheerios into my mouth. Chew. Swallow. "It's a college application." I procrastinated for three weeks before writing it. Ms. F. has been ridiculously patient with me, so even though the deadline is closing in, it was important to keep my word.

"Didn't you already apply online to Muni?" My father grabs a sponge.

"Yes." I clear my cereal bowl even though I've only had a few bites.

"Lily?"

My back is to him as I dump my breakfast into the sink, but I can feel his eyes. "It's not a big deal. Ms. Frey thought it'd be cool if I applied to a school with a stronger journalism program. I picked USC."

"I thought we talked about this."

I turn. He's scrubbing a stain on the counter that isn't there.

"What's the harm?" I ask. My dad's eyes bug out. When I was a little kid, I thought my father's eyes were superhero blue, but now they're just washed out, like his powers have drained away.

"The harm? Lily, I can't afford a California school."

"I could take out student loans. That's how Dr. Tinibu got her college degree."

"You have no idea how much pressure comes with owing that kind of money." He tosses the sponge into the sink. "USC is a really competitive school. Your grades are good, but they won't make that cut."

"I have a 3.4, plus Sawyer thinks my internship with the newspaper might help."

"Sawyer's a great kid, but he's top of your class, a star athlete and lives a very privileged life. He's not exactly in touch with reality. Sweetheart, even if you got into USC's journalism program, those students would overwhelm you. Cutthroat kids, like the ones who went to Cornell with me. It's a very tense environment."

I consider telling him that I know he snuck into my room. But it would lead to a larger fight. That wouldn't be good for me. "I want to have a bigger goal than Muni," I finally say. My dad tries to put a hand on my shoulder. I move out of reach.

"Lily, it doesn't matter where you go to college. You can make the most of any education regardless of how long you attend."

My world is a kaleidoscope. With a twist it comes into focus. My father doesn't think I'll make it through four years of college because he doesn't think I have four years of sanity left. I pick up the application. My hands are shaking, but I manage to shove the envelope into my backpack.

Calvin sighs. "I'll be ready in five."

"I'm getting a ride to school from Sawyer." I leave without looking back.

The aroma of Sawyer's morning latte wafts over me as I climb into his Jeep, grab the paper cup from his hand and take a big gulp. "Ow!" The roof of my mouth is seriously scorched.

"Okay," Sawyer says. "First, coffee is hot. Second, you don't drink caffeine."

"I just did."

"I saw. What's wrong?"

I pull the application out of my backpack. "I was going to apply to USC."

"What?" Sawyer pulls me into a sideways hug. "We are going to have so much fun!"

"First, I said I *was* going to apply. My dad took a massive crap on the idea."

"Why?"

"He's sure I won't be able to handle the pressure of loans or a competitive college."

Sawyer pulls onto Burnside Avenue, entering the flow of morning traffic. "He's wrong."

I slide the envelope back into my pack. "He's probably right."

"Then why'd you want to apply?"

"It's stupid."

"I love stupid."

"Fine. When I gave Dr. Tinibu the check—"

"Which wouldn't have happened if you hadn't thought of the contest."

He is so my best friend. "Thanks."

"Okay. Back to Dr. Tinibu and the check. Go."

"It's just, when she saw the amount, she almost cried."

"Because she loved the name?"

I flick his head with my index finger. "No, because Dr. Tinibu has a passion for what she's doing. She watched her father kill elephants, so now she has a mission in life to protect animals from extinction."

"So you want to save elephants?"

"Shut up."

"Sorry. Go on."

I fiddle with my glasses. "Ms. Frey said she wanted me to have something I love if...you know. She thinks it'd help me fight to find my way back. I've thought about it for a few weeks... This is going to sound dumb, but maybe my *thing* is going to a really good college so I can be a solid journalist who writes about stuff that matters."

The muscles in Sawyer's jaw clench hard. It must be extremely annoying for him to have to constantly listen to drama-queen me. Even I'm annoyed. "Forget it," I say. "What time is your game?"

Sawyer jerks the wheel, hard, throwing me into the gearshift. He pulls to the curb, jams the Jeep into Park. "Give it to me," he says, holding out his hand.

"What?"

Sawyer digs into my backpack, pulls out the application. He's out of the car and running before I have the chance to say anything. He stops at the mailbox on the corner and tosses the envelope in. Then he does a touchdown dance. People laugh as they walk by. A super cute well-dressed guy doing a sidewalk dance is funny. An unwashed homeless woman doing the same thing is threatening, because she might be high or mentally ill. He gets back in the car, holds up his hand for a high-five.

"Even if I get in..." I start to say.

Sawyer forces me to slap his hand. "Want another sip of my latte?"

I take a careful sip as he pulls back into traffic. "Huh."

"What?"

"It's cooler. It didn't kill me. In fact, it tastes pretty good. I might develop a coffee addiction."

"You're from the Pacific Northwest, so it's, like, your birthright. But trust me, only decaf after 1:00 p.m. or little caffeine soldiers will march inside your brain battling all night to keep you awake."

A Foo Fighters song comes on the radio. They're my favorite band. I sing along with Dave Grohl.

"So, Cushing suggested I get an apartment."

I snort. "Yeah, right." But when I look over at Sawyer and see his expression, a pang shoots through my chest. He's not kidding.

"He says it's about the money, about not living by his rules, but—"

"I can try to get the money back."

Sawyer's hands tighten on the steering wheel. "Lily, it's not about the money."

I fiddle with the radio stations until I find an SJ song. She sings, *I like it slow, slow, slow...* "If you think about it, this is kind of amazing," I venture. "I mean, I'd give anything for my own place." My voice is pitchy, which means I'm trying too hard, but I plow forward. "Sawyer, you're being handed total freedom on a silver platter. You can get an apartment in the Pearl District, or Hawthorne, maybe? Both have super cool coffeehouses and great restaurants. You can have parties, stay up all night and play Swift Jones so loud the windows break."

"He probably doesn't really mean it," Sawyer says.

"Well, I'd be there, like, all the time, watching *Naked and Afraid* marathons."

Sawyer reaches for my hand.

"Um. Why are you holding my hand?"

He stares straight ahead. "It's the coffee thing. I'm so proud."

We head down the tree-lined entrance to Grable. Sawyer parks in the school lot, first row, because when you're Sawyer Thompson the universe conspires to always have a prime parking space waiting.

Jonah is at the front entrance. He's leaning against the brick wall, pretending to read something on his iPhone. I know he's pretending because, unlike me, his glasses are so thick that they distort his brown eyes, and right now he's not wearing them. Jonah is probably waiting until the last possible moment so he can run into his classroom just as the bell rings. For an hour he'll be safe from the track team and the general cruelty of kids. Jonah's day must be very long.

"What if I do get into USC?" I ask as Sawyer pulls open the school's door.

"We'll fight for it." Sawyer looks over his shoulder. "Come on, Jonah, you can walk to class with me."

Relief colors Jonah's freckled face. "Dude," he says. "Really? Thanks." He scurries through the door behind us.

"Later," I say to my friend and his freckled disciple for life.

A tall silhouette with a ponytail of thinning hair stands at the end of the hall. My father is pretending to read a poster, but I know he's waiting there to make sure I showed up at school. I grab books from my locker and go the long way to chemistry so I don't have to face him.

9

I manage to avoid my father all day. After the last bell, I escape out the back exit of my school just in case he's waiting for me in the parking lot. When I get to the *P-Times* newsroom, Mr. Matthews is sitting on the desk beside Shannon's eating jellybeans by the handful from a crystal bowl. He holds out the bowl. I take a blue one.

"Lily, do you know how many emails, tweets and letters we've gotten since your elephant contest?" Mr. Matthews asks.

"No."

"Neither did I," Mr. Matthews says, "until this morning, when the doofus we have collecting readers' letters finally told me." He holds up a crayon drawing of a big gray rock beside a little gray rock. "It's from Kaylee, age eight, Mrs. Kendrick's first-grade class."

I squint. "What is it?"

"Raki and Swift Jones," Mr. Matthews says. He hands me a thick folder. It's stuffed with hundreds more drawings. "They're not just from schools in Oregon," he says. "Kids in

Washington State, California, Kentucky, even tots in Maine, keep writing us."

"How do they know about Raki?"

"Do you two ever talk?" Mr. Matthews asks, turning to Shannon.

"I told her a few weeks ago that her little article was picked up by the Associated Press," Shannon says without looking at me.

"Please tell me that you know what the AP is?" Mr. Matthews asks.

I have a vague idea, but I wait for Shannon. No help there. "They dispense news stories?"

"The AP is a not-for-profit, independent cooperative of news organizations that finds, reports and distributes news to half the world's population every day," Mr. Matthews says. "The *Pennington Times* is a member, along with thousands of other US and international newspapers. Your elephant story was picked up by the AP national wire, so it's been reprinted in other newspapers around the country, intriguing kiddies in every state of our great Union."

"Why would they care about Raki and Swift Jones?" I ask.

Mr. Matthews shrugs. "Hell if I know. What matters to me is that we've collected over three thousand emails, letters and pictures. It impresses our board of directors. Anyway, Dr. Tinibu agreed to a more in-depth interview and to photos. Four hundred and fifty words." He slides off the desk. It groans in thanks. "The interview is in an hour."

Shannon turns back to her computer. "Go see Jack."

"Who's Jack?"

"The photographer for your article and your ride to the zoo. He's in the break room."

A scruffy guy in skinny jeans and a black T-shirt looks up from pouring himself a coffee when I walk into the break room. He's cute in a hipster kind of way. I've taken a vow of celibacy for the next twelve years, but I can still look. "Jack?"

"Guilty."

"I'm Lily. Ready?" We head into the gray Oregon afternoon and climb into Jack's beat-up Volvo wagon. The car smells like stale french fries and wet wool. Jack grabs the offending pile of wrappers and workout clothes at my feet and tosses them into the back. "Where'd you go to college?" I ask on the drive to the zoo.

"Berkeley. Dual major. Creative writing and journalism. Are you going to college next year?"

"Probably Muni, but I'm also applying to USC. It's a long shot."

"If you want to get into USC's journalism program, then fight for juicier stories," Jack suggests. "Animal stuff is cute, but it's not going to get you noticed."

The rest of the drive goes by in silence, which is good because I need to think of some questions. By the time we pull into the zoo's lot, I'm ready. Addie's door is open when we get to her office, so I give the frame a little knock and she waves us in.

"Thanks so much for the interview," I say. "Jack is *P-Times*' photographer."

Jack shakes Addie's hand. "Just ignore me," he says.

"Why don't we start the follow-up on the way to the elephant exhibit," Addie suggests. "That way you can see the calf while we talk." She grabs a rain shell from the back of her chair. We follow her into drizzle. "You're both very lucky. The exhibit is closed to the public until Swift Jones is two months old."

Jack looks interested, but I've already seen the calf. I pull out my list of questions. "Can you tell me more about the conservation center you worked for as a kid?"

"The Henry Shaw Wildlife Trust," Addie says. "Their mission is to aid in the preservation and protection of all wildlife. They have an orphan project created to save the baby elephants left behind after poachers kill their mothers. There are similar orphan projects in Asia that also do this kind of work."

It starts to rain harder, but Addie stops walking, so I keep taking notes. I try not to look at the animal exhibit behind her. The orangutans have both an indoor and outdoor enclosure. Outside, it's a two-story-tall, chain-link-enclosed area half the size of a school gymnasium. There are some trees, suspended tire swings and rope walkways. I've seen the apes on sunny days, leaping, swinging and calling to each other. But right now, only one rain-bedraggled ape is outside. He's hunched on the rope bridge, orange fur soaked through, head hanging low. I appreciate that zoos do their best for each animal, that they're trying to educate and protect. But still, it's pretty sad to see animals that should be free and wild forced to live in artificial exhibits to keep their species alive.

"The first orphan I saw was named Mbegu," Addie continues. "He was found on the Masai Mara standing beside his dead mother. She'd been killed by a poacher's poison spear. Her tusks had been sawed off, leaving gaping, bloody wounds.

Mbegu was circling the body, using his tiny trunk to try to move his mother."

"Can a baby elephant survive without his mother?" Jack asks.

"Of course he can," I say. They both look at me. "Sorry. Go on."

"Mbegu was only two months old when his mother was killed. He didn't stand a chance of survival because the older females in his herd had not recently given birth so they had no milk to share."

"A calf can drink milk from an elephant who isn't her mom?" I ask.

"I've seen it work," Addie says, "but there's no guarantee."

"But you said he was rescued."

"Mbegu was flown to the Wildlife Trust, where a team of specialists waited. He hadn't been without milk for long but was so traumatized from watching his mother die that he wouldn't let our handlers come near. We tried to bottle-feed him but despite the love of handlers, tireless veterinarians and the comfort of the other orphan elephants in the stockade where he was kept, Mbegu continued to refuse the milk. He died a week later."

"Why wouldn't he drink?" I ask.

"In many ways elephant calves are more complex than humans," Addie explains. "They can die of a broken heart."

"But a lot of orphans do survive?"

Addie walks on. "Some orphan calves do survive, but the point of my story is that even with all the work conservationists do, saving the elephant from extinction is an uphill battle. Every win counts. Swift Jones's birth is a huge win."

"Aren't elephant breeding programs in zoos controversial?" Jack asks.

"One elephant dies somewhere in the world every fifteen minutes," Addie says. "Zoos like ours breed in the hopes that we can preserve a handful of elephants if conservation efforts fail and those in the wild become extinct."

"Why do you love elephants so much?" It's not one of my questions, but I want to steer Addie back to a topic that makes the crease between her brows disappear.

"Off the record because it's both personal and not pertinent to your story?"

Jack and I both nod.

"I told Lily already that my father was a poacher. He was a very cruel man. He beat my mother almost daily. He beat his children, too. We had no power in the world. As a child, working at the Wildlife Trust, I learned that elephants form the perfect family."

Addie pulls open the door to the elephant exhibit. We follow her inside. The air is warmer, thick with the miasma of sweet straw and the heavy musk of elephants. She leads us down the hallway.

"Back on the record," Addie says. "A herd is led by the oldest elephant matriarch and consists of her sisters, daughters and their calves. The older female elephants help the younger ones when they give birth. The entire herd looks after the babies. They're there for each other in every situation, and never overlook even the smallest member's needs."

"Where are the adult male elephants?" Jack asks.

"When the bulls reach adolescence they break away from

the herd and travel with other males. They seek out a herd only when it's time to mate—"

"Addie!" Steve runs down the hallway toward us. "I've been calling you."

Addie pats her jacket pocket. "I forgot my radio. Sorry. What's wrong?"

"Raki tried to crush her calf. If we don't get SJ out of the enclosure, Raki may kill her."

10

Steve and Addie take off down the hallway, leaving Jack and me alone. "Well. I guess the interview is over."

Jack shakes his head. "We're still on the job. Come on."

Addie and Steve disappeared through the farthest doorway on the right. Jack heads that way but my feet are rooted in place. Jack's right, this is my job. But Addie didn't invite us and I don't really want to see what's happening.

"You coming?" Jack calls.

I take a step toward the exit. Whatever is going on doesn't involve me. There is no way witnessing Raki kick the shit out of her daughter fits into my Twelve-Year Plan.

A plaintive cry that sounds almost human echoes down the hall and suddenly I'm running beside Jack.

We stop on either side of the slightly ajar outer barred door and peek our heads around it. Raki and Swift Jones are in the same enclosure where the calf was born. Raki's ears flap like they're on overdrive. She trumpets so loudly that it hurts. Swift Jones stands in the center of the room. Blood dribbles down her front leg from a cut on her chest. Her miniature trunk swings side to side. She calls out to her mother, high-pitched, forlorn. Steve, several staff members and Addie stand inside the smaller cage in the far right corner.

"I darted her over ten minutes ago," Steve says. "Since then she's been pacing, not attacking, but every time we try to run in and grab the calf, she charges us. She's too fast to risk it. We'll have to wait for the sedative to kick in."

"What'd you use?"

"One cc of Etorphine. Enough for a standing sedation."

Addie grips the cage's bars. "Yesterday Raki was the perfect mother. What changed?"

I'm in a hospital room, my forehead stitched, bandaged, eyes closed against the room's bright overhead light.

"What changed?" the policeman asks.

"I don't know," Daddy says. "Violet has always been a great mother."

"There were posters, scribbled messages on the walls of your apartment."

"My wife is an artist."

The policeman clears his throat. "Did you know she'd gone off her medications?"

"No," Daddy lies.

I wonder why my daddy isn't telling the policeman that Mommy no longer speaks to us with her own words. She's stopped showering. They scream at each other every day then cry. Mommy refuses to cook because Mrs. Berg, an old lady who lives down the hall, is poisoning our food.

"Are you taking notes?" Jack whispers.

I nod. Scribble on my pad. But I don't need notes. Traumatic situations burn their details into my brain.

"We both know that elephants who breed in captivity sometimes reject their calves," Steve says. "We'll work through it. But first we need to make sure SJ is safe."

Beside me Jack's camera clicks. I flinch. It feels wrong to document this private moment between mother and daughter. With an earsplitting trumpet, Raki charges her calf and head-butts her in the torso so hard that Swift Jones flies several feet through the air, hits the ground, rolls. Raki kicks her repeatedly, her body flipping down the length of the room until she's ten feet from us. The calf is motionless, her eyes closed.

Raki runs to the other side of the pen then turns and stamps the ground, winding up for a full speed attack. Every nerve in my body fires... I don't remember running into the enclosure. But I'm looking up at Raki, who is less than fifty feet away. Behind me I hear Swift Jones whimpering. The sound peels the skin from my bones. In the distance someone calls my name...

> "T. Lily, stop crying," Mommy says.
>
> On the street below, people point up at us. "But I can't fly."
>
> Mommy squares her shoulders. "'You just think lovely wonderful thoughts...and they lift you up in the air.'"

Raki trumpets. Her eyes roll in their sockets. They're too bright. *Fireworks.* She stomps the floor, bellows, then charges me. The ground trembles, or maybe it's me. She's about to crush me…and then she stops. Literally stops, less than ten feet away. She's still standing but swaying, legs splayed wide, trunk dangling, eyes glazed. I swallow hard, tasting only my own sour spit.

Addie shakes my shoulders so hard that my head snaps back and forth. "What the hell were you thinking?" she shouts. Spittle dots my face. "You could've been killed!"

"I'm sorry, I'm sorry, I'm sorry," I whisper.

Swifty wobbles to her feet. She's not dead. There's only one cut on her body. The calf looks up at Raki. She makes a sad, bleating sound. Steve kneels by her then runs his hands over her body like he can't believe she's alive either. "Get the calf and that girl out of here so I can reverse the sedation before Raki falls," he says, then approaches Raki with a small syringe. The massive elephant doesn't even register that he's there; that any of us are there.

"What happens if she falls?" I ask Addie. I know my voice is too calm for what just happened.

"A fall could injure her."

"She tried to kill her calf."

"It's not her fault," Addie says, leading us both out of the enclosure.

"Whose fault is it?"

Addie closes the barred gate. "Why'd you do it, Lily?"

I don't have an answer I'm willing to share.

11

Jack talks nonstop during the ride back to the newsroom. I pretend I'm listening but really just focus on breathing in and out.

"You doing okay?" Jack asks as we walk into the newsroom.

An elephant almost killed me. Hysterics are appropriate, but I feel...fine. "Just thinking."

"It's going to be a great article." Jack pulls out his camera and laptop, sits down at the desk to my right. "I'll work on the photos. Let me know when you've got a draft."

"Just so you know, I'm not writing about Raki's attack."

"Yeah, right."

Opening my laptop, I click on Word. "Seriously. I'm not."

Jack opens a file filled with photos of Swift Jones's ordeal. "Look."

I blur my eyes so that Swift Jones's image is just a gray mass. "Addie asked us not to write about the rejection."

"Lily, you do know that it's not her call, right? The rejection is news. News you were sent to cover."

There's a chemical taste in my mouth that's been there since Raki charged me. *This is the taste of stress.* "I was sent to write a follow-up story about Swift Jones. Not to torpedo the zoo's breeding program."

Jack leans back in his chair. "Why the hell did you run in there? You could've been trampled. You were seconds away from it. Seriously? Craziest move ever."

My face gets hot. "Raki was hurting her calf. I wanted to stop her."

"Raki is an *elephant*," Jack says. "She probably weighs about nine thousand pounds. What are you? A hundred and ten soaking wet?" Jack clicks on a photo. He whistles. "Look at this one."

It's a photo of me standing between Raki and her calf. Raki's front right foot hangs prestomp. My face is milky white, framed by escaped curls. My eyes are open wide. They appear much greener than they actually are. "I don't give you permission to use a photo of me."

Jack slams his hands on the desk. "Why the hell not?"

I recoil like he's hit me. I could tell him that the last time I was in this paper, the article was about Violet attempting to toss me off a building. Filicide is nothing new to me. I don't want someone to drag up my past, make the comparison. Also, my dad would be beyond freaked out by what I did. "I'm a reporter. I can't be part of the story."

"But you *are* part of the story."

"Not the one I'm writing."

"This is your chance to get noticed by USC. Hell, they'll probably give you a scholarship!"

"As journalists we're supposed to minimize hurt, balance

the public's need for information against the harm we might cause."

"But these are the most incredible photos I've ever taken!"

"Sorry." I get to work. It's only four hundred and fifty words, so it doesn't take long.

Baby Elephant Swift Jones Turns Three!

Swift Jones turned three weeks old today! She weighs 329 pounds thanks to her mother Raki's nutritious milk. "She's healthy, happy and figuring out how to use her wriggling trunk," Dr. Tinibu, director of the Pennington Zoo, said.

Not all baby elephants have such a peaceful existence. "I worked for the Henry Shaw Wildlife Trust in Kenya, Africa," Tinibu explained. "Their orphan project is dedicated to saving baby elephants whose mothers had been killed by poachers. The first orphan I saw was named Mbegu. He was found on the Masai Mara beside his dead mother, whose tusks had been sawed off, leaving bloody holes. The calf was brought to the orphan project where a team of specialists waited. Despite the love of our team, Mbegu died a few weeks later."

According to Tinibu, even with all the work conservationists do to try to decrease poaching and protect the species, saving elephants from extinction is an uphill battle. Every win counts. "Swift Jones's birth," she said, "is a huge win."

To learn more about Dr. Tinibu's breeding program and how you can donate to help Pennington Zoo's elephants, visit penningtonzoo.org/elephants.

No typos. The story makes sense. "Done," I tell Jack.

"Then go home. You looked wrecked."

"I told Shannon I'd wait for her to get here in case she wants me to make any changes."

"Just leave it on her desk with a note to call if she has any questions."

Jack thinks I'm a huge loser. He's right, but I'm unwilling to change the story so I don't bother defending myself. "I'll shoot it to her email."

"A little secret?" Jack says. "Shannon is old-school. She prefers hard copy for editing."

"Okay." I print out my article and put it on Shannon's desk. "See you later."

12

In the *Pennington Times* elevator I call Sawyer. His phone rings four times before he picks up.

"What?"

"Sawyer?" It's his voice but he sounds wound up way too tight.

"Get off the goddamned phone," a man in the background shouts.

My skin prickles. "Is that Cushing? What's going on?" I've rarely heard Cushing talk to Sawyer, let alone yell.

"Can I call you back, Lily?"

I should say no, because everything isn't okay. "Yeah."

Cushing yells, "I won't allow that kind of perver—"

Sawyer hangs up and I step into the rain, silently cursing myself for not having a jacket or an umbrella. Or a spine. I'm soaked before I walk half a block. Ten minutes later, Sawyer calls back.

"What's up?" His voice is hollow, like he's been carved out.

I'm instantly nauseous. "Do you want to talk about it?"

"Distract me."

I tell him what happened. "Was it so terrible? What I did?"

"Which part?"

"The part where I ran between a stampeding elephant and her calf."

"It was a lot of things. It was, at the least, a very bad idea."

"What was it at the very most?" I ask my best friend.

"It was totally Lily."

The light changes. Skirting a puddle, I cross the street. "Meaning?"

"Fierce."

"Yeah, right. I haven't been fierce since I punched Gary."

"Lily, you are fierce every single day of your life."

I stop walking. "Excuse me? You're speaking to T. Lillian Decker, life coward."

"Lily—"

"Hang on." The light is red but I chance it and run across the street in front of an oncoming Mercedes. The white-haired driver honks at me. "It's Oregon," I yell at him. "Pedestrians always have the right of way!"

"Tell me this."

"What?"

"Were you scared when Raki was charging you?"

"Terrified."

"Good."

I don't tell him that one of Hannah's YouTube videos flashed through my mind as Raki charged me. It was the one where she explained how she felt right before a violent hallucination: *like hot vinegar is surging up my throat.* I was half expecting that taste, and it was way more terrifying than getting trampled to death.

"Lily?"

"Yeah?"

"Don't do it again."

It's raining so hard that water streams down my face. "So what's up with Cushing?"

"Want to go look at apartments tomorrow after school?"

"Excuse me?"

"Apartments. My father wants me out in two weeks."

"I thought he wasn't serious."

"Turns out he is."

My skin feels like it's the wrong size. "Are you—"

"I'm thinking a corner unit, floor-to-ceiling glass windows, an outdoor deck for parties with a fireplace and pizza oven, of course, and at least three bedrooms so you have one and the third can be our movie room."

Sawyer still doesn't sound right. If my teeth weren't chattering I'd try a song. "There are some cool buildings near our apartment," I offer. "The Standard around the corner has a sign advertising gourmet kitchens with high-end appliances."

"Betty won't be there," Sawyer says.

What he doesn't say is that it's not really about Betty's cooking. She's the only adult in his life who pays any attention to his schedule and actually cares. "If it's not about the money for Cushing, maybe if you talked to him about the boat thing?"

"The boat thing," Sawyer says in a flat voice.

I dodge a cyclist. "Watch it!" I shout. "Why is he wearing all black? Is he, like, daring a car to hit him or trying to run over pedestrians?" I get to the front door of our apartment building and key in the code then stand in the atrium, making a puddle on the concrete floor and shivering. “I need a hot shower. Talk to Cushing if you don’t want to move out, okay?”

“I’ll figure it out,” Sawyer says, sounding almost normal. “Movie at seven?”

“Huh?”

“For film class. Our paper is due tomorrow. Betty made us caramel popcorn.”

“Crap. I’m exhausted. I’d just fall asleep, you know?” The line is silent. My nerves vibrate. “Sawyer?”

“No worries. I’ll sign your name.”

“You’re the best.”

I take a hot shower, but it doesn’t wash away the sticky feeling that something is way off with Sawyer. Dinner with my dad consists of broiled chicken—with paprika!—rice and green beans sprayed with Bragg’s Liquid Aminos. My dad says I look bushed. For once, I agree and head to my room. In addition to the film paper, I have a quiz in history tomorrow and a project proposal due for French class but instead of pulling out my homework, I get into bed without undressing. I’m almost asleep when my phone rings. I find it on the fifth ring at the bottom of my backpack. “Hello?”

“It’s Shannon.”

I sit up.

“Just wanted to check in on you. You okay?”

“Sure. I’m fine.”

“Good work on the article. Night.”

“Night.”

13

I wake in the exact same position as when I fell asleep. I'm super stiff as I shuffle my way into the kitchen. My dad sits at the counter with his head stuck in the newspaper. "Morning," I say after gulping down a glass of fresh-squeezed OJ. "You do know that you can read the paper online, right?" He doesn't look up. My Cheerios are already set out. Today there are fresh blueberries on them. They're out of season so they must've been expensive. I make a mental note to be nicer to my dad. He tries. "Thanks for the—"

"Were you going to tell me?"

My mouth is full of Cheerios. "About what?"

My father carefully closes the paper, folds it in half so that the bottom of the front page is faceup. There's a close-up photo of Swift Jones with blood running down her chest. Beside it is a large photo of me standing between Raki and SJ. Raki's trunk is held high; one massive foot stamps the ground. Even in black-and-white her eyes look wild. Even in black-and-white, my face looks...resigned?

"I don't understand—"

"That you ran between a furious nine-thousand-pound elephant and her calf? For crying out loud, Lily!"

My dad's cheeks are red. His fingers grip the edge of the counter. I scan the headline. Elephant Raki Tries to Kill Baby, Swift Jones. For a second I can't compute what I'm reading, because it's not the headline I wrote. Then I remember Shannon's call last night. *I just wanted to check on you...good work on the article.* Shit-shit-shit. Shannon wouldn't have complimented me on the shallow article I wrote.

"Lily? I want an explanation. Now."

My throat closes as I scramble for one. Jack said I looked wrecked. He said Shannon wouldn't have any real changes to my article. He told me to print it instead of sending it via email like I've done in the past. He sent me home. He wanted to use his own photos. He's worse than a liar, because he's made me his accomplice. I grab my iPad and read the article he wrote using my byline.

The Pennington Times

OCTOBER 21

BY T. LILLIAN DECKER, INTERN

Elephant Raki Tries to Kill Baby, Swift Jones

"Raki tried to crush her calf," zoo veterinarian Steve Cohen yelled as he raced toward Dr. Addie Tinibu, director of the Pennington

Zoo. "If we don't get SJ out of the enclosure, Raki may kill her."

They ran off, leaving *Pennington Times* photographer Jack Bell and me, *Times* intern T. Lillian Decker, alone in the hallway of the zoo's elephant exhibit to witness what happened next.

Raki was given a strong sedative, but its effects had yet to take hold. She stood in the corner of her pen, ears flapping, bellowing so loudly that the floors vibrated. Her calf, Swift Jones, was in the center of the enclosure. The three-week-old bled from a cut on her chest and made high-pitched mewls.

Suddenly Raki charged her baby, head down, striking hard. Swift Jones flew several feet through the air then hit the ground. Raki kicked her repeatedly then retreated to the far side of the room, preparing for a full-speed, possibly fatal, attack.

I acted on instinct, raced into the pen, standing between the hurt calf and Raki in an attempt to protect Swift Jones. The mother elephant charged. She was only a few feet from me when the sedative she'd been given kicked in. Raki froze, legs splayed, swaying, her trunk limp, eyes glazed.

"You could have been killed," Dr. Tinibu shouted at me.

This event leaves Swift Jones's survival in question. "In many ways elephant calves are more complex than humans," Tinibu said. "They can die of a broken heart."

Tinibu and Cohen plan to slowly reunite Swift

> Jones with her mother, Raki. "Hopefully," Tinibu said, "this is a onetime occurrence."
>
> Pennington Zoo board member Alfred Conway was reached late last night for comment. "The board plans to thoroughly review the Pennington Zoo's policies," Conway said, "and in specific, its elephant breeding program."

I'm sick to my stomach. Addie is going to hate me. Kids at school will bring up my past. "I didn't write this article."

My dad slams his hands on the counter. "I don't care about the article. I care that my daughter ran in front of a charging elephant. Lillian, for God's sake, it's something Violet would've done!"

My stomach cramps. "Except Violet wasn't acting strange!" I shout back. "She was normal right up until the time she tried to fly me off the roof!"

All color drains from my father's face. "What?"

"So what I did, trying to save that calf, is crazy? But what Violet did, scribbling on every wall, talking to us like she was freaking Peter Pan, doesn't rate on the insanity scale?" I don't know when my cereal bowl shattered, but there are shards of glass on the floor and blood drips off my fingers.

"Lily, what I said? Back then? Dammit, how can you even remember? You were in the hospital with a concussion. I was in shock. My wife had been arrested. My daughter almost fell off a roof."

"Almost *fell*? Bullshit!" My pulse is so fast, it's tripping over itself. I close my eyes, take deep breaths, but Violet is there waiting…

"Will you fly away with me?" Mommy asks.
"Where?"
She points to the sky. "'Second to the right, and straight on till morning.'"
"I want Daddy!"
"I love you, T. Lily, but you're hard to like."
The rooftop door crashes open. We both flinch. I want to look but I'm shaking too hard.
"Violet?" Daddy calls out. "Honey? It's okay."
Mommy sobs. "It's not."
"I love you, V," Daddy says. "Come down. We can figure this out together. You and me forever, right?"
"Please don't cry," I say. "I'll fly—I'll fly."
Mommy looks over her shoulder. "Calvin, I love you most!"
I can tell Mommy means it. But I'm standing next to her, so even though she doesn't love me most, she picked me to fly. Her nails dig into my wrist. Blood trickles down my arm. I swallow my sobs and try to be a tiger. Mommy bends her knees and pushes off. I go up, too, then down like a pumpkin. My head cracks open.

"Lillian, talk to me!"
My cell rings.
"Let it go."
"Hello?"
"We need you at *P-Times*," Shannon says.
"I didn't wri—"
"Now."
I hang up then rinse the blood from my palm. The cut is

shallow. No stitches this time. "That was my boss. I have to go over to the *Times*."

"We're not done talking," my dad says. "And it's clear you need to quit that internship."

"Why?"

"Because it's threatening everything we've worked so hard to achieve!"

My bones fill with lead. "What have we actually achieved?"

"Lily—"

"No. More likely than not, I'm going to get schizophrenia. Paranoid, catatonic, schizoaffective disorder, hebephrenic. It doesn't matter which one, because they all suck."

"We'll cross that bridge if—"

"A Freyism?" I shout. "That's all you've got?" He doesn't have another answer. "So when I lose my grip…I'll be able to look back on great memories, right? Newsflash. There aren't a ton of them. I'll battle to regain…what part of my life? Does any part, other than my friendship with Sawyer, warrant much of a fight?"

"Sawyer and I will both be there for you."

He doesn't get it. All the anger leaks out a hole in my heart. "By the time I lose my mind, Sawyer will be a professional athlete, an astronaut or a movie star. He can't be my lifeguard or I'll drag him down with me."

"Lily, why can't you understand that I'm doing everything I can to save you?"

I know that I should feel sorry for him because he loved her but couldn't save her, and all he's left with is me.

I grab my backpack and walk out the front door.

14

The *Pennington Times* boardroom is wood-paneled with swivel chairs around a fourteen-person, highly polished table. The leather seat I slide onto is cold. "Really great photographs," I tell Jack, as he sits down beside me. "They're probably the best you've ever taken." His Adam's apple bobs as he swallows the fake compliments. Across the table are Shannon and Mr. Matthews. My boss unwraps a breakfast burrito from El Rinconcito, the Mexican food cart around the corner. "First, Lily, good article," he says with a full mouth. "Second, what the hell were you thinking?"

I was thinking that I'd write a bogus story so Addie's program wouldn't be destroyed.

"I don't condone what you did, but damn, it made great copy." Mr. Matthews takes another bite. Salsa dots his chin. "Since this is your baby, I want you up to speed."

My baby? Jack shifts in his chair like he can't get comfortable. My bet is that he's dying to come clean, take the glory.

But if he tells the truth, that he hijacked my article, he'll probably get fired.

"We have a conference call with Dr. Tinibu in two minutes," Mr. Matthews says. He points to the open laptop on the table. "Skype. She called me this morning at 5:19 a.m. That woman knows many curse words. She's demanding a retraction. Threatened a lawsuit. So I gotta know," he says, "anything I need to be worried about?"

Jack leans forward. "Everything in that article is true."

"I'd like to hear that from the gal who wrote it," Mr. Matthews says.

"Yes," I say. "It's all true." I now understand the cliché about throwing someone under the bus. The wheels have just run over Addie's body with a sickening crunch.

"Well, get ready, Lily. Dr. Tinibu insisted that you be here for this call. Your ears will be bleeding by the time we're done," Mr. Matthews says.

The next ten minutes go by in a blur. And then things go from really bad to horrible.

"You have no idea the damage you've done," Addie tells me, nostrils flaring. "The bull used to inseminate Raki was on loan from Wild Walker's Circus in Haven, Florida."

Shannon leans forward. "Do you have a contract with them regarding offspring?"

"For now, this is off the record?" Addie says.

Mr. Matthews nods. "Agreed."

"Yes. We have a contract." Addie holds up a thick document. She flips a page then reads: "Should any calf born from Walker's sire, Lorenzo, be shown to be in imminent danger then ownership of said calf immediately reverts to Wild Walker's Circus."

There's a buzzing in my ears. "You're going to lose Swift Jones?"

"Thanks to you, yes. Unless we can talk the circus into giving us another chance."

"Why wouldn't they?" Jack asks.

Addie leans forward, her brow furrowed. "Because baby elephants sell tickets."

"Maybe it will be a better home," Shannon says.

Addie crosses her arms. "Wild Walker's Circus travels most of the year, transporting their animals in semi-trucks. Does that sound like a better home for Swift Jones? Their elephants are either chained or *freed* to spin in circles on pedestals or do other tricks counter to their nature, which they've been taught through the use of an ankus."

"What's an ankus?" I ask, trying to ignore the sensation that I'm trapped in a room with the water level rising and no way out.

"A pole with a hook and spike on the end," Addie says. "It's used to pull, push and punish elephants by poking and scraping the sharp ends against the most tender places on the elephant's body."

Mr. Matthews holds up one hand. "I agree that a circus isn't optimal, but zoos aren't exactly great for animals either."

"Zoos aren't perfect," Addie says. "But we are the best and only option right now to protect animals like elephants that are being decimated in the wild. And we don't torture them."

"You're saying Walker's does?" Shannon asks.

Addie runs a hand across bloodshot eyes. "I don't know for

certain. But Wild Walker's has never cared for an elephant calf this young. In addition, they have ten male elephants. No females."

"You're acting like that circus won't do everything they can to keep the calf alive," Shannon says.

"The calf refused most of her bottles of formula last night. She's traumatized, which can lead to depression. Our best hope for her survival is a slow reintroduction to Raki. Our second-best hope is to care for her around the clock in the way only people who have experience can do." Addie points at me. "Lily's reckless article may have taken away those chances."

I want to crawl under a rock. But. Everyone is watching me, so I fold my hands on the table. "What are you going to do?" I ask.

"Pray that Walker's doesn't invoke their right to our calf," Addie says.

I try to swallow but can't pull it off, because I'm out of saliva. "If they do?"

Addie's eyes lose their hard veneer for a split second. "Swift Jones may very well die."

"We'd like to do a follow-up article," Mr. Matthews says.

"For fuck's sake! Haven't you done enough?" Addie explodes.

"It might help," Shannon points out, "if public opinion is swayed toward your cause."

"Would you do that?" Addie asks.

"We'd report the truth," Shannon counters.

Addie's eyes turn to stone. "Fine. But Lily has to write it."

I lurch back in my chair. "Why me?" The last thing I want is to spend time with Addie.

"Because I want you to see, in person, what you've done."

Mr. Matthews rubs the stubble on his chin. "What do you have in mind?"

"We're understaffed. Swift Jones requires round-the-clock care. Lily can take this Tuesday's night shift."

I hold up my hand like I'm waiting to be called on by the teacher. "I have school."

"You'll go tired," Addie snaps. "I want her article on the front page of the paper, just like the last one."

Mr. Matthews nods. "Done."

15

I'm afraid to go home. It's too early to head to school so I call Sawyer and he picks me up outside the newspaper's office. I fill him in as we drive to his house.

"What're you going to do?" Sawyer asks.

"You're the smart one in our dynamic duo. Get me out of this." My voice is an octave too high.

"People would kill to spend a night with Swift Jones."

"Not funny. This is not in any way part of my plan. In fact, it can probably be found on the first page of the Anti Twelve-Year Plan." I bounce my head against the seat. "If I were to make a list of things that would be stress inducing, a night with a depressed elephant calf whose mother has rejected her—who might die because of an article I didn't write but might as well have because the blame will fall on me—would be in the top five."

"Breathe."

Every muscle in my body is tensed for flight. I can't suck in more than a ragged gasp.

Sawyer takes the exit ramp, downshifts then turns right. "Lily, I know you're freaked out. But another article is a great thing. Think about your college application, okay?"

"Don't you remember Zara?" I practically scream.

Sawyer jerks the wheel, pulls to the side of the road and puts the car in Park. He looks directly into my eyes. "You are not Zara."

"I could be." Zara was another schizophrenia YouTube star. She went to Harvard Medical School, and six months in the stress flipped a switch in her brain. She had hallucinations that she was having sex, all the time, day and night, fully clothed. Three years after her first episode, she'd attempted suicide twice, was addicted to cutting and lived in her stepmother's basement.

"You are not Zara," Sawyer repeats.

My face burns. I'm so ashamed of what I might become. Will I be one of those disheveled women sitting on the sidewalk, smelling of urine and babbling nonsense? The kind of homeless lady that people walk around like she's a leper or, even worse, make fun of? Or will I be institutionalized, unable to find the right combination of meds, seeing monsters morph out of walls, believing I've been abducted by aliens, the FBI is after me...or hearing voices that tell me I'm so worthless that I should kill myself before someone does it for me? Will I know what's happening? Will anyone be kind to me?

"Lily, lots of teens who have a schizophrenic episode never have a second one."

It's true. And there are cases of people taking antipsychotic meds after their first episode that result in normal brain activity if they're willing to stay on the medications for life. But Sawyer doesn't know about the letter. I look away. "Don't be disappointed in me, okay? I'm not going to take care of Swift Jones. And I think I should go to Muni, live at home."

Sawyer gets back on the road. He takes a left onto his street, stops by the keypad outside massive, iron gates and types in the code. We pass perfectly trimmed hedges, several fountains and a line of maple trees blazing autumn's oranges before pulling into the circular drive in front of Sawyer's house. He turns off the car but neither of us gets out. I stare out the window at a gardener expertly cutting back the prodigious rose bushes.

Taking a deep breath, Sawyer puts a hand on my shoulder. "Lily, no matter what you choose to do about Swift Jones, or where you go to college or decide to live, whether you keep your Paddington Bear clock, even if you dress in baggy clothes, wear your hair in a messy knot, you'll still be eighteen, and nineteen next year, twenty the year after that. You'll still grow up."

Sawyer has never said this to me before. His last sentence brings to mind a judge imposing punishment on a criminal. *Bam!* goes the gavel. I have been found guilty of having fucked-up genes. The sentence is for life. No possibility of parole. We sit in silence. My best friend is probably wondering if I even heard what he said. I did. I know. I have to try. Within reason, like Ms. Frey said, because the train is leaving the station. Even if I'm not on it, I'll end up wherever it's going. I cling to my imaginary superpowers. Logical. Emotionless. Responsible. Balanced.

"I'll take care of Swifty for one night. Period. And if I get in to USC, I'll go. Even if I don't get a scholarship; even if I have to take out loans that will put me in debt for the rest of my life."

"If I still have a trust fund, I'll help."

I shake my head. "I need to do it on my own so that it matters to me more than anything in the world."

Sawyer pulls me into a hug. I don't fight it, because he seems to need it. "What happened with Cushing? Did you tell him you want to stay?"

"Nah, I decided you were right. I need the freedom to blast Swift Jones until my eardrums bleed."

I pull back to see my friend's eyes. They're shiny. "Cushing doesn't deserve you." Sawyer nods but doesn't say anything else.

We get out of the car and climb the flagstone steps. Inside the massive front door, white and black squares of marble form a checkerboard pattern. They lead to a double stairway that swoops upward around a crystal chandelier the size of my loft's kitchen. Its prisms catch the light from a towering window on the far wall that looks out over the mansion's landscaped grounds. I believe this is what people mean by a "territorial view."

The mansion feels like a museum, filled with antique furniture and priceless carpets in deep crimson and sapphire hues and decorated with giant oil paintings hanging in gold frames. Sawyer gets the entire fourth floor. Besides his huge bedroom with a gargantuan closet, he has a home theater. His bathroom is my favorite. It has a rectangular glass shower with sprays and nozzles reminiscent of a car wash, and another TV. An intercom system connects the entire mansion.

I've never heard anyone but Betty and Nadine, the housekeeper, use it.

We head into a kitchen that's any chef's stainless-steel wet dream to see what high-calorie treat Betty has made. Strawberry-rhubarb tarts are set on a plate in the center of the soapstone island. They're still warm. When I bite into mine, the combination of sweet and sour makes my mouth water. "I love Betty." I truly mean it.

Mirabela floats into the kitchen. Sawyer's mom is dressed in black Lululemon yoga pants with a matching black top that shows off cut abs. Sawyer says they're spray-tanned on, but they look real to me. In fact, if you didn't look at his mom's face, she has the body of a thirteen-year-old gymnast who hasn't hit puberty.

"Sawyer," Mirabela says. "And?"

Sawyer's mom has met me about five thousand times, but my name just won't stick. I don't take it personally. Between all the Xanax she eats like candy plus the plastic surgery that's starting to make her look like a hammerhead shark with eyes tugged toward her temples, I figure she either can't see me or is too relaxed to care.

"Mom, it's Lily," Sawyer says. "My best friend. Since second grade."

"Of course," Mirabela says. She rolls a bright green shark eye toward me. "How're your mother and father, dear?"

I try to meet one of her eyes. "They're great! Mom sends her best and a new cookie recipe I've already given to Betty."

"Wonderful." Mirabela opens the glass door of the refrigerator. Everything inside it is lined up in perfect rows. She takes a fat-free yogurt off the shelf and has two spoonfuls, before tossing the container into the garbage. "Darling, your father told me some very disturbing news."

All color drains from Sawyer's face. "Ah—"

"You cannot take his BMW without permission. You have a perfectly good..."

"Jeep," I fill in.

"Thank you, Lisa," Mirabela says.

"Did you hear Sawyer is moving out?" I ask.

Mirabela turns toward her son. "Really?"

Sawyer nods. For once his mom appears focused. "I thought he'd drop it," she muses.

My mouth falls open a little bit. Mirabela and Cushing actually talked? I look at Sawyer. For a second he's nine years old again—big feet, bowl haircut, deer-in-the-crosshairs look.

"Mom?" Sawyer asks.

"Well, what'd you expect? You pissed him off, dear. You're his son, his legacy, blah, blah, blah. The video didn't help."

Sawyer's cheeks redden. "I was just—"

Mirabela pats his shoulder then wanders toward the doorway. "I left home at nine for boarding school. Growth experience. Maine is lovely this time of year." She drifts out of the room.

"Video?" I ask my friend.

"I might've left a DVD of some guy-on-guy porn on Cushing's office chair."

I shake my head like I heard wrong.

Sawyer turns away. "Drop it, Lily."

"But—"

"Seriously. Drop it."

So I do the only thing I can think of. "Race you?" I run

through the hallway, leaping up the right staircase, gaining a few seconds due to my surprise attack.

"Cheater," Sawyer shouts.

He passes me on the left set of stairs. By the third floor he's a half flight ahead. I'm gasping. We run into his room and throw ourselves onto the king-size bed. The housekeeper has been here. The bed with its snow-white cover is perfectly made. The area rug, a rich blue edged in chocolate brown, has been vacuumed. All the books on the built-in mahogany shelves are arranged tall to small. Pens and pencils have been collected in a crystal glass and set in the right-hand corner of an antique desk. The posters of Swift Jones's album covers—*Cat Eyes*, *Split*, *Elbows & Knees*, *Secret Places* and *Forget to Remember*—that hang on the walls are all professionally framed.

"You okay?" I ask.

"Yeah," Sawyer says. "It's for the best."

"What can I do?"

"Help me find an insane apartment."

My phone rings. It's my dad so I toss my cell to the floor.

"How are you going to get him to let you go on Tuesday night?"

"I'll tell him I'm studying at your house then call at eleven, say you fell asleep so I'm just going to stay in the guest room."

"Wow, Lily. Lying comes really naturally for you."

I grin. "Is that a compliment?"

"If the shoe fits, put on the other one," Sawyer says.

I snort. He cracks up. For just a second, all is right with the world.

Then the reality of my impending night at the zoo hits like an icy wave.

"Come on," Sawyer says. "We've already missed homeroom and I have a physics test second period."

I follow him downstairs even though I want to stay safe in his bedroom, hide beneath the covers. But it wouldn't work. I can't stop time.

16

Tuesday night comes way too fast. Sawyer drops me at the zoo with words of encouragement I can hardly hear over the hum of my fears. Addie is waiting outside the elephant exhibit. In silence, I follow her down the hall and into an enclosure the size of a small garage with bars instead of walls. The calf stands in the far corner looking very small. There are large canvas cushions plus several straw bales placed throughout the pen. Four red plastic garbage pails, a pile of wool blankets, a refrigerator and a shovel rest against the bars. The smell of wood shavings, straw and urine rises with each step I take. Flip-flops were not a good choice of footwear. In the distance, elephants wander a gymnasium-sized indoor hall that's filled with dirt piles that they climb, descend and then climb again. A floor-to-ceiling window frames sheets of rain. The empty enclosure to the left of Swift Jones's pen has five-foot-tall chain-link fencing fastened at the base of the bars.

I pull out a notebook and pen. "What's the chain-link for?"

"So that we can place Raki close by her calf without risking a negative interaction."

I swallow. "Raki doesn't want to be touched by her own calf?"

"It's still important for Swift Jones to be close to her; to hear, see, smell her. We've also been bringing the other adult female elephants into the nursery for visits, so that Swift Jones feels loved by her extended family. Right now we have to tread lightly, but given time, Raki's maternal instincts will kick in."

"Why did Raki reject Swift Jones?"

"Elephant births in zoos are rare. Raki had never witnessed one before."

"But she did fine with the birth and it's been three weeks. What changed?"

"I don't know." Addie walks over to the refrigerator. "Raki won't tolerate being milked, so that means Swift Jones isn't receiving the nutrition she needs. We have to provide her with a very specific replacement milk formula that's vital for her health." Addie opens the fridge. It's lined top to bottom with giant baby bottles.

"How many should Swift Jones drink each feeding?"

"One bottle—that's three pints, every feeding, for a total of up to twenty-four pints a day."

"Seems like a lot."

Addie sighs like it's taking a huge effort to educate stupid little me. "Calves can dehydrate very quickly. If a calf drinks little or no fluid, she won't survive more than a week. We've managed an average of nineteen pints with Swift Jones, which can sustain her, but we're hoping to up that number. So far we've been most successful with feeding her every three hours. But if she wants a bottle more often, give it to her. Calves can't be overfed."

"How long do calves drink their mother's milk?"

"They're not fully weaned until they're at least three years old."

"If the reintroduction doesn't work, that's a long time for hand-feeding."

Addie's lips compress. "Yes. It is."

I flip to a new page in my notebook. "So how does the caretaking process work?"

Addie takes off her glasses, rubs red-rimmed eyes. "In a perfect world, we'd have six caretakers each day rotating shifts. But we're sorely understaffed. I worked the last two shifts alone. Which is a problem."

"Why?"

"When a calf loses her mother, that mother must be replaced by both elephant and human caretakers who are the new family. But human caretakers need to be rotated so no strong attachment forms."

"But you're creating a new family. Don't you want the calf to bond with you?"

"If Swift Jones bonds too much then loses us, she'll plunge from sadness to depression. Refuse her formula."

Bullcrap! I shake my head. If I survived, a baby elephant can live, too. It's not a choice. It's just an instinct. "I'm sorry, but aren't you being kind of melodramatic?"

Addie shakes her head. "Life-threatening problems can be triggered by psychological grief. I've told you that elephants are more complex than humans. What people say about them never forgetting is true. Decades after a loss in their herd, they'll return to the exact spot where their loved one died to mourn."

"How do you know that they're mourning?"

"They cry," Addie replies.

Bullshit. "Raki isn't dead."

"For Swift Jones, she might as well be. That's why a successful reintroduction is so vital for the calf's survival."

Holy condescension. "If you're telling me these things so that I'll write that Swift Jones needs to stay put, at the zoo, I can't promise that. My job is to write a factual article, not an opinion piece."

"I'd expect nothing more from you," Addie says.

We stare at each other for a few seconds. "Is there a trick to getting her to drink?"

"Swift Jones is uncertain, so it's not easy."

Addie says it like she's positive I won't succeed. "Okay, what do I need to do?"

"Do you have a phone?"

"Yeah." I pull it out of my backpack.

"Set the alarm for midnight, three and six in the morning. Feedings take between one and two hours."

Clearly, I won't be sleeping tonight. There's no bed in here, not even a chair. The straw on the floor smells foul. I set my alarm. "Done."

An alarm on Addie's watch pings. It's 9:00 p.m. She takes out a bottle then sinks to the straw, leaning against one of the canvas pillows. Swift Jones peers at her like a shy kid on the playground, taking five minutes to shuffle over, her trunk wriggling around like it has a mind of its own. SJ nuzzles Addie's neck. "They know your heart," she says.

What she doesn't say but means is that my heart is a lump of coal. I'm the Grinch and Swift Jones will figure out that I'm not worthy.

"Calves have a nursing position that's most comfortable. Swift Jones usually rests her trunk on our necks."

It takes three tries for SJ to get her trunk onto Addie's shoulder then another few to curl it around the back of her neck.

"It will be months before she figures out how to precisely work her trunk."

The calf drinks from the bottle. Formula soaks Addie's sleeve. *Gross.* It dribbles down the calf's chest, her gray skin resembling a wet piece of paper that has been folded too many times. "More," Addie coaxes. The calf slowly makes her way through half the bottle then wanders back to the far corner. As she walks she dribbles urine, the smell permeating the pen. Addie hands me the half-empty bottle. It's sticky, but I resist the urge to wipe my hand. "Don't give up until she empties her bottle. Use the blankets to cover her when she sleeps."

This is getting ridiculous. "Seriously? She needs a blanket?"

"In the wild a baby shelters beneath her mother for protection from the sun and to feel safe and warm. Make sure her ears are covered; that just the front of her face is visible."

I point to the far wall. "What are all the buckets for?"

"Fresh water to clean Swift Jones after feeding, soapy water to clean off urine or diarrhea. The empty bucket is for soiled straw."

Urine? Diarrhea? Soiled straw? "The last can is for?"

"Calves can be playful. They have bursts of energy but they're hard to redirect, so this pen is childproofed so that Swift Jones can't hurt herself. The empty plastic can is basically a toy that can be used to redirect Swift Jones's energy until she learns the meaning of telling her *no* when her excitement gets the best of her." Addie walks toward the door. "You have my cell number. Call if there's a problem."

"What? Addie, you're leaving me? Alone? In here with her?"

Addie frowns. "Please call me Dr. Tinibu. And yes, I'm leaving you alone but I'm five minutes away in my office, trying to catch up on work. I sleep there now."

I get the implication. Dr. Tinibu sleeps at the zoo because of the article she thinks I wrote. I consider telling her I didn't write it; that I wrote a crappy article to protect her stupid program. But it wouldn't matter. I'm the enemy now. That's fine. You can't be logical, emotionless, responsible and balanced if being liked is a priority. I'm a journalist, not her friend. Dr. Tinibu steps through the door. It clangs shut behind her.

"One night," I whisper. "Anyone can do one night."

17

I listen to Dr. Tinibu's footsteps fade, then turn to face SJ. "Hey," I call. The calf turns her back, wedging her head into the corner like if she can't see me I'll disappear. Holding up the bottle, I shake it so that she can hear the formula swishing. Nothing. I walk toward the calf then stop. I forgot to ask Addie—Dr. Tinibu—if Swift Jones can hurt me. Does she have teeth? Will she try to charge me? Maybe that's Dr. Tinibu's plan to punish me.

"Hi," I say from where I stand three feet away. From here the calf smells like freshly turned earth with the sour note of urine. "You need to drink your bottle." She doesn't turn around. I approach her from the right then the left side but she turns her head away, like a kid refusing to eat peas.

It's time for a new strategy. "How about the real Swift Jones?" I sing a few lines of a new song I've memorized for Sawyer. It's from *Elbows & Knees*. "'You're made of sharp edges, elbows and knees, there's no soft space, no love lace,

no good way to please because your every move cuts me.'"
The calf doesn't budge. "Sawyer will be very disappointed."

After two hours I give up. The next feeding is only forty-five minutes away. Maybe she'll be hungry enough by then. Maybe she won't. When the new caretaker arrives tomorrow morning, he can pick up the slack because I can taste how tired I am. I abandon brushing my teeth, grab a blanket and spread it by the door. When I lie down straw prickles my back. Sawyer was right. I should've borrowed his sleeping bag. But who knew Addie wouldn't even have a cot in here? There probably is one—she just hid it from horrible me.

The lights have switched to dim, I should be able to sleep, but I'm suddenly wide-awake. I pull out my iPad, click on a link about elephants. "Elephants have a highly convoluted neocortex, just like humans, apes, some dolphins. That's why they're so smart." SJ turns. Head low, she watches me. "You're not smart or you'd be drinking your milk." The calf drags her trunk back and forth in the straw. "I'm not buying your act. You're just not hungry enough yet."

A bird lands a few feet away. Its head bobbles left then right as it looks for food. "I remember my first meal AV. That's After Violet," I tell the calf. "It was green Jell-O. A nurse tried to make me eat it, but I held out two days for macaroni and cheese. I couldn't taste it, though. Nothing tasted for, like, a few months." My alarm goes off. Groaning, I haul myself to my feet. Unfinished bottle in hand, I head toward Swift Jones. She spins, pressing her forehead back into the corner. I get on the ground, crawl beneath her head, but she won't open her mouth for the nipple. Urine saturates the knees of my jeans. Runnels of sickly sweet–smelling formula soak my arm. “Screw this.”

I sit down a few feet away from the calf. “You’re going to make me look bad,” I tell her. “This situation? It’s not my fault. It’s Dr. Tinibu’s fault for having a breeding program. It’s your fault for doing whatever it is you did to flip a switch in your mom’s brain. It’s Raki’s fault for not flipping that switch back. Seriously, I’ve got problems that make yours look like peanuts. So give me a break. Drink from your freaking bottle, okay?”

S. Jones turns halfway toward me. “That’s it,” I say. “Come and get it.” Rapid-fire bursts that sound like gunshots cut through the quiet. I leap to my feet. Swift Jones races away. She’s bleeding from her backside, blood gushing down her legs. My phone is on the blanket. I lunge for it, dial Dr. Tinibu. But then a stench unlike anything I’ve ever smelled invades the air. “You have got to be kidding me!” It’s not blood. It’s diarrhea. The stink is so strong that I can actually taste it. I gag, but don’t make the call. I won’t give Dr. Tinibu the satisfaction of thinking I can’t take one night with a freaking elephant calf.

Swift Jones watches as I soak a towel in the soapy bucket. “We need to get you clean.” When I’m close to her, she bolts. We circle each other for the next forty-five minutes. I threaten, but eventually resort to begging. At some point SJ decides to stop being chased and to chase me instead. Her trumpet sounds like a weak bugle before she runs straight at me. She might be a baby, but that’s three-hundred-plus pounds of solid animal hurtling like a missile. When I try to use the plastic trash can to redirect her, it’s like I’m wearing red and she's the bull. I end up in the corner where the worst of the diarrhea steams. It oozes over my flip-flops, warm on my skin. I throw up in my mouth.

The calf stops a few feet away, looking over her shoulder like she's the one being chased. My heart pounds so hard that it's going to leave a bruise. When SJ glances over her shoulder again, I bolt for the door, slam it shut behind me. The calf wanders to the center of the enclosure. She looks small, lost...too bad.

My feet are painted brown with feces. I leave vile prints as I walk down the hallway to the bathroom. There's a low metal counter. Hopping up, I put my feet in the stainless-steel bowl. As the water hits, the smell actually notches up, making me gag repeatedly. It takes me a while to scrape the crap from beneath my toenails. I shiver, because the sink has only cold water. My jeans are clammy against my skin from the wet towel I carried while chasing the stupid calf.

"What now?" I stare into the hazy mirror—both eyes are tracking in the same direction. I check the lower half of my face to make sure it doesn't look like a bear has mauled me. No blood, tatters of skin, missing teeth like Hannah's hallucinations. My eyes are red, puffy. When I was yelling, did Swift Jones see fireworks in them? I lean closer to the mirror. Do I?

"This night is not worth the risk." My reflection nods at me. I need to call Dr. Tinibu. Bail. I tried to modify my Twelve-Year Plan for one night, but being here, with Swift Jones, is not *within reason*. If I do a bit more research, there's enough information to write my article. "I'm outta here." Unfortunately, my backpack is still in the pen.

When I get back, Swift Jones is standing beside the formula

bottle I dropped after World War Diarrhea. She's trying to pick it up with the little finger at the end of her trunk, but can't pull it off. She circles the bottle, stepping on her trunk, lets out a thin, high-pitched wail. I sit down in the hallway, resting my head against the bars. I should walk to Dr. Tinibu's office right now, but… The calf makes tiny noises. It's the sound little kids make when they're ramping up for a cry. But she's not a little kid. And if she cries, it doesn't mean the same thing as a real person. I throw her a last bone anyway. "It's not like I don't know how you feel," I say softly. "My mother tried to kill me, too. It's awful. It'll always be awful." The calf can't possibly understand what I'm saying, because she's three weeks old. And she's an animal. I'm eighteen, human and I still don't totally get it.

I rest my forehead against the cold steel and stare at a piece of straw on the floor. "I won't tell you that you don't need your mom. But you can survive…if you let people help you." Something brushes my hand. I jump. Swift Jones stands on the other side of the bars. She's managed to swing her trunk onto my open palm. It's soft as a pencil's eraser, tiny hairs tickling my skin. This close the calf's eyes are the color of dark chocolate, ringed by impossibly long lashes. "You're advanced for your age," I tell her with a nod at her trunk.

When I reenter the pen to get my backpack, Swift Jones doesn't run. Instead, she watches, her head slightly tipped to one side, as my iPad, phone and homework get packed. "So," I say, heading to the door, "it's been an experience. Good luck. I hope everything works out for you."

The calf follows me back to the door. I look at her. She glances back at her bottle. "One last try, but if you're just teasing me then I'm outta here." I get the bottle. Sit down in the straw. The calf sidles right next to me, her lined face looking impossibly young, old and fragile. When I run my hand along her side, I can feel her heartbeat thumping against skin that reminds me of worn jeans. My heartbeat slows to match her rhythm. "It's going to be okay," I say. "Either way." I'm not lying, because I'm not promising her the world—just *okay*.

SJ manages to flop her trunk over my shoulder, squiggling it until it's around the back of my neck. Her trunk feels soft, warm against my bare skin. It's kinda like being hugged by a little kid. She drinks from the bottle, tentatively at first, then in big gulps. Formula drips down my arm. "Holy messy eater." But I don't really mind. She finishes the bottle. I grab another because she's still trying to suck milk from the empty one. She tries to get closer to me while she's feeding, until she's pushing hard against me, almost on my lap. "You are too heavy for that, you little porker," I say. My shirt is now soaked.

When the bottle is drained, I soap a towel and Swift Jones lets me clean the dried crap off her butt, and then follows me around as I use the pitchfork to put all the soiled hay in a pail. It's 2:00 a.m. by the time I'm done. "We should get some sleep." I lay a blanket down for the calf ten feet from my own. She seems to know what to do, because she lies on her side. When I cover her with another blanket, I make sure to tuck it around her neck. After a few quick photos with my phone, I fall onto my own blanket. "Go to sleep," I tell Swift Jones.

My eyes slide closed… Something plops onto my face. It's the calf's trunk. I sit up fast. Swift Jones lurches back. "Sorry," I say, "but you scared me." I reach out my hand, wait for the calf to come forward. One. Two. Three steps. She crumples onto my blanket. “No way,” I say, trying to shove her off. “You have your own very nice bed over there.” I can’t budge a three-hundred-pound elephant, so I curl up on the little bit of blanket left then cover us both. “Sleep,” I command. Swift Jones manages to get the tip of her trunk into her mouth. She looks like a little kid sucking her thumb. I breathe in the smell of fresh soap, sweet straw, and the calf’s earthy musk. We both drift off.

18

It's 5:45 a.m. and Swift Jones wants to play. I'm trying to study, but it's hard because she's racing around the pen. If I don't chase her, she runs at me, swings her trunk so it smacks me then runs away in her version of tag. "Seriously?" I ask. "School is in a few hours. I have a math for dummies quiz I haven't studied for, a French chapter I haven't read, plus a chemistry assignment I'll never figure out. Oh, and it's freaking important to look rested or my father will know I lied."

SJ smacks me in the back of the head with her trunk. "You asked for it!" I leap to my feet, chase her around the pen, dodging then weaving. She's fast. Suddenly she changes course and she's running after me. I leap over the garbage pail but make the mistake of looking over my shoulder then tripping on the landing, hitting the straw hard. Swift Jones stands above me, running her trunk along my body like she's making sure I'm okay.

I stand up. The calf looks at me expectantly. "Stay," I say, holding up one hand. I take a few steps back. She follows me.

"Stay," I repeat. This time she hesitates. I whistle a birdcall my father taught me in another life then hold my arms out, beckoning the calf. She runs right to me, almost knocking me over, but in her defense she tried to brake but had the timing wrong. "Stay," I say again, then move a bit farther away. I whistle. Swifty comes running. This time she stops before hitting my thighs. We practice until I can cross the room. She's smart.

I head back to my homework, but Swift Jones is looking over her shoulder at the refrigerator. "More?" I count the empty formula bottles. Four. "Okay, but don't complain later when you can't fit into your bikini." I pull another bottle out of the fridge. "Easy, Swifty," I say as she swings her trunk over my shoulder then tries to inhale the bottle's nipple. Formula soaks my shirt yet again. "You are a pig."

"Morning." Dr. Tinibu opens the pen's door. She steps inside.

Swifty finishes her bottle in a giant gulp then runs over to Addie for a scratch behind the ears that must feel great by the way she's twisting her head to make sure the other ear gets some attention, too.

"How'd it go last night?"

"Five bottles. She had diarrhea after the first one but none since."

"Did either of you sleep?"

I pull straw out of the tangled mess of my hair. "A few hours, I think."

"You call her Swifty?"

I gather up my stuff, shoving it into my backpack. "She's fast."

Dr. Tinibu unzips her rain shell and tosses it onto the straw. "It was wrong of me to leave you alone last night."

My eyebrows shoot up. An apology is the last thing I expected. "It turned out okay."

"It's not. Okay."

I push a curl from my eyes. "Then why'd you do it?"

"You don't grasp the consequences of your article." Addie tugs at the gold hoop in her ear. "I wanted you to literally feel them." She points to a small camera mounted in the far corner. "In my defense, I checked in on you."

My face gets hot. She must have loved the diarrhea part. I heft my backpack. "Good luck with everything."

"What are you going to write?"

"I don't know. But it'll be fair because, believe it or not, I'm not the enemy."

Dr. Tinibu kneels. The calf nuzzles against her. "Wild Walker's Circus called. They're giving us one chance to reunite Raki and Swift Jones. If it doesn't work, they'll claim our calf."

I absorb what she's just said. "On the record?"

Dr. Tinibu exhales like she's just run a marathon. "Why not?"

"When will you try?" I ask.

"They've only given us three days. So Friday."

"That's not much time."

Dr. Tinibu looks right through me. "I told you—baby elephants sell tickets."

"Will reuniting them work?"

"I don't know."

"Have you considered the idea that Raki just might not

be mother material?" I venture. "Maybe the circus will be good for the calf."

"Go home," Dr. Tinibu says.

Swift Jones watches me leave the pen. I hesitate. "You don't have enough caretakers."

"That's not your concern."

"I'm volunteering."

Dr. Tinibu kisses the calf's forehead. "So you can write another article? You've already done enough."

"She drank five bottles with me. Has anyone done better than that?"

"No."

"You said that more caretakers will make it easier for Swift Jones, if she goes."

Dr. Tinibu stands. "Fine," she says. "Friday night."

My chest puffs a little bit. Despite everything, Dr. Tinibu thinks I'm good with the calf. I don't say that she won't need me Friday because Raki and Swift Jones are going to successfully reunite. It's pretty clear she's not sure.

Sawyer is waiting for me in the parking lot. When I get into his Jeep, he opens all the windows despite the cold air and rain. "You reek!"

"Sorry." I'll have to clean the dried formula off my shirt in the school bathroom. The good news is that no one has high expectations for my fashion sense.

Sawyer nods at a duffel on the back seat. "Mirabela sent a change of clothes for you."

"Seriously?"

Sawyer laughs. "Mirabela doesn't even know who you are. I raided her closet. In case."

"I'm a foot taller than her," I say, unzipping the duffel.

"Lululemon fits everyone. Just remember, Lycra is a privilege not a right."

"Says who?"

"Mirabela."

I pull out Mirabela's size zero yoga pants and a long-sleeved light pink top with a V-neck. The tag says *one size fits all*, but if I rolled the shirt into a ball it'd fit in the palm of my hand. "I'll stick with my own clothes."

"You smell. Plus, if your dad sees you like this, he'll know you lied about staying at my house." He nods at the duffel. "There's makeup I swiped from Mirabela's beauty bar. I doubt it'll hide those dark circles completely, but it'll help."

"Did you do my homework for me, too?" I ask as I strip in the front seat and attempt to squeeze my long limbs into Mirabela's daily uniform. Sawyer glances at me, grins. "If this is your idea of a joke," I mutter, "it's not funny."

"First, there wasn't much to choose from in my mother's closet. It was either yoga clothes or cocktail dresses. But there's a silver lining," Sawyer says. "You look hot."

"Yeah, right."

He reaches into the back seat and hands me a folder.

"What's this?"

"It's from Lux-A Realty."

"And they are?"

"The number one rental agency in Pennington. I called them for a list of possible apartments. We have an appointment with a Realtor after school. She's going to show us five places. Two are already furnished, which would be helpful since I have no idea how to decorate an apartment. Two are penthouses with floor-to-ceiling glass and massive decks. The final one is a giant loft, which could be cool."

Sawyer is smiling and actually seems excited, so maybe he pushed things with Cushing because he was actually ready to move out after all, Betty or no Betty. My insides slump. "Um."

"What?"

"I can't go this afternoon."

Sawyer's grin crumbles. "Come on, Lily."

"I have a deadline with the paper and if I don't spend, like, all afternoon and night studying then I'm looking at Cs in three of my classes. I'm sorry. Seriously, I'd love to go, but you want me to try to get into USC, right?"

Sawyer gives me a sideways look. "Do something with your hair."

My curls are so knotted that all I can do is knot them further by securing them into two pigtails with the elastics on my wrist. The result is really not good. I look like a perverted version of Annie but brunette and freakishly tall. I use the visor mirror to put on Mirabela's concealer. Sawyer was right. It helps, but nothing is going to make my circles entirely go away.

"Well?"

"Well what?"

"How was Swift Jones?"

Sawyer usually drives with his left hand but he's gripping the steering wheel with both. "She hates her name," I deadpan.

"If you don't tell me what happened last night, I will stop this car."

"Nutshell?"

"Fine."

"Dr. Tinibu rescinded my right to call her Addie because she hates my guts. She left me alone all night with the calf. Swift Jones rejected my attempts to feed her. Elephant diarrhea *reeks*. Trust me on this—it's super hard to get out from under toenails." Sawyer looks at me, sees I'm serious and bursts out laughing. "I finally got the calf to drink. In fact, I got her to take more bottles than any other caretaker. She practically slept on top of me. Oh, and I taught her a trick."

Sawyer puts on his blinker. "Are you leaving out any big details?"

I close my window because the rain is pelting me. "I might've sung the calf a song from the real Swift Jones."

Sawyer slaps his hands on the wheel. "*What?* Which one?"

"'Sharp Edges.'"

My best friend's face clouds over. "But your voice..."

He's actually worried that Swift Jones, the calf, didn't hear a good representation of Swift Jones, the singer. "I didn't hear any complaints."

"She *is* locked up," Sawyer points out.

I slug him in the shoulder, but he has big muscles so it just hurts my knuckles. "One more thing," I add. "Wild Walker's Circus called. They're giving the zoo three days to reunite the calf with Raki. If it doesn't work, they're going to claim her."

"That's kinda awful," Sawyer says.

"Why? I mean, it's pretty obvious that Raki has a screw loose. Maybe getting the calf away will save her life. Zoos aren't perfect either. The animals are locked up, as you pointed out. Swift Jones might have a great life at the circus. Maybe she'll be a star." Sawyer gives me a skeptical look. "Quit it. She's just an elephant."

"So you're done?"

"I might've volunteered to go back for another night."

Sawyer makes a ticking sound on the roof of his mouth. "Lily, do you think—"

"Asa," I say.

"What?"

"That's your new girlfriend's name. She's from the House of Saud, which is the royal family of Saudi Arabia."

"That sounds way too easy for Carla to cyber snoop."

"The family has thousands of members. Oh, and Asa goes to Stanford. Freshman year. She plans to be a doctor. Pediatrician."

"And you figured all this out when?"

"Somewhere between getting soaked with formula, cleaning diarrhea off an elephant's butt and feeding Swifty."

"Swifty?"

"She's fast."

The Pennington Times

OCTOBER 24

BY T. LILLIAN DECKER, INTERN

Raki's Last Chance

On Friday, October 25, Pennington Zoo's Asian elephant Raki will be given a chance to reunite with her three-and-a-half-week-old calf, Swift Jones. As reported, Raki rejected her calf last week.

"Sometimes when animals are taken from their natural environments they don't learn important behaviors, like raising a calf," Dr. Tinibu, director, the Pennington Zoo, explained. "Given time, Raki's maternal instincts will kick in."

Unfortunately, a slow reintroduction will not be possible. Swift Jones's sire, Lorenzo, is owned by Wild Walker's Circus and was loaned to the zoo for breeding purposes. The contract between the zoo and circus states: "Should any calf born from… Lorenzo be shown to be in imminent danger then ownership of said calf immediately reverts to Wild Walker's Circus."

The circus has given the zoo three days to successfully reintroduce Raki to her calf. If Raki fails to accept her calf, the circus will take ownership of Swift Jones.

"We are loath to separate a mother and her baby," Wild Walker's Circus's publicist, Otis Walker, said in a statement to the *Haven Gazette*. "But if the calf is in danger we must act quickly to ensure her safety."

For more information on the calf, Swift Jones, and the Pennington Zoo's breeding program, visit penningtonzoo.org/elephants.

19

My dad was pissed when he saw my byline above the latest Swift Jones article. I told him it was a phone interview, super low-key. That I'd realized anything more is too stressful. He believed me. Like Sawyer said, I'm a good liar. I didn't mention that the AP again picked up my story, because my father won't care. But there's no way to cover the next lie.

Mr. Matthews convinced Dr. Tinibu to let me watch today as Raki is reintroduced to her calf, so Calvin will eventually know I was there. If things don't work out, I'll stay at the zoo and caretake Swifty tonight. Sawyer will cover for me by calling my dad to say I've fallen asleep in one of his mansion's many guest rooms. But when the articles are printed, my dad will know the truth. The good news, though, is that by then I'll have written my articles and hopefully they'll also get distributed by the AP. I'll have a nice package to send to USC, my Twelve-Year Plan will still be intact and my stress alleviated.

When I arrive at the elephant building it's late afternoon. Dr. Tinibu's nostrils flare when she sees me. I've figured out that's her *tell.* She's still pissed and doesn't want me here. The last thing I want to watch is a mother elephant kick the shit out of her baby, but Dr. Tinibu and I have something in common. I'm using her to get into USC. She's hoping to use me to get Wild Walker's Circus off her back.

I'm sure Dr. Tinibu was mad about my last article. But there are good reasons that I didn't include all the negative things she said about Wild Walker's Circus. Mainly, I couldn't get any of them substantiated. I did call Walker's ten times for comments about her allegations. Their publicist, Otis Walker, finally returned my last call. I was in the shower, hair in suds, but leaped out to answer my phone.

"May I speak with T. Lillian Decker?"

"Yes. That's me, Lily."

"Otis Walker. You've left ten voice mails."

"I... Sorry about that, deadline, um—"

"Super busy day. Can you cut to the chase?"

"I'm a reporter for the *Pennington Times.*"

"That was in every message."

Otis's tone is transmitting that I'm an irritating mosquito. "I'd like to talk to you about Swift Jones. The elephant calf that—"

"My family is deeply concerned about."

"There has been... Can you tell me if your trainers use any negative—"

"We don't comment on unsubstantiated claims made by animal-rights organizations seeking publicity. Anything else?"

"Well, I guess what I meant was—"

"Thank you for your call."

★ ★ ★

Otis Walker hung up. Admittedly, I wasn't exactly prepared for the call, my notes buried somewhere in my backpack, but his tone, his impatience? Asshat, I decided. After washing the soap from my hair and burning eyes, I looked up his bio on LinkedIn. It said he'd been the circus's publicist for three years, was only twenty-one. Maybe that's why he's so bad at his job. He's young, was probably given the position only because he's a Walker. Still, Otis gave the *Haven Gazette* a good quote, which felt like a total slight, and he was beyond rude. He's lucky I adhere to the Journalist's Code.

I push away thoughts of Otis and focus. Raki stands at the far end of an eighty-foot-long, narrow enclosure. There are ropes holding her left front and back feet. "They're for Swift Jones's protection," Dr. Tinibu says. "They don't hurt Raki, just keep her from charging her calf."

A gate on the far wall slides open. Steve plus two other guys I've seen working in the elephant building bring Swift Jones into the far side of the pen. The calf wears a chest harness attached to a thick rope. When she sees Raki, she snaps up her head, eyes brighter than sunshine, trunk wriggling, a goofy grin on her face. Slowly, the men pay out the rope, letting the calf get closer and closer. At first Raki ignores her calf. Swifty is fifty feet away, then forty, thirty, twenty, ten… Raki's ears were casually flapping when her calf entered the pen; now they're moving at high speed, making a thwacking sound. I'm pretty sure that's her *tell.*

"Her ears," I say.

"There's a fine line between excitement and agitation," Dr. Tinibu says.

"How can you know which it is?"

"We can't. But we do know that terrible things can happen fast. Steve and the other keepers are ready to pull Swift Jones back if need be."

My mouth goes dry. Raki stamps the ground with her free front foot. Swifty is only five feet away. Steve is sweating. My own muscles are wound so taut that they're bound to snap. Raki trumpets. Her eyes flash. Violet is waiting…

"'Not the pain of this but its unfairness was what dazed Peter,'" Mommy says.

"Are you talking about when Captain Hook bit Peter?" I ask.

Mommy nods. "'Every child is affected thus the first time he is treated unfairly.'"

"Hook shouldn't have bitten Peter," I agree.

"'After you have been unfair to him he will love you again, but will never afterwards be quite the same boy.'"

I know the next line by heart. I jump up and down with my right hand raised. "'No one ever gets over the first unfairness; no one except Peter.'" Mommy smiles even though her eyes don't. She takes my hand, leads me out of our loft, up the stairs to the rooftop, because she says I'm *not* Peter. I'm glad, because Peter isn't a real boy. This means Mommy finally sees me.

Swift Jones is only a few feet from Raki. She stares up at her mother. The calf's smile fades. She makes a high-pitched mewl. Raki tries to kick her with her free back leg. She misses but it's close. The mother elephant strains against her ropes, head down, attempting to butt her calf away. When she realizes she can't reach, Raki lashes out with her front leg. She misses Swifty by inches.

"Let's take her out," Steve says. The three men pull the struggling calf away from her mother. Swifty cries, the pitch higher and higher as the distance between her and Raki increases.

Addie takes off her glasses, swipes at her eyes. "That's it."

Steve walks Swift Jones down the hallway. When they reach us, Swifty stares through the bars at her mother. Raki turns her head away. Tears pool in Swifty's eyes. They course down her cheeks. The salty tracks drip onto the floor. Drip. Onto. The. Floor.

"It's despair," Dr. Tinibu says. "I need to speak with Steve. Lily, take her to the farthest pen. Please."

I slowly walk down the hallway, whistle. Swift Jones shuffles after me. I rest a hand on her head as we walk. "You don't need Raki," I say softly. But the calf keeps crying. When we enter the last pen, I kneel in front of SJ. Tears drip down the velvety folds of her face. I wipe them away, but they keep coming. When I lick my wet finger, it tastes like salt. "Okay, here's the deal," I say. "Of course you need your mom. But you can live without her." Grabbing a blanket, I drape it over the calf's shoulders. She shuffles in a circle then lies down. I take a photo of her miserable face, because Mr. Matthews made me promise to get a few more shots.

Shrugging off my backpack, I sit beside Swifty, rubbing her back like she's a little kid, even though I understand that she's not. "Brought you something." She stares at me with red-rimmed, leaking eyes. I pull out a battered stuffed animal. "His name is Nibs." The rabbit was once snow-white but is now a dingy gray. Most of his stuffing is gone. His ears are droopy. "He only has one blue eye," I explain, "because when I was six, I flushed the other one down the toilet. I wanted to see the magical place where all my goldfish lived."

I hid Nibs in a suitcase along with my mother's dog-eared copy of *Peter Pan* the day my father tore all the Escher posters to shreds and painted over Violet's rambles. He was erasing Violet. I thought that meant he'd take the stuffed animal she'd given me. Nibs remained in that suitcase until last night. "He's for you, Swifty." I hold out the stuffed bunny. It takes the calf a few tries to coordinate her trunk enough to touch Nibs. Its end quivers as she sniffs the rabbit. Then she wraps her trunk around the bunny, pulls him close. I take another photo—just of her trunk twisted about the stuffed animal. I lie down a few inches from her, face-to-face. She's still crying. "Fuck Raki."

Dr. Tinibu walks into the pen. She kneels beside Swift Jones, her fingers gently stroking the calf's head. "What now?" I ask, sitting up on the opposite side of Swifty.

"Raki isn't ready to accept her calf. She may never be."

"She's acting like she doesn't even know Swifty." I sound angry, not balanced.

"Lily, your perspective is skewed toward your human experience that all mothers instinctively do the right thing."

I laugh. At first it's just a chuckle, but then it's full-blown, rip-roaring laughter that cramps my stomach, makes me hiccup repeatedly. Dr. Tinibu looks at me like I'm nuts. I try but can't stop. She leans over Swifty and pats my cheeks frantically. My laughter slowly subsides.

Addie looks alarmed. "It's okay," I say, gasping, catching my breath. "I'm okay. No big deal."

She drops her hands and hesitates, then nods at Nibs. "Yours?"

"I brought it, just in case."

"Why were you laughing?"

"Violet gave me Nibs."

"Violet?"

"My mother. When I was seven years old, Violet was arrested for attempted murder."

Dr. Tinibu rocks backward. "I'm sorry."

"Don't be. I'm the one she tried to kill."

Dr. Tinibu recoils, like my words are an invisible slap to her face. "So when I said your perspective was skewed toward mothers doing the right thing?"

My face heats up. "It's not funny. But, yeah."

"What happened to her?"

"The jury found her guilty. She was sentenced to fifteen years in prison."

"That's terrible."

Her eyes meet mine and it's like I'm naked. My skin burns. "So…so what happens to Swifty now?"

"Wild Walker's Circus will arrange a plane to transport her to Florida," Dr. Tinibu says. "They've agreed to let me stay for a week to get our…to get the calf settled and make sure their elephant trainer knows how to care for her."

"That's good."

"So you'll write about this?"

"That's the plan."

"Then you should write about Swift Jones in Florida, too."

For a second I feel kind of sorry for Addie. This is over, but she's still trying to find a way to keep the calf. Swifty whimpers. The sound burrows under my skin. "I'm sure there'll be a reporter from the *Haven Gazette* who'll do a story," I offer.

Dr. Tinibu shakes her head. "You started this situation, you should see it through to the end."

We're back to this being my fault. Maybe it is. But the idea that I'd willingly go to Florida with an elephant calf who is currently devastated is so far removed from my Twelve-Year Plan that it's like asking me to fly.

But.

No, I tell my brain. Trying to fly definitely did not work out well for me. "Walker's won't want an intern reporter from the *Times* around," I say. "Their PR guy could barely bother talking with me."

"I'll tell them that you'd mainly be there as one of Swift Jones's caregivers, which is true. You're the best we have. Truthfully, Lily, I need you."

Swifty's trunk is curled around Nibs, and her eyes are swollen and red. I visualize cutting the imaginary thread I can almost feel connecting me to the calf, because our stories are not the same. She's a baby elephant. I was a seven-year-old human child. "I'll talk to Mr. Matthews," I hear myself say. There's no way Otis Walker is going to agree to this…but if he does, the AP might pick up another story of mine. It'd be stupid to give up another chance to get into USC.

"You'll need a week off school."

"I'm sure that can be arranged." I'm eighteen years old. My father can't stop me.

I set my phone's alarm to go off in three hours. Then I take a spare blanket, spreading it far from the calf. I pull homework from my backpack. I need to write a paper in French.

Dr. Tinibu doesn't say good-night. I listen to her footsteps fade as she walks down the hallway. A door opens then closes. Silence descends.

"Psst."

My head snaps around. The hallway beyond the bars is empty. Zoo sounds. But I wait a long moment before returning to my book, just to make sure no one is there.

The Pennington Times

OCTOBER 26

BY T. LILLIAN DECKER, INTERN

Swift Jones Rejected Again

On October 25, Pennington Zoo veterinarian, Dr. Steve Cohen, attempted to reunite Asian elephant Raki with her calf, Swift Jones. Although Raki was restrained for the calf's safety, she was at first disinterested then aggressive toward Swift Jones.

"Raki's hostility means the Pennington Zoo has lost ownership of Swift Jones to Wild Walker's Circus," Dr. Tinibu said. "We cannot break our contract with the circus even though life-threatening problems can be triggered by the calf's psychological grief over the loss of her mother that the Pennington Zoo is better equipped to handle."

Swift Jones will be transported to Walker's winter home in Haven, Florida, via chartered plane. Dr. Tinibu and her staff will spend a week at the circus getting the calf settled and educating circus personnel on proper care.

The *Pennington Times* has received thousands of emails, letters and tweets of concern for Swift

Jones. One reader has been circulating a petition on Facebook to keep Swift Jones at the Pennington Zoo. He has more than five thousand signatures.

Walker's publicist, Otis Walker, stated to the *Haven Gazette* that Howard Walker, the circus's elephant trainer "has a deep respect and appreciation for the animals he works with and strives to create a loving bond with these magnificent creatures."

20

Things are moving way too fast. Wild Walker's Circus has agreed to let me accompany Dr. Tinibu as a caretaker and even write a few articles about the calf's transition. It was the PR guy Otis's decision. I assumed he'd say *hell no* and already dislike him for putting me in this situation, which is well beyond a huge deviation from my plan. Still, as long as I can remain detached, professional, this trip could propel me closer to USC and away from Calvin.

"We need professional photographs," Mr. Matthews growls into the phone.

He and Shannon sit on his desk eating ice cream from the Ben & Jerry's cart next to the *Times* office. Shannon's is bright green pistachio in a cone. Mr. Matthews's bowl is piled so high with broken Oreo cookies that I can't tell the flavor.

"Dr. Tinibu, she's not a photographer…No. Okay. Fine." Mr. Matthews hangs up.

Jack looks up from the camera lens he's cleaning. "All set?"

"Give the kid a quick lesson," Mr. Matthews says with a nod at me.

"What?" Jack and I say in unison.

My boss takes a giant spoonful of ice cream. Somehow he gets it all into his mouth. He holds up a finger until it melts enough that he can talk around the Oreo crumbles. "Obviously it's not my first choice. But that Tinibu gal has a way with words. Impressive. Is she single?"

"She wears a gold ring on her right thumb?" I venture.

"Kid, it's called multitasking," he growls. "Either Lily goes alone," he says to Shannon and Jack, "or she doesn't go at all."

"So your school is good with this?" Shannon asks.

"My English teacher is giving me extra credit for a paper on my experience." I don't say that my chemistry teacher threatened to fail me.

"And your dad?" Mr. Matthews asks.

We aren't talking. "He's good, too." If I didn't need to pack, I'd spend the night at Sawyer's.

"This story needs great photos," Jack argues.

"This story has caught the nation's attention. Charlie fucking Hamilton from CNC can't get an interview. He called me last night," Mr. Matthews says. "Nice guy. Believe me, Charlie has tried his best, but Dr. Tinibu is a tough nut to crack. Every article Lily writes gets scooped up by the AP, read nationally, even with her crap iPhone pics."

"The one with the stuffed animal," Shannon says between licks, "didn't stink."

That's the first compliment she's given me, so even though it's sort of a noncompliment, it counts. Mr. Matthews used it on the bottom of the front page even though he told me it had *shit lighting*. Another noncompliment. But that's two.

"Sorry, Jack. Teach Lily how to point and click."

"The *Times* cameras are Canon 5D Mark IIIs," Jack says, gingerly handing his to me. "Send me what you get at the end of each day. I'll try to make your shots look decent."

"Where's the On button?" Jack jabs his finger at it like he'd rather be poking me in the eye. "Do you have an instruction manual?"

"No," Jack says, looking at Mr. Matthews. "Because I don't need one." He points at another button. "HD video recording. And this is the slot for the memory card. There are two more in the case."

Mr. Matthews scrapes up the last ice-cream-soaked crumbles of cookies. "I expect three articles during your time in Florida, all with photos. The public can't get enough of that elephant. Let's give them what they want then hope the AP follows suit."

"I still think it should be more personal," Shannon says. "An 'our intern was there' kinda thing."

"No," Mr. Matthews and I say in unison.

I'm not sure why he agrees with me, but if he hadn't I would've refused to go, USC or no USC. I'm already taking enough risks. The tension in our loft, one being low and ten being high, is at twenty-three.

"Kid?" Mr. Matthews asks.

"Yes?" I say, hoping it was a yes-or-no question I missed and that I got it right.

"Are you sure you're up for this?"

No. "Yes. Thank you for the chance. It means a ton." I carefully put the newspaper's fancy camera into its padded bag.

"Then get outta here," Mr. Matthews says. "And find out if Dr. Tinibu is single," he adds. "I like a gal with spunk."

I start to jog home. For once, it's not raining. I pause at a streetlight and wait for it to turn green, cross Everett Avenue then dial Sawyer and tell him about the meeting. "Do you have everything you need from me?" I ask. Sawyer is getting copies of my articles. He'll mail the package to USC on Monday morning, because I'm going to be on a plane.

"No worries," Sawyer says. "You have time to check out my final two?"

"Final two?"

"Apartments. I can pick you up in an hour and we can swing by both."

I leap over a puddle. "I wish. I still need to email my French teacher a paper and pack. But spill." Sawyer is quiet. "Please?"

"It's either the loft or the furnished penthouse on Couch Street, which has a bocce court on the deck."

"I don't know what bocce is, but I vote for the penthouse. It already has a bed. Sorry I can't see it," I say. "Really." I take a deep breath.

"What?" Sawyer asks, because he can basically read my mind.

"You sure that I can do this?"

"One thousand percent," he says without hesitation. "I know you're scared, but you've been stuck in one place for a long time. When you stop taking risks, you stop living life."

"That's definitely not a Freyism."

"It's a Sawyerism."

"Right back at you," I say.

"What does that mean?"

There's something in Sawyer's voice that's off. "Well. I'm risk averse, which has been holding me back."

"You said, right back at *you*."

"It's nothing." A car honks. I back onto the curb. A really short guy walking a black Great Dane passes by. "I'm just distracted, that's all."

"But?"

I'm trying to backpedal with a guy who's way smarter than me. "But nothing?"

"Say it," he snaps.

Sawyer isn't going to let me off the hook, which kinda pisses me off because I'm about to step off a cliff without knowing if I'll ever land and he's safe as usual. "You play it safe," I say.

"Fuck you, Lily."

The light changes, but I don't cross the street. My feet have morphed into lead weights. "What? Seriously?"

"You think you're the only one with problems?"

This can't be a fight, can it? I reach for a joke. "You're right. You might not score *all* the goals at your next lacrosse game." I wince because it's clear that this isn't a joking situation. I get that I need to come up with something better, some way to support him, but I can't find the words.

"I don't understand what it's like to have schizophrenia hanging over my head, but my father is basically disowning me," Sawyer says. "Cushing is an asshole, but he's the only dad I have. My mother hasn't even considered sticking up for me. She's too busy starving herself and getting plastic surgery to give a shit. And my best friend, who I've been there for since, like, forever, doesn't even spend a second thinking that for once, I'm the one who needs some support."

This isn't happening. "I didn't realize you were keeping score," I blurt.

"It's not hard to count to zero."

"Sawyer, I tried to talk to you about moving out!"

"Yeah, right. You diverted the conversation then made it all about you, like always."

"That's not fair!"

"Like you always say, life's not fair."

There's a car sitting on my chest and it's hard to talk around the massive lump in my throat. I manage to croak, "You didn't have to push Cushing—"

"Jesus, Lily. You really don't get it."

I start to retort, but Sawyer has already hung up.

21

Calvin is waiting for me when I get back to the loft. Not pretending to sleep or cook or clean the kitchen. He. Is. Waiting. For. Me. He's drinking Scotch. By the half-empty bottle on the counter and the bleary look in his eyes, he's had way too much. I haven't seen him drunk in a long time, not since the last few months with Violet. Mostly I remember the smell of his breath; the way he walked like the ground was tilting. I'm too exhausted for another fight, so I head to my bedroom to pack.

"What do you bring to wear at a circus?" I mutter. "It's Florida in October so it'll be hot, right?" I grab two pairs of cargo shorts, two T-shirts, two sweatshirts and then realize I'm stuck on the number two. I pull out seven pairs of undies, because I'm not planning to do laundry. A baseball hat Sawyer got me that reads: I Like You but if Zombies Chase Us I'm Tripping You goes into my duffel along with a toothbrush, toothpaste, brush, elastics and fake Ray-Ban gold-wire sunglasses I bought at the dollar store. I pause. That's a mistake, because the second I stop moving all I can think about is Sawyer. He hates me, which is nothing I've ever experienced. I dial his number. He sends my call to voice mail. I try again. Voice mail.

I head into my closet and dig beneath a pile of dirty clothes to find a pair of flip-flops. My fingers brush the edge of a book. It was in the suitcase with Nibs. I haven't looked at my mom's copy of *Peter Pan* for years. It's ninety-four pages but it feels heavier. The paper is worn soft, dog-eared, stained with tears, food and specks of brownish blood. That's from when Violet and I pricked our fingers. I vaguely remember that the reason we drew blood had to do with the Lost Boys and Captain Hook.

The pages flutter against my fingertips. During our last few weeks together, if I asked Violet a question she'd frantically leaf through this book looking for answers. I'm not sure whether she couldn't find her own words, or if she thought J. M. Barrie's were better. The book falls open to a page. This was one of Violet's favorite games, even before she went off her meds. She'd ask a question and then let the book fall open to reveal the answer. I close the book. "Am I giving up all I've achieved?" I whisper. The book falls open to page ninety. Violet underlined one sentence on this page: "Years rolled on again, and Wendy had a daughter. This ought not to be written in ink but in a golden splash." I close the book. There's no truth in *Peter Pan*.

"Lily?"

My father comes into my bedroom without knocking. He looks down at me in the closet, swaying slightly on his feet. I throw the book into my duffel. Not because I want to bring it, but because he's seen it. If I leave Violet's copy, it won't be here when I return. "I need to get some sleep. Early start."

"What can I say to stop you?" The ice cubes in his glass clink with each word.

"Nothing."

"I could call your editor or the zoo woman and tell them this situation is a threat to your health."

"I'd never forgive you."

He moves unsteadily to my bed, drops down on the corner. "I wanted to be a furniture maker. Not the simplistic stuff I have the kids make in the shop class the administration makes me teach. I wanted to create with every type of wood, live-edge, exotics, have a huge studio to work in and openings, like artists have." He takes a gulp of Scotch. "Violet was going to do all my advertising and sales. She'd work out front, with the customers. I'd be in the back, creating, crafting. It was going to be perfect, because why wouldn't it be? She was smart, beautiful and I was driven, talented. That's the stuff fairy tales are made of, right?"

He's slurring. "Right," I say, because telling him that life is not a fairy tale seems redundant.

"We were going to have at least two more kids because both Violet and I were only children. My parents died young and hers…" He looks at me with bloodshot eyes. "Well, you know about her parents."

"Yeah."

My father hangs his head. "I wish I hadn't kept that letter."

"Why did you?"

He shrugs. "As a reminder."

"That I'm related to her?"

"I could've forgotten," he continues like he didn't hear me, "because you were such a bright light. Even after. You were precocious without being obnoxious, imaginative, and you had a way of seeing the world with fresh eyes." He stares at the amber liquid in his glass. "But I had to remember, because I'm your father. It's my job to protect you."

It feels like the world has stopped spinning. I'm afraid to move, to start it up again, because this is the most honest conversation we've ever had about how he sees me. What he said about protecting me is like a piece of the bigger puzzle sliding into place. "I think...I think that's what Violet tried to do, too," I say. "Protect me."

He shakes his head. "That's not—"

"Listen, okay? I've hated her for that day, for what she said, did, and all the stuff that came after. But maybe it's simple. She was mentally ill. Her way of protecting me was to throw me off the roof before I grew up, because she didn't want me to grow up to be like her."

"That's ridiculous."

"It's not. And your way of protecting me is to keep me inside a box. But you're trying to protect me *from* me." I get up and sit beside him. "Neither way works."

"It will work if we stay the course."

I take his hand. "You believed in me enough to have me, even after you read that letter. I need you to believe in me now."

My father starts to cry. His shoulders shake. "I didn't know," he sobs. "I didn't know."

The world begins to spin again. I'm just along for the ride. "What do you mean?"

"Violet had moved into my apartment at Cornell. She intercepted her father's letter."

"When did you find it?"

"A few days before the roof."

It takes all my strength not to pull away my hand. "If you had known about Violet's family, about her history?" We live in a house of cards. I'm trying to place the final one, the Queen of Hearts, without everything collapsing. "If you'd known?"

My father opens his mouth then hesitates. Our eyes lock, and I hear the words he can't bring himself to say aloud. *Yes, I would've aborted you.* He looks left and right, like he's trying to find a place to hide, but I've already seen him.

Something inside me breaks. The pieces are so sharp that they draw blood. A line from the article that ran when Violet was found guilty of attempted murder bobs to the surface. "'As previously reported,'" I quote, "'Gomez grabbed the child's ankles as she fell. Decker caught his wife.'"

"Lily?"

"Just for the record? You never protected me from her." I let go of his hand.

22

"We're almost there," Howard Walker says. His muscular arm hangs outside the truck's open window, calloused hand tapping against the side. He picked us up from the small airport in Haven, Florida, wearing a white T-shirt tucked into worn green cargo pants, looking like the kind of guy who'd appear in a backcountry outfitter's advertisements. Late twenties, olive-toned skin that's seen a lot of sun, square strong jaw, rugged vibe. Not that it matters to me, but a girl can notice.

Swifty's trunk drops onto my shoulder. When I run a hand over her soft skin she leans into me. I let her for a few seconds then pull away, because she's not supposed to bond too much with us. She has a new family now. Humid salt air mingles with the gummy reek of hot tarmac as we drive along a two-lane road, passing only a handful of other cars, most of them pickup trucks. Dead grass and sickly palms border both sides of the road. It's the opposite of our evergreen, rain-soaked Pacific Northwest. To me, it radiates abandonment, desolation. In the near distance a narrow band of blue is the only real color in the landscape. I take a few photos, trying to capture the heat mirage floating above the asphalt. The tip of Swifty's trunk invades the shot.

"Walker's winter home is less than a mile from the beach," Howard says. "On hot days, I take all my elephants to the ocean to play."

"So you take them every day?" Addie asks.

Howard laughs. Addie hates him for claiming her calf, but if he gets that, he's not showing it. I'm not on Team Circus or Team Zoo. Raki might've killed her calf. Wild Walker's Circus won't be perfect, but it might be okay. Okay is better than dead. Howard looks at me in his rearview mirror. I smile because Addie has been super passive-aggressive since we landed but he's being nice anyway.

Your smile is made from barbed wire and nails, the real Swift Jones sings in my head. Sawyer would love that SJ has joined forces with Ms. Frey in my brain so that together they can comment on my life. I wish I could tell him, but I texted a tentative hi? when we landed, and he didn't text back. Our first fight is an ugly snarl in my brain. I don't know how to untangle or fix it, because we both said things that can't be taken back. Swifty's trunk flops onto my head, making more of a mess of my already drool-stiffened, straw-invaded hair.

Swifty was not a well-behaved flier. The only way to stop her pacing her small travel pen and repetitively trumpeting was to climb in with her. Addie never offered to help me during the six-hour flight. She wanted me to "fully experience the consequences of my actions." But she did say I could call her Addie again. That's something.

Addie took a photo when I did a handstand to entertain

Swifty and the calf put her head down on the straw, trying unsuccessfully to copy me. We both toppled. Addie actually laughed. The calf lay beside me, gazing into my eyes. I had the urge to tell her that there's a relief when you no longer have to prove to the most important person in your life that you're worthy. But Swifty is an elephant, not a little girl, so it's like comparing apples with sneakers.

Four hours into the flight, I asked Addie if she was single. She looked at me like I was nuts. "Sorry, Mr. Matthews wanted to know. Just FYI."

"FYI? If he wants to know, he should fucking ask me himself."

"We're here," Howard says, one arm outside the window to point up. The truck rolls beneath a red banner stretched between two stone columns. Winter Home of Wild Walker's Circus is written in white block letters. The reality that Swifty will never return to Oregon hits. An invisible band tightens around my chest. Swifty's trunk reaches out the window toward the sign. I take some shots with her trunk cutting across the frame, like I'm seeing everything through her eyes.

The road becomes a wide, single lane. We roll by white houses of varying sizes with green-trimmed windows set above covered porches. The grass around them is burned brown, but the window boxes are filled with yellow, red and white flowers. Some of the houses have swing sets. A ponytailed, rosy-cheeked woman in running shorts and a jog bra pushes a giggling little boy high into the air.

"That's Heather. She does an act with standard poodles." Howard nods at the homes. "They're for family members and featured performers—trapeze artists, teeterboard athletes, acrobats, contortionists, bear guy. Tiger trainers, too—that's my folks, Tina and Maximus, who's also ringmaster—and the horse- and dog-act gals." He points to the fourth house from the end. "That one is mine."

"It's big," I say.

"Not to brag," Howard says, blushing a little, "but my elephant act is a huge draw. It brings in as many people as the tigers."

We pass the final house. It's by far the smallest. "That one?"

"My little brother, Otis. He's our public relations guy," Howard says. "He's not a big act, but he's family."

The way Howard says his brother isn't a *big act* makes it sound like he doesn't think Otis should have a house at all. "Where does everyone else live?"

"About a mile down the road we have an apartment building for the clowns, showgirls and workers."

Swifty nuzzles my neck. "Workers?"

"They do all the heavy lifting," Howard explains.

"How many people live on your campus?" Addie asks.

"About one hundred and fifty, give or take a few clowns. We hire additional help at each venue. No need to feed and house them here."

"I notice you don't have gates, security," Addie says.

"There's a very small town, just one street, about ten miles from here. You've seen the airstrip, and there's nothing else around. We know just about everyone in these parts."

I scratch behind the calf's ear as we roll by several low, brick buildings with numbers on them. She tilts her head, gives a snuffle of appreciation, then tips her head the other way. "Bossy," I say, but scratch behind the other ear. "Where do the kids whose parents work for you go to school?"

"They're homeschooled. We live in Florida three months a year so we can put together a new show each season. Joe Public demands change. The rest of the time we're on the road. Wouldn't want to break up families, so it's the best option."

"That's hard on them," Addie notes.

Howard shrugs. "Most of the kids get their GEDs by the time they're sixteen. My little brother got his at fourteen."

"Impressive," Addie says.

Howard hitches one shoulder. "I guess. But there's a difference between being book smart and life smart."

His comment is tossed so lightly that it sounds like a simple observation, but there's an undercurrent, a tug, that makes me think it might be a dig.

"And you?" Addie asks.

"Embarrassed to say I never got mine. Sometimes the world has other plans." An enormous yellow-and-white circus tent looms to the right.

A group of young women wearing matching bikinis made more of sparkles than material run by. They have the kind of bodies I thought were the result of photoshopping in magazines; the kind that make mere mortals want to cover up in baggy clothes.

"Those are a few of our showgirls."

Addie grimaces. "Small costumes."

Howard laughs. "You're right, Dr. Tinibu, to think they're eye candy. But they're also talented athletes." He turns right at the next corner, away from a cluster of low stucco buildings. "Those are filled with props, construction materials, veterinary supplies, food," Howard explains. "You can check them out later if you want, but right now we're heading to the animal building to get Swift Jones settled."

Addie raises one brow. "All of your animals are in one building?"

Howard nods. "It's easier that way. We have six bears, about twenty different types of dogs, a few llamas, a unicorn that's really a goat with an off-kilter horn, two potbellied pigs for the clown acts, thirteen Bengal tigers, a dozen Arabian horses, and right now, ten elephants." He grins. "Swift Jones makes it eleven."

"All male," Addie says.

"Yup. Trust me, they weren't easy to come by and most were in bad situations. But together we've overcome their pasts. My guys are happy and really docile. They're not mothers, but they'll love this calf."

Howard pulls the truck in front of a large, cinderblock building. The far corner is two stories. The rest is a single story with open squares where the windows should be. Howard parks then bounds out of the truck to let out the calf. His moss green eyes, so round that they remind me of pebbles in a creek, shine. He pushes one of three red buttons on the right side of the truck. The lift gate comes down. Hopping up, he raises the back door of the truck. Inside, Swifty pushes her bottom into the far corner.

"Come on, little lady," Howard says. Swifty doesn't budge.

Addie pinches the bridge of her nose. "Whistle."

I do, but the calf glances at Howard, holds her ground. "Sometimes she's kinda shy," I say. "Maybe if you, um, move out of sight?"

Howard runs a hand through short, black hair then hops off the gate, goes to the side of the vehicle. I whistle. Swifty comes right toward me, stepping onto the lift gate. Addie pushes the bottom button and the calf is lowered to the ground, her trunk knotted around Nibs.

"You're home," Howard says, kneeling beside her.

Swift Jones hides behind me like she's a little kid who just wants to go back to her mom. "Lead on," I say to cover the uncomfortable moment. Howard walks toward the front of the animal building. Wariness plucks at my shirt. Swifty's trunk wraps around my leg and I hesitate, but Ms. Frey pipes in, *Don't look back, you're not going that way.* So, Swifty beside me, I follow Howard into the building.

23

The smell hits me, so thick that I can taste it. Straw, bark chips, the tang of urine, fresh feces, the mingled, rich musk of different animals. It's hard not to gag. The sounds come next—neighing horses, barking dogs, the scrape of shovels, an elephant's trumpet, men's low laughter, a throaty growl. It's overwhelming, like too many animals, too much humanity, has been packed into a very small box.

Howard's work boots clomp on bare concrete as we head down the wide hallway to our right. It's lined with horse stalls. Each stall has buckets of food, fresh water, super clean floors, and a horse with a glistening coat. The horses look really well cared for, which makes the band around my chest that tightened on our arrival loosen. Swifty's eyes widen when she sees the animals. She's seen only elephants and people, so the horses must look strange. Still, the calf reaches her wriggling trunk toward a bay hanging its head over a half door. I crouch beside Swifty, take a photo of her trunk touching the horse's soft nose.

"She's a curious one. That means she's smart," Howard says. He reaches to touch Swifty's head but the calf shuffles back. "Take the next left," Howard says.

We approach a four-way intersection. There's a long train of steel cages connected together like giant wagons. Inside are tigers. Bengal tigers. The one in front is massive, its orange, black and white–striped fur bristling as it takes us in. Long whiskers frame gigantic canines. Violet would've wanted to reach through the bars to bury her fingers in the animal's fur. All the tigers pace their rectangular cages. There's just room for their length, enough width to turn around.

"The first one is Benny," Howard says. "He's a sweetheart as long as he's eaten."

I take a step forward to get an even better look.

"Stop," Addie says. "He'll spray you."

"Sure enough. It's how they mark their territory," Howard explains. "Sorry I forgot to mention it. Tina and Maximus, my folks, own the circus and they're the tiger trainers. They wanted to be here to greet you, but they're in Cook City today with the bean counters."

"Bean counters?" I pull out my phone and take a quick video of a Bengal. This close, he's one of the most beautiful animals I've ever seen.

"Accountants," Howard explains. "This is a family-run business and no one works harder or wears more hats than my folks. But if they were here, they'd tell you that they're very proud of their part in the conservation of Bengals."

"How are they conserving them?" Addie asks.

Howard smiles. "The same way a zoo does, Dr. Tinibu."

Addie takes off her glasses. Methodically, she cleans them. "Do you have a breeding program?"

"Animal activists don't believe anyone has the right to breed endangered species," a voice behind us says. "Unless their offspring are released back into the wild."

Howard grins. "Ah, my little brother finally arrives."

I turn and my mouth falls open a little bit. Otis Walker is at least six-foot-two with jaw-length, light brown hair tucked behind his ears. I flash to a TV show Sawyer was obsessed with, *Friday Night Lights.* This guy looks like Tim Riggins, the bad-boy football player. His skin is lightly tanned and he's wearing a green T-shirt, faded Levis and flip-flops. His eyes are dark blue. He introduces himself, shakes Addie's hand, then mine. The tips of his long fingers rest along the soft skin on the inside of my wrist. Can he feel my pulse? It's racing because, well, he's the hottest guy who has ever touched me. I remind myself how terse he was on the phone. The memory gets my heartbeat under control.

A dog brushes against my leg. It's the size of a terrier with ratty brown-and-white fur, a crooked snout, one ragged ear flopped over its left eye like it's paralyzed. The thing sniffs my jeans. "Um." I nibble my lower lip. "Is he going to pee on me?"

"Maybe." Howard laughs.

"Flea is just being friendly," Otis says.

"Flea?" I take a step back. When I was six a miniature collie bit me. Since then dogs make me nervous. "I don't like dogs."

Otis half smiles. "Elephants, but not dogs."

I stare at my flip-flops, because I'm pretty sure he's making fun of me and I don't have a snappy retort.

"Dr. Tinibu, you were curious about our Bengals," Otis continues. "Walker's didn't get ours from their native environments. They came from roadside safaris, private owners who couldn't handle them, zoos that kill their surplus animals."

"Zoos that kill surplus animals are extremely rare," Addie says.

"Well, we both know that the media overreacts to sad but sometimes necessary measures," Otis says smoothly. "Regardless, the Bengals Wild Walker's owns are well fed, intellectually challenged and live in humane environments."

Addie looks at the cages. "Humane?"

Otis is unruffled. "My parents use this train car to transfer their tigers into the ring where they will play and learn for hours before returning to their enclosure for dinner."

I kneel slightly behind Swifty, taking shots of her standing in front of Benny. The lead tiger is mid-yawn, his massive fangs glinting as the shutter clicks.

Otis puts a hand in front of the lens. "If you'd like to take photographs of any animal besides Swift Jones, call my office."

"This is just for the readers at the *Pennington Times*."

Otis smiles but his hand doesn't move. "T. Lillian Decker. Lily. Intern. I know."

"My baby bro takes his job seriously," Howard says. "Let her take a few pics, O."

I watch the brothers. They sound friendly; their voices are light and Howard is still smiling, but there's tension, electricity beneath the surface. Howard doesn't seem like he has a lot of respect for his little brother or Otis's job.

"Public perception of how animals are treated at a circus tends toward the negative," Otis says. "I'm sure Lily wouldn't want to mislead her readers by showing our Bengals being transferred to the ring." He takes his hand away, meets my gaze. "Call. We'll set up a more appropriate time."

"You're not exactly helpful when you return phone calls." This time I keep my chin up. Addie twists the ring on her thumb. I'm probably embarrassing her.

"I had a great conversation with your boss, Mr. Matthews," Otis says, leafing through the folder he's carrying. "This is what we agreed on. I just need your signature."

He hands me a printed document, a map of the Walkers' property and a pen. A few buildings and areas on the map have been circled in green, but not the massive tent where the performers must practice their acts. Also listed are *approved* interview subjects. "You have me interviewing a costume designer and a clown?"

"Also Esmerelda—she's a trapeze artist—Tina and Maximus, and Howard," Otis says. "That will give you some background on our performers and the show." He takes the paper back, prints another line then hands it back to me.

"No videos?"

Otis smiles. "That's right. Or photos without my approval. That includes the one you just took of our Bengals. Correct me if I'm wrong, but your job is to help Dr. Tinubu and write a few articles on Swift Jones, not post photos of tigers on Instagram for your friends."

I open my mouth then close it when no words come out. The video thing is actually no big deal. The *P-Times* wants photos. But this guy is beyond condescending. It ticks me off enough to untie my tongue. "Some of these interviews aren't pertinent for my articles."

Otis shrugs. "They'll give you perspective, but you're the intern."

My face burns. "What if I want to wander around?" Otis raises one brow like he's surprised I'm pushing back. Irritatingly, I again can't help noticing he's very good-looking. I don't allow myself to be drawn to any guy. So why am I focused on the dimple in Otis's cheek that briefly flashes when he talks?

"I'm sure you can understand that putting together a new show requires secrecy," Otis explains with a half shrug to convey it can't be helped. "Plus, there are wild animals here. We need to ensure you don't get hurt. If you'd feel more comfortable having an escort, I can assign one of our staff."

Otis's attitude, like I'm an enemy, ticks me off. "I think I can manage it."

"Terrific," Otis says, smiling. "This is a busy place and all of our staff have real jobs. If you want to interview anyone else, just ask and I'll try to arrange it."

"If you have some time, I'd like to interview you," I say.

Otis reaches down to pet Flea. "I'm pretty sure I'd bore you."

"My brother's right. He's just a pencil pusher," Howard says with a wink.

"It seems like he doesn't want a reporter here," I say before I can stop myself.

Howard laughs. "Tina and Maximus run the show, right, Otis? While my brother is paid to be the worrier of the family."

"Pragmatist," Otis interjects. "Speaking of which." He nods at the pen.

I look to Addie. She shrugs. Still, I hesitate. Signing away my autonomy isn't part of the Code.

Otis smiles. "No hard feelings if you're not comfortable with this." He pulls out his phone. "I can have someone escort you off Walker's campus."

Mr. Matthews already agreed and he's my boss. I start to scribble my name at the bottom of the paper then stop. "What about your circus's veterinarian?"

"Dr. Robertson?" Otis asks. "What about her?"

I square my shoulders, trying to look confident. "The *Pennington Times*' readers want to know that Swifty is being well taken care of, that she's healthy." Otis takes the paper, prints Dr. Robertson's name on the approved list. I finish signing and hand it to him with the sweetest smile I can muster.

"As I was saying," Howard continues, "Otis is a pragmatist, but our folks are very proud of how we run our circus, the animals we caretake and all the joy we bring to people. Sometimes my brother forgets that, so apologies. You're here as our guest, Lily. And I, for one, am thrilled at the chance to show off my elephants."

I watch Otis's face to see how he's going to react to Howard's criticism, but it remains an impassive mask.

Flea prances over to Swifty like he's some kind of show dog instead of a mutt with patchy fur. The calf has dropped Nibs. Flea mouths the rabbit. He stands on his hind legs, offering it back. Swifty's first attempt to grab it with her trunk topples the mutt. He tries again. Swifty manages to get her trunk around the bunny. My heart lightens as they playfully tug the stuffed animal between them. Flea lets the calf have it. He winds through Swifty's legs like a cat then sits down beside her.

"I think your dog likes Swift Jones."

"Who chose that *interesting* name?" Otis asks.

"There are kids around the country who love that name and aren't thrilled that your circus has taken Swift Jones from the zoo," I say. It's the least I can do for Sawyer. A hundred grand should buy him more than a crappy friend.

"So it'd be a bad idea to rename the calf?" Otis asks, like he's trying to understand.

My cheeks are blazing hot. "Yes."

He smirks. "Well, thanks then for helping me do my job."

Howard stares at his brother like he's a total ass. But maybe I'm the idiot. Now the circus's PR guy hates me.

"Let's move on," Howard suggests. He glances at Otis. "We can take it from here, O."

"Come on, Flea," Otis says over his shoulder. But his ugly mutt stays by Swifty's side.

We follow Howard down the left corridor. Dozens of dogs, mostly standard poodles and little terriers, are in wire pens. There are two men in tank tops shoveling soiled straw out of empty cages. Their arms are slick with sweat.

"Sorry about Otis," Howard says. "Off the record?"

I nod.

"The kid had a rough childhood. Sad stuff our family doesn't talk about. Bottom line is that he wanted to be the elephant trainer but didn't have the ability to emotionally connect with the animals. He tried bears. That was even worse because they could smell his fear. Makes him kinda bitter, you know?"

I don't feel particularly sorry for Otis, but at the same time his brother throwing him under the bus seems pretty disloyal. I let it go. I'm not here to figure out why there's friction between the Walker boys. "Is it always so hot?"

"Sometimes it's even hotter," Howard says with a laugh.

Swifty's ears flap hard against her head, but she's watching Flea prance beside her with bright eyes. The dog is a good distraction. She needs only one friend.

My camera hangs at my waist from a shoulder strap. I try a few shots just as an F-you to Otis. They'll probably be too dark or frame my flip-flop. Addie notices what I'm doing, but she doesn't say anything. Maybe she feels the same way about Walker's PR guy.

"How do you train your elephants?" Addie asks.

"Free contact, but I never use an ankus. Don't need one. I work right next to my guys so we can accomplish a lot. They respond to my touch because we have mutual respect. I don't have to tell you how smart elephants are. They know when someone really cares. And it doesn't hurt to carry high-value treats," he adds. "My guys deserve a reward when they learn a new trick."

Addie grimaces. "Some would say that teaching animals to do unnatural tricks creates a high level of stress."

Howard smiles. "Some would say that putting them on display in zoos creates both stress *and* boredom. I think we'll have to agree to disagree." He stops at the end of the hall. "Here we are."

We're in front of a twelve-by-twelve-foot interior pen with a door made of steel bars. A fluorescent bulb hangs overhead, because there's no window to let in light. Fresh straw lines the floor. There's a bucket of water, two straw bales, a canvas pad, a plastic pail, a pile of wool blankets and a fridge. The walls are gray cinderblock. Howard opens the door. He ushers Flea inside the enclosure. Swifty follows the dog. She turns to watch Howard shut the door with a metallic clang. The calf looks through the bars at me. My stomach clenches at the idea that this is Swifty's new normal.

Addie's nostrils flare hard. "This is her new home?"

"Only until she's old enough to join the rest of the elephants," Howard says. "Then she'll spend time socializing, learning in the ring and swimming in the ocean with her new friends. Don't worry. Swift Jones won't be alone. She'll have caretakers day and night, just as you requested, although it'll probably be just one person per shift. We've already prepared the exact formula you specified, plus the plastic can for play, blankets, and I even had a canvas pad made." He puts his hand on Addie's shoulder. "I'm going to do everything I can to make sure our calf is healthy and happy. By the way," he says, glancing at me, "I love the name."

The band around my chest has tightened again, making it hard to get enough oxygen. "Um. Thanks." I look away from Swifty's upturned face.

Addie steps sideways, so that Howard's hand falls from her shoulder. "Lily is going to take the first night shift. I'll expect one of the circus's caretakers to join her, though, so she can show them how to take care of the calf at night. I will instruct more of your staff during the day."

"Of course," Howard says. "The first caretaker will be me."

My skin prickles as I think about spending the night in a small pen with a man. I mean, the only guy I've ever slept beside is Sawyer. That doesn't count because it's not like he looks at me *that way.* My scalp itches. I pull a piece of straw out of my dirty hair. It's hard not to laugh. Of course Howard isn't going to look at me *that way* either. He's a grown man and good-looking. Duh. *Focus.* I have a job to do. I have a goal. Three articles. I'll be back home in seven days.

Swifty stands in the center of the pen, her trunk slightly swinging. Nibs rests in the straw by her left foot. Otis's ugly dog sniffs around the enclosure. I take a deep, cleansing breath then crouch to Swifty's eye level, snapping a few photos through the bars. Hopefully, the light sensor is right. Howard doesn't stop me.

"All set?" Addie asks.

"Yes." I glance at my watch. It's 7:15 p.m. "Swifty ate on the plane so she doesn't get fed again until nine," I tell Howard. "Could you come back then so I can get my math homework done? Sorry, it's just...I have to email it to my teacher in the morning."

"No problem. You a junior?" Howard asks.

"Senior."

"Going to college?"

My cheeks get warm because he's looking at me like I matter. "I hope so."

Howard smiles. "Maybe we'll convince you to join the circus instead."

24

"Good girl. A little bit more, okay?" Swifty refuses to drink the second half of her bottle. "A plane, a truck, showgirls, tigers, horses, a new home. It's a lot." She tilts her head like she's trying to understand, then bats long lashes. "You're not as cute as you think," I say. "What you are is trouble." Drool has soaked the front of my T-shirt. I wring it out. "Trouble and a very messy eater." But I don't really mind. Addie kind of unnerved me, talking about the fragility of calves.

Swifty squeals. Flea has grabbed Nibs. The calf races after him. The mutt drops the stuffed rabbit. Swifty picks it up. They race in the other direction, running in circles. Worries fade like the sunset as I watch them play. The calf drops the bunny. The game reverses once again. Laughing, I scramble to the corner of the pen, take at least fifty photos. Hopefully Jack can work his magic on them, because it'd be cool for the newspaper's readers to see that even though Swifty's new home is dreary, she's already made a friend.

There's no sign of Howard yet. My thoughts swirl. A lot

has happened in the past twenty-four hours. Sinking cross-legged, I dial Sawyer. One ring and then direct to voice mail.

"This is Sawyer. You know what to do."

"It's me. I'm at Walker's…it's pretty dismal… Swifty's pen, I mean… How are you? I'm sorry…" It's a disjointed message. I should erase it and start again—

"What a cutie-pie!"

I jump to my feet and rock back from the looming shadow in the hall's murky light. Swifty runs to the corner and presses her butt into the cinderblocks. A guy opens the metal door. He's so muscular that his T-shirt stretches to the point of ripping around his biceps. The acrid scent of nicotine wafts off him.

"Sorry! I didn't mean to startle you. Name's Clem. I'm supposed to help with Jones."

"Swift Jones," I correct. I put my phone away.

"Yeah. That's it."

"Lily," I say as we shake. Swifty's eyes dart from him to me.

"Howard apologizes," Clem says. "Work. He asked me to take the first bottle."

"She's already had it."

"Oh. Damn. Howard'll be here for the next bottle, sure thing. Anyway. I'm one of the guys who'll be the elephant's caretaker. So maybe you can show me the ropes?"

Clem runs a hand over his head, a gleaming white dome shining with sweat. Both his sunburned arms are covered in half-finished tattoo sleeves that look messy enough to be homemade. Gauges have stretched his earlobes into quarter-sized holes. A woven, black-wire hoop earring hangs from one of them. Apprehension needles me. Clem seems kind of tough to be a caretaker, but Sawyer looks like every girl's dream, and I don't look like my brain is going to implode, so clearly appearances can be deceiving. Clem pulls a pack of cigarettes from the back pocket of stained jeans. "Okay. Um. First? No smoking around the calf."

"Oh. Shit. Oh. Sorry for my French."

"No worries. Just. So. Swift Jones needs to drink one bottle of formula every three hours. Set an alarm, okay?"

"Sure." He fiddles with his plastic watch. "And...wait for it...done."

I go through everything Addie taught me. When I'm done, Clem takes a few steps closer. I fight the urge to back away. His fingers twist his earring. "Tiger whiskers."

"Excuse me?"

Clem tugs the black fibers. "They're good luck. Lots of circus folks think so. Make great ear or nipple rings. Next ones I find? I'll braid them for you."

I don't have a nipple ring. "My ears aren't pierced."

"Bracelet then."

"Cool. So. Do you like working for Walker's?"

Clem smiles. Three gold teeth, one on top, two on the bottom, catch the light. "My choices were limited, but it's good."

He sits down on the end of my sleeping bag. I don't want to be rude, so I sit a few feet away and pull out a pen and notebook. "What do you do for the circus, exactly?" Clem reaches over, gives a curl of my hair that's escaped a gentle tug. His hands smell like earth, oil and animals. His touch, when we're already confined to Swifty's small pen, is claustrophobic.

"You have really great hair."

I do my best not to obviously recoil, because I don't want

to insult Clem, but I lean back a little so my curl slides free. "Um. Thanks. So, your job?"

"I'm a worker. Means I shovel shit." He laughs. "Excuse me. I put up the big tent when we're on the road. Clean cages, ready the show rings. Drive cargo trucks to transport the animals. Load 'em and unload 'em. Pretty much do any heavy lifting that's needed."

"Sounds like you, um, work really hard."

"Yeah. But, see, guys like me? Hardworking guys? Get screwed by the system—"

"That's what they all say." Otis opens the pen's door.

"Otis," Clem says, frowning.

"Why don't you pack it in for the night?" Otis says.

Clem shakes his head. "Boss man won't like it. I'm supposed to help Lily care for her baby elephant 'til he shows up."

Otis smiles, but if he had a superpower it'd be the ability to both freeze and thaw with his voice. "First, it's *our* elephant now. Second, I'm your boss, too. I'm telling you to pack it in for the night."

I look from Clem to Otis. The charged air between them makes the hairs on my arms stand. Why don't they like each other? Flea growls. Clem stands up and sidles out of the pen. He makes sure he doesn't bump Otis, hands held up in the air like he's backing off from a fight. He strides away, and his footsteps fade. A door slams in the distance.

Otis leans against the wall by my sleeping bag. If I stand up he'll be too close. I'd have to back away, which would make it look like I'm uncomfortable, which I am, but I don't want him to know that. I stay seated, which is also uncomfortable, because I have to tip my head back to look at him. A bead of sweat trickles down my back. "Clem was supposed to help me." I make myself meet Otis's eyes. They remind me of the Pacific Ocean. It's impossible to see the sharks swimming beneath the dark surface, but they're there.

Otis reaches down and tucks my loose curl behind one ear. "It's best to keep a more appropriate distance from the workers."

My face gets hot, because he thought I was flirting with Clem and because when Otis's fingers skimmed along the edge of my ear, my insides twisted. Otis taps a cigarette out of the pack he pulls from his pocket. I say, "No smoking—"

"Around Swift Jones," Otis finishes. He flips the cigarette over his knuckles.

I change tacks, because everything I say to this guy comes out totally awkward. "As long as you're here, maybe I can ask you some questions about Walker's?"

"Sorry I'm late," Howard says, stepping into the pen. "Hey, little brother. Don't you have a press release to write?"

"Sure," Otis says.

He takes off without looking back, which shouldn't bother me. I mean, I'm glad to be rid of him. But I feel…a little disappointed, which makes zero sense.

"Clem do okay?" Howard asks.

"Yeah. Why doesn't Otis like him?"

Howard sighs. "It's not personal. Otis doesn't like any of the workers. Thinks he's better than them, I guess, but this circus couldn't run without their hard work."

Again, he's throwing Otis under the bus. I shouldn't mind, but it makes me uncomfortable. I grab a blanket to tuck in Swifty just the way she likes. When Howard leans down to tuck the end of the blanket around her back, the calf jumps up and scoots away from him.

"It's okay, girl," Howard says, walking toward the corner where Swifty stands, his arms held wide. Flea, Nibs in his mouth, trots over to the calf. The patchy fur on the mutt's back is up. He growls.

"Told Otis not to take in a stray," Howard says. "Kid can't even train a mutt."

Swifty gives me a sideways look. "Um. I think if you just hang out for a bit, she'll get more comfortable?"

Howard shakes his head like he's getting his thoughts in order, or getting rid of the ones that aren't useful. "Of course. She's been through a helluva day."

Swifty settles in the corner. I cover her again. "Once she's settled, I usually set my alarm for three hours and try to get some sleep, too."

"First, can I show you something?" Howard asks with a smile that looks like he has a secret. I hesitate, but Swifty's eyes have already closed. Flea lies down by the curve of the calf's trunk, his one visible eye fixed on me. "Um. Okay." Howard leads me out of the pen, down the hall.

"I want you to meet my boys," he says as we pass by a cage with two sand-colored, sleeping llamas.

We round the corner. The ceiling lifts to a story and a half. A line of huge elephants stands side by side on a thick rubber pad that stretches from wall to wall. Each elephant has a thick, dark gray iron cuff around its front right foot. A chain connects the cuff to bolts on the floor. The zoo used restraints to keep Raki from hurting Swifty. These elephants, though, are chained for the entire night. Most have their eyes open but a few are asleep.

The sight makes my throat constrict. "Why are they chained?"

"To keep them safe when I'm not around," Howard says.

I watch the elephants sway in unison, like they're hearing music in their heads. I've never seen this kind of behavior at the zoo. "Why are they swaying?"

"They do it a lot," Howard says. "Sometimes I think they're communicating with each other. Other times I imagine that there's an ancient song embedded in their bones. It stays with them for their entire life's journey, comforting them when they need it, reminding them of their true home." He looks away. "Sounds stupid, I know."

"It doesn't." It sounds like he really cares about his elephants...but they're in chains.

"I know you're used to the way your zoo does things, but it's important you understand that just because we do things differently here, it's not necessarily the wrong way. My guys spend the night like this, but unlike the zoo, they also get plenty of time outside this building, playing in the ring, learning and gaining a sense of accomplishment. That's really important for animals this smart."

"I'm keeping an open mind," I say, reminding myself that's what reporters are supposed to do. I'm here to follow the Code, write some articles, give myself options. And what Howard is saying does make some sense.

"You have a pretty smile."

Blood floods my face, but Howard is picking up a box of apples so he doesn't see. I follow him over to the first elephant. He's the tallest one, his skin a gunmetal gray that looks like it was washed until it faded. His eyes, ringed in long lashes, track Howard's every move.

"This is Bolo." Howard holds up an apple. Bolo wraps his trunk around it and puts it in his mouth, squirting juice with each crunch. "He came from a zoo in Connecticut. He was there for twenty years. The concrete floor in his pen gave him pretty bad arthritis." Howard taps the rubber floor with the heel of his boot. "Changed it to rubber when Bolo got here." He pats the elephant's chest. "Took a year to turn things around for him, but with our veterinarian's help, we did it."

"That's great. I mean, not the arthritis, but Addie, Dr. Tinibu, was worried you don't have a vet working here."

"We don't," Howard says. "But that's because our animals are rarely sick. Still, Dr. Robertson is only a phone call away."

"What about when the show travels?"

"We have vets on call in every city."

Bolo reaches his trunk toward me. I let him snuffle my hair, because it couldn't look much worse. The tip of his trunk tickles my neck.

"He likes you," Howard says.

I blush again. This time I'm pretty sure Howard notices. We move on to the next elephant.

"This is Jake. I got him from an animal safari in Tennessee. Some safari. They had a half-dead alligator, one mangy lion, plus Jake."

Pink scars crisscross Jake's right side. "What happened?"

"His owner used a whip." Howard holds out an apple, but the elephant doesn't take it. "He's been with me over a year. We're still working on trust. Elephants have long memories."

Howard puts the apple on the floor. Jake picks it up, eats it in two bites. "Attaboy."

We go down the line. Christopher Columbus sways with the rest of the line but remains asleep. His trunk is spotted like he has freckles—he came from a zoo in Alabama whose elephant exhibit was the size of a one-car garage. Vinnie's eyes open as Howard talks about him. He came from another animal safari. Some guy living near the Florida Everglades owned Digger and Wyatt. He used them to give people rides. "The scars on Wyatt's and Digger's trunks?" I ask.

"The guy used a cattle prod to train them." Howard rests his hand on Digger's shoulder. "I'm just glad I could bring them here together. The majority of elephants in the US have been taken from the wild. They lose their families. I don't have to tell you that family, for an elephant, is sacred. At least these two boys still have each other."

"The Pennington Zoo doesn't do that," I blurt. "They get their elephants from other zoos or private owners, just like you did."

"Maybe."

"Isn't taking an elephant from his family just what you did when you took Swift Jones from her mother?" Howard frowns. Crap. Does every thought in my head need to come out of my mouth?

"I think Raki made that decision." Howard scuffs the toe of his boot against the floor like a little kid. "Lily, I'm sorry she rejected Swift Jones, but I'm just trying to do the next right thing. And maybe taking elephants from the wild isn't your zoo's policy, but it happens. A lot."

"I guess," I say. Howard smiles like we've just settled an

argument and he's won. He gives Wyatt an apple. The elephant eats it in one big chomp. He reaches his trunk into the box for another.

Howard laughs. "Nope, big guy. Don't want you to get a stomachache."

"Which one is Swift Jones's father? Lorenzo?"

"His nickname is Romeo," Howard says with a wink. "He's been loaned to another zoo for their breeding program."

Howard skips a sleeping elephant and offers the next one, a smaller elephant with pale gray skin, an apple. This one's ear looks like a bite has been taken out of it. "Good boy, Chuck." He glances at me. "Did you know that elephants in zoos die decades earlier than elephants in the wild?"

"But—" I swallow my next words.

"But?"

"Zoos do have breeding programs?"

Howard shrugs. "Nothing is black-and-white. But the infant mortality rate for elephants in zoos is 40 percent. That's triple the rate in the wild." He walks up to the last elephant in the line. "Hiya, Tambor." Howard holds up an apple. The elephant turns his head away. There are a few red sores behind his ear. Howard frowns hard. "Freakin' designers."

"Pardon?"

He shakes his head. "Tambor's new harness is rubbing. The designers have promised the next one will fit right." Howard puts the apple at the bull's feet but the elephant doesn't reach for it.

"He doesn't like apples?"

"It's not that. He has some lingering behavioral issues because he came here as a four-month-old."

"That's pretty young."

"Yeah. I know Dr. Tinibu doesn't think we're capable of taking care of a calf, but we've done it before. Successfully."

"What happened to Tambor's mother?"

"She died at a Pennsylvania zoo from tuberculosis."

"TB?"

"It's not uncommon for elephants. They die from the herpes virus, too. Losing his mom was hard on Tambor. He started acting out. The zoo couldn't handle it. They were going to euthanize him when I stepped in."

Howard pats the massive elephant's leg. Tambor raises his foot. "Tambor can be a handful, but we've been together for decades. He's part of the Walker family." Howard steps back, but the elephant is still holding his foot in the air.

"When will he put his foot down?"

"When I tell him to. Down, boy." Tambor puts his foot back on the ground. Howard's face lights up. "Communicating with animals never gets old."

He closes the distance between us in two strides, putting his hands on my shoulders. "Lily, what you write matters. That's why we let you come with Dr. Tinibu. We can tell that you're not interested in gossip, that you're fair. That you have the calf's best interest at heart."

My headache has returned. "I'm just an intern at the newspaper." I shrug, hoping his hands will fall from my shoulders, but they don't. "As soon as a panda is born at some other zoo, people will forget about Swift Jones."

"Maybe. But I want your readers to know we already love her. Also, that while zoos spend hundreds of thousands of dollars to expand exhibits and breeding programs, Wild Walker's

Circus gives 5 percent of our net earnings to conservation programs in the wild."

I take a step back, because Howard's breath is overpoweringly minty. His hands fall away. "I should get back," I say.

Howard nods. "Sure. Just. Look, sorry if I came on too strong, but I'm passionate about what I do, how much I love my elephants. I hope some of that will come across in your articles?"

"Yeah, of course. Do you mind if I take some photos?"

"Why the hell not? I'll grab some Zs in my office before joining you for the midnight feeding."

When the clunk of Howard's boots disappears, Tambor turns toward me. His brown eyes watch as I pick up the apple by his foot. Gently, Tambor takes it from my hand and eats it.

"Psst."

I whirl, but there's no one standing behind me. The hairs on my arms rise despite the still damp blanket of Florida heat. "Hello?" I call. The only answer is the swooshing of the elephants' feet as they sway side to side and a slight buzzing in my ears, probably from the noisy flight. I take a few shots of the elephants then head back to Swifty's pen to get some rest.

I manage to sleep for an hour before my alarm goes off. Howard doesn't show up for the midnight feeding, which is disappointing. Swifty drinks less than half her bottle, which is more disappointing. No amount of bad singing can get her to take one more swallow. She plays half-heartedly with Flea for a few minutes then lies down. Flea burrows under the blanket beside her as I tuck the edges around Swifty's face so that her ears are covered. She looks so…vulnerable. "It was a long day," I remind us both. "Tomorrow will be a fresh start."

I consider trying Sawyer again, but instead pull out my iPad. I Google Wild Walker's Circus to find Howard's bio on their website. He's twenty-eight, loved elephants practically since he was born, apprenticed with Walker's former elephant trainer before taking over the act on his eighteenth birthday.

There are blurry photos of Howard as a kid riding bareback on an elephant, balancing on an animal's outstretched leg, orchestrating as Walker's elephants spin on pedestals. Howard looks so little, all skinny limbs, long hair blowing across his face, arms held wide, like he's hugging the entire herd. In one shot he stands in front of an elephant, hands pressed on either side of its face, their foreheads touching. I lean in, trying to see the look in his eyes, but the shot is too far away.

The last childhood photo jumps to Howard's eighteenth birthday celebration. He stands under Wild Walker's red banner holding a cake with the number eighteen encircled by candles. His hair is brush cut, darker. He's in shorts and a wrinkled, blue cotton shirt. It looks like he's wearing an ankle brace. Behind him are clowns, gorgeous showgirls in feathered hats and performers in sparkly costumes. The line beneath the birthday photo labels the people in the front row. Tina and Maximus Walker stand beside their son. Tina's blond hair is in a high bun. She wears a white sundress. Maximus towers over her. He's in a collared short-sleeve shirt with black, wavy hair falling well past broad shoulders. He's smiling hard, round eyes identical to Howard's.

I peer at a kid on the far left of the picture…long dark blond hair, striped T-shirt, baggy shorts. It's Otis. He's the only one not smiling. I click on Otis's bio. Unlike Howard's, which is four pages, Otis's has only two lines of copy. "Otis Walker, born November 7, is the youngest son of circus owners Tina and Maximus Walker. Currently Otis is in charge of Walker's public relations department."

The anxiety that's been a constant companion since we arrived gathers into a dull headache. I start surfing the Web. Howard was right about the infant mortality rates for elephants in zoos, but there's a ton of negative information about circuses, too, including that a lot of elephants get depressed because of cruel treatment and harsh conditions. I haven't seen that here. Howard Walker clearly cares about his elephants. But…I'm sitting in a windowless cell. Howard's elephants are chained. They're swaying, which one of the articles says is a result of boredom, even mental illness, and not some internal song.

"So what're the alternatives?" I click on a link. Animal-rights experts agree animals should be protected, preserved in the wild. But when they're already in the US, it's basically about choosing the best remaining option. From what I read, the luckiest wild animals end up at sanctuaries designed to recreate their natural habitats. They get to live on thousands of acres like they're almost wild.

I follow a link to an article written a few weeks ago about Daisy, a female Asian elephant from a zoo in Detroit. Her two-month-old calf suddenly died. Daisy became horribly depressed. She stopped eating. "Daisy was dying," Detroit Zoo veterinarian Betty Edmonds said. "So we contacted Viv Hemming's Elephant Sanctuary in Galton, Texas." The elephant sanctuary agreed to take ownership of Daisy. At the time of the story they were still trying to save her life.

When I look at Swifty, she's sucking the tip of her trunk

like a human baby. Flea sleeps halfway under her blanket. Both of them are touching Nibs. "He's an old stuffed rabbit, not magic," I whisper. Lying on my stomach, I take photos of Swifty from different angles. Something tugs inside my chest. After pulling my sleeping bag to the far wall, I crawl inside and imagine my questions are bubbles floating away...

It doesn't work, because Sawyer's accusation floats to the surface...*it's not hard to count to zero.* I dial him and get his voice mail. "It's me. Again. I'm sorry I didn't go look at apartments with you...and for anything else I didn't do. But come on," I say, trying to make my voice all jokey, "you have to admit having your mom try to kill you, impending insanity, traveling to the circus with Addie, who hates my guts, and an elephant calf who might die, trumps getting kicked out by your dad, right? Call me, okay? Please?"

Once again I try to sleep, but my mind spins like a washing machine. "Screw it." I pull out the notes I've scribbled and start writing my first article.

Swift Jones Comes Home to Wild Walker's Circus

After a six-hour flight, the truck carrying former Pennington Zoo Asian elephant calf Swift Jones rolled under a red Wild Walker's Circus banner.

"During your visit you'll see that we care for and protect our animals," Howard Walker, the circus's twenty-eight-year-old elephant trainer, told Pennington Zoo's director, Dr. Tinibu, who

> accompanied the calf to Florida to help with the calf's transition.
>
> Walker is proud to say that all of his male Asian elephants have been rescued from abusive or unhealthy environments. He uses a system of free contact to train his elephants. "But I never use an ankus [a tool for handling elephants with a metal point and sharp hook]," he said. "They respond to my touch.... And it doesn't hurt to carry high-value treats."
>
> For now, Swift Jones is housed in her own enclosure, a twelve-by-twelve-foot interior room in a large building that's home to all the circus's animals. The show's employees will work around the clock to ensure she's well cared for.

I do a quick proof then email my article and photos to Shannon. It's a few minutes after one in the morning. Two hours before the next feeding.

My dull headache now pounds like surf on sand. I hear Addie's judgmental voice in my head. Howard Walker argues with her. Ms. Frey twitters that there are *three sides to every story.* Mr. Matthews reminds me that *It's a local happenings beat. People want to get jazzed.* The Code sounds beneath it all. *Seek Truth and Report It. Minimize harm. Act Independently. Be Accountable and Transparent.*

"I won't let you screw with my Twelve-Year Plan," I tell all of them and close my eyes.

25

Ringing. Ringing. Ringing in my head. Not. My. Head. My phone. My heart leaps into the air and does a double flip. I slide off the lumpy motel bed onto shag carpet, fast-crawl to the chair where my jeans are crumpled, dig out my phone. "Sawyer?"

"You're sleeping?"

"Shannon." I lie on the stiff carpet, staring at the yellow water stains on the ceiling. My T-shirt is glued to sweaty skin because the AC window unit is all noise, no action. "I only got four hours sleep last night. Not. Continuous."

"You sound grumpy."

I could tell her that I smell like eau de animal—urine, feces, stale formula; that it's so freaking hot here that I've sweated out every ounce of fluid in my body; that Addie is still only speaking to me in bullet points; that my best friend isn't even my friend anymore; that Swift Jones drank a total of only two of her three bottles; that there's no way I'll have the energy in this swampland to go for a run, which I desperately need to keep my brain in working order; that there's a current of stress buzzing through my body that can't be good for me. Instead, I get up, empty a packet into the filter of a plastic coffee maker on the bathroom counter then fill the top with water. "What's up?" I ask.

"You're lucky I was in the office late last night," Shannon says, like she's on her fifth espresso, one sugar. "Managed to get your article into today's paper."

"Did you—"

"Like it?" Shannon finishes. "No. But the tweets and emails of concern for Swift Jones keep rolling in so Matthews is up my ass for copy. He wants more photos, too."

"Which ones did you use?"

"The calf touching the horse's nose with her trunk. The tiger. Damn, it's big. Swift Jones reaching toward the Walker's banner and looking through the bars into the calf's prison cell."

"It's not a prison cell," I say. But it does look and feel like one. *Stop.* Swifty is an animal, not a small child. Animals live in small places. At least Swifty will be let out of her pen to play and learn. "Four photos?"

"Don't gloat. Jack had to fix all of them. Still."

"Still?"

"Your perspective was interesting. Anyway, you're on the front page of the Entertainment section, below the fold."

"Cool." I do a little dance.

"If you're doing some kind of victory dance, stop. Your article was about an inch deep."

I stop dancing. "It's a human interest story."

"True. But it seems like you've landed on the circus's side."

"I haven't. But this is Swift Jones's home now. People need to know that she's safe."

"People want to know the truth."

She's wrong, but I don't say it. Outside the window, the sun beats down on a parking lot that's more cracks than pavement. A few sad-looking palms grow out of sun-scorched grass. "Today I'm going to interview the owners of the circus, Tina and Maximus Walker."

"Good. Find out their story, vision for Walker's, how a baby elephant fits into it. By the way, the AP already picked up your article."

I refrain from dancing. "That's great, right?" I'll send it to USC. Sawyer will… He won't care.

"All the AP proves is that a monkey can write about Swift Jones and get attention. Are you a monkey, Lily?"

"No."

"Then act like a real reporter. Write something that's freaking better."

She hangs up on me. I take a sip of coffee. I'm a newbie, but it's definitely horrible. I guzzle it down anyway. The phone rings again. It's Calvin's number, so I let it go to voice mail then check for, like, the tenth time to see if Sawyer has emailed. Nope. I listen to my father's voice mail.

"Lily. Call me. You have to understand. The love of my life turned into a woman I couldn't recognize. She wouldn't take her meds… Sometimes, I was afraid to come home from work. But I never thought she'd hurt you. She—she loved you so much. Christ, I must've called her parents a thousand times for help. They hung up on me, eventually changed their number. Lily, I was so scared—"

The message cuts off. I heard ice cubes in the background. Calvin was drunk again. My nose wrinkles. I can almost smell the peaty scent of Scotch. When Violet completely unraveled, it was always on Calvin's breath. After the trial, he mostly stopped drinking…until now. The space where I'm supposed to feel something is empty. *You have to understand?* No. Actually, I don't.

Peeling off my T-shirt, I head for the shower. It's cold, which is fine. But the nozzle only releases five trickles of water that are not enough to get the shampoo out of my hair. I settle for adding conditioner to the remaining suds in the hopes that a brush might make it through the tangled mess. When I gather the dark mass of curls and twist it into a bun, the threadbare towel tucked above my breasts falls to the linoleum. I bend to retrieve it.

"Psst."

My body snaps to attention. The only image reflected in the mirror is my own sickly white one.

"'I'll make you the gift of a secret…'"

My ears are filled with invisible bees. "It's not a new quote," I whisper. "It's not," I repeat, louder. "It's from *The Little Prince*." But was it my voice saying it? Was it? "Was it?" My reflection doesn't answer. "'I'll make you the gift of a secret,'" I repeat. "I. Will. Make. You. The. Gift." It was a young woman's voice. My voice. I'm pretty sure. I'm sure. "I have a kick-ass imagination," I say, channeling my former best friend's words. And then it hits me why my subconscious brought up that quote.

I can't count how many times over the years I've turned

to Sawyer for comfort. About a zillion, and that's a low estimate. Our friendship is well beyond lopsided. It's basically one-sided. "The secret is that you're incredibly selfish," I say, staring at the lower part of my face to make sure it's intact, blood-free, which I do realize, on an intellectual level, is pretty stupid because if I go nuts I'll have my own hallucinations, not YouTube Hannah's. Maybe I'll see devils' faces in trees like some suffering from schizophrenia do, or rooms filled with dead people, or maybe it'll just be a voice I think is God commanding me to do some really twisted stuff. "Again," I tell my thoroughly disgusted reflection, "all about me."

I throw on a T-shirt and shorts then rifle through my bag for a Luna Bar because the awful coffee is eating a hole in the lining of my stomach. No luck. There's no restaurant at the motel, but Howard said we could eat all our meals at Wild Walker's food cart, so my plan is to swing by the animal building to see if Tina and Maximus are around, figure out how to schedule an interview with Esmerelda then find the cart so I can eat. I grab my backpack and head into the sauna that is Florida.

It's a two-mile walk to the circus. I consider putting on my sneakers and running there, but instead opt for a fast walk. The air smells of brine and scorched earth, and the sidewalk's cracked asphalt radiates heat. I've sweat through the Koi Korean BBQ T-shirt Sawyer got me last Christmas by the time I walk beneath the circus's banner.

All around me there's activity, like Walker's is a brightly colored hive of people and animals in all shapes and sizes. Performers in clown shoes juggle pins between them as they walk along the road, kids play soccer in the front yard of a performer's house, a girl in a very short pink sequined dress leads two horses toward the big tent, their black coats gleaming in the sun. Trucks with Walker's logos unload what look like props in front of one of the buildings.

My phone beeps. *Please be a text from Sawyer.* It's Addie.

ADDIE: Training caretakers all day. You are on from 6:00 p.m. to 12:00

ME: I can take the whole night

ADDIE: No. I've given that shift to circus personnel

ME: I could help them?

ADDIE: No. FYI. SJ has only had half a bottle

ME: Offer the bottle to Flea if he's still there. Swifty doesn't like to share

I didn't eat much after the rooftop. According to Ms. Frey, food was the only thing I could control. I guess that goes for a little kid *and* a calf. Addie doesn't text back, so my suggestion probably worked. Still, uneasiness flops in my belly like a fish on dry land.

As I approach the animal building, I see an elongated golf cart down the road and recognize Tina Walker in the driver's seat. Beside her is Maximus, his long black hair now silver. Otis is talking to them. He points at me. Butterflies flutter. I'm just hungry. Otis nods at me then turns, walks away, and the butterflies settle. Tina drives my way.

"Hey," I call out. Tina pulls up beside me. Both she and Maximus are beyond tanned with very white teeth. A Wild Walker's T-shirt stretches tight over Tina's breasts. Max wears a matching T-shirt and sweatpants. The back of their cart is piled high with chunks of crimson-red, raw meat.

"You must be Lily," Tina says, holding out her hand. "We've been looking for you."

I shake Tina's hand. She smiles and the dimple in her right cheek reminds me of Otis's.

"Maximus Walker," her husband says, shaking my hand gently with his massive, calloused one. "Call me Max."

"We're scheduled for an interview today," I say. "Is there a good time?"

"Now works," Max says. He nods at the raw meat in the back of their cart. "Just can't be too long. We need to feed our boys then work with them once they're satiated. Keeps them from nibbling our toes," he says with a belly laugh.

"Before we start, I just want to say thank you," Tina says.

"For what?"

Her blue eyes radiate warmth beneath overly tweezed brows. "Howard tells me we have you to thank for Swift Jones."

No one has ever put it that way before. It feels…not that good. "Um. I guess."

"Howard will take wonderful care of her," Tina says, giving my arm a squeeze.

"Swifty, the calf, she's not drinking as much as she was at the zoo."

Max nods. "It'll take some time, but she'll adapt. Animals are like that. Flexible."

"What if Swifty's not? Flexible?"

"If you have concerns, please do bring them to Howard," Max says. "The wife and I have a policy not to interfere with our animal trainers. Treat them like we'd expect to be treated, once they've proven themselves of course. Howard has proven himself time and again. His act is a marvel. We're incredibly proud of his work."

"So you never get involved, even if there's a big problem?"

"Between running the business side of things and our own act, it's hard to find enough time in the day. Luckily, our trainers are top-notch, autonomous. If they need anything, run into difficulties, our youngest, Otis, steps in."

"So does your circus have a policy about, um, what kind of methods can be used in training your animals?"

"If you're asking if we abuse our animals," Max says, his smile fading, "absolutely not. But no matter how much we care for them, they are still wild creatures, not family pets. They're capable of killing us. We take precautions. But every trainer at Wild Walker's treats their charges with love and respect."

It feels like Max is trying a little too hard. "So, where are you from, originally?"

"Everywhere. I grew up traveling with my family's circus," Max says.

"Kentucky," Tina says.

I wait for them to elaborate but they don't. "That's a lot of meat."

Max chuckles. "Our tigers aren't cheap to feed. We're responsible for making sure they're healthy."

Tina nods. "We're their shepherds. They may be big, have sharp teeth, but we love them like you love your dog."

I don't have a dog, and it's hard to imagine that, if I did, it'd be the same as a tiger. "Have you both always known you wanted to be tiger tamers?"

"Trainers," Max corrects. "The word *tamer* brings to mind

the stereotype of a man with a whip and chair. We only use positive reinforcement."

"As for always knowing I wanted to be a trainer, hell no," Tina says. "I just knew I wanted to escape the piss-hole town I grew up in."

"So you ran away? Joined the circus?"

"When I was sixteen," Tina says, "Wild Walker's Circus came to my town. One look at Max with his tigers, and I would've followed him anywhere. His act was sexy as hell. When the circus left town, I went with them."

"And you fell in love with the tigers?"

Tina laughs. "I fell in lust with Maximus. Loving the tigers was a slower process."

"Why?"

"Do you know how tigers hunt?"

"Um. No."

Tina leans in, like she's about to tell a secret. "They ambush their prey from behind then bite the animal's neck. Sever the spinal cord. Usually it's an instant kill." She giggles. "I was terrified of turning my back on them for the first few years."

"Let me guess your next question," Max says. "Is it humane to keep tigers in cages?"

I was actually wondering if Violet knew about the way tigers hunt. Would it have scared her, or made her like them even more? "Is it?"

He sighs. "Kiddo, the tigers at your zoo are in cages, too, just bigger ones. At least our Bengals aren't dying of boredom."

His tone has a whiff of annoyance. It's not my job to decide what's right or wrong about a circus or the zoo, so I move on. "You must be proud that Howard is following in your footsteps? As a trainer?"

"Of course," Max says, his eyes lighting up.

"But he chose elephants?"

"Not at first," Tina says. "Howard loved the tigers. That boy had no fear at all. Still doesn't."

"What about Otis?"

"Otis doesn't have the right temperament to be an animal trainer," Max says, frowning.

I notice that Tina's smile slips away, too. "That must be kind of disappointing… I mean, since it's the family business?"

"Off the record," Tina says.

I nod. "Sure."

"It's extremely disappointing. Otis has a stubborn streak, like his dad. Hopefully he'll have a change of heart somewhere along the line, maybe when Max and I retire."

Max shakes his head. "Doubtful. You're too young to understand this, Lily, but sometimes, no matter what you do, kids don't turn out how you'd hoped. Luckily we have Howard. He's the future of Wild Walker's Circus." Max claps his hands together. "Now if you'll excuse us, we need to make sure our hungry tigers haven't torn off a worker's arm." He winks. "That's a joke, kiddo."

I watch them drive off, feeling like the only story I got was the one they fed to me.

26

On the path to the far side of the giant circus tent, two guys in tank tops that accentuate massive muscles and myriad tattoos pass me—they're pulling wagons piled with colorful pedestals.

"You're the reporter, right?" one of the guys asks, stopping.

"Yes."

The second guy scratches a nose broken so many times it looks like a staircase. "Otis asked us to keep an eye out for you, help you find your way."

"Just heading to the food cart," I say with a smile, hiding my annoyance that Walker's PR guy is keeping me under watch. The smell of grease hits by the far corner of the big tent. My mouth floods with saliva. The food cart is painted bright purple with a sliding window on the front. A girl bustles around inside. "Hey," I call out. Pretty eyes circled with thick liner study me. The girl's brow and nostril are pierced with tiny gold rings that complement her bronze-toned skin.

"What can I get you?"

"Lunch?" I reach into the pocket of my shorts for money.

"Your food is free."

"What? I can pay."

"Not what the family wants." The girl flips her braid over one shoulder. "Anyway, we don't take cash. Performers eat on credit. Workers use coupons."

"Coupons?"

The girl shrugs. "It's none of my business."

"Meaning?" She gives me a flat look. *Okay, moving on.* "I'm Lily."

"Esmerelda. Soirez. My family is the featured trapeze act. Six generations. We're from Venezuela."

"You're on my interview list."

"Otis told me."

"Mind if we talk now?"

Esmerelda shrugs. "Guess not."

She does not seem thrilled. "So you do that? Trapeze?"

"I flew before I could walk." Esmerelda eyes me. "I'll make you a burrito, extra cheese, avocado and double rice. You're too skinny."

I pull out a pen and my notebook. "Isn't it terrifying?"

Esmerelda scoffs. "Flying? No. It's in my blood."

I think about saying it's in my blood, too. "Does *anything* scare you?"

"You mean like the dark or something?"

I mean like hearing a man's voice telling you to drive your car into a group of little kids, watching your best friend's face morph into a monster or people screaming so loudly in your brain that you consider taking a hammer to your own head to crush the voices. "Yeah," I say, "like the dark."

Esmerelda laughs. "Nah. Only thing that scares me is failing."

Jealousy slithers through my belly.

"You can come watch us. Practice starts in twenty minutes in the big tent."

"That'd be cool. Hey, how old are you?"

"Fourteen."

"Can I take your picture?" She nods, so I take a few shots while she finishes making my enormous burrito. The first bite is beyond delicious. "Mmm. Thanks. So you love working for Walker's?"

Esmerelda's smile disappears. "I know about zoo people. You look down on the circus. But Wild Walker's is the best thing that ever happened to my family. I've got a Twitter account. I read what people are saying about your little elephant not belonging here. She's just an animal. Real people work here with real kids who get an education in the United States of America and the chance for a better life. Think about that before you write something shitty about our circus."

She turns her back. I guess we're done. There's a shady spot down the path so I sit on the grass, finish my meal even though part of me wants to go back, explain that my goal here is only to get into USC, away from Pennington and Calvin. My article was picked up again, monkey or not. A quick search on my phone yields USC's admissions office number. Since Sawyer is no longer on Team Lily, I need to step up.

"Ben Jackson, USC Admissions," a man answers on the third ring.

"I, um, I'm applying to your journalism program for next

year. I have a recently published article I'd like to email to be included with my application?"

The poodle lady walks by with two prancing black dogs heeling perfectly by her side.

"Just email it to me, Ben Jackson-at-USC Admissions-dot-edu."

"Great. It's been picked up by the AP."

"That's nice."

Nice doesn't sound very promising. "Thank you for taking the—" I start, but he's already hung up.

Sawyer once explained what it felt like to throw a Hail Mary shot in lacrosse. How, from the corner of his eye, he could see the time running out on the scoreboard in blinking red, that his muscles tightened like an overly tuned guitar, the way the release of the ball toward the opponent's net left him suspended, breathless. The thing is, Sawyer almost always made those shots. For mere mortals, what we feel is the plummet back to earth, the hard landing.

I call Sawyer. As I wait for the recording—because by now I get he's not going to answer—I wave off a mosquito feeding on my shin. It leaves an itchy red dot beside the other bites. "Florida sucks," I grumble.

After four rings, Sawyer's message kicks in. "It's Sawyer. You know what to do."

"You listened, nonstop, gave me advice, let me sleep over when I needed to escape Calvin, stayed my friend even after you became übercool, and in return I sang you SJ's songs, off-key. But I do care. If it's any consolation, Florida is a humid, smelly swamp. Okay. I miss you. I'm sorry. You don't have to be my friend anymore, but please don't hate me because—" I get cut off. A robotic voice asks if I'm satisfied with my voice mail. I'm not, but I leave it anyway.

"That's quite a frown."

The man looking down at me is mostly bald with a neat, gray goatee. Tinted purple sunglasses don't quite hide a scar that bisects his left eyebrow all the way down to the middle of his ruddy cheek.

"It's too nice a day for a pretty girl to be upset. Tell Uri what's so wrong." He sits down on the grass, pats my thigh like we're old friends.

I hold out my hand. "I'm Lily." We shake.

"Ah, the zoo girl who writes newspaper articles."

The way he says it, with his thick accent, makes me smile. When he rolls up the sleeves of his cotton shirt, there are scars running along his muscled, ropy forearms.

"What do you do here?"

"I am the Great Gregorvich," he says with a half bow. "I perform with six black bears."

"From the looks of it, your bears don't like you very much."

Uri breaks into a grin. "Young lady, bears love me. Sometimes they just don't know it."

"Where are you from, originally?"

"Romania."

"How long have you been working for Walker's?"

"Twenty-seven years."

"Wow. That's a long time."

"Longer than you've lived?"

"Yeah." Uri pretends my words are a knife in his heart. I laugh, which feels good after the past few days of gloom. "So, you knew Howard and Otis as kids?"

"Is this an interview?"

I take a sip from my water bottle. "You're not on my approved interview list, so I guess it's off the record."

Uri picks at a patch of clover, pulls the top off a flower and flicks it. "Otis used to be my favorite. He had a true gift with animals."

"Otis? I heard Howard is the gifted one."

Uri looks at me sideways. "Who told you that?"

"There are tons of photos of him as a kid with the elephants, like he was practically born to be their trainer. Otis has no photos with animals."

"Young lady, you're supposed to be a reporter."

"I heard that Otis worked with you?"

"That was Maximus's idea."

"What happened?"

"My bread is only buttered on one side. But I will tell you that young Otis used to follow around the elephant trainer like a puppy. Damned if he didn't sleep with those giants most nights. Especially the one that came to Walker's real young. Miracle that kid wasn't crushed ten times over."

"So why isn't Otis the elephant trainer?" Uri doesn't answer. Two showgirls run by. Their suntanned legs are long, lean, and the feathers in their hair make them look like exotic birds.

"Caged birds accept each other but flight is what they long for," Uri says.

"Pardon?"

"Tennessee Williams, an old American playwright, said that, not me."

Despite the heat, goose bumps appear on my arms. "What made you say it?"

Uri's eyes twinkle. "The way you were looking at our showgirls. Seems like it'd be more fun for a young gal to make news instead of just telling other people's stories."

I've been on both sides of that coin. It's preferable to put on fake glasses, keep my head down and avoid risks. But the guy trains bears for a living, so my guess is he won't understand playing it safe. "On the record, do you love your job?"

"Sometimes." Uri takes off his sunglasses. His left eye is missing.

The eye socket isn't gross, just saggy, pinkish, an empty shell. But it is weird to see an eye without its eyeball. "Did a bear do that?"

Uri chuckles. "No. A woman I thought I'd tamed."

I don't know what to say.

"Don't frown, little girl." Uri slowly gets to his feet. "The one certainty in life is that it changes."

That, I don't tell him as he walks away, *is what keeps me up at night.*

27

The sun overhead is so hot that my skin is already turning pink. I head for the circus tent. It's not on Otis's list of places I'm allowed to go, but Esmerelda invited me so I act like I know where I'm going, wait until there's no one around then quickly duck inside the tent before one of Otis's spies can stop me.

The area inside the tent is divided into three massive rings that are surrounded by a circular row of bleachers climbing at least four stories high. It's got to be ten degrees cooler in here, which still makes it in the low eighties, and the air smells of animals, mingled body odors, plastic. I pause to let my eyes adjust to the dimmer indoor light before climbing up the bleachers for the best view.

In the center ring Esmerelda's family balances on two platforms high in the air. There are five men and four women, all different ages, in silver outfits that hug lean bodies. Two trapeze bars swing between the platforms above a wide net made from woven ropes. One of the men lets out a yip. An aerialist from each side grabs their bar, launching a few seconds apart. The woman releases her bar, flips, spins. The man, now hanging upside down from bent knees, arches to meet her, hands clasping her forearms. For the first time I wish my glasses weren't fake, because it's impossible to see if the girl is Esmerelda. I take them off and zoom in with my camera. It's not her.

The first pair returns to a platform and a new pair steps to the edge. One is Esmerelda. The camera's shutter clicks as she swings several times, reaching higher, her body gracefully arcing through the air. When she releases the bar, she spins in a tightly tucked ball…one, two, three, four and… The man swinging toward her stretches his arms to catch her. Their timing is off. Esmerelda spins again, her body no longer tucked, before landing on her back in the net. I remember to breathe. She somersaults to the ground, runs to the ladder to climb back to the platform, like what just happened is no big deal.

"You don't have permission to be in here."

I almost drop my camera. Otis stands in the row above me. What is he, a freaking tiger? The butterflies in my stomach once again flutter multicolored wings. Stupid butterflies. "Why are you here?" I blurt.

"I'm a Walker," Otis says like he's talking to someone who is mentally challenged. "As we discussed, I'm happy to arrange for you to take some photos, but we're putting together a new show so I need to control what you see."

Note to self: stop forgetting that Otis is a total asshat. "Esmerelda invited me to watch."

"I don't think—"

"I won't write about it. Promise." Esmerelda reaches the platform. "What she does? It's amazing."

Otis hesitates. "Yeah. It is."

It's hard to look away from his eyes, which have suddenly thawed, but I force myself to watch Esmerelda grab the bar. Someone yips. She swings, gains height, releases, spins… Otis leans forward and squeezes my shoulder. Fingers of heat seep beneath my skin and a blush I hope he doesn't notice creeps across my chest. Esmerelda misses the catcher's hands and somersaults down to the net.

"Damn. She almost had that one," Otis says, withdrawing his hand.

"What's she trying to do?" I ask, still feeling the imprint of his touch. He climbs over the bleachers and stands beside me, so close that the blond hairs along his tanned arm brush against my bare skin. It's hard to focus.

"Not that long ago, fliers used to call triple somersaults salto mortale, the deadly leap. The speed they needed to rotate three times made their brains lose track of where they were in space. Even seasoned artists sometimes broke their necks when they missed the catcher and fell. Esmerelda is working on five rotations. That skill has been successfully performed by only a handful of fliers in the world."

Out of the corner of my eye, I watch Otis as Esmerelda again swings. His jaw muscle clenches. This time Esmerelda's hands touch her catcher's but slip. She falls at an angle, barely landing at the edge of the net.

"If five somersaults are so dangerous, why do Esmerelda's parents let her try it?"

Otis chuckles. "You met her. She's a force to be reckoned with. I doubt her family could stop her even if they wanted to."

I shake my head, trying to understand a world where parents encourage their children to follow their dreams, even if they get hurt or die trying to achieve them.

"You don't approve," Otis says.

"It's not that. It's—"

"My mistake. I thought reporters were supposed to be nonjudgmental."

"If you think the trapeze is so amazing," I say, "why don't you do it?"

"Because I was born into a family of wild-animal trainers."

"You don't do that either."

Otis's face shifts into a flat mask. "If you want to watch, interview other performers or take photographs, I'll set up some times for you," he offers. "But I've already given you a chance to talk to my folks and Esmerelda, even though they have nothing to do with your elephant."

"She's *your* elephant now. I'm just trying to give people a glimpse of her new world."

Otis leans down until his lips brush my ear. I don't back away. I won't give him the satisfaction of thinking I'm scared.

"Tell the truth, T. Lillian Decker," he says, his breath hot. "You're looking for dirt on us."

I don't know where I find the balls, but I ignore the sweet scent of his sweat and whisper back to him, "You have no idea what I'm looking for." We stare at each other, inches apart, and even though sweat is trickling down my back and my pulse is thrumming, I refuse to break first. A commotion below turns both our heads. Howard walks into the tent with three of his elephants. I recognize Jake and Tambor. Howard moves his elephants to different spots in the side ring with only the touch of his hand.

"If you'd prefer, I can get someone to escort you out," Otis offers. "How about Clem? You seemed to like him."

This time I definitely break first, square my shoulders and descend the metal steps. No wonder Max is disappointed in his son and Howard has zero respect for his brother. Otis Walker is a total jerk. Stepping into the harsh Florida sunlight instantly coats my skin with sweat. It must be over a hundred degrees. I really, really hate Florida. A bee buzzes by my ear. I run, because if it gets caught in my hair I'll never get it free. Been there.

A text chimes.

ADDIE: Text me after 6:00 p.m. feeding. Local vet will come in the morning

My uneasiness instantly returns. It's like watching from the shore as someone struggles to keep their head above the water's surface, unable to swim out to save them because if I try, I'll drown, too.

With three hours left until my shift, I do the only thing I can...find a shady spot on the far side of the tent, take out my iPad and start working on the second article.

Swift Jones's New World

Swift Jones's new world isn't just filled with tigers, bears, llamas, dogs and a herd of male Asian elephants. She will be surrounded by some of the most talented human performers in the world.

Esmerelda Soirez, age fourteen, is the youngest member of the Flying Soirez Family, sixth-generation trapeze artists from Venezuela.

"Wild Walker's is the best thing that ever happened to my family," Soirez said. "Real people work here [Wild Walker's Circus] with real kids who get an education in the United States of America and the chance for a better life."

Tina and Maximus Walker, owners of Wild Walker's Circus and the tiger trainers, also strive to be top-notch and are proud of the circus and their animal trainers.

Over the past forty-eight hours, Swift Jones has made one new friend, a dog, Flea, who never leaves her side. Soon she'll meet the male elephants that will be her new family. Howard Walker is certain that once the calf gets used to her new environment, she will thrive.

At the time this article was written, Swift Jones was refusing to drink enough of the formula that is imperative for her proper nutrition. A veterinarian will visit tomorrow to assess her condition.

I attach photos of Maximus and Tina Walker driving their cart, Esmerelda in the food truck, Swifty and Flea curled together beneath a blanket and the calf sucking the tip of her trunk. With the push of a button, article number two goes to Shannon.

When I dial Sawyer, I know he's not going to answer. But I still need to talk to my best friend, even if he's not my best friend anymore. "Fine," I say. "You don't have to talk to me, but just so you know? Otis Walker, who looks like Tim Riggins from your favorite show, is a total dirtbag. Total." I stop, because talking about myself is exactly what I shouldn't be doing. "How's your new apartment? Have you had a blowout party yet? Anyway. I have to head for my shift with Swifty. She's not doing great, by the way—" His voice mail cuts me off again. Which doesn't really matter, because Sawyer is probably erasing my messages without listening to them.

A mosquito lands on my hand. I watch it suck away, bloating from my blood, then smash it. When my phone rings, it's Calvin. I pick up. "Tell me again, did I almost 'fall off' the rooftop of our building?" Silence. "Tell me again how you were certain that Violet would never hurt me, even after you brought me my coat on a freezing day at the zoo, even after you saw the bruises, even after she scraped a dead skunk off the road and cooked it for dinner, even after she screamed at me until she vomited. You were afraid to come home, but it was okay to leave your seven-year-old child with a woman you'd stopped recognizing?" Silence. "That's what I thought."

I hang up, mouth bone-dry, and wait until my pulse slows, then walk toward the building where Swifty waits, hoping I don't fail her like my father failed me.

28

Flea and Swifty lie on their bellies. The calf's trunk is twined around Nibs's neck. The mutt has one furry, gray ear in his mouth. When I step into the pen, Swifty gets to her feet. "Hey there." I scratch behind her ears. Her trunk wraps around my leg like a little kid. Pulling out the camera, I take a few shots.

"I tried to take her for a walk, but she won't leave the pen," Addie says.

"Well, there are tigers and bears out there."

Addie doesn't smile. "Text to let me know how much she drinks."

I want to say that this isn't a disaster, but the word *yet* pops up at the end of my unspoken sentence and I know that anything I say is going to sound hollow, because neither of us will totally believe it. Swifty returns to Flea and Nibs. She's moving a bit slower. "The vet comes tomorrow?"

Addie nods. "Lily, just so you know? These things can happen quickly."

My stomach burns, a combination of acidic coffee and a

sense of impending doom that I push away. But it's like trying to get rid of my own shadow. When Addie leaves I take a few more pictures of the calf then pull out a bottle. Swifty shuffles next to me, her trunk wrapping around the back of my neck like we're old friends. I guess in her short life, we are. Each time she takes a sip she gets a kiss. The hairs running along her chin tickle my lips. "Good girl," I whisper then offer the bottle to Flea. The mutt's tail wiggles. Swifty takes another sip. We manage to get through half a bottle before she refuses more.

"Fine, just remember you forced me to do this." I clear my throat. "'Even when I'm alone, you're always there, we're 2-strong, 2-deep, 2-loved, 4-ever can never take you away...'" I'm butchering the real SJ's song, but maybe Swifty will drink just to stop my singing. The calf's trunk moves spastically toward my mouth like she's actually trying to shut me up. "Oh no you don't," I laugh. "'4-ever is our happily-ever—'"

Flea barks at the barred door then jumps up, tail thwacking. Otis leans against the doorway, the picture of casual cool, effortlessly good-looking, fully amused. My face burns. "How long have you been standing there?"

"Long enough to know that you are not a good singer."

Total mortification. TOTAL. "I wasn't— I know—it helps Swifty sometimes."

"Swifty?"

I hold the bottle out. The calf takes a half-hearted swallow. "She's fast. Why are you here?"

"It's my shift."

Could this day get any worse? "Fantastic."

Otis chuckles. "Sorry to disappoint. I was Howard's last choice, too. No one else was free."

"Why were you his last choice?"

Otis enters the pen and gives his dog a scratch. "So."

"So?" Otis's light brown hair has streaks of blond from the relentless Florida sun. He runs a hand through it and for a second, I imagine what his hair feels like. Then, worse, I picture his fingers running along my scalp and shiver. This is not the way to adhere to the Journalist's Code.

"So you're supposed to tell me what to do," Otis says.

"Sure," I say, getting down to business, because this is about what Swifty needs. "One bottle every three hours."

"What else?"

"Play with her. Cover her when she sleeps. Give her lots of hugs—"

"Hugs?"

"She needs to feel loved." I meet his eyes even though it's really hard. "If you can't handle that, please find someone who can. We're out of here in four days," I say, my voice a little unsteady. "Then Swift Jones's health is Walker's responsibility."

Otis sits down a few feet from Swifty. She doesn't run from him like she did Howard. "Has she been drinking all of her bottles?"

"She was. In Oregon." It's mostly true.

"And here?"

"On average, half of each one at best."

"Is Dr. Tinibu worried?"

"Yes."

Flea lies with his head on Otis's lap and again my mind

crosses the PG line. What the hell is wrong with me? Am I actually one of those girls who are attracted to dark, moody guys?

"Two years ago he showed up covered in bites that were infected, hardly any hair from mange." Otis runs a hand along the mutt's ratty fur. "He moved from porch to porch, hoping for scraps, some water. He was all bones, more flea than dog. My house is the last in the line. When I opened the door he shot inside, hid under the couch, growled when I tried to pull him out. We spent a few weeks that way. I'd put out food and water every night. He'd creep out, eat, sneak through the side door I left ajar to do his business, then race back inside and hide again. I think he was afraid that once I got my hands on him, he'd get tossed."

As Otis talks, it's like he's opening a window, giving me a peek at what's really inside. He's nicer than I thought, at least to stray dogs, which makes him even more attractive. *Quit it*, I tell myself. Nowhere in the Journalist's Code does it say a reporter should think about how hot one of the subjects of her story is. "Would you have kicked Flea out of your house if you'd caught him?"

"Probably," Otis says then chuckles. "Nah."

Swifty is watching Otis, her head tipped like she's listening to the cadence of his words. I'm once again trying not to focus on his lips. "How'd you finally get Flea to trust you?"

"He came when he was ready."

Otis picks up the bottle, toys with it. Swifty shuffles toward him. Her trunk swings until it touches his hand then retreats. He extends the bottle, but she doesn't go for it.

"Hold it up higher, by your shoulder," I suggest, adjusting his arm. My hand remains on his bicep for a split second too long. When our eyes meet, my cheeks get warm. I'm an idiot. Looking away, all I can hope is that Swifty's swinging of her trunk a few times before flopping it over Otis's shoulder drew his attention from my stupid blush. She takes a sip from her bottle.

Otis slowly smiles. "There you go." She takes another sip. He gently runs fingers along her side. "Anything else I need to know?"

It's beginner's luck, but also impressive. For a second I actually feel jealous that Otis is tracing circles along Swifty's skin with his long fingers. "Keep the straw clean—" As if on cue, an explosion of gas comes out of Swifty. I know what's coming next. Runnels of diarrhea course down her back legs. Otis calmly walks out of the pen. Just a second ago I thought he wasn't a total jerk, but obviously, I was wrong. "It's okay, Swifty." The smell is disgusting but I give her a hug anyway. "These things happen, girlfriend. I'll find something to clean you up."

Otis comes back in with a bucket of soapy water. I try not to let my surprise show as we clean the muck off Swifty's backside. A few times I gag but keep working. At one point, our hands touch. I don't pull away, because contact with his skin feels...almost magnetic. Then I remind myself that I'm cleaning diarrhea off an elephant's butt and that nowhere in my Twelve-Year Plan does attraction to a guy with a major chip on his shoulder fit in. When we're done, Otis takes the soiled straw out of the pen. He returns with fresh straw and spreads it along the floor. Swifty wanders over. When he sits on the canvas pad, she plops down beside him, rests her head on his thigh.

"You're good with her."

One side of Otis's mouth tugs upward. "Your singing wasn't that horrible."

I laugh. "Sawyer says it's an insult to the real Swift Jones." I tuck a blanket around Swifty then sit down on her other side.

"Sawyer your boyfriend?"

"No. My best friend." He was, anyway.

Picking up a piece of straw, Otis twists it into knots. "I'm sorry…about before…in the tent. It's my job to protect Walker's."

His apology catches me off guard. "I'm not trying to hurt your circus. Honest."

"What's the *T* for?"

"What?"

"T. Lillian. Your byline."

"It's stupid."

"I heard you sing," Otis points out. "How much worse could it be?"

My cheeks heat up again, which is beyond annoying. "The *T* is for *Tiger.*" I'm not sure why I tell him. Maybe I just miss having a friend to talk to.

Otis's eyes widen. Beneath the harsh light, flecks of sky blue are visible in his cobalt-colored irises. "You're kidding."

This conversation was a mistake. "Forget it."

Otis grins. "Like the character Tiger Lily in *Peter Pan*?"

I shake my head. "My dad never would've gone for that."

"So who came up with Tiger?"

"My mom thought tigers were cool." Holy understatement. When Violet wasn't making me practice my tiger roars at the zoo, we'd play a game in our loft of trying, on all fours, to move like the massive cats…for hours. “Anyway, my dad didn’t like the name so it was relegated to a *T*.”

“And Lillian?”

“My dad’s mom was Lillian. I didn’t know her, but he said she was great at math, easygoing and an amazing cook. He hoped I’d take after her.”

My phone rings. I look at the caller ID. It’s Sawyer. A wave of actual terror rolls over me. I’m beyond afraid of what he’ll say.

“Do you need to get that?” Otis asks.

“Um… I’ll call him back. Who are you named after?”

“Maximus.”

“But everyone calls you Otis?”

“Yeah.” He pulls my glasses from his shirt pocket.

My fingers fly to my face. I’m so used to wearing my glasses that I assumed they were still on. “Where’d you find them?”

“You left them in the tent.”

I quickly put them on. There’s a smudge across the right eye but I don’t wipe it clean.

“Why do you wear them?”

“To see.”

“They’re fake.”

I blush yet again. It’s getting really, really old. “You wouldn’t understand.”

“Try me.”

“They make me feel…safe.” Otis doesn’t say anything, so my stupid rationalization just hangs in the air. “I met Uri, the bear guy?”

Otis’s eyes narrow. “Oh yeah?”

"Yeah." I run light fingers along the gentle humps on the top of Swifty's head. "He has so many scars."

"A bear is the only wild animal that doesn't always signal before it attacks."

"Good to know. Is that why you didn't want to work with them?"

Otis looks up from the piece of straw he has twisted into a dozen knots. "Who said I ever wanted to?"

My skin prickles like a warning. "Uri said… He said that when you were a kid, you were really gifted with animals. That you loved elephants."

Otis shrugs. "All little kids love elephants." He picks up Nibs, fingers toying with the rabbit's ears. "Was this yours?"

"Yeah. Nibs."

"Ha! Named after one of the Lost Boys?"

I can't help smiling. Otis smiles back at me. It's like a ray of sunlight on my face. "You really read *Peter Pan*?"

"Yeah. I used to read it to…it doesn't matter. Every kid wants to fly away," he says.

Not every kid. Some want to keep their feet firmly planted on the ground. Some want their mom to stop pinching, slapping and punching them, because without any warning it hurts twice as much. Some wish their only fear was missing a new trapeze move, because that's an achievable goal. It's impossible to bend crazy to your will. It wins, hands down.

"Howard said something about you having a messed-up childhood. Is that why you aren't the elephant trainer?" Is that why I sense we have more in common than what's floating on the surface?

Otis's eyes frost over. "I have no idea what you're talking about."

"I'm…I'm just trying to know you better."

"Why?" he asks.

Reasons pop into my head. I miss my best friend. I need to talk. Swifty won't let Howard touch her. "I need to know that the one person at Walker's that Swifty seems to like actually cares."

Otis tosses Nibs to me. "Swift Jones is an elephant, not a little girl. You're not doing her any favors treating her like one."

I watch him leave. Flea watches, too, but stays with the calf. I guess when you're a Walker your shift can end anytime you please. I squash my totally inappropriate disappointment. I'm not here to have any kind of feelings about Otis. I'm here to scratch out some kind of future. Glancing at my phone, I see that Sawyer has left a voice mail. I'm afraid to listen to it. Afraid he'll tell me that he no longer wants to be my friend. I'm unworthy, but that doesn't mean I'm ready to hear those words. My fingers tremble a little as I dial for my messages.

"Did it ever occur to you," Sawyer says, "that I invited you to all those parties because *I* needed *you* there? Most of the time I go to parties for, like, fifteen minutes, just so everyone sees me there, then leave before Truth or Dare or worse. And you weren't a pity date for homecoming. I wanted you there because you're my best friend. And because then I wouldn't have to get a hotel room with my date like all the other senior guys determined to get laid. Did you ever think that if I did get a hotel room, my date would tell her BFFs and everyone at school that I couldn't get it up? And you act like I can't wait to throw ragers at my new apartment but—"

My voice mail cuts off the rest of the message but I can guess what it said. I'm beyond a shitty friend—the scum at the bottom of the shitty-friend bucket. I don't bother wiping my tears or the snot running from my nose as I listen to Sawyer's message again, because I deserve it. But the fourth time through, I hear something new… Sawyer called me his best friend.

Without giving myself time to chicken out, I call his phone. When voice mail kicks in, I do the one thing I've never done before. I tell him the truth. "You're right," I say, talking fast. "I'm a horrible friend. But I do care. Immensely. I've never pushed you outside your comfort zone. Part of that is being super self-involved. No excuses, my life sometimes overwhelms me. I'm going to work on that. But another part is that I don't want to make you feel dissected. And the third part is because the idea of you getting hurt by anyone—Cushing, the kids at school, *anyone*—makes me unbearably sad and horribly uncomfortable. So instead of forcing you to talk to me, I sang you stupid songs…well, not stupid, because you love SJ. I get that this can't be fixed with a simple sorry and I hope I'm not too late. But. How are you, *really*? And why did you leave porn in Cushing's office? Was it a big fuck you, or something else—" The system beeps: *If you are satisfied with your message…* I think about calling again, saying more, but it's a start.

29

The alarm for Swifty's 9:00 p.m. feeding goes off. At first she doesn't want to get up. I pull off her blanket and she grudgingly stands. She drinks only a third of her bottle before lying back down, closing her eyes. My insides slump. Flea, who I haven't seen leave this pen since our arrival, fixes his one eye on me. "What?" I demand. "I'm trying." I hold out the bottle to the mutt. "You think you can do better?" In response, he picks up Nibs then burrows beneath Swifty's blanket until only the tip of his ratty tail is visible.

"Fine." I lie down on my blanket, close my eyes. Two cups of bad coffee, Swifty's diminished appetite and my conversation with Otis make sleep impossible. I give it a totally frustrating hour before sneaking out of the pen to find the bathroom. At the last second I grab the camera, slinging it over my shoulder like I'm some kind of rebel journalist in a war zone instead of a girl who just wants to take some decent photos and get the next few days over with.

There's no one around. The air vibrates with the snorts of

horses, a low growl and some gruff barks. It's like the building is alive, more animal than cinderblock. As I wander down the one hallway I'd yet to travel, black eyes gleam behind the crisscrossed bars of the bear cage. Otis said they don't signal before they attack. He's just like them. I take a few photographs in the dark that probably won't turn out, then move on.

A tiger snarls when I approach its cage. My heart skips a beat. Addie was right—this cage is too small, more like a big dog kennel, and each tiger is kept separate from the others. Their buckets are filled with water, though, and their floors are clean. Bones lie scattered on the concrete. I make sure not to get too close, but manage a few shots of their amber eyes.

At the next intersection, the elephants are at the end of the hall to my left. Bathrooms are to the right. Chains jingle; a low voice carries on the air. I sneak forward, pressing against the wall so that whoever is with the elephants can't see me.

"Shhh, big guy," Otis says. "Let's go."

I hold my breath as Otis leads Tambor out the sliding barn door of the building. The air is electric and I'm drawn forward like a magnet. A half-moon illuminates a winding dirt road leading into dense foliage. The two walk side by side, like they both know where they're going. Once the mangroves swallow them, I follow. Weak moonbeams filter through gnarled roots and branches. It's slow going, because if I take the trail Otis and Tambor walk and they turn, they'll see me. Roots twist then turn, arcing in stiff tangles. The ground is moist, spongy, the air a miasma of rotting, wet earth. When the maze of roots bars my way, I climb them to keep Otis in my sight. I reach for a handhold, and a thousand tickles race up my arm. There's a massive, gray termite nest in the shape of a beehive a few inches from my fingers. Termites skitter down my back. I stifle a scream. Spastically, I shake out my shirt then look for the small opening still visible far behind me, because I'm about to hightail it to safety.

Our greatest weakness lies in giving up, Ms. Frey whispers.

Unless you, too, have termites crawling in your private places, shut up, I tell my counselor. But I don't turn back. Otis is well ahead of me now. I snag my foot then topple forward. A horizontal root catches me in the ribs, suspending me about a foot above the ground. I don't cry out from the sharp pain, but the air escaping my lungs makes an *oomph* sound. Otis's and Tambor's footsteps stop. Dangling head down over the ground, I hold my breath. I hear them shuffle off again. By the time I've untangled myself their footsteps are gone.

I'm not afraid of the dark. Still, it's eerie being in the mangroves, surrounded by weird noises. I creep forward, trying to keep myself from looking for wild animals, monsters and the devil's face, because, let's face it—this situation is just about the perfect recipe for my first hallucination.

The mangroves lighten up ahead and then I'm out of the root system, standing on the edge of a beach. About twenty-five yards away, Otis and Tambor are knee-deep in the surf. Moonlight paints their skin silver. Otis is naked, his T-shirt, shorts and flip-flops discarded in the sand. My insides melt and twist. I should look away, but I don't. It's not the first time I've seen a naked guy. I mean, I've seen Sawyer plenty of times. We skinny-dip in his pool late at night when his parents are away or asleep. But it's the first time I've seen a naked guy who doesn't know I'm watching him. Technically, that's uncool. But my eyes still travel from his broad shoulders to his lean waist, pretty much perfect butt and muscular legs.

Otis splashes the elephant. Tambor sucks water into his trunk and sprays him back. The sound of waves crashing mingles with laughter. I turn on my camera. The shutter's clicks are drowned out by the waves. Tambor follows Otis through the foam like a puppy, dodging, weaving, stomping. When Otis does a somersault into the ocean, Tambor waits for him to surface, then fishes him out with his trunk. They stand in the waves, staring at the ocean's endless expanse, Otis's hand on the elephant's shoulder like they're best friends. Looking up at the stars, I make a wish. *Please take me back, Sawyer.*

Blinking back the grit in my eyes, I focus the camera's lens on Otis and Tambor. The bull bends a massive leg. Otis uses it to hop onto the elephant's back. They wander down the beach. My skin tingles like it's covered in fairy dust. The two of them, together, are magic. I zoom in, trying to capture the feeling. When Otis leaps off Tambor's back to catch a wave and bodysurf to the shore, the elephant stamps his feet, like he wishes he could do it, too. Otis holds out his arms. Tambor walks over, lowering his head. They rest their foreheads together, Otis's hands on the sides of the bull's face. My heart squeezes. Their silhouette is the most beautiful thing I've ever seen. I crouch, trying hard to get the right focus, because this moment is lightning in a bottle. Unfortunately, I can't risk using a flash, so I repeatedly change the settings in the hopes one of the photos will come out.

"Hey!"

Otis gets bigger and bigger in my lens as he runs toward me. Adrenaline floods my body, sending sharp pinpricks over every inch of skin. I consider running, but it's clearly too late to escape.

"What the hell?" Otis grabs his shorts and pulls them on fast.

His look makes me feel like I'm the one who's naked. A flood of supreme embarrassment threatens to drown me. "I'm sorry," I mumble, eyes glued to the sand. I know what it's like to be spied on, scrutinized for signs of fracture. There's no excuse for making someone else feel violated. "I'm really, really sorry." My voice is shaking.

"Forget it," Otis says gruffly.

I venture a look up. Tambor's ears slowly flap as he studies me. "Hi, Tambor." I hold out my hand. He lightly touches my palm with his trunk. "Sorry, no apple this time."

"Do you always spy on people?" Otis asks.

"I wasn't. Okay, I was. Spying, I guess. Not at first. At first I was going to the bathroom. But then I heard you. And—"

"You followed us."

Otis runs a hand through wet hair. His shirt is still off. Even though it's totally inappropriate of me to notice, his stomach is ripped, shorts hanging below the indentation of his hips. I've just horribly violated this guy's privacy. What the hell is wrong with me?

"Are you going to tell Howard?"

"What? No. Not if you don't want me to. But he takes the elephants swimming all the time, right? I mean, he wouldn't mind—"

"Just. Don't."

"I won't." Otis is staring at me like I'm a huge loser. I shouldn't care what he thinks about me, but for some reason

I do and I'm dangerously close to crying, which is horrifying. "None of this is what I expected, what I wanted to happen," I blurt. "I came here to help, write a few articles and get away from home."

Otis's body slowly relaxes. He traces a circle in the sand with his bare foot. "Why do you want to get away so bad?"

I sink to the ground, grains of sand sliding through my fingers. "It's complicated. Why do you hide how much you love elephants?"

"It's complicated," Otis says, sitting down beside me.

I can feel the heat of his body only inches away. "Tell me one thing and I'll tell you one," I finally say. "Off the record."

"This isn't a game of truth or dare."

"If it was, I'd dare you to run naked into the water. But you've already done that."

Otis actually laughs. He lies back on the sand and stares at the stars. "I remember when Tambor was brought to Walker's. He was angry. Rebellious. Dangerous, even though he was still young." He glances at Tambor. The elephant is nibbling mangrove leaves. "I was six. Every single night I snuck out of our house, went to see him. I read him my favorite stories."

I lie down beside Otis. *"Peter Pan?"*

"Yeah. That was one of them. I also liked *The Giving Tree*, and *Horton Hears a Who!*"

When Otis moves his hand in the sand, his pinkie brushes mine. We stay like that, barely touching.

"Anyway, one day Tambor reached through the bars of his pen with his trunk, ran it over my face like he wanted to know me. I opened the door, went inside. My parents found me sleeping next to him in the morning. We've been friends ever since." Otis looks at me. "Your turn."

"My mom died when I was seven. Ever since then, Calvin, my father, has been afraid."

"That you'll die, too?"

"No," I say, my voice snagging. "That I'll turn into my mother." Otis's hand finds mine. That simple act of kindness puts a little lump in my throat.

"Was she that bad?"

"Sometimes." Otis licks his lower lip and I can't help imagining how it tastes, can't help noticing there's a tiny chip on the edge of one of his lower teeth. I breathe in the air between us. "Um. Anyway, since then there hasn't been a whole lot that has made my life worthwhile. I had my best friend, my father, but there was nothing...nothing purely my own." I'm afraid Otis is going to make a joke, but he doesn't.

"Swifty?"

I shake my head. "She's a means to an end, a way to have the articles I write noticed so I can get into USC, move away from my father, study journalism and create a career I'll fight for if—"

"That's why you wrote the article about Raki rejecting her?"

Otis withdraws his hand. The empty space where his fingers were woven through mine feels like a loss. There's an edge to his question, an implied judgment that puts me on guard. "Baby elephants sell tickets. You should be thrilled about my article."

"Yeah. You can see what a great life Tambor has," Otis says.

His sarcasm throws me off balance. I thought everyone at Wild Walker's wanted the calf. "I didn't write that article."

Otis frowns. "What are you talking about?"

"I wrote an article about how happy Swifty was, because I didn't want to ruin her chance to reunite with Raki. But there was a photographer with me during the attack. He'd taken these great shots—"

"And convinced you to write about the attack."

I raise my hands. "Let me finish?"

"Sure. Fine."

"The photographer wrote the article. He switched it behind my back. By the time I found out, it'd already been published."

Otis sits up. He claps his hands. "Congratulations. You're off the hook."

I sit up, too, his scorn making my temper flare. "What the hell is your problem?"

When Otis smiles, his eyes remain flat. "Don't worry, Lily. In a few days you'll be out of here. You can forget all about Swift Jones and Wild Walker's. You'll be free to get on with your big college plans."

"That'll be great." But my stomach hurts all the time now, and it's not because of the sucky coffee. I doubt I'll ever be able to forget Swifty—the way she looks at me through the bars of her pen, how it feels when her trunk wraps around my leg, her hugs, earthy smell, chocolate-colored eyes. She's smart, sweet and loving despite my repeated efforts to push her away. But there's nothing I can do for her. Nothing.

Tambor twists his trunk around Otis's wrist, pulling him up. They leave me on the beach. The sound of their feet in the sand, the brush of branches as they enter the mangroves, slowly fades. Waves crumble on the sand, recede, strike and crumble again. The night sky is filled with stars. One falls, trailing an ephemeral orange blaze.

"Psst."

I don't bother looking away from the pinpricks of light.

"'If you love a flower that lives on a star, then it's good, at night, to look up at the sky. All the stars are blossoming.'"

Again, it's a quote from *The Little Prince* in my own voice, though I sound a bit more…innocent. That's wishful thinking on my subconscious's part. *Giggle.* The laughter is as light as wind chimes, a young girl's. Mine from a time before Violet tried to kill me, before I read my grandfather's letter, before my father admitted he would've erased me because I'm damaged goods, before I turned eighteen and the world opened its maw like a monster ready to devour my brain. "I didn't want to grow up," I tell that girl. "But it happened anyway."

By the time I get back to the animal building, Tambor's front foot is cuffed in iron and chained to the cement floor. Otis is gone. A new worker waits for me outside Swifty's pen. His name is Mark. Addie has already taught him what to do. My shift is over, but I still stay for the midnight feeding. Mark and I try for several hours, but Swifty refuses to drink any of her formula.

30

"She's not getting enough nutrition," Dr. Robertson says, running a hand along Swifty's face. "We shouldn't be able to see the shadows around her cheeks or this much depth in her eye sockets." She pinches the skin under Swifty's eyes. When she releases it the skin stays pinched. "She's also dehydrated." The vet runs a finger inside Swifty's mouth. "Dry and sticky. Another sign of dehydration."

SJ stands beside Addie, toying with the nipple of her bottle. Addie coaxes her to drink. "Did she drink anything at her morning feedings?" I ask.

"Not much," Addie says. "It wasn't Mark's fault. He's a good guy, gentle. He was up all night trying."

"I should've stayed longer. She drinks more with me."

Addie shakes her head. "I need to rotate in as many new caretakers as possible before we leave. This calf has had enough loss."

The band around my chest is back. It cinches tight. I want to scream that Swifty is an elephant, not a human. But that argument has been lost. The way the calf looks at Addie? The way she looks at me? We matter to her. She matters. "How'd she do for her early-morning feedings?" I ask Addie.

"Less than half a bottle." She pinches the bridge of her nose. "What about intravenous fluid therapy?"

The vet gets to her feet. She's broad shouldered with short gray hair that matches her complexion. "SJ's been through the ringer. I'd rather not stress her out more by putting her in restraints."

I take a step closer to Swifty. "Why would she need restraints?"

"So I can get a butterfly catheter into the vein behind her ear then secure it with sutures. The catheter is the conduit for us to deliver fluid therapy. For now, let's watch and wait. But if this continues, we'll need to do something. My preference is hydration with a rectal enema before taking more extreme measures."

"An enema?"

"The colon's function is to process waste from the body and to reabsorb fluids. When we want to rehydrate animals, fluids delivered rectally can be very effective."

"So if you can keep Swifty hydrated, then she'll survive this transition?"

Dr. Robertson's mouth twists to the side. "Not exactly. Even if Swifty is hydrated, if she doesn't drink enough formula, get enough nutrition, she may not survive because as she gets weaker, she'll also be more susceptible to illness."

My eyes are gritty. I'm so tired I can taste it. I didn't get back to the motel until two thirty in the morning, then I set my alarm so I could be here when the vet came. I am playing with fire. "Okay. How can you tell if she's getting sick?"

"We look for certain things," Dr. Robertson says, ticking them off on calloused fingers. "Slow-moving ears, lethargy, no or slow trunk movement, lack of appetite, abnormal temperature, sleeping too much, weight loss, eye discharge, pale pink mucous membranes."

"And?"

Dr. Robertson takes off her red-framed glasses, cleans them with the edge of her shirt. "SJ's membranes look okay, not great, no temp, but she's lethargic, has slow ear movement, little appetite and is disinterested in her surroundings. She is, at the least, very depressed."

I tighten the elastic holding my hair. "Okay. That's sort of good. I mean, we can deal with depression, right?"

Addie sighs. "Lily, I've told you that elephant calves are fragile—"

"I know. But depression is something Swifty can get over." Addie and the vet share a look, which pisses me off because no one knows more about what a daughter can survive than I do.

"I'd actually prefer Swift Jones had a virus," the vet admits. "At least there's medicine. Depression is tougher. A calf, especially one this young, needs female elephants around her or other calves who can call to her, caress her, let her know she's not alone. Sadly, it's not uncommon for calves to die from a broken spirit."

The doctor turns to Addie. "Can you talk to the Walker family?"

"I spoke with Howard an hour ago. He believes that SJ will

settle in, be fine. He's planning to introduce her to the male elephants, has high hopes that will help her. Then I called Tina and Maximus, but they deferred to their son's opinion."

The vet sighs. "I've worked with the Walker family for fifteen years. They're a stubborn lot."

"Any advice for getting through to them?" Addie asks.

"We'll just have to take it day by day. If the calf doesn't drink at least half of her bottles today, go ahead and give her an enema. Use a hose in her rectum, about a foot-and-a-half deep. Just make sure the water is warm. Body temp is optimal. Fill her until the water comes back out. That should take ten to fifteen minutes. Do it one or two times a day. See if it helps."

"Hang on," I say. "Will that hurt her?"

"Actually, calves don't seem to mind it." Dr. Robertson hands a business card to Addie then another to me. "Call if you need me. Anytime."

Addie shakes the vet's hand. "Thank you for coming. Lily, you have the 6:00 p.m. to midnight shift."

I leave the pen without saying goodbye. At the motel, I don't bother taking off my clothes, just close my eyes, fall onto the bed and dive straight into sleep…

Otis Walker sits on the edge of my bed. He looks around the motel room. "This place is a dump."

"It's only for a few more days. I just need to write one last article."

He runs a hand along his jaw. "Haven't you done enough?"

I sit up. The sheet falls away. I'm naked but more upset

that my hair has come loose; that he's seeing the part of me that's most like Violet. She always wore her hair down. It was beautiful until she stopped washing it. The black curls matted into dull twists. "Why are you here?"

Otis looks up from beneath long lashes. "To make sure you know."

"I didn't write that article."

Otis moves closer. "Does it matter anymore?"

He has faint freckles along the bridge of his nose, like he sunburned it as a kid. His scent is fresh soap. "Did you bring Swifty?" I ask.

Otis reaches out, his fingers twisting one of my curls. "Swift Jones is with Howard. She's his calf now."

Goose bumps dance across my skin. "It's okay. He loves elephants."

"How do you know?"

"The rubber mat, the apples, the photos. Ever since Howard was a little boy, he's loved elephants."

Uri appears in the doorway. "I thought you were a reporter." He shakes his head, walks away.

Otis presses his palms against my cheeks, like he did with Tambor. He rests his forehead against mine. The warmth of his breath dusts my face, swirls inside me. I start to melt.

"What's love?" Otis asks.

Our lips are inches apart. His fingers drift down to trace my collarbone. My skin is on fire. "I don't know."

"What's love?" Otis repeats.

Our lips brush, soft, fleeting. His mouth travels along my neck. Everywhere he touches comes alive.

"What's love?"

"Swifty," I finally say.

Otis pulls away. His eyes are glacier blue. "Then your love is death."

Buzzing. Buzzing. Buzzing. I open my eyes. My muted phone is vibrating on the bedside table. It's Calvin's number. I pick up but don't know what to say anymore. I'm wrung dry. He's the only parent I have left, but the distance between us has become an abyss.

"Lily?"

"Yes."

"Please. What do you want from me?"

"The truth."

Calvin sighs. "Ask."

"You knew she was hurting me?"

"At first I was in denial. Yes."

"Why didn't you stop her?"

"No excuse will be good enough," Calvin says. "I tried to get Violet help. Force her to take medication. Get her committed. But that's much harder than it sounds. I considered telling the authorities what she was doing…with you, but they would've taken you away from us. That would've pushed Violet over the edge."

"She was already miles over the edge."

"Hindsight is twenty-twenty," Calvin says. "Lily, I was in over my head, drinking too much. Our life was a roller coaster of extreme highs and lows that I never wanted to ride, couldn't get off. I was… I was so trapped."

"Because of me?"

"Violet. Me. You."

I swallow around the knot in my throat. "That day on the roof you saved her, not me."

Calvin clears his throat. "Yes."

"Why?"

"Violet was the absolute love of my life. She was this bright light, beautiful, funny, so funny, creative, smart…" His voice catches. "I watched her unravel, powerless to help, but still, the need to save her was all-consuming."

"What about me?"

"It happened so fast."

"Bullshit."

My father exhales like he's been hit hard, hands on knees, struggling to recover. "It doesn't mean I don't love you, too."

My chest constricts. "You would've aborted me."

"In a logical, theoretical world?" A sob strangles his voice. "Maybe. But only to save you from what Violet went through."

"To save yourself."

Calvin is crying hard. "The second you were born and I looked into your eyes? I would've chosen to have you a thousand more times. And once I held you? There's no way in hell I ever would've let you go, even if I'd known the challenges we'd face. Lily, life isn't black-and-white. People are flawed. I'm fallible. But I do love you."

"Controlling me isn't the same thing as loving me."

"Something in me broke after what…after Violet tried to kill you. And every year that passes, it's like the clock on a bomb is ticking down. I'm calm on the outside but inside, I'm waiting for you to turn into her. I'm waiting for our world to shatter again. And that thing inside me, no matter how hard

I try? It's still broken. But I'm here for you. I will be until the day I die."

"Do you..." The words stick but I have to say them so I try again. "Do you think I'm going to have schizophrenia?" Calvin is sobbing. I wait.

"I don't know... Probably."

I thought hearing his response would be a brutal punch to the gut, or a plunge into ice water. Instead, it makes only a slight ripple across the surface of my life. There's a strange sense of release from hearing what I knew he believed but never said, aloud. "Thank you for telling me the truth." I hang up, then hold the phone tight to my chest. The chasm between my father and me widens until I can no longer see him on the other side.

31

I wanted the truth. Calvin gave it to me. Still, it's like I've been put in a tiny boat, set adrift in an endless ocean with no idea how to sail home and no idea where home even is anymore. The need to call Sawyer is palpable, but I don't. I've already asked way too much of him.

A cold shower doesn't wash away my nightmare or the conversation with my father, but at least my skin is less sticky. *When you let go you create space for something better,* Ms. Frey murmurs. I hope she's right. After turning off the shower's uneven stream, I dry off and push away the conversation. Calvin wants me to give up, come home and hide. Hiding didn't work for him. It didn't work for Violet. It *probably* won't work for me.

"One more article." With a weak cup of coffee in hand, I sit at the laminated desk by the window. I have enough time to write my third article, grab a burrito and still be at the circus in time for my 6:00 p.m. shift. There's an itch at the back of my mind. *Ever since Howard was a little boy, he's loved elephants.*

Focus.

But the itch won't go away. *I thought you were a reporter.*

Drop it.

My ringer was off while I napped, so I check my phone before I begin writing. There's nothing from Sawyer, three voice mails from Calvin, one text from Shannon: Call me. ASAP.

She answers on the second ring. "It's about time."

"Sorry. I didn't get much sleep last—"

"I care because?"

"What's up?"

"Your second article was picked up by the AP," Shannon says.

"Great." I wait for Shannon's criticism.

"Mr. Matthews wants you to take some videos."

"Of what?"

"A rocket launching into space."

"The performers are working on new acts, so Otis Walker won't let me tape them." What I don't say is that I allowed Otis to add *no videos without approval* to our agreement then signed on the dotted line. Shannon would go ballistic.

"You. Are. A. Reporter," Shannon says very slowly. "You. Are. Supposed. To. Find. A. Story."

I stare out the grimy window. "I have. I am. I'm about to write my third article."

"Let me guess. How high the poodles jump. How beautiful the dressage horses are when they move together. How much Howard Walker loves his elephants."

"I'm not here to do an exposé on the circus."

"Give me the phone."

My stomach flips. It's Mr. Matthews.

"Lily, you're there to tell the real story about a baby elephant whose mother tried to kill her, who was flown to a circus across the country where there are no female elephants to help her get over her grief, who is going to be a show animal for screeching kids for the rest of her fucking life," Mr. Matthews says.

"Your photographs?" Shannon says. "They're actually really good. Not technically, but visually. They tell the real story. Your words fall well short of that mark."

"Do better," Mr. Matthews says. "And take some goddamned video we can post online, because the petition floating around Facebook to *Save Swift Jones* has something like ninety thousand names on it. A lot of them are or have become *Pennington Times* readers."

Crap. "Okay."

"And I want the third article. Today."

"I can do that, Mr. Matthews. But it won't have video."

"Why not?" he demands.

"I won't have time," I lie.

"Photos?" Shannon asks.

"Yes."

"Fine. But write a fourth article," Mr. Matthews says. "Delivered by tomorrow night. With photos, videos, plus in-depth information. Don't disappoint me, kid."

Crappity. I'm going to disappoint him. Maybe I can get Otis to approve a video of Swifty playing with Flea or something else that's rated G, innocuous. "I asked Addie."

"Asked her what?" Mr. Matthews says.

"If she's single."

"And?"

"She said you should fucking ask her yourself."

Mr. Matthews guffaws. "See, kid? You can multitask after all."

They hang up. I check for emails—nothing from Sawyer. Taking a deep breath, I open my computer, start doing research. I can write what Mr. Matthews wants but still be balanced and stick to my approved interviewee list. After I finish researching, I dial Otis's number because the circus side of things needs a quote or my story is lopsided.

"Otis Walker."

My face instantly burns. He didn't actually kiss me. But I wanted him to, which should worry me more than the voices in my head. "It's Lily."

"What can I do for you?"

"I need a quote from the circus about Swift Jones's health."

"We are doing everything we can to ensure the health of our newest addition."

He's back to his PR voice. "Swifty is drinking even less of her formula. The veterinarian your family uses came to see her this morning. She said she's lethargic, depressed and—" I hear papers shuffling, like he's working on something else. "Hello?"

"Dr. Robertson is depressed?"

"Swifty." I wait for Otis to say something, but he doesn't. "You obviously don't care, but Dr. Robertson thinks Swift Jones could be in serious trouble." There's a tapping sound, like Otis is bouncing the end of a pencil on his desk.

"Has Dr. Tinibu spoken to Howard?"

"Yes."

"And?"

"Howard said Swifty will be fine." Again, silence. "Otis?"

"Just use the quote I gave you."

"Okay. I also wanted to see if I can take some—" He hangs up.

Okay. Fine. I call Addie to run some quotes and statistics by her.

"This isn't your usual article," she says.

"It will be fair."

"I'd expect nothing more."

A Tough Transition for Swift Jones

Four-and-a-half-week-old Asian elephant calf Swift Jones, who was rejected by her mother, Raki, and claimed by Wild Walker's Circus, has now spent three days at her new home in Haven, Florida. The transition has been difficult despite around-the-clock caretakers from both the zoo and the circus.

"She's not getting enough nutrition," large-animal veterinarian Dr. Ellie Robertson said after examining Swift Jones.

Elephant calves drink up to twenty-four pints of their mother's milk each day. According to Robertson, the calf's appetite has diminished to fourteen pints a day. "Even if Swifty is hydrated, if she doesn't drink enough formula, get enough nutrition, she may not survive because as she gets weaker, she'll also be more susceptible to illness."

The calf is showing other signs that worry Dr.

Robertson, including lethargy, weight loss and signs of depression. "It is not uncommon for an elephant calf to die from a broken spirit. A calf, especially one this young, needs female elephants around her or other calves who can call to her, caress her, let her know she's not alone."

All the elephants at Wild Walker's Circus are adult males. However, the circus's elephant trainer, Howard Walker, believes the calf will be fine once she becomes part of his elephant herd.

Animal-rights advocates are pushing for both zoos and circuses to phase out many of their wild animal exhibits, especially elephants, because neither can provide enough space or varied habitats for an elephant's well-being.

So where does that leave Swift Jones? "For now, we watch and wait," Dr. Robertson said.

I attach several photos—the vet examining Swift Jones, a close-up of the calf's face, Swifty's trunk wrapped around my leg. Everything goes to Shannon. It was fair, what I wrote. But Addie and the Walker family won't like it.

Running sneakers tied tight, I lock the motel room door behind me and jog down the concrete stairs because, hot or not, I need to pound pavement, tire out my brain before returning to the circus.

Ever since Howard was a little boy, he's loved elephants... I thought you were a reporter.

"The photos."

Sinking onto the last step, I pull out my phone, click on

Wild Walker's website then Howard's bio. There are so many photographs of him with the elephants. Toddling beside them, playing beneath their bulk, orchestrating intricate moves in the ring. He's just a tiny kid, all elbows and knees...and dark blond hair. I enlarge the shot of the little boy with his hands on either side of an elephant's face, their foreheads pressed together.

It's Otis.

32

"Good, you're here early," Addie says. She's standing behind Swifty with a hose in her right hand, her left holding up the calf's tail. "Turn the red lever on the hallway wall for me." Swifty glances over her shoulder at Addie, head tilted, curious.

"I thought Dr. Robertson wanted to wait."

"So far today? SJ has had only three-quarters of one bottle. Total."

There's a buzzing in my ears. "It's supposed to be warm water."

"The hose has a warm and cold option, the red lever is the warm. It's ninety-five degrees, which is close to Swifty's own body temperature."

I can't stall any longer so I turn on the water then watch Addie slide more than a foot of hose into Swifty's rectum. The calf doesn't react, instead watching Flea pounce on Nibs, toss the stuffed animal into the air, then pounce again. It's hard not to think that the mutt is actually trying to distract her.

Addie holds the hose in place until brown water finally starts running down Swifty's legs. It smells pretty foul.

A metal bucket sits beneath the industrial-sized sink on the far side of the hallway. I fill it with warm water and soap; bring it back into the pen. Addie has turned the hose off. She collects all the wet, dirty straw while I clean Swifty's backside.

"Give her another enema tonight," Addie says. "A Walker's employee will be here to help."

"Um." I focus on toweling Swifty dry.

"Are you saying you can't do it?"

There's no way I'm going to tell Addie I can't do it. "No problem." Swifty lies down, like the entire process exhausted her, so I cover her with a blanket, making sure it's tucked perfectly around her little face. She reaches out her trunk. The tip touches my knee. Our eyes meet. *Sadly, it's not uncommon for calves to quite literally die from a broken spirit,* Dr. Robertson murmurs in my ear. "Will the enema really help?" I ask Addie.

"It can't hurt."

The line I once imagined connecting Swifty and me pulls tight. It's still invisible, but I can no longer deny it's there. "I'll be back at six, SJ. We'll have dinner together." I kiss the calf's forehead then shove my hands in my pockets because they're shaking. When I get outside the animal building, I hesitate. Tina and Maximus own the circus. Should I go directly to them, tell them Swifty is in trouble? They'd tell me to talk to Howard. Addie already tried both approaches and failed. If none of them listened to her, they won't listen to me. I hear Max's words: *Our trainers are top-notch, autonomous. If they need anything, run into difficulties, Otis steps in.* "Great," I mutter.

At Otis's front door, I waver. This isn't my battle. I have a plan, a code to live by, potentially a lifesaving goal. *My* life.

I pound on the door.

"Hang on," Otis calls.

His shadow approaches. The door opens. He's on the phone and holds up one hand to silence me. "Thanks for doing that, Ellie. I will."

I wait until Otis disconnects and lowers his phone. "Why'd you lie?"

"Hello, Lily."

Everything about him infuriates me. The way he says my name like it's a joke. How he's so comfortable in his skin. The richness of his eyes, because they make people think he's a mile deep instead of an inch. The fact that I want Otis to be more than he obviously is. "Why did you lie?"

"What, exactly, did I lie about?"

"The elephants."

"You have my quote." He starts to close the door.

I jam my sneaker in the doorway so he can't shut me out. "It's not about the stupid quote."

"Would you like to come in or would you rather rant on my front porch?"

Over his shoulder I glimpse scarred wood flooring, worn-in leather furniture, a laptop on the kitchen counter beside stacks of folders. The walls are painted white with no pictures or photographs, but floor-to-ceiling shelves are filled with books. "I'll stay outside."

"Fine." Otis hangs his thumbs from the front pockets of his jeans. "Say what you came here to say."

"Why is Wild Walker's Circus so intent on Howard being seen as the son who grew up loving elephants?"

"What are you talking about?"

"The photos. On your website. All the pictures of Howard with the elephants are actually of you."

Otis comes outside. He leans against the porch railing, pulls out a cigarette but doesn't light it, instead spinning it along his knuckles. "Why does it matter?"

"Because you're the one who cares the most."

"So?"

"Addie just gave Swifty an enema."

The cigarette stops its perpetual motion. "Excuse me?"

"Grow up," I snap. "Swifty is seriously dehydrated. If the enema doesn't work, Dr. Robertson is going to have to put a catheter in the vein behind Swifty's ear to deliver IV fluids, which will stress the hell out of that calf."

Otis spins the cigarette along his knuckles.

"Look at me," I demand. He does. "Someone needs to step up, do what's right for Swift Jones. If you're the one around here who really loves elephants, then it should be you."

Otis watches a string of horses led by a worker trot into the big tent. "So I played with elephants as a kid. Big deal."

"And Howard?"

"He was into the tigers."

"So what changed?"

Otis's gaze goes arctic. "We grew up."

We glare at each other. "Go to hell," I say before descending the porch steps.

"I thought Swifty was just a means to an end," Otis calls down.

"At least I don't pretend she's not suffering."

"Where are you going?"

"To find your parents." It's a long shot but I've run out of options.

"Why?"

"This is *their* circus, not yours. Maybe, if I talk to them face-to-face, explain how bad things are for Swifty, they'll have the balls to do something to help her."

Otis laughs. "They'd never tell Howard what to do."

I turn and actually stamp my foot like I'm ten. "Why not?"

Otis flicks the unlit cigarette to the ground. "It's complicated."

"Try me."

"All you need to know is that he's the prodigal son."

Frustration strangles my throat. "This isn't about which of you Tina and Max like better."

"No contest there."

My head pounds like it's going to explode. "So you're a big fucking disappointment to your parents. Join the club. Ask them to talk to Howard. Ask them to let Swifty go."

"Go where?" Otis asks.

"I don't know, but not here."

I look everywhere for Tina and Maximus but can't find them. I'm stopped three times by employees of Walker's who offer to help me find my way, obviously Otis's spies. My stomach is on fire from the bad coffee I drank. I'm a million miles from hungry but need to put something into my belly before it gets any worse.

"Psst."

"Get lost," I tell my subconscious.

"Can I help you?" a woman with a thick Southern accent

in full clown makeup, red nose, frizzy purple wig and massive polka-dot shoes asks.

"Sure. You can tell Otis that I'm just heading to the food cart," I snap, striding away.

Esmerelda's not working. There's a guy behind the counter who looks like he could be her brother. His nose crooks to the left, broken at some point but never fixed. The smell of grease makes my stomach growl. "Cheese quesadilla, please?"

The guy nods. "Sure thing."

"Hey, lovely Lily."

I whirl. It's Clem. "Hey. Have you seen Tina or Max?"

"They're doing a supply run a few towns over," he says. "Stuff for their kitty cats." Clem leans into the cart's window. "Burger and fries, please." He hands the guy a red coupon.

"Why do you pay for your food with coupons?"

Clem rolls his eyes. "The powers that be think the workers can't handle too much cash."

"Because?"

"Some of the guys have drug problems. Too much cash equals too much trouble for the family. So they give us coupons to pay for our food, take lodging out of our pay, plus taxes, etcetera. End of the month there's not much left. Definitely not enough when we go on the road. Most of us have to sleep in the trucks."

The initial conversation I had with Addie after the article was published, after this whole catastrophe was triggered, floats to the surface.

Wild Walker's Circus travels most of the year, transporting their animals in semi-trucks. Does that sound like a better home for Swift Jones?

I pull out my pad, knowing this probably won't make a difference but grasping at anything that might help me sway Tina and Max, get them to step in to help Swifty. "Can I ask you a few more questions?"

"Is it going to get me fired?" Clem asks. "I need this job—got a bunch of kids."

"I won't use your name," I offer.

Clem moves out of earshot of the food cart then glances around to make sure no one else is close enough to hear him. "Shoot."

"Do all the workers travel with the show when it goes on the road?"

"Only the ones who ain't on probation. Most of us have done some time and, like I told you the other night, have limited options. The Walker family don't care about anything 'cept us being legal when we cross state lines."

"Are you? Legal, I mean."

"I've been off probation for eighteen months, so I got to hit the road with the show last season."

"What, um, did you do?"

Clem looks away for a second. "Drugs. Got hooked. Made some stupid choices." Clem smiles, gold teeth flashing. "I got the midnight shift with the little elephant tonight. You gonna be there?"

The guy in the cart walks over with my quesadilla and Clem's burger. I wait until he leaves to continue. "Yes, I'll be there. Hey, how long does it take to get to each arena?"

"Depends. Sometimes hours, sometimes days."

"What do you do with the animals when it's a long trip?"

"They stay in the trucks the whole time. It's too much trouble taking them in and out. Specially the tigers and elephants."

"What if it's super cold or hot?"

Clem takes a huge bite of his burger. "No diff. Last year a few of the elephants got a little frostbite. A few years ago I heard one of the llamas died from heatstroke."

"So on a long drive, how do you guys keep the animals' cages in the trucks clean? Shovel them out on the side of the road?"

"We don't. They're just animals."

One of the circus vans rolls to a stop in front of the food cart. "Clem, stop flirting and get your ass in the truck," the driver calls.

Clem digs something out of his back pocket. "Hit the gold mine. Three tiger whiskers. I'll weave them into something special for you."

"Um. Okay." I find a bit of shade and sit to eat, but instead Google how to take videos with my camera. It's not rocket science. My stomach growls but the smell of the quesadilla is making me nauseous. After a couple of bites, it goes in the trash.

When I get to Swifty's pen, there's a guy inside shoveling dirty straw into a wheelbarrow. "What are you doing?"

"Cleaning," the guy says without looking up. "It's my shift."

Goose bumps rise on my arms despite the oppressive heat. "Where's the calf?"

"Howard came by. He took her into the ring with his elephants."

The heart I thought was hollow fills with blood and presses

painfully against my chest. Every beat is excruciating. "She's too weak. Why didn't Dr. Tinibu stop him?"

"The elephant?"

"Howard."

The man looks up from his work. "She wasn't here. But it wouldn't matter. No one tells Howard Walker what to do."

33

I slip into the big tent unnoticed and silently climb halfway up the bleachers. Twenty rows above center ring, mostly hidden in the murky light, I slide onto a metal bench. Howard stands in the center ring with all his elephants, including Swifty. The calf holds on to Tambor's tail with her trunk like it's a security blanket. Pulling out my camera, I turn the settings to video. My nerves jangle. I haven't gotten Otis's approval. If he catches me he'll be furious. "Too bad," I mutter. Howard will make his little brother approve the video, because he's so proud of his elephant act. More important, Mr. Mathews will be happy.

Trying to keep my hands steady, I track the calf as she moves around the ring. There are bright silver pedestals placed at irregular intervals. The older elephants know exactly where to go, when to spin in circles, raise a leg, or trumpet. It's pretty impressive, given their size, that Howard has trained his elephants so well. A few of them wear harness-like contraptions with feathers on their heads.

Out of the corner of my eye I see Howard walk over to Swifty. The calf doesn't let go of Tambor's tail. The bull turns, putting his mass between Howard and the calf. Howard squares his shoulders, barks out a command I can't quite hear. Tambor still doesn't move. Swifty's ears flap faster, like she senses tension, but Howard backs off, jogging to the bleachers on the other side of the ring. He stumbles midway then gets his balance, his body off-kilter, then trips again, almost falls. The way he's moving reminds me of my dad when he's had too much Scotch.

What the hell is going on? Why is Howard working with the elephants when he's been drinking? Tambor runs his trunk over Swifty's body, almost like Raki did when the calf was born. In the distance, Howard reaches beneath the first row of bleachers. He pulls out a wooden rod with a metal curved hook near the top. I zoom in with my camera. The hook and the rod's pointed end have been honed into sharp spikes. I've never seen one before, but I know it's an ankus.

Every muscle in my body is taut. Like Sawyer making a Hail Mary shot. Except this isn't a game. This isn't a goal. And I'm not a high school lacrosse star; I'm just a girl standing at the edge of a cliff. But I can no longer hold on to the idea that Swifty will survive the circus if I just find one person here to care. I take a desperate breath but it's not enough to fill my lungs.

All the clues were there. The sores behind Tambor's ears, the fact that the gentle elephant wouldn't take an apple from Howard, the photos, Otis's lies, Clem's admissions all spell out that Wild Walker's is a dangerous place for its animals. But I didn't want to accept it. That would get in my way.

Disgusting. I'm beyond disgusting. But what am I supposed to do now?

I wait for Ms. Frey, Calvin, Swift Jones and Violet, even my inner voice, to whisper the answer in my ear. My eyes sting like my tears have turned to acid. My voice, even if I wanted to hurl obscenities down on Howard's head like lightning, fry him to a crisp, is buried deep beneath fears that have created the impotent girl I hate yet struggle to protect. What would shouting do anyway? Wild Walker's owns Swifty. She's Howard's now. Period. Even if I wanted to save the calf, there's nothing I can do except leave so that what happens next won't be burned into my brain.

I steady the video camera. I'm a selfish coward, but this is my Hail Mary pass.

Howard swings the ankus toward Tambor, catching him on the soft top of his foot. The elephant dodges left, eyes rolling. Blood trickles over his toenails. Howard swings again, connects behind the bull's delicate ear then rains rapid-fire blows down on the bull's feet and trunk until Tambor finally backs away. Rivulets of bright red run down his shoulder, trunk and feet. Swifty loses her grip on the bull's tail. She stands alone. *Alone.* Howard raises the ankus, leaps toward her. He drops the spike onto her foot. Blood wells from Swifty's wound. Her eyes dart as she clearly looks for a way to escape. A scream claws its way up my throat.

"Stop!" Otis runs into the ring. "What the fuck?"

"Hey, Saint Otis," Howard drawls. "Can I help you with something?"

I hold my breath and zoom in on Otis's face. His eyes are no longer ice. They're burning up. He steps between his brother and Swifty. Relief courses through my veins. Otis is going to stop Howard; he's stepping in, doing what's right. He's exasperating, rude, moody as hell, but he's going to protect Swifty. He does care. That's all that matters.

Howard's backhand comes out of nowhere, like a bear attack. It catches Otis in the jaw, snaps his head sideways. He doesn't go down but it's close. Despite the blood on his lower lip, Otis keeps his hands balled at his sides. I stand, the fight instinct I haven't felt since Gary Haycox kicking in. Otis's head jerks toward me then back to Howard. Did he see me?

"Wow. Now you're a tough guy," Howard notes. "Too bad you weren't tough when you were seven."

"How long am I going to have to pay for that?"

Howard grins. "As long as I can remember what happened to me for four years because of you."

They stand toe to toe, Howard a few inches taller. I zoom in on Swifty. She's hiding behind Otis. Tambor takes a few steps toward the calf but Howard waves the ankus. The bull stops, ears madly flapping.

"You promised you'd lay off the booze."

Howard smirks. "Oops." He turns his back to Otis. "Get lost."

"You put a mark on Swifty—"

"Swifty?" Howard hoots. "You already gave her a nickname? You're predictable if nothing else."

"The zoo people will be all over you."

"You think I care what they think?" Howard asks, still walking away. "She's *my* calf now, baby bro. And she needs to be broken in, learn that I'm the boss. Only way to stay safe once she's grown."

Otis opens his fists, hands loose by his sides. He relaxes his shoulders. "You're right," he agrees, his tone casual, conversational. "But she's dehydrated, weak. Let her get stable. Otherwise you won't have her for long."

Howard turns. He's smiling but his eyes are daggers. "Say please."

"Please."

"Fine. Take her back. But, Otis?"

"Yeah?"

"Don't interfere with my training process again."

"Sure," Otis says. "Mind if I take Tambor to lead your calf back?"

Howard's smile slips away. "The bull stays."

Otis shrugs. "Sure."

Swift Jones follows Otis, glancing over her shoulder at Howard until she's out of the ring.

"Psst."

I listen, because I need help.

"Here is my thecret. It's quite thimple: One thees clearly only with the heart. Anything ethential is invithible to the eyes."

It's from *The Little Prince*, again. The voice still sounds like mine, but it's definitely a younger me, and some words that begin with an *S* have a slight lisp. I turn off the video, quietly descending the stairs, and slip out the back of the tent.

34

"Yes, Lily?"

"Howard uses an ankus." Silence. I switch the phone to my other ear. "Addie? Did you hear what I said?"

"Lily, you need to calm—"

"I have it on video. He was drunk and used it on Tambor at least a dozen times. For no reason! Then he hit Swifty. She bled." I'm outside the big tent. It's almost dark but I can see Otis in the distance leading Swifty back to the animal building. "What are you going to do?"

"Lily, there's nothing I can do."

Her voice is a slap. "You knew."

Addie exhales. "I saw signs of abuse on his elephants. But I wasn't certain if it was Howard or a previous owner."

"We have to stop him."

"A lot of circuses, even some zoos, still use an ankus. While it's not my preference, if an ankus is used responsibly..."

"Didn't you hear me? Howard didn't use it responsibly. We have to tell someone. Get Swifty back."

"Lily."

"What?" There's so much pressure in my brain it feels like my head is going to split open.

"I signed an NDA."

"A what?"

"It's a nondisclosure agreement."

"Meaning?"

"I can't disclose anything negative I see at the circus to outside sources. It was the only way to get the Walkers' permission to accompany Swift Jones. It was my only chance to teach the circus how to care for her."

"So what? You signed a stupid agreement. Break it."

"If I say *anything* negative about what I've seen at Walker's, the Pennington Zoo will be sued. The circus will win that lawsuit. I can't put all of our animals at risk over one elephant calf."

"Fine. I'll tell everyone."

"Lily, you signed an agreement for approved interview subjects, locations and videos on the first day we arrived. I was shocked Otis didn't make you sign an NDA, too, but I guess that would've looked like he was overtly trying to control the press. Instead, he used the excuse of ensuring your safety and protecting the circus's creative work to control who you talked to, what you saw, where you went."

Certainty drains from my body. I can't write about what I saw, because it happened in the big tent. And there's no way I can use the video.

"Listen to me," Addie says. "If you talk about any of this or share that video, you can forget about going to college because Walker's will sue you for every penny you have."

"What if I don't care?"

"They'll go after your father. Would you really do that to him?"

I'm deep underwater. My chest hurts like it's being crushed. "It's so wrong, Addie."

"Agreed."

"So we just walk away?"

"Yes, to fight other battles. Battles we have a chance to win."

"That's it?"

"I'm sorry, Lily."

"Swifty won't survive him."

"Probably not. But she might not have survived Raki either."

I hang up and run toward the animal building.

35

"Dr. Tinibu signed an NDA. You signed an agreement, too. The big tent isn't an approved location."

It's the first thing Otis says when I enter Swifty's pen. He saw me in the tent. Now he's sitting, calm as can be, beside Swifty with a bottle of formula in his hand. The calf takes a few sips while Flea watches, one paw resting on Nibs. Somewhere between Pennington and Haven, the rabbit lost his remaining eye.

"Did you take a video?"

I cross my arms. "Yes."

"You can't use it."

Incredulity makes my voice too loud. "That's all you have to say to me?"

"Yes."

Otis's lower lip is split. There's a bluish bruise at the corner of his mouth. He adjusts the bottle. Swifty takes another swallow of formula. I sit down across from them. Flea brings over Nibs, wet with saliva. I push the stuffed animal away. "I don't care about what I signed."

"You should. We'll crush you, the paper and your family."

"You sound proud."

"I do my job. You have no right to judge me."

I meet Otis's gaze. It's no longer hard, because I hate him. "Okay," I say. "Why don't *you* judge you, then? What do *you* think about a guy who loved elephants so much when he was a kid that he slept beside them? Even the most dangerous one, who came to the circus too young and needed a friend. But when that boy grew up, he became so callous that when another young elephant needed his help, he turned away. He not only let her get hurt, he was willing to let her die rather than take a stand. How would *you* judge that guy?"

Otis presses his back against the wall. "You have no idea what you're talking about."

"I know that your family is willing to let Howard hurt Swifty rather than step in, take away his big elephant tamer title."

"Trainer."

"I recognize the distinction. You're all cowards."

"Howard would agree." Otis picks at a frayed spot on his jeans. "Your articles have gone national. You've gotten what you wanted. Go to a fancy college. Become a great reporter. Live the dream."

He's right. The AP will pick up my third article, because it's way better than the first two. USC admissions will read it; they'll see I'm capable of writing a good story. I may actually get into their journalism school. Sawyer would high-five me right now if he still cared. "Swifty is no longer a means to an end," I say. It's true. She matters more than my own selfish goals.

Otis shrugs. "It doesn't matter."

"What are you so afraid of?"

"Just drop it, Lily. You're out of here in two days. Erase the video. We'd never let your newspaper use it anyway. If you send it to the *Pennington Times*, their lawyers will tell your boss there's no way he can post it. And if you try to post it yourself, our lawyers will get it taken down and then sue you and your family. Trust me, they'll throw a ton of money at this one."

"Because it's Howard?"

"Because it'd be a PR nightmare for all of us."

"Leave," I say.

"It's my shift."

I storm out of the pen, drag the hose coiled in the hallway back. "Hold this." I shove it into Otis's hand, go back, turn the lever on the wall to warm, then return to stare at the calf's behind, heart racing. Otis is watching me. Steeling myself, I slowly ease the rubber hose into Swifty's butt. There's not much resistance, but still, it's pretty freaky. We stand there in the most uncomfortable silence ever. Swifty glances back at us. "It's just an inside bath," I tell her. "We'll be done soon." When the water flows freely around the hose, I slide it out. A trickle of sweat rolls down my back. But I did it.

Otis gets a bucket of soapy water from the hall. We work together to clean Swifty's legs. While Otis gets rid of the soiled straw, I help the calf lie down and cover her with a blanket. Her trunk wraps around my wrist, drawing me close. I trace the horizontal lines that band her trunk. "Doesn't she matter at all to you?"

"It's complicated," Otis says.

"Try me."

"Why would I tell you anything?"

"Because you're not on my approved interview list," I snap, "so your secrets are safe with me." He slides down the cinderblock wall, pulls up his knees, resting his chin on them. He looks more than beat-up; he looks bone-tired, totally alone. It strikes me that Tina Walker has Maximus—they're a united team. Howard clearly has his parents' love and approval. But Otis's family doesn't respect him and there's no evidence they care. He's watching me, eyes narrowed, like he's trying to figure something out. The look in his eyes is recognizable—he's adrift in an ocean, too. "There's another reason," I say quietly. "Maybe you don't have anybody else willing to listen."

"I tell you one truth, you tell me one?"

"Yes."

"Off the record?"

It doesn't matter anymore. "Yes."

"When I was seven, one of the workers took an interest in me. I was the kind of kid pedophiles target. A loner. Ignored by my parents. Looking for attention beyond what I got being with the elephants."

Otis meets my gaze. I don't say anything; giving him the time to find the words.

"The guy took me fishing, bought me candy, which is such a fucking cliché, but it's true. One night I was sleeping outside Tambor's pen. I woke up to the guy unbuttoning my jeans. Nothing happened. But it was heading that way."

"I'm—"

"Shut up," Otis says. "You wanted to know. Howard was in the building late, messing with the tigers probably. They were his obsession. Tina and Max ate that up with a spoon. Even let him take cubs home, sleep with them in his bed. Anyway, Howard came around the corner. He saw the guy trying to get into my pants, launched into the creep. The guy was on his back, scrabbling away, when Howard jumped on him, bashed his head against the concrete."

"You don't have to tell me the rest."

"I'm just getting to the good part." The cut on his lip cracks. He licks away dots of blood. "When the guy tried to break free, Howard hit him so hard I heard his jaw break. Howard kept punching. I lost count. But the sound was wet, like water sloshing in a bowl, you know?"

I don't know. So I don't say anything.

"The guy was out cold, but Howard kept going. Blood splattered everywhere. Howard's fists were dripping with it. There was a puddle of red under the guy's head. I screamed at my brother, tried to stop him."

"Did he? Stop?"

"Yeah, to grab a pitchfork. Howard stabbed the guy twenty-two times. I can still hear the sound of the tines going through skin, muscle, hitting bone. Maybe the guy was dead before that. I hope so."

"What happened next?" My mouth is so dry that each word makes a clicking sound.

"Howard was charged with manslaughter."

"Even though he was defending you?"

Otis laughs, the sound joyless, brittle. "That's the thing. Howard hated me, even then. Not big-brother stuff. Hate. Maybe it was because he wanted Walker's all for himself. Maybe he was jealous because of how I was with the elephants. I don't know. But when he killed that guy, he wasn't doing it for me."

"How can you be sure?"

Otis meets my gaze. "Because he was smiling."

He taps out a cigarette, spins it over his knuckles. "I was supposed to testify on Howard's behalf. Say that the worker had molested me before; that he was going to do it again; that I was begging him to stop when the whole thing went down. But the guy hadn't. He didn't. He probably would have. But he didn't get the chance. Max tried to literally beat it into me with a belt that I was a victim, but I knew I wasn't. Least not the way he meant. So I refused to lie to the DA. I was just a kid, you know? I had no idea what was going to happen to my brother."

How long am I going to have to pay for that?

As long as I can remember what happened to me for four years because of you.

"Howard went to prison?"

Otis nods. "He was sentenced to ten years. Four at a juvenile facility, then, when he turned eighteen, he was supposed to go to an adult prison for another six."

"He deserved to go."

"How much do you know about juvenile correctional facilities?"

"Nothing."

Otis picks up a piece of straw, slowly tearing it in half. "In Florida, at least at the time, they were all privately operated."

"Meaning?"

"They weren't subject to full oversight by public officials. Howard was at a facility with a history of more sexual abuse scandals than any of the others. He wasn't a runt, but he wasn't strong yet. He went through hell."

The photo of Howard's eighteenth birthday runs through my mind. "He was supposed to go to prison for ten years. But he was out by his eighteenth birthday?"

Flea climbs onto Otis's lap. He runs a hand along the mutt's back. "Howard was released early for *good behavior.* I think my folks made some kind of deal not to sue or go public about what'd happened to my brother in juvie, if the state agreed to an early release. They also sealed Howard's record so he wouldn't spend the rest of his life as a convicted felon." Otis tosses the piece of straw. There are gray smudges under his eyes, like the story just aged him.

"Howard served the final year of his sentence under house arrest," Otis says.

The ankle brace Howard was wearing in his eighteenth birthday photo suddenly makes sense. It was a tracking device used for probation. Other things make sense, too. "When Howard got out of prison, he chose elephants."

"Yeah, to hurt me. After what happened to him? My parents weren't going to deny Howard anything. Max also wanted to punish me for not standing up for my brother. He tried to push me into working with the tigers or bears, but I wasn't interested. That pissed my father off even more."

"You're better with the elephants. Doesn't that matter?"

"Not really. Tina and Max blame me for how Howard has turned out, can't let it go, and refuse to acknowledge that he was always *off.* Plus, there's a heavy kind of guilt associated with not being able to protect Howard from what happened to him in jail."

"So Max and Tina let him abuse his elephants?"

"They're pragmatists. Howard's act is a big draw. Tina and Max don't approve of his drinking, but most of the time Howard does keep it in check. My folks also have a different perspective. They know that wild animals are dangerous, that there's a fine line between training and abuse."

"A fine line?" I demand.

"Lily, Bengals do not naturally leap through rings of fire."

"Max said he only uses positive reinforcement." I hang my head, fingers digging into my scalp. "I'm an idiot."

"If it's any consolation, I think Howard loves his elephants in his own way."

My head snaps up. "Are you seriously defending him?"

"I'm just..." Otis sighs. "No."

"Just in case it's not crystal clear," I say, "that's not love. You have to stop him."

Otis shakes his head. "What happened to Howard, while he was incarcerated? I can't even imagine it. Lily, I'm not afraid of him. I owe him."

"You were seven years old."

"If—"

"If wishes and buts were candy and nuts we'd all have a Merry Christmas." Otis looks at me like I'm already insane. "Sorry. My counselor's favorite sayings pop up sometimes."

"Counselor?"

"It's complicated."

"Try me."

"When I was seven, my mother tried to kill me." Otis doesn't react. He just spins the cigarette over his knuckles. I realize it's his *tell.* He's absorbing, thinking.

"How?"

"She tried to throw me off the top of our apartment building."

"Did your mom die then or later?"

"Later. She committed suicide in prison." The cigarette makes another trip over Otis's knuckles. It's not as bad as I thought, telling Otis the truth. But it's not the whole truth. I trace the soft folds of Swifty's ear. "She deserves better."

"I'll keep an eye on her. Step in when I can."

Swifty peers up at me. The line connecting us tightens, constricting the blood flow to my heart. "We're giving up on her."

Otis places Swifty's half-empty bottle back in the fridge. "I'm sorry, Lily." He walks toward the door. "For what it's worth, I hope you get into USC."

"I don't care about USC anymore."

"You should. It's attainable."

The walls of Swifty's pen close in. So this is it? Her life *if* she survives? Chained beside the adult elephants. Swaying. Not to an ancient song embedded in their bones. That's bullshit. Swaying out of boredom, fear or, worse, a broken mind. Because isn't that as bad as it gets? Losing who you are? Who you're meant to be? "Otis."

Otis stops in the doorway. "Let it go."

But I can't. I can't just let Swifty go. My brain is tangled yarn. Bits of memories, random thoughts, useless quotes form a snarled ball. *Daisy was dying...so we contacted Viv Hemming's Elephant Sanctuary in Texas...* I pull out my phone.

"What are you doing?"

I Google *Elephant Sanctuary, Texas.* Click on the telephone number when it appears. Someone answers after three rings. I put the call on speaker.

"Hemming's Elephant Sanctuary, can I help you?"

"Daisy," I say. "Is she still alive?"

"May I ask who's inquiring?"

"Oh. Sorry. My name is Carla. I'm in grade six, from Detroit? I love elephants so I'm doing a school paper on Daisy. I read about her calf. Super sad. So I wanted to write a paper about how Daisy is doing now that she's with you guys."

"Hi, Carla. My name is James Chi. I'm the staff veterinarian at the Sanctuary. And yes, Daisy is holding on. She's still pretty sad, but she's been eating more. The other female elephants here are doing their best to make her well. Emotionally, it will help when her milk dries up."

"Thanks so much." I hang up.

"You're a good liar."

Okay, not very flattering. But he's right. "An elephant in Detroit lost her calf a few weeks ago. She stopped eating. She was dying. So the zoo gave her to Viv Hemming's Elephant Sanctuary in Texas. They've been trying to save her life."

"How do you know any of this?"

"Research. Otis, Daisy is still alive. She has milk. She needs Swifty and vice versa. They could save each other if we—"

"First, *we* are not a team. I work for Wild Walker's Circus. They're my family. Second, I already told you that Howard isn't going to let Swift Jones go. Not to a zoo. Definitely not to a sanctuary."

I scramble to my feet. "Why not? Once she's healthy, he can take her back. She'd be older, maybe able to handle things better. At least she'd still be alive."

Otis shakes his head. "That's not the way sanctuaries work. Once they take an elephant in, they won't return them to a bad situation. At least not without a fight."

"Then we don't ask Howard."

"You're insane."

"Texas can't be more than a few days' drive from here."

Otis looks down the hallway. "Lower your voice. What you're saying, what you want to do? It can't happen."

"Why not?"

"How would you get Swifty there?"

"Truck."

"Whose?"

"Walker's. Except..."

Otis shakes his head. "Just for entertainment, except what?"

"I don't know how to drive."

Otis steps back into the pen, puts his hands on either side of my face, just like he did in my dream, except this is real. He smells like soap with a hint of cinnamon.

"I get that you love Swifty. But you can't save her."

"Not alone."

"I can't help you."

"I understand that you're afraid of losing everything you've always known, that your family will turn its back on you. That if you're not Otis Walker of Wild Walker's Circus you'll be lost. But you'll still be you. Maybe just closer."

"Closer to what?"

"The you that you want to be."

Otis paces the small enclosure like he's a trapped animal. "How do you know any of that?"

"Because I'm afraid of some of the same things. But Swifty is more important than all of them."

"You'll get arrested. Swifty is worth a lot of money. You could go to prison."

"I've been told by Esmerelda that I'm too skinny. Stripes will be flattering on me."

"This isn't a joke," Otis says. "You signed an agreement that is legal, binding. And you can't just steal a calf in one of our trucks. The cops will pull you over within hours."

"I'll figure something out. Get a different van once Swifty is away from here."

"You're what? Eighteen? You can't even legally rent a car."

"Then I'll borrow one."

Otis rolls his eyes. "Now you're a car thief? Lily, maybe Swifty will be okay."

"Would Tambor agree that *okay* is enough?" It's a low blow, and he flinches.

"What if Hemming's Sanctuary won't take her?" Otis asks.

"You're the PR guy. Call them. Don't give them a choice."

"If they have advance warning, time to convene their board of directors, talk to lawyers, they'll definitely say no."

"Then we just show up with a sick calf. They'll have to let us in."

"Lily, to do this right? It'd take weeks to plan."

"I have two more days here. After your family reads my last article, they might kick me out before then."

"What'd you say?"

"I made it clear that Swifty isn't doing well at Walker's, implied that Howard is ignoring the facts, and that Swifty might die."

Otis hesitates. Suspended. My hope grows wings, desperate to take flight.

"I'm sorry, Lily. I can't."

Otis leaves without looking back. I sink down beside Swifty, rest my forehead against hers. Flea watches us, Nibs in his mouth. Even if I still wanted to take Swifty, steal a truck, somehow drive to the Sanctuary, I can't. Otis would stop me. His family comes first; Howard comes first. The realization is like being run over by a truck. "It's over," I tell the calf, my voice a croak. We've lost.

36

"Hey there, pretty lady," Clem says, stepping into the pen.

I look up and wipe away my tears.

"Why are you crying?" he asks, forehead wrinkling.

I shrug. "I'm just sad that I have to leave Swifty. She's… She matters to me. What are you doing here so early? You're not on until midnight."

"I couldn't wait." Clem slides a bracelet made from tiger's whiskers around my wrist, smiles as he spins it. "It's good luck."

I think about telling him that there is no such thing. Instead I say, "Thanks."

"Has Swifty eaten yet?" Clem asks, pulling a bottle out of the fridge.

"No. Why don't you give it a try?"

Two hours later Swifty has had two sips of her formula and I've learned that Clem has three ex-wives, got hooked on heroin when he was thirteen, switched to meth because it was cheaper, got arrested for dealing and spent eight years in prison, where his nickname was Squash. Swifty is lying beside Flea, the tip of her trunk in her mouth. I cover her, tuck in the blanket and put Nibs against her chest.

"Wish I could've done better," Clem says.

"It's not your fault." I attempt a smile but can tell it's pitiful. My curls have staged a revolt, a lot of them escaping from my ponytail holder. I pull the elastic free, start to twist my hair back into a low knot.

"Sorry to interrupt," Otis says, stepping into the pen.

I jump, pulling the elastic too hard. It breaks. "What do you want?" I refuse to meet his gaze.

"Just looking for Clem. Maximus forgot one of his bags at Little Bit Ranch Supply in High Springs. He wants you to go get it."

"It's a two-hour drive," Clem says. "They'll be closed by the time I get there."

"You know how my father is about the tigers' supplements. He got the owner on the phone. They're staying open for you."

"Guess I gotta go, then." Clem winks at me. "Later, Lily."

Clem's footsteps fade. A door opens, closes, then silence. "Go away," I say, curling up beside Swifty.

"The key is public perception," Otis says. "That and finding a place to hide out until Walker's is forced to do the right thing."

I sit up so fast it makes me dizzy. "Why?"

"Why what?"

"Why would you do this, help Swifty?"

Otis looks down, kicks at the straw. "Ask me why I didn't have you sign an NDA."

I scowl. "You thought I was a lightweight reporter, that you could control me with your approved interview list, locations and spies."

Otis shakes his head. "You ran between a stampeding mother elephant and her calf. You risked your life to save an animal you barely knew." He rubs the back of his neck like it hurts.

I'm beyond confused. "So you're saying that you wanted me to expose Howard?"

Otis shakes his head like he's confused, too. "It wasn't a plan or anything. But…I guess there was a little part of me that hoped you'd figure out a way to save Swifty again. Do what I couldn't."

"And now?"

Otis looks up, his eyes steely beneath a furrowed brow. "This place? I can't do it anymore. I won't. I want to be closer to the person I want to be."

I let his words sink beneath my skin then take a deep breath, allow hope to unfurl her wings. "We're doing this?"

Otis exhales. "Yes."

"If the key is changing public perception, I'll post the video of Howard on YouTube."

"Using an ankus isn't illegal."

"Howard was drunk, and the way he used it was cruel and barbaric, especially on a traumatized baby elephant. People will be furious."

"It won't look good for Walker's," Otis agrees. "But you'll get sued for posting it."

"I have six hundred and seven dollars in my bank account."

Addie's words float to the surface… *You'd do that to your father?* "Can Walker's sue my dad over what I do?"

"You're eighteen?"

"Yes."

"Legally, you're an adult. They might try to go after your father, but they'd probably have to settle on you, the newspaper or the zoo."

"Addie has no idea what I'm planning."

"Are you paid by the zoo?"

"I'm a volunteer. Same with the newspaper."

"Then my best guess is that it'd just be you. But Walker's won't only go after your savings. They'll tie the damages lawsuit to future earnings. You could be paying Walker's for the rest of your life."

I almost smile. "Let's do it."

Otis holds up his hands. "Slow down. Another problem is that our lawyers will make YouTube take your video down pretty fast."

"I can send it to animal activist sites."

"A lot of people don't believe what they read on those sites because their views are extreme. It'll be easy for lawyers to make them take that video down, too. You said something about a petition?"

"It's on Facebook. Created by people who want Swifty returned to the zoo. Last I looked there were over ninety-seven thousand signatures. I can post the video of Howard on their wall."

"That won't work either. Walker's lawyers will force them to erase it. And they'll force you to wipe out the link." Otis keeps pacing. "The best way to do this is to upload the video to an anonymous, offshore file-sharing site where lawyers can't find it without serious footwork. Footwork that'll take more time than Walker's has to keep public perception under control."

"How do we post the video on an anonymous site?"

Otis stops pacing. "That's easy. I can do it then give you a link to the video. You can post that link on Facebook and send it to activist websites. After those sites are forced to wipe it, people who saw the link will still be able to share it because it'll remain active. That is, if anyone is actually interested."

"They are. What if it's still not enough to force Walker's to let Swifty go?"

"Can you write more articles?"

"The *P-Times* wants at least one more. I'll throw out being balanced. Tell the real story."

"Not about what Howard did to that guy or his time in prison," Otis says. "You can talk about Swifty, her needs, even about how our circus is no place for wild animals. But nothing about my brother beyond that video."

"But—"

"It's a deal breaker."

We glare at each other, but this is impossible without his help. "Okay. Where do we hide out?"

"I know a place."

I hold out my hand. We shake. The touch of his skin sends tingles down my arm.

"I already picked up more formula from the cold storage building, a cooler, ice and put it all in the truck around back," Otis says.

Wow. He's been busy. "Let's go," I say.

Otis grabs my shoulder. Our faces are inches apart. For a moment I imagine leaning in, kissing him to seal the deal. Otis's fingers dig into my skin.

"Lily, there's no going back. We might both end up in jail."

"Are you scared?"

"Yeah."

"Me, too. Let's go."

It's after eleven, dark, so the area behind the animal building is empty, warm air alive with the thrum of frogs and crickets' chirps. Getting Swifty into the truck with the lift gate is easy, because Flea gets on first so the calf follows. I cringe at the whine of the motor as the gate lifts, but there's no one around to hear it. Swifty follows Flea into the back of the truck. Otis has lined the floor with a thick bed of straw and tossed in extra bales. We tuck a wool blanket around the calf, covering her ears, ease the rolling door down and then climb into the front seats.

Headlights off, we slowly drive past the performers' homes. I'm no longer the same girl who saw them for the first time. That girl had her eyes closed. "Is there any security at night?" I whisper.

Otis shakes his head. "Since we're in such a remote location, and we all live on campus, there's no need. Once in a while we get wind of an animal-rights demonstration heading our way and hire a local security company, but usually the animal-rights groups stage their protests at the venues for optimal coverage."

"What about performers?"

"This place is a ghost town after nine. We're in the midst of putting together our new show, so people get up early, work hard all day then fall into bed exhausted."

Despite what Otis says, I strain to see in the dark, nerves tingling. A few of the houses have TV screens flickering silver and blue. Others are dark, the performers probably dreaming of their next dangerous stunt, the roar of the crowd, their names in record books.

"Duck," Otis says, shoving me down into the footwell then tossing his jacket over me.

"What?" I whisper. Otis's electric window goes down. My pulse is a runaway train. Is this over before we've even driven off Walker's grounds?

"Hey, Otis."

"Hey, Esmerelda. You're up late."

"Gotta get that new trick," Esmerelda says. "What're you up to?"

"Heading to the bar for a drink."

"Want company?"

"You're fourteen."

Esmerelda giggles. "Can't blame a girl for trying. You know your headlights are off?"

"I'll flip them on soon as I'm off campus. Don't want bright headlights in a window to disturb anyone's sleep."

"Another reason you're my favorite Walker," Esmerelda says. "Have a good night."

"You, too."

I stay hidden as Otis puts the truck in gear. A pang of guilt hits. What I'm doing, what we're about to do, it's going to impact all the performers at Walker's. If we're successful in turning the public against the circus, people like Esmerelda who don't train animals, who are hardworking and talented, might lose their jobs. If that happens, will Esmerelda's family be sent back to Venezuela? Will she still get an education, survive the unrest and thrive? Am I wrong to put Esmerelda and others like her in jeopardy? I don't want to hurt anyone… But. But Swifty matters, too.

"You can come out," Otis says.

We exit the circus grounds, round the bend. The campus lights quickly fade away and we're swallowed by Florida's sticky darkness. Otis pulls to the side of the road. He turns off the truck's engine. My stomach slides to my feet. He's changed his mind. Reaching beneath the seat, Otis pulls out a thick roll of duct tape. "Um. What are you doing?"

"Give me a sec." He gets out of the truck.

I hear duct tape being paid out, ripped then stuck on Otis's door. He comes around the front of the truck to my door and does the same. He's covering the Wild Walker's Circus emblems. "Where are we going?" I ask once we're rolling again, this time with headlights on.

"Cedar, Florida. It's a three-hour drive."

"Why there?"

"I know a girl."

A twinge of jealousy hits. It's ridiculous and totally inappropriate. "How do you know we can trust her?"

"A while ago I helped her out." Otis nods at my pack. "Start writing that article. You'll have to ditch your iPad and phone in about an hour."

"Why?"

"Because both can be tracked by the police. I'll ditch my phone then, too."

"Then how will I post the video link?"

"Keep the camera. I'll set up the file-sharing site once we're hidden for the night. Then you can post the video. But I'm going to cut out the part with me in it."

Otis is risking a lot to help me, but that's still a little bit disappointing. "Okay. Does your girlfriend have internet?"

"Limited. But yeah." He looks over at me. "She's not my girlfriend."

I duck my head, using my curls to hide a blush. Does Otis have a girlfriend? It shouldn't matter. But it does.

"It looks cool."

"What?"

"Your hair. Why do you always wear it up?"

I think about lying. "My mom had the same hair. I never wanted to look like her."

"Do you?"

"Yeah. The spitting image."

My phone vibrates. It's a text from Sawyer. He's finally answering what I asked in my last voice mail about why he left porn in Cushing's office.

SAWYER: Because I wanted Cushing to talk to me, love me. Because living a lie is making it hard to breathe.

It hits me like a kick to the gut. My perfect, athletic, brilliant, kind, beautiful, incredibly considerate best friend doesn't have the choice to bury his secret so that he can remain home. That secret is crushing him. And no matter how much he wants to change himself—not because he thinks being gay is wrong, but because he desperately wants unconditional love from his parents and to fit in—he can't. I'm used to powerlessness, Sawyer isn't. I take a minute to collect my thoughts then text back.

ME: I get it. Finally. You succeed at everything you touch. But you can't change who you are inside for your dad

ME: Here's the crappy truth. Cushing may not be capable

of loving you unconditionally. But I do and always will. And so will a ton of people that you haven't met yet

ME: And eventually, you'll love you, too. We will figure this out together. Promise

SAWYER: Gotta go

I think about telling him what I'm doing but decide against it. First, it'd be making things about me again. Second, it might get him into trouble. Despite everything, one side of my mouth crooks up. We're a long way from okay, but we're texting. That's something.

Otis pulls onto a dark bypass road then Highway 19. I start writing, not worrying about the length of my article. Mr. Matthews will print all of it, because I've kidnapped a baby elephant.

The Pennington Times

BY T. LILLIAN DECKER, INTERN

Swift Jones Struggles to Survive

Swift Jones, the Asian elephant calf rejected by her mother at the Pennington Zoo, claimed by owners Wild Walker's Circus, has spent three days in her new home in Florida. She is showing serious signs of deterioration and depression.

Swift Jones, nicknamed Swifty, is now consuming less than ten pints of milk a day. Normal consumption is up to twenty-four pints.

I dig out Dr. Robertson's card and dial her cell phone. "Hello," a sleepy voice answers on the fourth ring.

Crap. I forgot it's late. "Dr. Robertson? I'm so sorry to wake you. It's Lily, from Oregon? The newspaper? I'm taking care of Swifty tonight?"

"Is everything okay?" Dr. Robertson asks, now sounding wide-awake.

"I guess. But I'm still worried."

"I'll tell you what I told Dr. Tinibu," Dr. Robertson says. "Less than ten pints of milk a day will not sustain that calf."

"How long can she survive?"

"Given her depression, a week or so, if she continues to drink some formula. Less if she refuses it."

"Even with the enemas?"

"I'm sorry, Lily. I can tell how attached you are to Swift Jones. But if she wants to die, she'll die."

"Thanks for talking to me. And sorry again for waking you."

"I'm sorry I don't have better news."

"May I quote you?" I can almost hear the cogs in Dr. Robertson's brain spinning. Howard Walker might get angry. She could lose a ton of work.

"Yes."

> According to the circus's veterinarian, Dr. Robertson, "less than ten pints of milk a day will not sustain that calf." When asked how long Swift Jones can survive if her situation remains the same, Dr. Robertson said, "Given her depression [Swifty has] a week or so if she continues to drink some formula. Less if she refuses.... If she wants to die, she'll die."

I glance at Otis.

"What?"

"I'm just at a hard part."

> Today I witnessed Howard Walker, Wild Walker's elephant tamer, who was previously quoted in this newspaper saying, "I never use an ankus. Don't need one," use an ankus (a rod with a sharp steel hook and a pointed end that resembles a fire poker) on one of his adult elephants, Tambor. The bull was trying to protect Swift Jones. Howard Walker, visibly drunk at the time, swung the ankus like a baseball bat, connecting with Tambor's most tender spots—the back of his ears, feet and trunk. He drew blood each time.
>
> An elephant's skin is so sensitive that they can feel the pain of an insect bite. Howard's blows caused Tambor,

"How much does Tambor weigh and how tall is he?"

"Almost ten feet. Over eleven thousand pounds," Otis says.

> a ten-foot bull weighing more than eleven thousand pounds, to retreat in pain. Walker then turned the ankus on Swifty, puncturing the soft skin on the top of her foot.

I do a Google search for more information to substantiate what I want to say next and quickly find what I'm looking for.

"Does Walker's have ZA accreditation?"

"No," Otis replies.

I pull up the Pennington Zoo's website, find what I'm looking for after a brief search.

> The ZA (Zoo Association) published a guide for institutions to measure their success in caring for elephants. If zoos and circuses follow those guidelines, they receive ZA accreditation. The Pennington Zoo has ZA accreditation. Wild Walker's Circus does not.
>
> All the animals at Walker's, including the elephants, are transported in trucks to arenas for shows. They travel forty weeks a year, covering an average of twenty-three thousand miles. According to a circus employee who asked to remain anonymous, "[The animals] stay in the trucks the whole time. It's too much trouble taking them in and out. Especially the tigers and elephants." While traveling, no trucks or cages are cleaned. When asked what happens when the temperatures gets too hot or too cold, Walker's employee said, "Last year a few of the elephants got a little frostbite. A few years ago, I heard one of the llamas died from heatstroke."

I read what I have about travel and Clem's quotes to Otis. "True?"

His hands tighten on the steering wheel. "True."

"Can I quote you on that?"

"No."

I glance over my shoulder. Flea and Swifty are playing a

gentle game of tug of war with Nibs. Returning to Google, I dig deeper into the ZA guidelines to prove Walker's isn't in compliance and what that means for their animals.

> What does this mean for Swifty? Elephants at Walker's have no bathing water, or any type of mud or soil to aid in their temperature control. When not performing, they're kept chained by one leg in a cinderblock building without heat or air-conditioning, which can result in dangerous issues, including severe depression, viruses and foot infections.
>
> Wild Walker's Circus has been apprised of the decline in Swifty's health, but Howard Walker has refused to consider alternatives that might help the calf survive. Otis Walker, publicist for Wild Walker's Circus and a member of the family that owns the show, declined to comment.
>
> To save Swifty's life, I've taken her somewhere safe. She'll have as much formula as she's willing to drink and fluids to keep her hydrated. My hope is that I can keep her alive until Wild Walker's Circus gives up their claim. Then she can go to a new home that will give her all the support and love she needs to thrive.
>
> Please share this article. On Facebook's Save Swift Jones page, I've also posted a link to a video that I took of Howard Walker using an ankus on Tambor and Swifty. Please sign the petition on

Facebook and copy the link and the video to as many other sites as you can.

Lawyers will get involved quickly. They'll force Facebook to take down the link, and sites like YouTube to delete the video, but by sharing and copying it to other sites, you'll keep it alive.

Write letters to the *Pennington Times* care of Shannon McDaniels, to your own newspapers, magazines, Facebook pages, Instagram, even your senators asking for Wild Walker's to give up their claim to Swift Jones.

Thank you,
Lily Decker

I read the rest of my article to Otis. "What do you think?"

He meets my gaze. "That I had no idea how fierce you are. Now hold the wheel."

"What? Did I mention I don't know how to drive?" But his hands are already off it so I do my best to keep us in the same lane.

Otis takes my iPad, copies the article then sends it to an email address.

"Who's Christine West?"

"My friend. We'll send your article from her place."

"Why not send it now?"

"Because your boss might alert my family or the cops. We need to be off the road when it goes out."

"Note to self—good liar, bad at the clandestine stuff. I can improve."

Otis actually grins. "Good to know."

"Won't the police use your friend's email to figure out where we are?"

"It would be hard for them to track her. She kind of doesn't exist."

I turn sideways, facing Otis. "Then how does she have an email account?"

He doesn't look at me. "There are ways."

"Does Christine even know we're coming?"

"Yes."

Otis opens his window. He tosses out my iPad. It explodes on the asphalt. His phone is next, then mine. I watch them shatter. Irreparable damage, but I feel lighter. My subconscious has gone silent, which means that I'm finally doing the right thing for the right reasons. I've just stolen a baby elephant. I'm on the run with a guy I barely know. My father and probably Sawyer, too, are going to think I've finally lost it when the news hits. But for first time in my life, I don't feel like I'm on the bleeding edge of crazy.

37

It's after two in the morning when we drive along the deserted main street of Cedar. The wooden buildings are gray from the salty ocean air. The lack of streetlights makes the small town feel even more desolate. "How many people live here?"

"Around two hundred."

"Your friend must not be very social."

"She's not."

We pass only one person, a guy wearing a frayed gray poncho over pedal-pusher jeans. He's focused on changing a flat tire. There's a closed coffee shop, a few restaurants serving seafood and a bait store whose roof looks like it's slowly collapsing. About a mile outside of town, Otis turns onto a dirt trail bordered by trees. It looks more like a bike path than a road. The truck lurches over roots, branches scraping its sides as we wind around trees threatening to take back the road. Swifty's trunk reaches over the back seat, stretching toward me. The little finger on the tip tickles my neck. An hour ago

I climbed into the back and gave her a bottle. She drank only a fifth of it. "How much farther?"

"A few miles."

"So Christine is a hermit?"

"She likes her privacy."

The headlights finally illuminate a trailer. It might've been white at one point, but now it blends into the trees surrounding it. The sides sport muddy runnels, rust, moss and hungry branches that are on the way to swallowing it whole. A woman steps outside. Two things are apparent in the wash of our headlights. One, Christine is very attractive. Two, she's holding a shotgun.

Otis stops in front of the trailer. He turns the ignition off. "Wait here."

He gets out slowly, like he's giving the woman time to get used to the idea. She lowers the gun, resting it against the sagging deck railing. Otis walks up the rickety steps. They hug...for a long time. "Come on out," Otis finally calls.

As I climb the stairs, it's clear I was wrong. This woman isn't attractive. She's beautiful. Thick, auburn hair runs well past her shoulders. Add a cleft in her chin, and a body, beneath leggings and a camisole, that is beyond perfect, and she's pretty much the most gorgeous woman I've ever seen. Her dark green eyes scan me, head to toe. "I'm Lily." I hold out my hand but she doesn't take it.

"Christine, we need to use your phone and internet," Otis says.

"What's mine is yours."

She has an accent I can't place, but it sounds familiar. "Where are you from?"

Christine looks at Otis. "Cedar." She opens the metal screen on her door. The inside of the trailer smells delicious. Homemade breads line the counter. Chili boils on the stove. Boxes filled with dozens of muffins are set on a rough, wood table. The floor is yellow linoleum, the furniture Salvation Army plaid, but the place is spotless. Christine points to an old Mac in the corner set on a makeshift desk of crates. Otis gets to work.

"If you're hungry," Christine says, nodding at the chili.

She hands me two bowls. I make one for Otis that he eats while working. Mine I take outside so I can give them privacy. Flea and Swifty step onto the lift gate together. Once down, they wander the yard, side by side. When Flea stops to pee, lifting his leg so his stream hits high on a tree, Swifty attempts to do the same. A small amount of urine dribbles down her back leg.

"Otis wanted me to tell you that your third article has been picked up by the AP."

I jump, because Christine moves like a freaking spook. I didn't even hear the screen door open or her steps on the deck's stairs. "How does Otis know?"

"It's in the *New York Times*."

My mouth hangs open for a second. The *New York Times*? I'm stunned, but more stunning is that I really only care because of Swifty. We watch the calf trail Otis's mutt. Her trunk drags on the grass like she's forgotten it, or it's too much effort to lift. I'll have to give her more fluids tonight.

"What you're doing? It could get Otis into a lot of trouble."

"You don't approve."

"This is not a game."

"I know."

"Do you?" Christine's eyes glint in the dark. "For Otis, this isn't an adventure or a road trip to brag about to his friends when he's back in his middle-class, safe home with Mommy and Daddy to tuck him in at night. Wild Walker's Circus is the only life he's ever known, the only life he'll ever have."

"He has other options."

"No money. No job. No family. No financial or emotional safety net, possible prison time. It's nice to see you care so much. And what will you lose?"

I think about telling her that I've probably lost my best friend, learned things about my father that I'm not sure I can forgive, and now I'm risking the one thing I've spent my entire life desperately trying to hold on to, my sanity, but she doesn't know me so she won't care.

"How long have you known Otis?" Christine asks.

"A few days."

"I've known him for seven years. He has trouble saying no to a pretty girl."

Definitely a backhanded compliment, but it's obvious she cares about Otis so I bite my tongue. "Right now, no one knows that Otis is helping me. My plan is to keep it that way. He's not in any photos, videos or in my articles, except as Walker's PR guy who, in print, definitely doesn't support the Pennington Zoo or stealing Swift Jones. If things go well, this will be over in a few days."

"If they don't?"

"Then I'll make sure Otis isn't with me when I get caught." Christine's eyes gleam. Not with tears. She's too mean for that. Maybe it's venom. "Satisfied?"

"Swear it on that stupid little elephant."

I'm losing patience, especially after the word *stupid*, but Christine is giving us a place to stay. At least she cares about what happens to Otis. "I swear on Swifty." Christine's eyes narrow, like she's trying figure out if I'm a liar.

"You smell," she finally says. "There's a clean T-shirt and shorts in the bathroom. I'll find something for Otis, too. I only have one extra toothbrush so you two will have to share."

"Lily?" Otis calls from the front door. "Ready when you are."

We post the link to Facebook's Save Swift Jones page, and then send my article to Shannon along with the link. "I should call her. Let her know so she can get it into tomorrow's paper."

Christine hands me a cheap cell phone. "It's a burner," she explains, then hands Otis another phone. "Just in case."

I can't remember Shannon's cell number. I have to write down different combinations until one looks right. Otis rolls his eyes.

"Who memorizes numbers?" I ask. Shannon doesn't pick up, probably because the number is blocked. I try five times in a row before she finally answers. I put her on speaker so Otis can hear the conversation.

"Hello?"

"It's Lily. Decker."

"Can you stop saying your last name when you call? I know who you are. Why aren't you calling from your own phone and have you forgotten it's almost midnight here?"

"I dropped it and I know it's late, sorry."

"Did you see that your article was in the *New York Times*?"

"Yeah."

"A little excitement is actually appropriate. It was in the *Post*, the *LA Journal*. Basically? Every-freaking-where. Good job, kid. Seriously. You're turning into a reporter, and the photos? Lily, they were better than the story. Matthews is bitching about video, though. It better be attached to your next article."

"Shannon?"

"Yeah?"

"I just sent you the fourth article with photos plus a link to a video." I can tell Shannon is checking the time or the print schedule or her email because she's moving around.

"If it doesn't need major work, Matthews might be willing to move some things, squeeze it in for tomorrow. Maybe it'll be in Entertainment again."

"Um."

"What? You sound weirder than usual. Spit it out."

"Read the article. Watch the video. I'll call you back in five minutes."

It's the longest five minutes of my life. Otis goes outside to check on Swifty. That leaves me with Christine staring a hole through my chest. Her superpower, it turns out, is the ability to make someone feel like a total piece of shit. "Lots of bread and muffins," I finally say.

"I sell them to the coffee shop."

There are burn scars on the inside of her arms. They're perfectly round. "Have you always been a baker?"

"No."

Okay then. I dial Shannon. She picks up immediately. Otis comes in so I push Speakerphone.

"Holy motherfucking shit," Shannon says.

I wince. “Okay.”

“Lily?”

It’s Mr. Matthews. Shannon must’ve called him, put us on three-way. Any shred of confidence I possess leaks out with the perspiration that’s trickling down my back.

“You can’t do this,” Mr. Matthews says. “Wherever you are? Go back. Apologize. Then get on the next plane home.”

“I can’t.”

I hear Shannon in the background. “It *is* news.”

“Screw the news,” Mr. Matthews roars. “She’s going to wind up in jail.”

“I won’t take her back. If I do, Swifty doesn’t stand a chance.” No one says anything for a few seconds.

“Lily, if we print your story and that link, Wild Walker’s, their lawyers and the cops are going to be all over us,” Mr. Matthews says. “Does Dr. Tinibu know what you’re up to?”

“No.”

“Do you have a plan for Swifty that might keep her alive? Beyond publicly shaming Wild Walker’s Circus into letting her go?” Mr. Matthews asks.

“Yes. I hope so. They deserve it.”

“You realize this might get personal?” Shannon asks.

She knows about my past. Of course she does, because it was front-page news in her paper. Any journalist, after tomorrow, can dig it up. But I’m pretty sure the story will stay focused on Swifty. People are fascinated with her, and all of this, what we’re doing, is about her, not me.

“Lily?” Mr. Matthews says.

“Yes. I do.” Otis raises one eyebrow. I shrug it off.

“You could end up in court,” Shannon points out.

"It'll give you something to write about," I say. It's gallows humor but she chuckles. My pulse speeds up. Without the *Pennington Times* this will be harder, maybe impossible because it will take too long to get traction. Swifty doesn't have unlimited time. "So? Will you print my article?" I can hear Mr. Matthews breathing, because it takes a lot to move his mountainous chest.

"Front page, with the link," Mr. Matthews barks. "But we're going to have to take out the part about sharing the link and copying the video, because that crosses the line. Don't worry, people will do it anyway."

I can't help myself. "The paper might get sued."

"It'll give our fancy lawyers something to do besides count their piles of money."

"Why are you willing to do this?"

"It's news," Mr. Matthews says. "Plus, I owe you one, kid."

"You owe me one?"

Mr. Matthews puffs out a cloud of air. "I was a new editor at the *Times* when your mom tried to fly you off that roof. Shannon was my star reporter. The attempted murder and trial were news, but we squeezed hard, made an already shocking story more sensational than was professional, kept it alive way too long. Apologies, kid. Stay safe. Keep that elephant breathing."

They hang up.

Now I know why Shannon picked me for the *Times* internship out of all the other applicants. It would've mattered to me, before. And now? I don't care as long as it gets my article printed.

"How long are you going to stay?" Christine asks Otis.

"One or two days," Otis says. "Is that okay?"

"You sure no one could've followed you?"

"Yes."

Christine nods. "Okay."

I wait for more, but there isn't any. "Do you have a hose outside?" I ask.

"Yes."

"Any chance it has a warm-water option?"

"It's rainwater from a cistern so it's about air temperature. If I want a cold glass of tea I have to use ice."

I'm sticky from the heat so it must still be in the low nineties outside. "That'll work."

"You sure she needs it?" Otis asks.

"Yeah." Swifty is at the bottom of the stairs with Flea. "Hey, sweet pea." Violet used to call me that…in the mornings, when she'd climb into my bed to snuggle before breakfast. The words hang in the air, shimmer. The true sound of my mother's voice comes back to me…then fades away. The calf starts to climb the trailer's stairs, but I don't think the steps can hold her so I scoot to the bottom one. She nuzzles into my neck. "I know," I say. "But it's going to get better. Promise." I hear the screen door open. Otis comes down the steps.

"I'll get the hose," he says.

We work together. When we're done and Swifty has been cleaned up using some baby shampoo Christine had in her shower, we help the calf back into the truck and cover her with a blanket. Flea jumps into the truck, lying down at her head like some sort of mutant guard dog.

I sit down on the lowest stair of the trailer. Otis sits, too, taps out a cigarette and spins it over his knuckles. "Do you even smoke?"

"Nope. Disgusting habit."

"So why carry around cigarettes?"

Otis spins the cigarette forward then back. "The motion calms me. They're like worry beads."

I look over my shoulder. Christine is moving around the kitchen, cleaning even though it's already spotless. Suddenly I realize where I've heard her accent. It's the same as Uri's, the bear guy. A chill slithers down my spine. When I asked Uri if a bear clawed out his eye, he'd said no…that it was a woman he thought he'd tamed. "Christine was married to Uri," I say.

Otis nods.

"The burns on her arms?"

"He did that and worse."

"You helped her get away?"

"He would've killed her eventually," Otis says. "So I researched how to make her disappear, create untraceable accounts. Unfortunately my paltry savings weren't enough to get her very far or set her up in style."

"You saved her life." Otis shrugs like it's no big deal. But it's a huge deal. I'm seeing deeper into the real him, and it only makes him more attractive. "I promised Christine that if things go wrong you'd be long gone."

"You can't—"

"Shut up." Surprisingly, he does. "No one knows you're helping me. You're not in the video or my articles, other than as Walker's PR guy. I doubt your family will tell the media you're missing."

"You may be overestimating my family."

I shake my head. "I'm not saying they'd do it for you. It'd look bad for them if the media finds out that their publicist—their own son—has joined forces with the kidnapper."

"You sound like a B-movie villain."

I laugh, then snort, then blush. "It's my first crime. I'm learning as I go." I hold out my hand. "Promise me you'll let me take responsibility."

Otis reaches up, brushes a curl from my cheek. Instead of promising, he kisses me. It's my first *real* kiss. There's a furious Romanian woman living under an assumed name taking her anger out on kitchen pots. I just stuck a hose up an elephant's butt. Swifty's drool has dried in splotches on my T-shirt. It's still the best kiss of my life. Otis pulls back, runs his thumb over my lower lip. My skin is alive for the first time in my life. It's like being woken up after eighteen years of trying to feel nothing.

"You're beautiful."

I believe him.

We each take a quick shower, then meet at the truck. Together, we pull the dirty straw out then put fresh straw down from one of the bales Otis threw on the back seat. The four of us sleep in the back—Flea in the curve of Swifty's neck, the calf's trunk resting on my arm; Otis behind me, his body curled into mine, arm wrapped around my waist with just enough pressure to let me know he likes me.

"Good night, Tiger," Otis whispers in my ear.

"Good night." But I stay awake long after his breathing settles into a rhythm, because despite everything, this is the greatest night of my life.

38

I wake up to Otis's breath tickling my ear. It makes me want to freeze time even though Swifty's drool is dried in streaks on my arms, the wool blanket is itchy, and Flea, despite his small size, is an extreme bed hog.

"Hey," Otis says.

He kisses me good morning. My teeth are furry, my breath must be horrendous, but he doesn't seem to mind. Me neither. We get Swifty down from the truck. It's a relief to see that Christine's car is gone. Swifty presses against my leg. I check the skin beneath her eyes; it's still tenting. The inside of her mouth is sticky. Plus, she only peed a tiny bit on the straw last night. This morning her urine is dark yellow. No poop at all. She must not be drinking enough formula to make any. Flea pees by Swifty, then together they wander the yard, Swifty trailing behind the dog.

"I'm starving," Otis says.

"You think she's okay out here?"

"Yeah."

Neither of us says what we're thinking. The calf doesn't have the energy to go far. Christine left us coffee, fresh bread and a few muffins and left her computer on, waiting. I grab Swifty's next bottle, a cup of coffee and two muffins. Otis pours himself a mug, slathers jam on bread and brings the computer outside. He sits on the lift gate while I feed Swifty. It's a totally preposterous situation, us, together, taking care of an elephant calf whose guardian is the ugliest dog in the universe, yet it's strangely right.

Swifty gives up after a quarter of her bottle. "No way. You need to drink more." She refuses. We give her another enema while Flea distracts her with play bows and spins. The circus's fancy standard poodles have nothing on Otis's mutt. "You're a really good dog," I tell Flea. I swear he nods. When we're done, I scatter kisses all over the calf's face while Otis cleans her hind end. Then we sit on the tailgate, Otis searching for my article while Flea draws Swifty into a walk around the yard.

My article is on the digital version of the *Pennington Times*, front page with the link. Mr. Matthews is going to get in trouble. Big trouble. The article has also been reprinted in the digital *New York Times*, *Wall Street Journal*, *LA Press*, *Chicago Tribune* and eleven other major papers across the country. I should be elated but relief is the prevalent emotion—that, and concern. "It's not in their physical newspapers."

"Tiger, there wasn't time. Don't worry, way more people read the news online."

He called me Tiger again. I smile. That name no longer makes me cringe. "Um. Any comments from Walker's?"

Otis searches. "It's in the *NY Post*. 'Wild Walker's Circus's elephant trainer, Howard Walker, stated, "I am devastated by the kidnapping of Swift Jones. She is already a part of Walker's family, loved by many, including her fellow elephants. The video taken by Lily Decker is a malicious fabrication. Our family plans to sue Decker. For now, we're working with law enforcement to find Decker before Swift Jones suffers any more harm.'"

There it is. "They can have the few hundred dollars in my savings account," I say. "The more important question is, who will people believe? Howard or me?" What I don't say is that Calvin is going to freak. I'm sure there's a stack of voice mails on my exploded cell phone. Part of me feels guilty, but even if I could go back, I wouldn't.

Otis returns to surfing the Web. "The Save Swift Jones Facebook page has been renamed Save Swifty. There are 122,417 signatures." He wraps his arm around my waist, kisses my cheek. "'Wendy, one girl is more use than twenty boys.'"

I laugh. Snort. Peter Pan said that to Wendy Darling. This time I'm the one who leans in to kiss him. No one ever told me that the touch of another person's lips could send ripples of heat through my skin. "What now?" I ask.

"We wait."

Swifty wanders over. Flea drops Nibs right next to her, but she doesn't even reach out her trunk to touch the stuffed bunny. We guide Swifty onto the lift. She lies down in the back of the van. Flea gets under the blanket with her, snuggled tight against her chest. "It's going to get better," I again promise the calf. After seeing my article, hearing how many people have signed the Save Swifty petition on Facebook, I believe it's true. We head inside the trailer to charge Christine's computer. Otis flips on the TV, running through the channels. He stops on the big cable news channel, CNC. Charlie Hamilton is doing a special report. The banner on the bottom of the screen reads: Save Swifty?

"Damn." Otis turns up the volume.

"...is riveted by the real-life drama of T. Lillian Decker and Swift Jones, nicknamed Swifty, an Asian elephant calf whose mother rejected her, triggering a clause in her contract that led to Wild Walker's Circus legally claiming ownership," Charlie Hamilton says.

Hamilton's sky blue eyes stare into me. His superpower is making every single person feel like he's talking directly to them. He adjusts rectangular glasses.

"The video you're about to see is graphic, disturbing," Hamilton says. "Our experts have made certain that it has not been tampered with in any way. Decker, age eighteen, an intern for the *Pennington Times* and the only reporter who has had access to Swift Jones, took this video yesterday."

The video runs, cutting off just before Otis races into the ring although I can hear the first two letters of him shouting, *Stop!*

"There is currently a petition on Facebook with—" Hamilton glances down at the flat screen in front of him "—125,027 signatures demanding that Wild Walker's Circus give up their claim to the baby calf, which is suffering from both depression and malnutrition as a result of refusing to drink her formula. The *Pennington Times* has declined to comment at this time about how and when they received Decker's article or whether they are still in touch or know her whereabouts. We will keep you posted as developments unfold."

Otis turns off the TV and pulls me toward the couch. This time the kiss isn't tentative. This time our bodies are drawn together like magnets. He takes off my glasses, unknots my hair so that curls tumble free. His hands travel along my skin, leaving a trail of warmth as he traces my curves. He cups my breasts, his thumbs instantly making my nipples insanely sensitive. He draws me onto his lap so that I'm straddling him, and I can feel how much he wants me. Me.

A week ago I was afraid to drink coffee. And now? I've thrown away my Twelve-Year Plan. Jettisoned the Journalist's Code. Confronted Calvin. Kidnapped a baby elephant. I've broken the freaking law. Me. Everything is happening so fast. And right now my body is reacting while my brain struggles to catch up, assess and make rational choices.

Do you think I'm going to have schizophrenia?

I don't know… Probably.

Where has rational ever gotten me? I run fingers through Otis's hair, lean in, lose myself. I'm more alive than I've ever felt, on fire. *But.* When I pull away it's like stepping out of the sun.

"Lily?"

I take a few breaths and let my mind catch up to my body, stare into the depths of Otis's eyes for answers. Clarity comes in a rush of adrenaline, fear and desire. This moment is the only thing in my life, in anyone's life, that's guaranteed. I refuse to squander it. I've wasted enough time.

Otis searches my face for clues. "It's okay. I shouldn't have assumed you wanted—"

"This is all new," I say, blushing.

"Then we'll take things slow."

I kiss him, losing myself in his taste, touch. He peels off my T-shirt and bra so gradually that it's hard not to help. I've never wanted to be touched by another person this badly. He slides me beneath him then bends, lips tasting the curve of my breasts, tongue teasing my nipples until I shiver from the sensation. My insides twist, ache with the thought of all the things I've never done and want to do.

"How'd you get this bruise?" Otis asks, outlining the purplish stain on my ribs with a light fingertip.

"I fell."

"On what?"

I half smile. "A mangrove root, um, when I was following you and Tambor. Sorry about the whole spying and seeing you naked thing."

"Really?"

"Really what?"

"You're sorry?"

I'm lying beneath Otis in only shorts. The instinct to cover myself comes then goes. This is overwhelming, scary, but in a good way. For the first time in my life, I want to be seen. "I'm not sorry."

"Me neither."

I pull off Otis's T-shirt, his skin butter-smooth beneath my hands. My fingers trace his muscled abdomen. There's a small scar beneath his belly button. "What's this?"

"Appendicitis when I was eleven."

I slide down, kiss the scar; flick my tongue over the slightly raised line. Otis shudders. Instantly my fragile confidence crumbles. “Did I do something wrong? I don’t— I’m sorry—”

Otis softly laughs, drawing me back up. “Tiger, you may be new at this, but you definitely aren’t doing anything wrong.” We kiss, bodies coming together, the heat from our skin radiating. I press my hands against Otis’s chest, not to push him away, but to anchor myself, because my body is so light I need to hold on to something solid or float away…

The cell phone rings. We ignore it. It stops then rings again. Stops. A third round of rings slices the air. Otis grabs it from the table. “Hello…okay…yeah…okay.” He kisses me one more time. “To be continued, hopefully really, really soon. That was Christine. Turn the TV on.”

We dress quickly. It doesn’t take long to find what Christine called about. It’s on Hivox News. A perky blonde interviews Addie outside the motel in Haven, Florida. My school photograph is in the corner of the screen. Round glasses, curls trapped in a twist, green eyes wary.

“Sally Quince for Hivox News standing a few miles away from Wild Walker’s Circus in Haven, Florida. Dr. Tinibu, you’re the director of the Pennington Zoo?”

Addie nods. “Yes.”

“So you hired T. Lillian Decker to accompany you to Florida?”

“Lily is not an employee. She’s a volunteer. I brought her because of her connection with Swift Jones. The calf loves her.”

The reporter shifts her microphone closer. “Did you have any idea what Decker was planning?”

“No.”

"Any truth to her allegations? Animal abuse? Horrible conditions? Is the video real or doctored?"

Addie's nostrils flare. "No comment."

"Any signs that Decker was prone to rash behavior?"

"Not until now."

Otis rolls his eyes. "Rash behavior because you want to save Swifty's life?"

Despite the heat, I'm suddenly chilled.

"Do you have anything you want to say to Lily if she's watching?" the reporter asks.

Addie looks directly into the camera. "Make sure you keep Swift Jones hydrated. Call someone who can help if anything seems wrong."

"It sounds like you're supporting Decker."

"No comment." Addie walks away from the reporter.

"Sally Quince for Hivox News," Quince says. "Back to you, Eric."

Eric, the concerned-looking anchor, thanks Sally then cues another reporter who's standing beneath a red umbrella because it's pouring. I recognize the dull lead color of an Oregon sky as well as the building behind him.

"Chip Paley for Hivox News. I'm standing outside the Grable, a private high school in Pennington, Oregon. Until a week ago, T. Lillian Decker was a senior here." Paley walks toward a group of students wearing the type of rain shells everyone in the Pacific Northwest owns. "These three students are some of Decker's friends."

It's Carla, Dawn and Jonah. Sawyer isn't there. His absence is like an open wound.

"Can any of you tell me about T. Lillian Decker?" Paley asks.

"We were friends," Carla says, "when we were little kids."

"Are you surprised that she's kidnapped Swift Jones?"

Carla sighs as if talking to the reporter is a burden. "Lily has always been…off. But who wouldn't be with her past?"

"Her past?" Paley prods.

Dawn nudges Carla. Clearly Carla thought the reporter already knew about my mother, because for a second surprise widens her big brown eyes. I guess Paley didn't have time to dig up my past when he was racing to get the first "friend" interview. I can't feel my hands or feet. "Otis, I need to—"

"Lily has always been really nice to me," Dawn says. "I don't think she's that weird."

Jonah enthusiastically nods. "She's not. Weird. And she was willing to be my friend when no one else would talk to me."

That's kind of Jonah. Not true, but kind.

The reporter looks at Carla like she's dinner. "If you know anything that will help the police find Lily, you need to tell me," he says. "There's an innocent elephant calf out there that desperately needs medical attention."

Carla twists the class ring on her pinkie. "I'm not sure I should say anything."

"If you don't, you'll be telling the police," Paley warns.

"Carla," Dawn says, "leave it alone."

Carla glares at Dawn. Her shiny dark ponytail swings from side to side, like plastic gears that form her brain are powering it. "It's not really a secret. I mean, anyone could do a little research. Lily's mother tried to kill her when we were, like, seven years old? It was a super big scandal in Pennington."

Otis takes my hand. "It's okay."

But it's not. I know what's coming next.

"Why did her mother try to kill her?" Paley asks.

"Her mom had schizophrenia. One time, she showed up at our elementary school naked. It was December. No joke. And Lily's school lunches, sometimes they were all candy, other times her mom would fill Lily's brown bag with slips of paper covered in drawings or weird quotes. Do you remember the roadkill lunch?" she asks Dawn, who shakes her head. "Liar. It was a dead squirrel."

"Shut up, Carla," Dawn says. "Lily isn't like her mom."

The look on Carla's face, after being told to shut up on national TV, spells trouble for Dawn. She might lose her spot in Carla's clique. "When we got older," Carla continues, "my parents told me not to be Lily's friend. Dawn's did, too, even though she won't say so. It's sad, but crazy is genetic, you know?"

Those three words again. *Crazy is genetic.*

The reporter chats with the news anchor about how worried they both are for Swift Jones, given this new development. Meaning, since they've learned I'm not playing with a full deck. A commercial runs, something about mattresses. At some point Otis let go of my hand. "Say it."

"You should have told me," Otis says.

There's distance in his tone, like he's already moved away from me. I stare at my empty hands. "I didn't lie."

"A lie by omission is still a lie."

I laugh. It's totally inappropriate but impossible to stifle. "You still would've helped me, right? Hey, Otis, I want to steal Swift Jones from your family, stir up a hornet's nest of heinous PR, drive the calf cross-country and convince an elephant sanctuary to take her in. Oh, and by the way, you should trust me because Violet, my mother, had paranoid schizophrenia with homicidal tendencies. When she went off her meds she papered our loft with Escher drawings, scribbled quotes on the walls and only spoke or answered questions with lines from *Peter Pan*. And if that isn't bad enough? When I was seven she took me to the roof, gibbered words that weren't even her own, then tried to fly with me in tow."

Otis is staring at me. I know what he's seeing—a freak; the babbling homeless woman on the sidewalk that people ignore; a girl bound for an institution where endless days are spent wandering aimlessly or pounding my head against the wall. He's seeing my future, and it's ugly.

I take a hitching breath because I'm going to finish this. "The cherry on top of Violet's attempted filicide? My father tried to save her, not me. Here's even better news! Pretty much every woman in my family ends up with schizophrenia, so I'm freaking doomed. But right now? Right now I'm not nuts." I pump one fist into the air. "So trust me! I've taken my monthly 'do I have schizophrenia yet' test, passed with flying colors. It's all good so let's go on a road trip!"

"Lily—"

"What?" I'm on my feet. I'm yelling. "I'm so fucking trapped. The worst part is that now no one is going to focus on saving Swifty's life. This has officially become a 'save an elephant calf from the crazy girl' campaign, and I'm an idiot for thinking the focus would stay on Swifty!"

Otis slumps on the plaid couch, only a few feet away, but a million miles from where we were twenty minutes ago. "I need a few minutes to process this." He heads out the screen door. It slams. Footsteps clomp down the stairs.

"Sure," I say to the empty trailer. My glasses are on a side table. I leave them there, because I can no longer hold on to the fantasy that they're some kind of protection from the eyes of the world.

"Psst."

"Go away."

"Psst."

I dig fingers into my temples. "I don't want to hear you."

"Psst."

"It's not my fault."

"It ith much harder to judge yourthelf than to judge others. If you thucceed in judging yourthelf, it's because you are truly a wise man."

My subconscious is once more speaking like a little girl with a lisp. Again, it's Antoine de Saint-Exupéry's words.

"... If you thucceed in judging yourthelf..."

She's right. What has happened is entirely my fault.

39

I wait for Otis to come back. He doesn't. The truck's engine hasn't been started yet, but I'm pretty sure he's sitting in the driver's seat. I wrap my arms around bent knees to keep the pieces together. A Breaking News: Save Swifty? banner scrolls across the bottom of CNC. The two men discussing some kind of financial crisis are replaced with Charlie Hamilton. I turn up the volume.

"Breaking news on the story of Swift Jones, the elephant calf kidnapped by eighteen-year-old Pennington Zoo intern T. Lillian Decker," Hamilton says. "Disturbing facts have arisen about Decker's mother, Violet Hanover Decker. CNC has learned that eleven years ago, Violet tried to kill her daughter, known as Lily, by throwing her off a rooftop. Violet had previously been diagnosed with schizophrenia. She'd stopped taking her medication. Luckily, the police were able to save both mother and child. Violet was convicted of attempted murder. She committed suicide in prison."

Hamilton adjusts his glasses. The same school photo as the

one Hivox News used is in the bottom corner of the screen. Tight bun. Dorky glasses. I'd think I looked like a wacko, too. "There has been speculation that Decker may also be suffering from mental illness," Hamilton says. "Calvin Decker, her father, has agreed to an interview on Skype to help shed some light on this situation."

The screen splits. There's Calvin. He's wearing the blue flannel shirt I gave him last Christmas. I'm torn between wanting to reach out, explain, or turn off the TV.

"Mr. Decker, thank you for talking with me," Hamilton says. "I'm sure you're worried about your daughter, her safety, and want this situation resolved quickly."

Calvin nods. There are dark circles beneath his red-rimmed eyes. His blond hair pulled into a ponytail makes him look more like a hippie than a teacher. Maybe that's what he'd be, if Violet and I hadn't torpedoed his life.

"Have you heard from your daughter?"

"No."

"Do you have any idea where she might be or who might be helping her?"

"No, I don't." Calvin leans forward, peering into the camera like he might find me inside it. "I agreed to this interview because I hope that my daughter is watching it. Lily, whatever is going on? Whatever you're going through? I love you. Please call me. The authorities have assured me that they don't want to see you punished, just helped. Everyone wants the best care for the elephant calf. Trust me on that. So call. Please. Come home."

"There have been accusations that your daughter has a mental health condition. Can you talk about that with us?"

"To my knowledge, she does not."

"But?"

"Because of...because of her mother, Lily has a higher risk of mental illness than a normal eighteen-year-old girl. Many things can trigger it. Drugs, alcohol, stress. Especially stress. This situation? It's beyond anything Lily has ever experienced. I'm very concerned."

Calvin ends the call. My entire body aches, like he's run over it with a truck. He didn't bring up the overwhelming history of mental illness in my mother's family, but it's obvious that he thinks I've become Violet.

Hamilton fills the screen. "It's clear we don't have all the information yet," he says. "Our hope is that this difficult situation can be resolved quickly for everyone involved and that both Lily Decker and Swift Jones are returned home safely."

Hamilton takes off his glasses. "I've never seen anything quite like this story. Swift Jones, a sick baby elephant, has captivated the world. We've received calls of possible calf sightings, emails from worried adults and children. They're not just coming from the United States. This story has been reported in Europe, China, even Russia. We promise to keep you posted."

"What a bastard," Otis says from the doorway.

My stomach lurches. I was so fixated on the TV that I didn't hear Otis climb the steps. "I thought Hamilton was pretty open-minded, considering."

"I meant Calvin."

"He's spent his entire life afraid that I'll turn into Violet. Now that he thinks it happened? He's scared. There's no parental manual on how to deal with your daughter's impending insanity."

"And the hits keep coming," Otis says, his eyes back on the TV.

A cute brunette reporter stands in front of Wild Walker's striped tent. "Bee Trenton from Haven News Six reporting. I'm here with Tina and Maximus Walker, owners of Wild Walker's Circus."

Otis's parents are dressed in blue, button-down shirts, pressed jeans, shiny cowboy boots. Howard isn't there. Maybe he's already on the road, searching for us. Maybe he's passed out, drunk. There's a group of performers behind Tina and Maximus. Esmerelda stares into the camera like an accusation. "I'm sorry," I whisper.

Max reads off a sheet of paper. "I'd like to address the kidnapping of our almost five-week-old elephant calf, Swift Jones, who the Walker family legally claimed after she was almost trampled to death by her mother, Raki."

Otis scowls. "They're already working with Tess Whitcomb."

"Who's she?"

"The best crisis manager in Florida. I had her on retainer."

I didn't think it was possible to feel any worse. But it is.

"Our family was shocked to learn that Lily Decker, a young woman we allowed in good faith onto our property in order to help Swift Jones with her transition from zoo to circus, has stolen our calf," Max says. "We're devastated that the life of Swift Jones is in the hands of a mentally ill young woman. Our calf has already been through the trauma of her mother's rejection. She's fragile. We fear for her life."

Nausea floods my mouth with saliva. The story is all about me now. Not Swifty. And it's going to screw up everything.

My Grable yearbook picture appears on the screen. Sawyer insisted that I wear something other than his baggy sweatshirt, so I'm in a cream-colored long-sleeved shirt, my hair still pulled tight, dark glasses a sharp contrast to pale skin that gives me the appearance of a nerdy mole.

Tina looks down at the notecard in her shaking hand. "We are asking for people's help. If you see Lily Decker, please don't approach her. We don't want anyone to get hurt. Call the police. Immediately. Please. We need to get Swift Jones home. We have a veterinarian on call waiting to take care of our calf upon her return."

"I want to add," Max says, peering straight into the camera, "that the authorities have assured us that they will prosecute *every* person involved with this crime. So if you are thinking about aiding and abetting Decker, think twice. Thank you."

"We will continue to keep our viewers up to date on this bizarre kidnapping story," the reporter promises. "I'm Bee Trenton reporting for Haven News Six."

If I were Joe Public, I'd see two devastated circus owners appealing for help in apprehending the unhinged girl who stole their fragile, defenseless calf. The part about prosecuting anyone involved with me was a clear message. They know Otis helped steal Swifty. They're telling him to get back home before he gets caught. This is over.

I busy myself putting muffins in a plastic bag then hold it out. "For the road." Otis doesn't move. What more does he want? "I'm sorry. Really." He's silent. "Look, I get that this has become a losing battle. That it's my fault. I can't stop you from taking Swifty back, and it's not like Christine will let me stay once you're gone." My nose burns, the precursor to what will be an epic ugly-cry. I dig my nails into my palm to push it off, because I have no right to feel sorry for myself. Otis risked it all only to get screwed, and not in a good way, by me. "Leaving now is the smartest thing to do," I say, trying to sound strong, certain.

Otis folds his arms over his chest. "I've never been that smart. Didn't even go to college."

His words are jarring, like the needle of an old-fashioned record player being dragged across a vinyl record. "You graduated high school at fourteen."

"Yeah. But I didn't live up to my potential."

I push away the curls threatening to swallow my face. "Look, I get that you hate me. I'd hate me, too. You should go. Seriously. Please go."

Otis taps out a cigarette and spins it along his knuckles. "Do you plan on developing schizophrenia in the next week?"

"Psst."

There's a buzzing in my ears. I shake my head to clear it.

"Lily. I need to hear you say it."

"No. But like Calvin said, stress can be a trigger."

"No worries there," Otis says.

I wave a hand at the TV. "I think it's safe to say we've lost the PR battle. The public is going to rally *against* me, not *for* Swifty."

"Then we have some damage control to do."

"Why?"

"Why what?"

"Why are you still willing to help me?"

Otis tosses the unlit cigarette into the trash. "Because Swifty deserves a chance, even if it's a slim one."

I get it now. He isn't doing this for me. I push down a sense of loss. It's impossible to lose something I never really had. "Tell me what to do," I say.

"People need to know you."

"I think they're pretty sure they already do."

"Change their minds."

"How?"

"By telling them the whole truth," Otis says.

In my head, a tiger chases his tail. "You didn't get the memo? They know the whole truth. That's the problem."

Otis picks up my camera, toys with it. "So make yourself the solution." He turns the camera on, switches the settings. "We're going to make a video."

"Of?"

"You, telling the world who you really are and why you've stolen Swifty."

This is a bad idea. "I don't think—"

"Our only chance is to try to turn the world's attention away from you, back to Swifty—to what's important. Introduce yourself."

Otis is not going to let this go. I pour myself another cup of coffee, sit cross-legged on the Formica counter, dig for strength, or at least a voice that doesn't shake. It's hard to know where to start. Who's going to watch this? Someone young? People my dad's age? Girls like Carla? The police? Calvin? The grandparents I've never met? Addie? Sawyer? Otis gestures for me to begin.

"My… I'm T. Lillian Decker. The *T* stands for *Tiger.* My mother, Violet Hanover Decker, was obsessed with the tigers at the zoo. So she named me after them. I think she hoped I'd be fearless, considering..."

"Go on," Otis orders.

"Um... By now a lot of people have seen the CNC and Hivox News interviews. There have been allegations that I'm mentally ill."

"Are you?"

"I'm just doing my best to save Swifty—Swift Jones—because she can't save herself. But my mother had schizophrenia. She had auditory hallucinations and—"

"Auditory hallucinations?"

"She heard voices. Mostly Peter Pan's. Sometimes Tinkerbell's. Maybe the artist Escher's."

"Do you hear voices?"

Invisible hands are squeezing my neck, trying to strangle my secrets. But I'm tired of keeping them. "Yes. I hear voices. But they're quotes from my past, things I've read, my subconscious chiming in, or lines from Swift Jones songs, which I used to hate, but I've become a fan. Voices, quotes or songs I already know don't constitute delusions or hallucinations. They just mean I have a kick-ass imagination. It's a quirk, but is anyone really normal?"

"Psst."

Not now.

"It ith much harder to judge a girl than to judge otherth. If you thucceed in judging yourthelf, it's because you are truly a wise woman."

Shut up, I silently command, but annoyance chews a ragged hole in my focus. The quote is wrong. It's "judge yourself," not "judge a girl." And it's "a wise man," not "a wise woman." *Leave it*, I tell my brain. But. But I know that quote, and that voice in my head…she's me, right? So how could she screw up the quote? I have a kick-ass imagination… Right? "Please," I whisper.

"Lily? Tell them what happened with your mother."

I try to smile, because people like people who smile. The effort is probably lopsided.

"Violet went off her meds. One day she took me to the roof of our apartment building because she thought we could fly to Neverland." I twist my hair into a knot, but there's no elastic on my wrist. Curls fall around my face and I know… I know my father will see Violet in this video. But I'm hers, too. He can't erase that, even though he tried.

"What happened next?"

I trace the scar above my brow. "Violet tried to make us both jump. The police saved us. My… Violet was convicted of attempted murder. A few months later she committed suicide." I dig fingernails into my thigh. "For a long time I thought she was a coward. But I get it now. Violet was psychotic, desperate as hell, but she tried to do the only thing she believed could save me from turning into her. She was brave."

"What you're doing now? That's not brave?"

"I'm just telling the truth."

"Why should people believe you?"

I stare into the camera's lens. "They don't have to. Watch the video of Howard Walker. CNC checked to make sure it wasn't somehow fabricated before they ran it. All the rest? The stuff about my mother, about me? It's just a distraction. What's important is that Swifty is a beautiful, intelligent being that creates lifelong bonds, craves family and is desperate for a mother. She deserves a chance at happiness."

"What can people do to help?"

"I think Mother Teresa said, 'I alone cannot change the world, but I can cast a stone across the waters to create many ripples.' I can't change the genetics that might eventually take *me* from me. But I can cast a stone. Create ripples. And if other people who care about Swifty cast a stone, too? Maybe we can save her life. Please sign the Save Swift Jones petition on Facebook. Email Wild Walker's Circus and CC everyone you know. Write letters to your local officials, newspapers, magazines."

"What will that do?"

"If Walker's has to decide between irreparably damaging their reputation and letting Swifty go? My hope is that they'll let her go."

Otis turns off the video. "Let's get a few shots of you with the calf."

We head outside. Swifty is in the back of the truck. I crawl in beside her. She rests her head on my lap; bottomless brown eyes stare up at me. Flea watches, waiting for me to fix the calf. I don't know if I can. The shutter clicks as Otis takes photos. "Make sure Flea's not in them," I say.

"Why?"

"If your dog is in the photos, your family will know you helped me. And don't forget to cut your voice out of the video." I curl my body around Swifty, like she's the Yin to my Yang. While Otis heads inside to edit the video, create a link and send it to anyone still willing to listen, I pull a bottle of formula from the cooler. "You're a golden splash," I tell the calf. She lifts her head and takes a sip.

40

"Lily."

It takes a minute to remember where I am. Then Swifty's trunk flops onto my chest. "Hey, sweet pea." She drank about a pint then wanted to snuggle. We both fell asleep. "How about stretching your legs?" Swifty wobbles to her feet and steps onto the lift. Down she goes to the grass. When she pees, brown urine dribbles down her back legs. Swifty looks back at me like she knows something is wrong. "It's okay. I'll see what Otis wants then get you cleaned up." Flea hops out of the van. "Keep an eye on her?" He chuffs.

I climb the porch steps. Otis holds open the door. It seems impossible that it could be steamier inside the trailer than out. It's early afternoon, the hottest part of the day. The T-shirt Christine loaned me is stuck to my sweaty skin along with her shorts. There's a row of mosquito bites down my legs. I hate Florida.

"You need to see this," Otis says with a nod at the TV. The channel is on CNC. Charlie Hamilton sits at his desk.

"Did you get the video out?"

"Yeah. The *Pennington Times*, YouTube, Facebook along with fifty other newspapers plus a few magazines."

"Thank you." Otis doesn't look at me.

Hamilton clears his throat. "We continue to follow the story of Tiger Lillian Decker, who goes by Lily, an eighteen-year-old from Oregon, who has stolen elephant calf Swift Jones. Sawyer Thompson, a senior at the Grable, Decker's high school, has agreed to talk with us via Skype to help us better understand this complicated situation."

I am the scum on the bottom of a garbage can.

"Sawyer, thank you for speaking with me," Hamilton says.

"Sure." Sawyer looks gorgeous, as usual, in a Grable lacrosse T-shirt and jeans, but just like Calvin, his bloodshot eyes reveal that he hasn't gotten much sleep.

"We've been told that you and Lily are best friends?"

"We are."

A sparkler in my brain goes off like it's the Fourth of July. *We are?*

"Have you seen the video she released this morning?"

"Yes."

"What did you think of it?"

"That it took more balls than most people have to be so honest."

Hamilton taps his pen on the desk. "Can you tell us a bit about Lily?"

"She's smart, really funny in a self-deprecating way and she's incredibly kind."

"Given her history—"

"Lily Decker isn't her mother."

Otis looks at me. "Sure he's not your boyfriend?"

"Why do you care?" I ask.

He looks away. "I don't."

"Point taken," Hamilton says. "Lily's father has said that her mental health is at risk. That stress can trigger a life-changing problem. Your friend has broken the law, stolen a sick elephant—she's hiding out somewhere. Are you worried she's mentally ill?"

"No."

Hamilton blinks three times. "Isn't that naive? She's high risk, right?"

"I know a ton about schizophrenia," Sawyer says. "I've talked with doctors, done research to make sure I'm educated and aware so I'm there for Lily if she needs me. Right now? She doesn't need me. She needs people to stand up for Swift Jones, for Swifty. Because if they don't? That calf is going to die."

Sawyer did research. Ten percent was a big number for him, too. I'm such a bitch.

"What do you want people to know about your friend?" Hamilton asks.

"That she's the bravest person I know."

"Then in your opinion the name Tiger fits?"

"Yes."

My eyes overflow. Embarrassed, I wipe tears away with the hem of Christine's shirt.

"I have to ask, are you romantically involved?"

"We're not. But there's no other girl in the entire world I'd pick. Not even the real Swift Jones. #SaveSwifty, #FreeSwifty, #GoTigerGo."

"Thank you for speaking with us," Hamilton says. "We now join the news conference beginning on the steps of the *Pennington Times*. Speaking is Mr. Markus Matthews, editor in chief of the *Pennington Times*."

There are at least a hundred people gathered in front of the podium where Mr. Matthews stands in a sweater and khakis, flanked by a gray-haired guy in a three-piece suit who must be the *Times*' lawyer. Flashes go off; sound techs hold out booms with additional mics. There are a dozen TV cameras filming. It's hard to believe all of this is because of Swifty. But it's not about Swifty. It's about the sensational details of *my* story. Who I am has ruined everything.

"Thank you for coming today," Mr. Matthews says. "I'd like to address the articles we've recently published by our reporter, Tiger Lillian Decker." The lawyer leans in, whispers in his ear. "Correction from the shiny shoes beside me," Mr. Matthews says. "Our *unpaid intern*, Tiger Lillian Decker. We adhere to the same standards as all legitimate news organizations. Our stories are responsible and vetted. That includes the link we posted of Howard Walker, Wild Walker's elephant trainer, abusing both his adult male elephant and the calf, Swift Jones." The lawyer leans in again. Mr. Matthews shakes his head. "We received *both* the article and the link from an offshore, untraceable site."

"That's not true. Whatever email address Christine uses, he has it."

Otis shakes his head. "He might think he does, but he's wrong. I set her up on the Tor network. It uses different relay proxies that redirect users along a random path."

"In English?"

"Her location and privacy are protected. Tor is a system that whistleblowers and abuse victims use. I learned everything I could about it so that I could help Christine disappear."

"Do you know where Decker is?" A reporter wearing a light gray hijab asks.

"I guess we've moved on to the Q and A," Mr. Matthews says. "I have no idea where she is, but of course the *Times* has been cooperating with the Florida law agencies investigating the kidnapping of Swifty Jones."

"It's Swift Jones," another journalist corrects.

"I like Swifty," Mr. Matthews says. "Has a nifty ring to it, dontcha think? Just like Tiger." The reporter actually nods. "Where was I?" Mr. Matthews asks. "If we receive further contact or correspondence from Tiger, we will turn over all information to the appropriate agencies."

"What do you, personally, think about what Tiger has done?" asks a hipster writer sporting a slouch hat.

"It makes a helluva story."

"Whose side are you on?" another reporter demands.

Mr. Matthews glowers at him. "Aren't we all on the side of truth? Or have we become so jaded that we're not concerned about saving a baby elephant's life?"

"Howard Walker plans to hold Tiger Decker responsible if Swifty dies," notes a journalist whose black beard completely obscures his mouth.

Mr. Matthews taps his lips like he's thinking. "Isn't he the guy who beats elephants with a barbaric weapon?"

"Save Swifty!" a few people shout.

"Aren't you minimizing the threat that Tiger may have had some kind of psychotic break?" the hipster asks.

I look at Otis. "They're all calling me Tiger." He nods but keeps his eyes on the TV.

"As far as I know, that kid isn't even remotely nuts," Mr. Matthews says. "To be perfectly honest, up until a few days ago I thought her most outstanding attribute was that she was quick to get my coffee, but after watching her video? I misjudged her. Tiger is willing to risk her future for what she believes in. What we should all believe in, if we're not callous, inhumane pricks."

An actual cheer goes up in the crowd.

"Do you feel it?" Otis asks.

I'm stuck on the fact that Mr. Matthews just defended me. "What?"

"The tide is starting to shift. The story is turning back to Swifty."

"Would you help Tiger evade the police if it meant getting more of her story?" the bald reporter asks.

Mr. Matthews shakes his head. "We will not thwart the law. Thank you for your time." He walks away from the microphone. CNC returns to its regularly scheduled news.

"Will it be enough?" I ask Otis.

One corner of his mouth tugs upward. It's not a smile, but it's a start. "Maybe—"

A coughing sound punctuates the air. I hear it again, strained, rattling. We both move quickly toward the screen door. Swifty stands at the foot of the steps. Her trunk twists into a knot, and she coughs again, harder, longer, harsher, then slowly crumples to the grass.

41

We kneel beside Swifty. As she coughs her trunk spirals like she's trying to get something out of it. Her stomach rumbles but there's no diarrhea, just foul smelling gas. Otis runs his hand over her belly.

"What's wrong with her?" I ask.

"I'm not sure."

Swifty starts trembling. I grab my backpack from the front seat of the truck, dig until I find Dr. Robertson's card.

"What are you doing?"

"During her interview, Addie said to call someone if anything went really wrong." I grab Christine's cell phone from inside the trailer and dial Dr. Robertson.

"She works for my family," Otis says.

I sit back down beside him. "I won't tell her where we are." The line rings three times before someone picks up.

"Dr. Robertson's office, how can I help you?"

I push the speakerphone button. "I need to talk to Dr. Robertson."

"She's with a patient right now. Are you an existing client?"

"No."

"I can take your name and number, have her call you back when she's free. Her schedule is pretty packed today so it'll probably be after five, or tomorrow morning."

"This is Lily Decker."

"Oh." I hear shuffling, the phone dropped, a door opening then whispered voices.

"Lily?"

"Thanks for taking my call."

"What's wrong, other than the obvious?"

"Swifty still isn't drinking much. She's had three enemas, but her energy is lower. She's started shaking, twisting her trunk, coughing—"

"Her stomach is rumbling, plus it's harder than normal," Otis adds.

"Ah," Dr. Robertson says, like a piece of the puzzle has fallen into place. "I thought it was your voice on that video. How's your family taking that, Otis?"

"Probably not well."

"What?" I stare at Otis, stomach plummeting because I don't want him to be a casualty, too. "You didn't cut your voice out? Otis, there's no going back!"

"In the past few days you fought harder for Swifty than I fought for Tambor my whole life. I didn't cut out my voice because this is my fight, too. And for the record, I don't ever want to go back."

We glare at each other. Swifty hacks again and both our hands reach to comfort her. "Okay," I say.

"Okay," Otis repeats.

"You two have that cleared up?" Dr. Roberston asks.

"Yes," we say in unison.

"Did you get that application in, Otis?"

"Yes."

"Let's hope it's still an option when all this is done. Now, does Swifty have gas but no diarrhea?"

"Yes," I say.

"Two things are going on. Calves who aren't drinking enough formula get hypothermia."

"How do we treat it?" I ask.

"Pile as many blankets as you have on her. Snuggle against her so she gets your body's warmth. If you have warm water bottles—"

"We don't," I say as Otis grabs blankets from the truck and piles them on the calf, tucking them tightly around her.

"Get some if you can. But that's not your biggest problem right now."

"What is?" I ask.

"I'm pretty sure Swifty has colic."

The calf coughs again. I run my hand along her throat, trying to smooth whatever's catching. "Is that a disease?"

"It's a sign, not a disease. Her dehydration has led to an inability to digest the formula. Her stomach is full of gas from the artificial milk fermenting in her gut. That causes a severe stomachache plus painful bloat. Can I convince you to let me come to you?"

"Ellie, we can't put you in that position," Otis says. "If you got caught, you'd lose your license."

"Otis, this is serious."

He clenches his jaw. "So tell us what to do."

Dr. Robertson sighs. "Continue the enemas. That will help make her gut secrete more mucus, which moves the gut, forcing the gas to pass, along with the undigested matter. Try to get her walking for fifteen or twenty minutes."

"She's weak," I say.

"Make her, and if you can? Get her Pedialyte."

"The stuff for babies?" I ask.

"It's a rehydration solution of sugar, water and salt that will replenish Swifty's missing electrolytes. It'll also help her intestines absorb more water. That will prevent further dehydration. Give it to her in half-strength, basically one-to-one with water."

"Okay. We can do that."

"Lily," Dr. Robertson says, "have you considered that your rescue attempt, as noble an idea as it was, may kill Swifty?"

It takes a second to find my voice. "Do you…do you think she would've died at Walker's?"

"That's not—"

"Psst."

I close my eyes.

"It's so thecret, the land of tears."

The correct quote is "mysterious" not "secret." I shove the voice into a deep drawer. "Tell me. Please."

"Yes. Once you and Dr. Tinibu left, my medical opinion is that Swifty would've died. But untreated colic will speed up that process."

My eyes open. "By how much?"

"My best guess? Days. What you two are doing is rash, unadvised. Frankly, it's insane. Sorry to use that word, given the details of this situation, but it is." Dr. Robertson clears her throat. "But…"

"But?"

"It might be the calf's only chance. A slim one, but still."

"Thank you for taking my call."

"You both know that I'm legally obligated to report this call to the authorities?"

I didn't, but it makes sense. "Do what you need to do."

Dr. Robertson exhales loudly. "Tell me you have a plan."

"We do," I say.

"I won't make that call and neither will my employee, but execute it fast."

"Thank you."

"Good luck to all three of you." Dr. Robertson hangs up.

Beneath my palm, Swifty's heart thuds. I can't tell if it's slower or faster now that she's so sick. I just know that it has to keep beating. "We need to drive to Texas, to the Sanctuary, now."

Otis shakes his head. "My family hasn't given up their claim."

"But you said the tide had changed."

"People are questioning Walker's. They're starting to focus on Swifty's plight instead of on you."

"So if we show up at the Sanctuary with a sick calf, they'll take her in."

"We won't make it there." Otis rests his chin on his knees. The bruise on the side of his mouth has darkened to purple. "By now my family has given the cops the truck's license plate number. They'll know what we're driving. Duct tape over Wild Walker's name won't fool the police. We'll be stopped within a few hours, maybe sooner. Lily, there're no more options. We hide out. Hydrate Swifty the best we can. Wait. Hope Walker's gives up their claim before we're discovered. Before it's—"

"Too late," I say softly. Flea brings over Nibs. Swifty scrunches her trunk, inch by inch, toward the stuffed animal but gives up even though the rabbit's ear is only an inch away. "We can't stay trapped." I dial another number. Put the phone on speaker. It rings one time.

"Tell me it's you," Sawyer says.

"It's me."

"Are you okay?"

No. "Yes. Are you?"

"Yeah."

"Sawyer? Seriously. Are you okay?"

"You were right," Sawyer says. "I've been stuck in one place, too. It's time to start living."

My eyes fill and overflow. I wipe away the tears. "The silver lining of this whole thing is that I'll have a ton of time to be a great best friend when I'm in prison."

"Looking on the bright side," Sawyer jokes, "nice. So where the hell are you?"

"Near Cedar, Florida. Hidden in the woods. The truck I have is the circus's. If I drive it, I'll get caught."

"You don't know how to drive."

"Otis does."

"Otis Walker?" Sawyer explodes.

"He's not like the rest of his family. Sound familiar?"

Sawyer's tongue ticks the top of his mouth. "Point taken. Is he there?"

"I'm here," Otis says.

"Why are you doing this?" Sawyer asks.

"For Swifty…and because Lily is the bravest person I know, too."

"We need money and a truck," I say.

"Lily, maybe you can stay put?" Sawyer asks. "The petition on Facebook has close to three hundred thousand signatures. Walker's will have to give up Swifty soon or they'll go out of business. Can she hold on?"

When I look at Swifty, even though I don't want to see it, it's obvious her eyes have dimmed. "I don't think so."

"Give me twenty minutes then call back."

"That fast?"

"Maybe. I have a lawyer on call, too, in case you need him."

"Who are you?" Otis asks.

"Lily's best friend. I'll hunt you down if you let anything bad happen to her."

I can't help grinning. "I love you, Wonder Woman."

"Lil? Charlie Hamilton gave me his phone number in case you called me. I can call him, give a message from you, if it'll help?"

"We'll keep it in mind," I say. "Sawyer?"

"Yeah?"

"I'm proud of you."

"I haven't done it yet."

"You will."

42

We manage to get Swifty to her feet. With Flea's help, the four of us circle the trailer for twenty minutes. We don't want to make Swifty get back into the truck so Otis tucks both dog and calf beneath blankets. I call Sawyer back. He picks up halfway through the first ring.

"I have to read you some tweets."

I put him on speaker. "Sawyer—"

"Tiger Decker is my hero," Sawyer says. "#GoTigerGo #SaveSwifty #FreeSwifty."

"I don't want to be anyone's hero."

"Calling all fans and famous friends," Sawyer reads. "Imperative! Sign Save Swifty petition. #FreeSwifty, #SaveSwifty. Lily? Swift Jones, THE VERIFIED SWIFT JONES, tweeted all of those."

"I don't understand what—"

"Lily," Sawyer shouts, "Swift Jones has fifty million followers! Only a handful of singers, Katy Perry is one, have more. What you're doing? It just skyrocketed to the moon. There's no way Walker's is going to be able to withstand this amount of pressure. Swift Jones, *the* Swift Jones, just buried them."

It's like my blood has turned to helium. "Otis?"

Otis looks like he's trying to keep his feet on the ground, too. "He's right. There's a real chance."

"We'll call you back." I hand Otis the phone. He dials then puts it on speaker.

"Wild Walker's Circus," a woman with a Spanish accent says.

"Carmen, transfer me to Tina or Max."

"Otis?"

"Yeah."

"Shit. Are you really with that girl?"

"I am."

"Amigo, your parents are worried and pissed off."

"I'm not surprised."

"They're in your father's office," she whispers. "Tina, Max, Howard and some crisis management lady named Tess."

"Thanks, Carmen. I'll talk to all of them, I guess."

Circus music plays for about three seconds before the line is picked up. "Otis?" Max asks. "That you?"

"Yeah, Dad, it's me."

"Are you okay?"

"Yeah."

"Then have you lost your mind?" Max demands.

"Saint Otis," Howard drawls. "How's the road trip?"

"Come home," Tina says. "We can work through this. Just come home before more damage is done."

"I hear you have Tess there. Has she told you that the singer Swift Jones tweeted her support for Tiger? She asked for all of her famous friends' and fans' help," Otis says. "With over fifty million followers who are retweeting that message as we speak and adding their own support, it'll be hard to survive the negative press if you don't let Swifty go."

"Otis, Tess here. Who knew when you put me on retainer that I'd end up working to get you out of the frying pan. Listen to me, son. Right now no one knows for sure that you're with that girl."

"Your point?" Otis asks.

"You can get out from under the grand larceny charges. Avoid prison. Kid, trust me, you don't want to go to prison in Florida."

"Maybe it'll be good for him," Howard says. "Character building."

Otis shakes his head. "This isn't about me. It's about saving Swifty's life."

"Otis, it doesn't matter anymore if the calf dies," Tess says. "It'll be Lily's fault, not yours or Walker's."

Howard laughs. "We win either way."

Otis closes his eyes like he's absorbing a blow. "Is there anything I can say to make you give up your claim on the calf?"

"After all Howard has been through? How could you do this to your brother?" Tina asks.

"Get your ass home," Max says. "Now!"

Otis ends the call. He twists the cheap phone, breaking it in half, and then pulls out the other phone Christine gave him.

I dial Sawyer. He answers immediately and I put him on speaker again.

"Well?" Sawyer asks.

"The Walker family won't give up their claim," I say. "We need a truck."

"To go where?"

"Viv Hemming's Elephant Sanctuary in Galton, Texas."

"Will they take Swifty?"

"I don't know. But Walker's isn't going to release Swifty, so they're our only hope."

"Are you going to call them?"

"No. We're going to show up at their sanctuary if you can get us that truck," Otis says.

Sawyer ticks his tongue on the roof of his mouth. "Okay. I talked to a guy in Glade, Florida, which is about ninety minutes from Cedar. He's willing to bring you his van."

"Can we trust him?"

"The Florida Youth Alliance oversees all the Gay-Bi-Trans clubs in the state. I told their outreach guy that I was moving to Cedar, wanted someone to contact from the nearest high school club. He gave me Wes Burnham's number. He's a senior on the football team—"

"So because he's gay and plays football we can trust him?" Otis asks.

"I'd say it's a fifty-fifty bet. Not great odds, but in Wes's favor? No one wanted him on that team. He had to fight for what's right. Plus, I offered him a serious amount of cash to help you and he said no. Actually, he told me to fuck off. That he was going to give you guys *his* money. Lily, it's the best I can do."

"It's a huge risk," I say to Otis. "Wes could call the police. And we might end up helping Uri find Christine."

Otis chews his lower lip. "It's too much of a risk for us

to leave, given that by now the cops will be looking for our truck. Wes is our best chance at this point, our only hope." He looks over at the trailer. Worry pinches his face. "I'll talk to Christine, make sure she's not here when Wes comes, that she has a fallback plan."

I wait a beat, just in case Otis changes his mind. "Okay. Sawyer, can Wes pick up some things?"

"I can ask."

"Bags of ice, warm blankets and a dozen bottles of Pedialyte. It's the hydration stuff they give babies. As many hot water bottles as he can find and jugs of water."

Otis gives Sawyer directions then hands me back the phone. I take it off speaker.

"Lily?" Sawyer says.

"Yeah?"

"You really okay?"

My heart pounds like I'm about to leap off a cliff with no certainty that there's water below. "Did I have a lisp?"

"What?"

"As a kid?"

My best friend ticks his tongue on the roof of his mouth. "No."

"You sure?"

"Yes."

My life is a long line of dominoes, each tile perfectly spaced, arranged in curves, diagonals, letters, images, spirals. It's a *new* person…a *new* voice. The quotes are wrong, because they're not coming from me. At least not the *me* I've been for eighteen years. I hold my breath, but the first domino falls anyway. The others follow in rapid succession until there's only one piece of me left standing. And then it topples, too. There should be a sound when a carefully constructed life literally collapses into ruin. But there isn't one. And no one is there to notice anything at all except me…and whoever the girl is who has invaded my brain.

"Lily?" Sawyer says.

"Give me a second." I've imagined this moment much of my life. I thought it would be different. Tears. Screams. Accusations. Immediate hospitalization. But it's strangely anticlimactic. Violet once punched me in the stomach so hard that I lost my breath. It's like that, without the pain. I wait for my lungs to inflate, wait for my new normal to settle onto my shoulders. It's heavy but bearable. It has to be bearable, because of Swifty.

Otis is staring at me. "Hey, Sawyer? Ask me questions seven and twelve from the test." My voice sounds almost normal. I hear a chair squeak, rustling, then something hits the floor and shatters.

"'Number seven. I can't trust what I'm thinking because I don't know if it's real or not. A, Not at all. B, Just a little. C, Somewhat. D, Moderately. E, Quite a lot. F, All the time.'"

"D."

"'Number twelve. I talk to another person or other people inside my head that nobody else can hear. A, Not at all. B, Just a little. C, Somewhat. D, Moderately. E, Quite a lot. F, All the time.'"

I take a deep breath. "D."

"Remember YouTube Emmy?" Sawyer asks.

"Yes."

Sawyer's tongue is ticking away again. He's trying to figure out if he can convince me to give up, come home, get help. “I love you,” he finally says.

“I love you, too.” I hang up, lean back against the trailer’s steps. Otis slides next to me, puts an arm around my shoulder.

“I was never angry,” Otis says. “I just felt...powerless.”

I nod. “I know what that’s like.”

“So your mom? She just changed one day? She became a totally different person?”

“It happened slower than that,” I say. “But yes, in the end I didn’t know her.” Otis is quiet. I imagine that, in his mind, he’s spinning a cigarette over his knuckles trying to process something I’ve struggled my whole life to understand.

“Do you know what freaks me out the most?” he finally says.

“What?”

“That someday you might not be you. Even then? I’m still all in, because you’re the most incredible person I know.”

They’re the most heartwarming and heartbreaking words I’ve ever heard. I lean in. Kiss Otis. He kisses me back. It’s not hot and steamy, although I still really like kissing him. This time? It’s more like a pact.

“What are questions seven and twelve?” Otis asks.

I think about telling him what’s going on in my brain. That I’m pretty sure I’m following in Violet’s footsteps.

“Lily?”

I could tell him about YouTube Emmy. She was a twenty-year-old girl whose mother had schizophrenia. One night a full moon caught Emmy’s eye and she was instantly certain that she could fly to it if she just leaped over her twenty-fourth-floor balcony. Emmy immediately went to a doctor and began taking antipsychotic meds. Five years later, and she's never had another hallucination. She has a job, a husband and a son.

Otis squeezes my hand. "You can tell me anything."

I could tell him about the continuing education talk by Lucy. Her schizophrenia hit during college when voices in her head started making demands and threatening her if she didn't follow their orders. After years of hospitalizations and failed attempts to find the right drugs, Lucy figured out how to discern between reality and her own delusions. She stopped fighting the voices—fighting always made things worse—and has a complex but good life.

But if I'm going to be honest, I'd also have to tell Otis that a lot of people with schizophrenia don't have a happily-ever-after. Many never find the right medications. Some go off them because the side effects are worse than the illness. YouTube Hannah talked about her memory being so bad from the medications that she couldn't recall her mornings during her afternoons. That could happen to me, too. I could forget Otis, Swifty. Sawyer. I could forget everything that ever meant anything to me.

I want to tell Otis that even if I end up with schizophrenia, there are some individuals who have one episode then never have another one. But it's also true that between 20 and 40 percent of those that have continued episodes attempt suicide and up to 10 percent succeed. Lives are derailed. Families are shattered. Dreams end. The only promise with schizophrenia is that there's both hope and despair.

I could tell Otis all these things, and someday soon I will, but for now this journey isn't about me.

There's a crunch of tires. Christine drives up to the trailer in a car that's more rust than metal. Otis gets up and follows her inside to warn her that she may no longer be safe living in these woods if the van delivery goes awry. Five minutes later, Christine briskly descends the steps with a duffel bag slung over one shoulder. She gets into her car without looking at me, does a quick U-turn and speeds down the road. I add Christine to the growing list of people who might end up hurt by my choices.

43

After the sound of Christine's tires fades away, Otis and I get beneath the blankets, sandwiching the calf between our bodies. We're roasting. Sweat drips down our foreheads. But there's no place else I want to be. My hand brushes Otis's. He twines our fingers together, holds tight.

"Do you think Wes will show up?" I ask.

"Yeah," Otis says, squeezing my hand. "You?"

"Yeah," I say. We're both kind of lying. "What application was Dr. Robertson talking about?"

"A five-year undergrad and veterinary medicine program. She wrote my letter of recommendation."

Otis was looking for a way out. I hope that he'll still get that chance.

"I wanted to quit being Walker's publicist two years ago," Otis says, "but I gave Christine every penny I'd saved. I needed more money to make school happen." His sigh is ragged. "In retrospect, I should've just gotten a job waiting tables. It would've taken longer but been better than ignoring what went on with our animals."

"If you hadn't stayed, you wouldn't have been there to help me, to help Swifty."

Otis squeezes my hand tight. Despite the sweltering heat, I slowly drift off. When I wake it's to Flea scampering out from beneath the blankets, barking at the dirt road. I scramble to my feet, Otis at my side, as a battered white van pitches over roots, coming toward us way too hot. Screeches fill the air as branches tear stripes down the vehicle's sides. The van stops ten feet away, kicking up dust. Flea growls like he's a German shepherd, instead of a thirty pounder with only one visible eye. I love that mutt.

A guy gets out of the van. He's Mr. Matthews big with a toothpick clenched between his teeth. Beefy arms stretch a gold-and-red football jersey tight, and a baseball cap rests on his brush-cut hair. "You're skinnier than you looked on TV," he says. "But that hair is intense. You look like some kind of hot war goddess."

My face burns, but not in a totally bad way. I go to push up my glasses, a nervous habit, and remember that they're still in the trailer.

"Where's the elephant?"

I nod toward the pile of blankets, pull them back to reveal Swifty. She blinks but doesn't move anything except the tip of her trunk. Flea growls like he's a rabid rottweiler.

"That little dog gonna bite me?"

"Maybe," Otis says. "He's protective of Swifty."

"Why you doing this?"

"Because if we'd left Swifty at Walker's Circus she was going to die," I say.

"She don't look so hot right now."

"She's really sick," I say. "That's why we need to take her to a place that can help her."

"Where's that?"

My heart bashes against my chest. Maybe Sawyer was wrong. Maybe we can't trust this guy. "Have you called the police?"

He kicks at the dirt like I just insulted him. "You nuts?"

"Some people think so," I say.

The guy's mouth splits into a grin, revealing a huge gap between his front teeth. "I'm Wes. Sawyer said you were on fire. You think you can save that baby elephant?"

"We're going to try."

Wes twists his mouth, the toothpick pointing sideways. "Pleased to meet you, Tiger." He eyes Otis. "And you are?"

"Otis Walker."

Wes frowns. "Walker as in Wild Walker's Circus?"

"Yes," Otis says.

"Don't you feel like a prick? Going against your family?"

Otis doesn't flinch. "No."

Wes tosses Otis his keys. "Cash in the glove compartment is from my whole football team, not just me. Don't worry, I didn't tell them where I was meeting you, even though they'd never squeal. There's also Pedialyte, ice, blankets, some junk food, Red Bull to keep you awake during your road trip, plus team shirts." He reaches into the passenger seat and pulls out four hot water bottles and a jersey. "Tiger, if you get the chance to meet the real Swift Jones, who is tweeting up a storm about you and that calf, you give her this shirt, you hear? Tell her the Glade Panthers love her."

I nod, because if I try to talk I'm going to cry. While Otis and Wes move the clean straw into the van, I heat a pot of water on Christine's stove and fill the hot water bottles. When I come back out, the guys are walking Swifty slowly toward the vehicle. "Wow," I say when I see inside it. The back windows have been spray painted black to ensure that Swifty will be hidden from other drivers. The paint is still wet in spots. The rows of bench seats are gone, replaced with a six-foot stack of wool blankets, lawn chairs, enough Pedialyte for ten elephant calves, jugs of water and the biggest cooler I've ever seen. Wes and Otis gently boost Swifty onto the fresh bed of straw. Otis places the warm water bottles along Swifty's belly, then we cover her with blankets a foot thick, her sweet face peering up at all of us.

Wes hands me his baseball cap. "Cover those mad curls."

I pull on the cap. "Thanks."

"Can I give Swifty a kiss?" I nod. Wes crawls over to the calf, kisses her forehead. "Stay strong, little warrior." He locks eyes with me when he climbs out of the van. "You, too, Tiger."

Otis gives Wes the truck's keys. "I don't need to tell you how important it is that you put as much distance as possible between us."

"I have a plan that includes the gnarliest back roads in the universe," Wes says, grinning. "Took 'em to get here and only saw two other cars."

He follows us down the narrow driveway. I glance back at Christine's trailer, where, once we're gone, she'll be able to return and remain safely hidden from Uri. I can't help thinking that she's as trapped in there as the animals at Walker's Circus. At the end of the road we take a left. Wes turns right. There's a map in the glove compartment, and I plot the shortest route to Texas. Given the distance, it should take about eleven hours. I turn on the radio so we can listen for news updates, then reach for Otis's hand. We drive into the darkness, toward the unknown, because there is still a chance for Swifty.

44

Violet sits on the edge of the roof, her bare feet dangling. Below are fire trucks, police cars with flashing blue lights, a TV crew with cameras trained upward. "'There is a saying in the Neverland that, every time you breathe, a grown-up dies,'" Violet says.

"I don't want you to die," I say.

"Then come with me."

My own bare feet, dangling beside Violet's, are no longer a child's. "You know I'd do anything for you."

"I know."

"But I'm like Wendy, not Peter."

"Wendy Darling chose to grow up. But you don't have to. Don't you see?" Violet asks. "It's up to you." The wind picks up, blowing dark curls away from our nearly identical faces, though Violet has fine lines around her green eyes.

"Lily?"

"Call me Tiger. I get it now. The name was your hope."

Violet smiles. "It was my gift. Tiger, can we talk about your father?"

"I guess."

"He gave up his dreams for both of us."

It's true. "I don't hate him."

"Then don't punish him for being flawed, for loving me most."

I reach for Violet's hand. "I'll try not to."

"Your father hung the stars for me even though he was terrified of heights."

"You were brave, too."

Violet blinks back tears. "I was always afraid."

"That's what made you brave."

Violet shifts forward, so that she's perched on the very edge of the rooftop. "I did love you."

"I know." I let go of her hand.

"Tiger?"

I open my eyes. The dome light above casts the back of the van in weak yellow light. It's pitch-black outside. I'm resting beneath a foot of wool blankets, arms wrapped around Swifty. Fear makes my heart lurch. I check for the calf's heartbeat. It thuds beneath my hand. She's asleep. "What time is it?"

"After four in the morning."

"Crap. Sorry. I slept through Swifty's last feeding." I sit up. Flea is stretched in his usual spot by Swifty's head.

"Didn't want to wake you," Otis says. "I took care of it."

"How much did she drink?"

"A quarter bottle of diluted Pedialyte."

"Has she peed at all?"

"No."

"Gotten up?"

"No."

Otis has parked on a deserted country road. Water heats on the camp stove Wes supplied. I open the back of the van, dump out the now-cool water bottles then help Otis fill them. We place them along Swifty's back and belly. "She's not shaking. That has to be good, right?" Otis nods. "How much farther?"

"A little over three hours." Otis pulls chips out of the junk-food bag Wes left for us. The smell of barbecue fills the van. My mouth is beyond dry, eyes gritty. I slug down a bottle of orange Gatorade from the cooler, eat a few chips then give the rest to Flea. In our rush to leave Walker's, we forgot his food so he's been getting people food, which might upset another dog's stomach, but Otis's mutt appears to have an iron gut.

"You were talking in your sleep. What were you dreaming about?"

"My mom."

"Was it a nightmare?"

"Psst."

It's okay, I tell the voice inside my brain. I understand my dream. "It wasn't a nightmare," I say. "It was a chance to say goodbye." The words *Glade Panthers* come over the radio. Otis dives to turn up the volume.

"...and in another strange twist, eight members of Florida's Glade Panthers, a high school football team that has won State the past two years, were stopped an hour outside Haven, Florida, by police. They were driving the truck stolen from Wild Walker's Circus by Tiger Decker. Police believe the vehicle was used to kidnap Swift Jones, now the most famous elephant calf in the world. The police questioned the football players separately, but all of their stories were identical. They found the circus truck six hours east of Haven and decided to return it to Wild Walker's Circus. Spray-painted in red and gold on the truck's side were the hashtags: Save Swifty, Free Swifty and Go Tiger Go.

"Currently the Panthers team members are outside Wild Walker's Circus's front gate, where they're participating in what the police are calling a peaceful sit-in. Several hundred protesters have joined the young men, all with posters that read Go Tiger Go and Free Swifty. The Save Swifty petition on Facebook now has over fifteen million names on it. You heard right. Fifteen million thanks, in large part, to the support of singer Swift Jones and her fans. We'll keep you posted as this story plays out."

An advertisement for miniature golf comes on. Otis turns the radio off. "Holy shit."

"Fifteen million names?" I repeat, stunned. "You did it, Otis. You turned the focus back to Swifty."

Otis shakes his head. "It wasn't me. It was you, Tiger."

I pinch the skin beneath Swifty's eyes. It's still tenting. "Come here, little one," I say, pulling out a bottle of Pedialyte. Swifty nuzzles me, half slumping onto my lap like a giant puppy. She gets her trunk over my shoulder but doesn't wrap it around my neck. She manages to swallow a third of the bottle then starts mouthing my curls with her sticky lips. "Are you trying to make me look even worse?" I ask. There's a twinkle in her eyes that reminds me of shooting stars. "You are naughty." The calf coughs, the sound rattling in her throat.

Otis repositions the straw and Swifty slumps onto it. We place hot water bottles around her body then cover her with the remaining blankets. Flea crawls under them, snuggling against Swifty's chest despite the sweltering heat. As Otis packs the camp stove into the back, I get into the driver's seat. "Teach me to drive."

"Slide forward."

Otis climbs behind me, his legs straddling mine, worn jeans soft on the bare skin beyond my shorts. He shows me how to push the clutch down with my left foot, shift into first. His hand covers the top of mine as we move the stick.

"Now ease up on the clutch as you press down slowly on the accelerator," Otis says.

I do, and we lurch but don't stall, slowly rolling forward.

"Now press the clutch down again with your left foot." Otis guides my hand from first, to second. "A little gas then clutch again."

We shift into third, then fourth gear. I've watched other people drive my entire life, so it's not hard. It's more of a timing thing.

"Now shift down."

I do.

"Again."

I manage it without lurching. The van slows.

"You're a natural," Otis says.

He drops his hand, moves his feet to the side, and I'm driving. A small smile lifts the corners of my mouth. "Swifty? Can you see me? I'm driving. I'm driving you to the Sanctuary. More than fifteen million people want us to get there because they love you." I glance over my shoulder. The calf is watching me.

"Why didn't you ever learn to drive?" Otis asks.

"I told people it was because I couldn't afford insurance, let alone a car."

"But?"

"When she was off her meds, my mom's driving was...erratic. I was scared she would hit a pedestrian. Then, when it was my turn, I decided it was too stressful having to worry that I might hurt someone, eventually."

"What made you change your mind?"

"Today this is something I can do."

Otis starts to slide away. "Wait," I say. For a few seconds I lean back, his chest warm, his arms holding me just tight enough. "Okay. I've got this." Otis goes back with Swifty, and I drive us toward Galton, Texas.

45

Massive steel posts strung with thick wire appear long before we get to a sign for the Sanctuary. The fences border rolling hills, some thickly covered with stands of pines, others filled with tall, golden grasses. I roll down my window. The air smells like freshly tilled dirt. Flea, perched on Otis's lap, sticks his head out the window, sniffing, then hops back to Swifty, like he wants to tell her about all the sights and smells. Her eyes open, but she doesn't move. I slow the van by a silver sign. It's set to the right of twenty-foot-tall gates made from twisted steel that forms the bodies of elephants, their trunks holding the tails in front of them. Through their outlines, I can see blue sky, the sun and white clouds. That's what elephants are made of—sunshine, endless sky, the strength of steel.

THE SANCTUARY
#1 ELEPHANT WAY
NO VISITORS

"THE QUESTION IS, ARE WE HAPPY TO SUPPOSE THAT OUR GRANDCHILDREN MAY NEVER BE ABLE TO SEE AN ELEPHANT EXCEPT IN A PICTURE BOOK?"

I turn the engine off. Neither Otis nor I move. The road on the other side of the gate climbs a large hill until it disappears. Somewhere in the distance is help for Swifty. Somewhere in the distance is her new home. "The Sanctuary has over three thousand acres. Plus a twenty-five-acre lake, heated barns, separate habitats for Asian and African elephants."

"Lily?"

"They believe that abused elephants can help each other heal if they have the freedom to move like they do in the wild, and if they can live without the fear of being hurt by humans."

"Tiger?"

"What if they won't take her?"

"It's time to find out."

I get out of the van, walk to the call box to the left of the gate, press zero. The box rings twice before being answered.

"Viv Hemming's Elephant Sanctuary," a man's voice says.

I haven't thought about what to say. I don't know what to say. My knees buckle. I kneel, my hands flat on the dirt, like I can stop the earth from spinning, freeze time. Because right now Swifty is still alive and there's a future for her. Right now I recognize the difference between reality and schizophrenia. Otis gets out of the van. He crouches beside me. "I'm afraid," I whisper. "What if I say the wrong thing? What if they turn us away?"

"What if they don't?" Otis asks. He puts his hands on my cheeks, presses our foreheads together.

I try to breathe. Otis waits. "Okay," I finally say, standing. I press zero.

"Hello?" the same man says.

"Tiger Decker to see Viv Hemming." There's no response.

"Hello?" Nothing. I press zero again. No answer. They don't want to talk to me. They don't want Swifty. They're calling the police. This is over.

Squeezing my shoulder, Otis points toward a speck at the top of the hill. We watch it wind down the road until we make out a white pickup truck. There are racks on top and the road crunches beneath its tires. Otis reaches for my hand. I can't even feel his touch. The truck gets closer and closer. It stops five feet from the gate. We can't see through the darkly tinted windows. The engine is cut. Silence punctuates our Hail Mary pass. Both front doors open in unison. The driver walks toward the gate. He's wearing a knit hat with the Sanctuary logo of intertwined elephant trunks over short, black hair, jeans and a gray, thermal long-sleeved shirt. My guess is he's in his forties, but his fair skin is unlined.

"Tiger?" the man asks.

"Yes."

"James Chi. I'm one of the veterinarians that work for Viv." He extends his hand through the gate's bars.

We shake, but he doesn't open the gate. Why isn't he opening the gate? The truck's other passenger joins James. She's in jeans, a plaid flannel shirt and worn cowboy boots. "Viv Hemming," she says. Her dark blond hair is pulled back in a ponytail. I'd peg her at close to sixty, but her deeply tanned face has that forever-young look where all the wrinkles are just character lines.

"And you are?" Viv asks Otis.

"Otis Walker."

"I wasn't expecting that." Viv shakes Otis's hand then mine. "You two have caused quite a stir."

"I'm sorry. It wasn't supposed to be about me," I blurt.

Viv's gray eyes sweep toward the van. "Swifty in there?"

"Yes," I say. "She's really sick. She had hypothermia. We've used blankets and hot water bottles for the past thirteen hours. She's stopped shaking, but she's still dehydrated and has colic."

James frowns. "Symptoms?"

"Sticky mouth, skin tenting, very little urine, stomach rumblings, coughing, twisting her trunk. We've given her warm water enemas and half-strength Pedialyte, but she's lethargic, weak. Please," I say, "can you help her?"

"Viv, they've been doing the right things so far," James says. "If we step in now, she has a real chance."

She frowns, shakes her head. "Our Sanctuary is supported by private donors. A board of directors governs us. This entire facility is built on federal land and the government granted us our tenure. If we open the gates, let Swifty through, we would put our tenure at serious risk. We could also lose most of our grant money and donors who don't believe in breaking the law or that the end justifies the means. Plus, we, personally, would be accessories to a crime."

I have to say the words. "Swifty is dying."

Two deep grooves appear between Viv's brows. "What about all the elephants we've saved? The ones we're still trying to save? Are their lives less valuable than your one calf?"

"Is Daisy still alive and producing milk?" I ask.

"You're the one who called?"

"Yes."

"Daisy is alive and still has milk," James says. He turns to Viv. "We've got to."

Viv shakes her head. "You know that I'm right about this."

"Since when did saving a struggling calf become a crime?" James asks.

"Since she was stolen," Viv snaps.

"If you're still giving her formula, stop," James says to me. "Until she's rehydrated it'll just continue to ferment in her belly. Push the Pedialyte. Continue the enemas." James hesitates, watching Viv. She says nothing. He stalks back to the truck, gets in, slams the door.

"He's a great doctor with a soft heart for the calves." Viv tucks a strand of hair back into her ponytail. "My best advice is to call your family, Otis. Ask them to give up their claim. If they do, we'll gladly open the gates." She meets my eyes. "Tiger, we want to let Swift Jones in. But if the Walker family won't release her, ask them to send a vet and plane transport so you can try to save her life."

"You know that won't save her life," I say.

Viv kicks at a stone. "I'm truly sorry."

"Are you going to call the police?" I ask.

"No. Believe it or not, I was rooting for you like the rest of the world," Viv says. "I'm sorry, Tiger. What you tried to do? It was for the right reasons. But some battles can't be won."

"Life isn't a fairy tale," I say.

Viv shoves her hands into jean pockets. "I know it doesn't matter to you right now, but the level of awareness you created on behalf of elephants was unbelievable, powerful. Last I checked, twenty-one million people from around the world had signed the Save Swifty petition. Powerful people, politicians, celebrities, even major news anchors like Charlie Hamilton are talking about the plight of elephants. Swifty may die, but other elephants will be saved. They'll gain freedom because of you." Viv walks back to the truck. James does a U-turn and the two people who might've saved Swifty's life drive away.

Otis and I sit in the dirt, leaning our backs against a gate that will never open for Swifty.

46

We open the back doors of the van. Swifty lifts her head but doesn't try to stand. At least she can see the clear, blue sky. We sit next to her, our hands running over her skin like Raki's trunk did when she welcomed her baby into the world. I try to memorize the feeling beneath my fingertip, the way the wrinkles connect like an ancient map.

Otis gets Swifty to drink ten sips of Pedialyte before she kind of crumbles onto her bed of straw and blankets. My chest hurts like a deep wound. The tip of Swifty's trunk wriggles. She's trying to make me smile. I do, for her, then sprinkle kisses along her hollowed-out cheeks. Flea watches me. He hasn't moved from Swifty's side in hours. He knows I broke my promise to her. "I'm sorry," I tell them both.

"Do you want me to call my family?"

I try to swallow around the rock lodged in my throat but can't. "Dr. Robertson said she'd die at the circus." I struggle with the part of me that's still a coward. "It would be the easy way out, not being there for her…in the end. Not bearing witness, you know?" Tears drip off my jaw. Otis is crying, too. "I knew this might happen, that she might...but I wanted it to be behind those gates," I say. Swiping at my tears, I force my chin to stop quivering. "I vote that we stay here, with Swifty."

"Agreed." Otis hangs his head. "From the time I was little, all I can remember is Max saying that our name meant everything, that we should have pride as a multigenerational circus family, never tarnish our legacy. Tiger, I helped shape that legacy." Otis slams his fist against the metal side of the van, denting it. "Right now I'm sure Max is raging about what I've done to darken the Walker name. But I'm just ashamed to be one of them."

There's an itch in my brain. I try to ignore it because I'm not sure how much longer I'll be able to sit by Swifty, feel the thrum of her heart, breathe in her scent. I scratch behind her ear. She smiles. She smiles for me. *Multigenerational, pride, family name, tarnish, legacy...* "Why was it so important to bury Howard's past? I mean, Max could've created a story about how his son was wrongfully accused, how he was protecting his little brother from a pedophile."

Otis shakes his head. "Anyone who read Howard's record would see that he mutilated that guy. A circus can't be advertised as clean family entertainment with a violent, convicted murderer as the elephant trainer. Who'd want their kids around that kind of monster? Plus, Max *believes* in his legacy. I'm not willing to train our animals. Howard is. That means Howard is Wild Walker's future. Max will live on through him."

"So your father did what it took to get Howard out of

prison. Then he had his record sealed so it could never be dug up to mar Wild Walker's reputation." Our eyes lock. We have one last chance. I grab the cell phone and dial Sawyer.

"Where are you?"

"Outside the Sanctuary's gates. They won't let us in because Walker's still refuses to give up their claim."

"Lily, I'm sorry. This probably isn't the time, but I did something—"

"Just listen! Call Charlie Hamilton. He has to interview us—"

"I already called him. He's in Galton, waiting for me to talk to you, to see if you're willing to let—"

The phone dies. "Crap."

"We don't have a charger," Otis says.

"It's okay." My best friend is the smartest person I know. While we wait for the news anchor from CNC to arrive, we make a plan.

47

Twelve minutes later a silver, two-door car comes down the road. It slows by the gate, parks. A lean man in jeans and a loose, white, button-down shirt steps out. A dark blue baseball cap covers closely cropped brown hair. Mirrored sunglasses hide his eyes. I peer down the road. No other cars appear.

"I took a private plane here last night," Charlie Hamilton says. "Got here as fast as I could without being detected. A CNC fixer—that's someone we count on when we need to fly under the radar—arranged for my rental car and hotel room. The key was in the car that he parked in the short-term lot. I didn't see a single person at four in the morning when I let myself into my hotel room. I stayed there until I got Sawyer's call. No one saw me leave the hotel or followed me here."

"Wow," I say. "This is the cherry on top of the Anti Twelve-Year Plan."

Hamilton takes off his sunglasses, laser-blue eyes studying me. We shake. "Good to meet you, Tiger."

"You, too, Mr. Hamilton."

"Call me Charlie."

"Okay."

"You've lost your glasses."

"Mr.... Charlie, they were fake," I say.

He smiles. "Mine are fake, too."

"Not to insult you, but how do we know you haven't called the police?" Otis asks.

"Sawyer drafted a confidentiality agreement that forbids me to disclose your location to anyone." Charlie shakes his head. "Kid his age had a lawyer on speed dial to vet it. I signed before he told me where you were. He loves you a ton."

"More than Swift Jones, the singer," I say.

"Yes," Charlie agrees. "I asked Sawyer for an exclusive interview with you, *if* you agreed."

"Agreed," I say.

He holds out his hand to Otis. "I'm sorry, you are?"

"Otis Walker."

Charlie blinks three times, like he's recalculating. "I'd like to interview you, as well."

Otis nods. "I was hoping you'd say that."

"First, do you want to meet Swifty?" I ask. Our plan hinges on the anchor believing she deserves a chance. Flea watches but doesn't growl as the news anchor climbs into the van and sits beside Swifty, gently touching her cheek.

"I'm sorry about all this, sweet girl," Charlie says. He looks at me. "Is she going to be okay?"

Otis and I sit side by side in the van. "Not without your help."

"Off or on the record?" Charlie asks.

"Off for now?" I ask.

"Okay."

"My family refuses to give up their claim on Swifty," Otis says. "They know she's dying. At this point they hope it happens before they get her back, so that her death will be Tiger's and my fault instead of their own."

"Whose fault is it?"

"It's complicated," I admit.

"Why?" Charlie presses.

"Because there is no perfect solution to animal care and conservation once animals are taken from the wild," I say. "But for now? Let's take it from the moment Walker's claimed Swift Jones. They should've allowed the Pennington Zoo to keep her. The zoo has a full-time, experienced veterinarian, dedicated caretakers and they planned to slowly reintroduce Raki to her calf. It was Swifty's best chance for survival."

"Why didn't Walker's let that happen?" Charlie asks.

"Baby elephants sell tickets," Otis says. "Also, my brother, Howard, wanted Swifty."

"And Howard carried a lot of weight in the decision?"

"To my parents, Tina and Max, Howard is the future of Wild Walker's Circus."

"What about you?"

"I refused to train animals."

"The abuse on the video?"

"Real and frequent." Otis leans in. "I'd like to say that Howard is complicated. That he loves his elephants, that he wants a great life for them, that he strives for the best outcomes in an imperfect situation, same as zoo directors like Dr. Tinibu. But Howard is a sociopath. He's been that way his entire life."

Swifty's eyes clench shut, her trunk writhes.

"Has she gotten sicker?" Charlie asks.

I nod. "Besides being depressed, she has colic. If it's not treated, it will kill her even more quickly than her other issues."

"And if it is treated?"

"If she's given great medical care and is surrounded by female elephants and calves? She has a chance. But unless the circus gives up their claim, the Sanctuary can't treat Swifty without risking the loss of their foundation."

"And what about you?" He studies my face. "How are you doing, Tiger?"

It's complicated. "I'm fine."

Charlie looks from Otis to me. "So what's your plan?"

"I want to call my family from your phone," Otis says. "Threaten to tell you the one secret that no amount of digging, whether you have fixers or not, will be able to turn up. We'd like you to film that conversation and let Walker's know that you're filming it."

"If they agree to give up their ownership in return for keeping the secret?"

Raw nerves make my skin tingle. "If Walker's Circus gives up their claim, then you don't get to know the secret."

"And this secret?" Charlie asks, not missing a beat.

A muscle in Otis's jaw clenches. "Would destroy my family's name and their circus."

Charlie hands Otis his phone then unzips the duffel at his side, pulling out a small video camera. "We have a deal."

I control the urge to hug the news anchor really hard.

"Wait, use my camera," I say. "That way you can't get into trouble over the tape."

He takes the camera and says, "Tiger, you're a natural."

Otis dials then puts the phone on speaker while Charlie videotapes him.

"Wild Walker's Circus. How may I direct your call?"

"Carmen, it's Otis. Put me through to Max."

The line rings once. "Otis, have you come to your senses?" Max says.

"Who's there?" Otis asks.

"Your mother, our crisis gal, Tess, and—"

"Hey, O," Howard drawls. "Starting to think somebody's big brother shoulda let his little brother get torn up after all. No good deed goes unpunished, I guess."

"Tiger and I are here with Charlie Hamilton," Otis says.

"Bullshit," Max says.

"FaceTime us," Otis challenges. Charlie crosses over to our side of the van, sits down beside Otis. The only background visible is the beat-up metal of the van.

Max appears on the screen. The anchor nods at him. "Mr. Walker? Charlie Hamilton."

"I'm hanging up," Max says.

"Wait." Tess appears over Max's shoulder. Her face is painfully thin and the same shade of gray as the hair she scraped into a low bun. "Mr. Hamilton, you do realize, sir, that you cannot record this phone conversation without our permission?"

"Otis and Tiger are taping it with their own camera. My guess is they're not worried about the legality of that decision, considering the trouble they're in."

"What do you want, Otis?" Tess asks.

"The Walker family to give up their claim to Swifty," Otis says. "Otherwise, I'm prepared to tell Mr. Hamilton the family secret that will ruin our name, our business and Max's legacy. You have ten minutes."

"Otis, wait," Tess says.

Otis hangs up. I rest my hand on his thigh.

Charlie presses a button on his phone. "Call Sam Boone." He puts the phone on speaker. The line rings once.

"Boone here. What's up?"

Charlie says, "I need a down and dirty contract."

"Spell it out."

"Wild Walker's Circus gives up all legal claim to the elephant calf, Swift Jones. Further, they agree to drop all charges against Tiger Lillian Decker and Otis Walker for the theft of Swift Jones or anything libelous they've said or done during that process. In return Otis Walker will not tell me, or any other reporter, the private information he has on the Walker family's secrets under penalty of blah, blah, blah."

Otis and I look at each other. We never thought about getting ourselves off the hook.

"Where should I send the contract?" Boone asks.

"990-555-7979," Otis says.

"When you get it back, signed by both Max and Tina Walker, send it to the Elephant Sanctuary in Galton, Texas. Attention Viv Hemming. Text me when it's done."

"Will do."

48

We've done all we can for Swifty. Her sand is running quickly through an hourglass. There's no stopping it. Charlie's hand rests on Swifty's foot. There's a scab on the top where Howard punctured it with the ankus. I trace the calf's trunk. Otis shifts to rest his hand on her head. Flea lies between Swifty's front legs, one paw on her chest like he's monitoring her heartbeat. What a strange, impossible, determined team we make.

Charlie picks up the camera. The red light blinks as he films Swifty's trunk wrapping around my wrist. She coughs, the force rattling her body. I spoon her, my arm hugging her belly. Her heartbeat thuds against my chest. "I love you. If you need to fly," I say, because I can't bear her suffering, "you can fly."

"Tiger, there are twenty-nine million–plus signatures on the Save Swifty petition," Charlie says. "What you've done, both of you, so quickly, is…it's unheard of."

That number is unfathomable. I know Charlie is trying to make us feel better. I'm glad he's still taking video. It seems wrong not to have a record of this day. "It's a huge number," I say. "Swift Jones's tweets made all those signatures happen and I'm—" I look at Otis "—we're really grateful."

"Swift Jones only became involved because of what you said," Charlie points out.

He's right, I guess. We started the ball rolling. But none of it matters anymore. "The thing I used to be most afraid of in the entire world," I say, "is hearing a person I didn't know talking in my head because that would mean I had schizophrenia."

"And now?" Charlie asks.

"Swifty dying. I would give anything if she were more than just a story. If her life could've mattered enough for Walker's to have seen she was more than ticket sales. I'd trade my future for hers."

"What about you, Otis? You've lost your family."

"I chose another one."

Swifty coughs again, her trunk repeatedly twisting. Tears fill then overflow her eyes. Charlie lowers the camera. "No. Keep filming," I say, letting the salty tracks run down Swifty's face even though all I want to do is wipe them away. "People need to see this."

"Why?" Charlie asks.

"I once thought that Addie—Dr. Tinibu—was exaggerating when she said that elephants cry for the same reasons humans cry. That they feel things just as strongly as we do, remember them even longer. After Raki rejected her, Swifty cried for hours. I want people to see her tears, to know that in any life, elephant or human, they mean despair."

"Tiger." Charlie clears his throat. "You've opened a dialogue about animals in both zoos and circuses and become an outlaw hero in the process. What does that mean to you?"

"An outlaw hero?" I trace the curled border of Swifty's delicate ear. "I didn't even start that petition. People who cared more about Swifty than I did started it. Dr. Tinibu, who's trying to save animals from extinction the only way she knows how, Viv Hemming, who fights for abused and sick elephants. All the animal activists out there are the heroes. Me? I'm a girl with an extremely uncertain future. There wasn't that much for me to lose." My thoughts coalesce. "I didn't really like who I was, before Swifty. Maybe because I did everything out of fear, you know? I was trying to stay in control, eke out as much time as I could before schizophrenia took me down. But if you don't feel anything, what's the point?"

"You tell me," Charlie says.

"Swifty has taught me that it's not about how long I live as me, it's about *how* I live that matters."

Charlie's cell phone chimes. He doesn't pick up until the third ring. "Hello?" he says, like he has no idea who might be on the line. "Let me put you on FaceTime." He hands Otis the phone, picks up the camera, filming.

Max's face fills the screen. "Agreed," he says.

I wait for joy to flood my body, but the moment is bittersweet, because we have what we wanted but it may be too late.

"Otis?" Max says.

"Yes?"

"We loved you the best we could, despite what you did. You're on your own now."

"Sign the agreement in the next minute," Charlie says, "or I'll start the interview with your son." He ends the call.

I meet Otis's gaze then look into the calf's bottomless brown eyes. "'I wonder...if the stars are lit up so that each of us can find his own, someday.'"

"You memorized *The Little Prince*?" Charlie asks.

"No. Some quotes just stick in my head."

"What about secrets?" Otis asks, his eyes the warm blue of the sea.

"What do you mean?"

"When this is over, consider telling Charlie my family's secret."

My heart aches because it's both breaking and expanding. "Otis?"

"I promised not to tell him, but I already told you. Do what you want with what you know. Fair warning, though—the Walker family will try to sue you."

I let the idea settle. There may be a chance to find Tambor a better home—maybe all of Walker's animals. It's a battle worth taking on.

"Psst."

Yes?

"People have forgotten thith truth, thaid the dog. But you mustn't forget it. You become responsible forever for what you've tamed." Antoine de Saint-Exupéry, but again the quote is wrong. It's "fox," not "dog." There's a soft buzzing in my ears. Just outside the van, I glimpse a blond-haired little girl. The edge of a white nightgown scattered with pink rosebuds catches my eye before she runs out of sight. It's my first visual hallucination, but I smile anyway because I will fight to throw as many stones, create as many ripples, as possible.

A text pings on Charlie's phone. He holds it up for us to see: Signed. Airtight.

This time the white truck comes down the road so fast that plumes of dirt rise at every corner. The gates are opened before it reaches us. We get out of the way as James and his team run over, climb into the back of our van. They try to push Flea out, but he growls like he's Cujo.

"He's her best friend," I say.

James glances back at me. "Then the mutt stays—you and Otis, too. Swifty will need all of you to help her fight her way back."

Flea settles by Swifty's head, Nibs in his mouth. Charlie films as the Sanctuary's team start taking care of the calf before the van is even started. I don't ask James if Swifty will live. He doesn't know. But beyond the gates is a mother who lost her baby. And there are other female elephants and calves waiting to welcome Swifty into her new family. She will never be afraid, hurt or lonely again. There will still be fences. Life isn't a fairy tale. But there are all different kinds of happily-ever-after.

The invisible line that connects the calf's heart to mine tugs hard. I welcome the pain. Swifty will take a piece of me with her, wherever she goes. I believe that neither of us will ever forget.

★ ★ ★ ★ ★

acknowledgments

It took a lot of people to bring *When Elephants Fly* to life. The first thank-you is always for my husband, Henry. He believes when I don't. He's my first and last reader, my partner in everything, absolute love and the best human being I know.

Thank you to my agent, Stephanie Kip Rostan of Levine Greenberg Rostan, and her associate agent, Sarah Bedingfield. They answered my query, read Lily's story and gave it wings. Steph, you are super smart, kind, supportive *and* you make dreams come true. How cool is that? I'm very lucky and incredibly grateful.

Thanks also to LGR's foreign rights director, Beth Fisher; business manager, Melissa Rowland; and contract attorney, Kristen Wolf.

To Natashya Wilson, editorial director at Harlequin TEEN, thank you for loving Lily's story and working so hard to make *When Elephants Fly* the best book possible! Every time you said you cried while reading, I was elated. Sorry! But knowing how Lily's journey affected you made me certain you were the right choice to publish her story.

Thank you to the whole Harlequin TEEN team! Copyediting, proofreading and production team: Heather Martin, Ingrid Dolan, Tamara Shifman, Kristin Errico, Nicole Rokicki and Peter Cronsberry. Art director, Gigi Lau. Publicity director, Shara Alexander. Publicity manager, Laura Gianino, and Publicists, Crystal Patriarche, Savannah Harrelson, and their team at Booksparks. Library marketing, Linette Kim. The Toronto marketing team: Amy Jones, Bryn Collier, Evan Brown, Krista Mitchell, Olivia Gissing and Aurora Ruiz. Natashya's terrific assistant, Gabrielle Vicedomini. My sincere thanks as well to the tremendous Sales team: Jennifer Sheridan and Jessie Elliott for the early support and enthusiasm, Andrea Pappenheimer, Kerry Moynagh, Kathy Faber, Jennifer Wygand, Heather Doss, Heather Foy and everyone else who worked so hard to put this book into the hands of readers.

Writing a book requires readers willing to slog through early drafts and criticize them without crushing an author's spirit. For *When Elephants Fly*, it also required sharing really personal stories, discussing legal and medical ins and outs and being a supportive friend willing to listen as I rambled on about story; plot; concerns about portraying mental health conditions with respect while still allowing Lily to be a teen with her own point of view and voice; and my fears about the future of elephants.

Apologies if I've forgotten anyone!

My thanks to Judy Frey and Michelle Goguen for their friendship, honesty and keen reading eyes through each draft. Sue Bishop (my sister) and Jane and Art Richardson (my folks), thank you for reading, always listening and being in my corner. I'm so very lucky to have you. Trent Burgess, Karen Ford, Colleen Jones, Eric Bernstein, Daryl and Doug, and Carol

Holdsworth, thanks for your spot-on feedback and support. Kristie Mitchell, thank you for our talks and being there when I needed you. Shannen Fogarty, thanks for that awesome trip to the zoo, your wicked sense of humor and for being Boone's second mom (joy!). Erin Burnham, thank you for being so supportive of my writing over the years and your medical expertise. Nancy Potter, thanks for the legal input. Rebecca Kenney and Tamson Weston, thank you for the early reads and ideas. Boone Fischer, thank you for the wiggles and unconditional love. And Ridgeway Cook, enormous thanks—you know why.

Mitch Finnegan, veterinarian at the Portland Zoo, you have an incredible, difficult and amazing job taking care of every animal at the zoo. It doesn't seem possible that all that knowledge can fit in one person's brain! The tour and education was an eye-opener, and your medical know-how kept Swift Jones hydrated on her road trip, perhaps saving her life.

It's so important to me that Lily's story, while fictional, be accurate and plausible from a psychiatric perspective. Dr. Rick Cohen, thank you for your time, insights and suggestions. I imagine your patients are very lucky to have you!

To the friends and family who have faced difficulties, struggled, sometimes failed, but never stopped trying, as well as everyone who shared their stories of mental health conditions, whether in books, films, videos, lectures or in person, my thanks are not enough. You bare your souls so that we can understand your battles. You are brave, intelligent, perceptive and deserve a life filled with love, laughter and wonder.

Please don't give up. There is always hope.

author's note

Everyone views mental health conditions differently. Some from the outside in, and others from the inside out. Regardless, there is no "normal" or "wrong" way to be. What matters is treating each other, despite our differences, with compassion and acceptance, and realizing that the words we use are powerful. This story illustrates that toss-away comments, words not even meant to hurt, can damage and shape self-perception.

Lily's family history and struggles can't possibly reflect all the experiences of individuals with schizophrenia. Her voice is just that, *her* voice, and her perceptions are solely her own. She's trying her best to shine a light, and I am, too. My hope is that Lily's journey does justice to the courage it takes to face mental health conditions. If her bravery helps someone dig deeper, fight harder, appreciate relationships, discover empathy and find magic in the moment, then *When Elephants Fly* has exceeded my dreams.

When Elephants Fly was inspired, in part, by family and friends who struggled to embrace life despite genetic histories of mental health challenges. Their stories made me think about how both physical and mental health conditions can shadow lives, impact families, pass down generations and affect myriad decisions from careers to friendships, relationships, marriage and whether to have children.

A story about one young woman struggling to survive an invisible threat gave me the chance to write a universal story. Everyone has to figure out how to have a fulfilling life despite fears, roadblocks, prejudice, or emotional or physical health. If we're lucky, those obstacles don't derail our lives. If we're not, then each day is a fight to be who we want to be. That battle requires love, support and empathy. For Lily, it also required finding something to fight for that was larger and more important than her own life.

Another inspiration for *When Elephants Fly*, and specifically for Swifty, was a real news story. In 2012, the *Seattle Times* published an article about an Asian elephant born at Portland's zoo. The zoo owned the calf's mother, Rose-Tu, but her father, Tusko, was owned and on loan to the zoo by Have Trunk Will Travel, a privately funded company that provides elephants for rides, special events, movies and commercials. Under the zoo's breeding loan agreement, Have Trunk Will Travel owned the second, fourth and sixth calves sired at the Portland Zoo by Tusko. This meant that the female calf (named Lily in a public vote) could be taken away from her mother and the zoo.

When the *Seattle Times* article was published, the public reaction was fierce. People were outraged that mother and baby might be separated, and also feared for Lily's welfare as part of a working group of elephants. The controversy ended when the zoo raised funds to purchase both Tusko and Lily.

When I dug deeper into Rose-Tu's story, I learned that Lily wasn't her first calf. She gave birth to Samudra, a male calf, in 2008. After the birth, zoo officials said Rose-Tu attacked her newborn. No one knew the reason for the attack. Some said it was because of the abuse Rose-Tu had previously suffered at the hands of a handler. Others blamed a birth in captivity that resulted in fear and confusion.

Rose-Tu and Samudra were separated and later successfully reunited. But the initial rejection made me wonder what would've happened if Samudra had been owned by an entertainment company and they'd claimed him. Would the zoo have fought to keep him? Would Samudra have survived being separated from his mother?

For Lily's journey, I had to find someone who desperately needed her help. Someone she could love enough to risk her careful existence in order to find purpose. After reading Rose-Tu's story, and relating to how much the public cared about her calf, I created Swifty as Lily's reason to fight. Empathy was key. So I had Lily witness Raki violently attack her baby. Almost being killed by her mother was something Lily could relate to, and it resulted in a bond that would eventually shake Lily from her careful existence and show her that regardless of how much time she might have, what she did with that time meant the most.

Was Lily right to forgo her careful life and risk her mental health? That's for each reader to decide. Regardless, I'm not advocating getting your medical information from the internet like Lily did in her younger years (though that's what a lot of us do!), stealing a baby elephant or risking your freedom or mental health. I can't say what drugs anyone facing a diagnosis like schizophrenia should take, or how to manage their lives. That's for the individual, their family and doctor to decide. I do, however, advocate that no matter your circumstances, you get involved in issues that are important to you. It's what makes life fulfilling.

Writing stories that change people's perceptions about mental health matters to me. Saving elephants matters, too. In my early twenties I worked as a writer for a large circus. The human performers were incredible athletes who passed their skills through generations. But seeing wild animals in captivity, chained in windowless arenas, transported long distances in questionable conditions, broke my heart. I quit that job after a year, and promised myself that somehow I'd find a way to make up for being a part of that circus.

The idea that elephants might become extinct in the wild in my lifetime is unacceptable. They are brilliant, loving creatures that deserve their freedom. The fact that they're caged in unacceptable conditions and forced to do unnatural stunts in traveling shows, hunted for sport or killed for the illegal ivory trade is abhorrent. Please do visit the websites in the Resources section if you want to make a difference and help save elephants from extinction!

Thank you so much for taking the time to read *When Elephants Fly.* My wish for every single one of you: live in the moment when you can. Find something or someone to love. Fight for what's important. Change the world one elephant calf at a time.

resources

There's no one answer for mental health concerns. Treatment is as personalized as the experiences of those with challenges. If you think you might have an issue, please talk to your family, a teacher, good friends, a coach, spiritual advisor or a mentor. *You do not have to face your problems alone.* Asking for help doesn't make you weak. It makes you smart and helps you control your destiny.

Below are a few websites that may prove helpful:

National Alliance on Mental Illness: nami.org

Mental Health America: mentalhealthamerica.net

The Trevor Project: thetrevorproject.org

The JED Foundation: jedfoundation.org

National Institute of Mental Health: nimh.nih.gov

Psych Central: psychcentral.com
psychcentral.com/quizzes/schizophrenia.htm

People who fight every day to save elephants from extinction have a heartrending task. Each elephant orphaned by poachers that they rescue, circus they shut down, country they convince to adopt a ban on ivory sales, brings the world one step closer to saving the beautiful, intelligent, devoted and deserving elephant from extinction.

If you want to learn more and help in the battle to save elephants from extinction and inhumane conditions, please visit the sites below. If you're inspired to join in the fight, all these sites have donation pages.

Space for Giants protects Africa's elephants from immediate threats like poaching while working to secure their habitats forever in landscapes facing increasing pressures. Their vision is to develop new conservation models to enable people to support and sustain populations of large wild animals and the natural landscapes they depend on.

spaceforgiants.org
spaceforgiants.org/our-work/wildlife-protection

March for Giants—a Space for Giants campaign. One elephant is killed every twenty-five minutes in Africa. In the last decade, a third of all elephants have been wiped out. Join #MarchforGiants for $8 and you can protect an elephant in the wild for one month. Your personalized digital elephant will join the "herd" and travel across social media platforms worldwide making "live" appearances on digital billboards and relaying location information back to its sponsor so you can track its progress.

www.marchforgiants.org

Every August 12 the annual World Elephant Day campaign brings the world together to help elephants. The mission of WED and its World Elephant Society organization is to raise awareness and ignite action to save African and Asian elephants from extinction by educating the global public about the plight of elephants and the conservation solutions required to protect them.

worldelephantday.org

Reteti Elephant Sanctuary in northern Kenya is home to the first community-owned elephant orphanage in East Africa. The sanctuary is designed to rescue orphaned, injured and abandoned elephant calves with the goal of releasing them back into the wild. Reteti also empowers young Samburu women to be the first-ever women elephant keepers in all of Africa. Reteti is redefining wildlife management into a community effort that benefits both elephants and people.

www.retetielephants.org
blog.conservation.org/2017/11/to-save-elephants-it-takes-a-village

Performing Animal Welfare Society (PAWS) is at the forefront of efforts to rescue and provide appropriate, human sanctuary for animals that have been the victims of the exotic and performing animal trades.

www.pawsweb.org
www.pawsweb.org/meet_the_animals.html

The Wildlife Conservation Society uses science to understand the natural world and engage and inspire communities, supporters and decision-makers to take action to protect wildlife and their environment. Their goal is to conserve the world's largest wild places, home to more than 50 percent of the planet's biodiversity.

www.wcs.org
www.wcs.org/our-work/species/asian-elephants

Big Life Foundation employs hundreds of Maasai rangers to protect two million acres of wilderness in East Africa. Their mission is to prevent the poaching of elephants and all wildlife by partnering with communities to protect nature for the benefit of all.

biglife.org/about-big-life
biglife.org/donate/other-ways-to-give